Susanna Gregory was a police officer in Leeds before taking up an academic career. She has served as an environmental consultant during seventeen field seasons in the polar regions, and has taught comparative anatomy and biological anthropology.

She is the creator of the Matthew Bartholomew series of mysteries set in medieval Cambridge as well as the Thomas Chaloner books, and now lives in Wales with her husband, who is also a writer.

SUSANNA GREGORY
The Chelsea Strangler

sphere

SPHERE

First published in Great Britain in 2015 by Sphere

1 3 5 7 9 10 8 6 4 2

A CIP catalogue record for this book
is available from the British Library.

ISBN 978-0-7515-5283-6

Typeset in Baskerville MT by Palimpsest Book Production Limited,
Falkirk, Stirlingshire

Printed and bound in Great Britain by Clays Ltd, St Ives plc

Papers used by Sphere are from well-managed forests
and other responsible sources.

Sphere
An imprint of
Little, Brown Book Group
Carmelite House
50 Victoria Embankment
London
EC4Y 0DZ

An Hachette UK Company
www.hachette.co.uk

www.littlebrown.co.uk

For Chris and Annie Wilson,
dearest of friends.

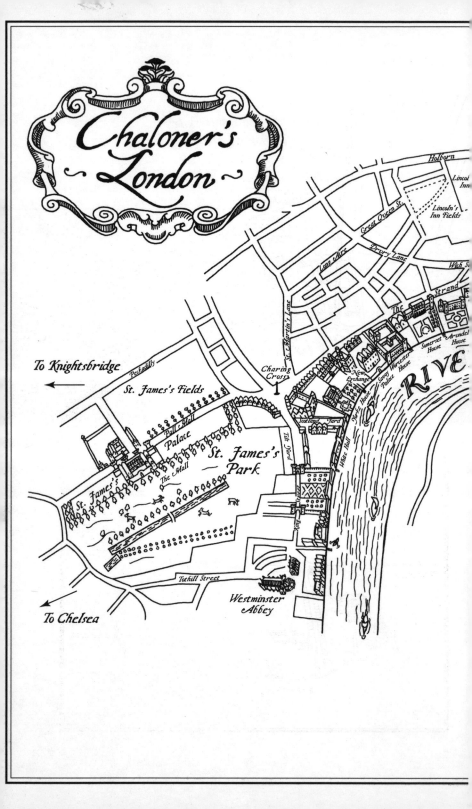

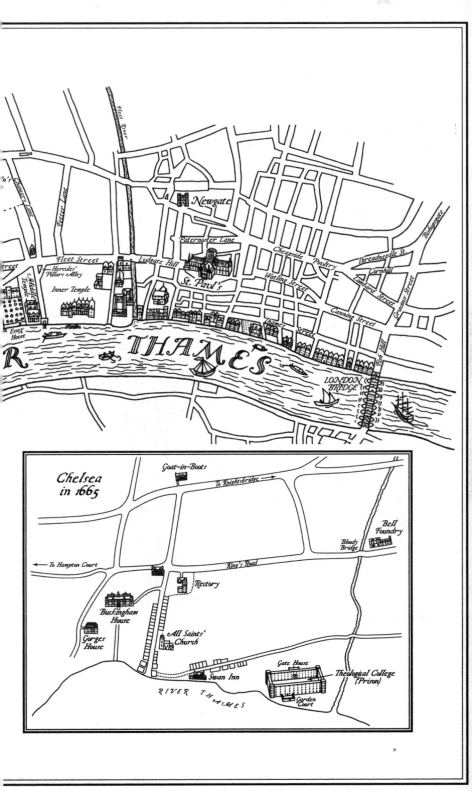

Prologue

The port of Harwich was *en fête*, flags flying from every house and cheering crowds hurrying towards the quayside. The English were victorious, while the Dutch fleet was slinking back to Rotterdam and Friesland with its tail between its legs. Aboard HMS *Swiftsure*, limping towards the shore with a gaping hole in her portside and her sails pock-marked from cannon fire, Thomas Chaloner could not share the noisy jubilation. He had spent much of his life fighting for one cause or another, both on land and at sea, and had thought he was immune to the horrors of warfare, but the scale of the carnage under that bright summer sky a week ago had shaken him to the core.

More than two hundred of his countrymen had been drowned or blown apart by the enemy's fusillade, but the Dutch casualties were in the thousands, many hideously burned when English fire-ships had careened into their midst. Chaloner had been half-deaf from the roar of great guns as he had helped drag the survivors from

1

the sea, but while the screams had been eerily muted, his other senses were working, and there had been no escape from the stench of charred flesh, the slippery feel of fresh blood on sea-chilled bodies, and the sight of corpses – and parts of corpses – bobbing amid burning wreckage.

'Thank God we have made safe passage.'

Chaloner turned at the familiar voice of Captain Lester, master of *Swiftsure*. 'Were we so badly damaged, then?' he asked in surprise. 'I thought you said it was mainly superficial.'

'I mean the prisoners.' Lester nodded towards the holds, where the Dutch had been kept since they were rescued. 'They outnumber us five to one, and when I was not worrying about an attempt to take my ship, I was afraid that the extra weight might capsize us.'

'They would not have tried to escape,' said Chaloner, recalling the dull, cowed expressions of the captives as they had been herded below. 'They know what Admiral Berkeley thought about you saving them – he would have tossed them overboard at the first sign of trouble.'

Lester grinned. 'Of all the orders I failed to hear in the heat of battle, ignoring his instruction to let them drown was the one that gave me the most pleasure.'

'God only knows how we managed to win with *him* in charge of the squadron.'

'Luck, and an inequality of fire-power,' explained Lester. Then his expression grew bitter. 'We could have ended the war if we had given chase and smashed the Dutch fleet once and for all, and I still cannot understand why the command was never given. It was a tactical mistake of enormous proportion, and will cost us dear in the future.'

'It is what happens when aristocrats are given charge of the navy, instead of professional seamen like you,' shrugged Chaloner. 'They think they know best, and disaster inevitably follows.'

He and Lester looked towards the quarterdeck, where the youthful Admiral Berkeley was talking to Sir Thomas Clifford, a politician who had eagerly volunteered his services when war had been declared, but who had spent the battle cowering in his cabin, pretending to study charts.

Lester grimaced. 'It makes me sick just thinking about it, so let us discuss something else. Your assignment – did you find that thief you were hunting?'

Chaloner switched his thoughts to the task he had been set by his employer, the Earl of Clarendon, wondering whether he would have followed the culprit's trail quite so assiduously if he had known it would pitch him into the violent, bloody encounter that was the Battle of Lowestoft.

'I found him,' he replied, 'but too late to see him on the gallows. He was cut in half by a cannonball, and you buried him at sea the next day.'

Lester's eyes widened in shock. 'My clerk? Are you sure?'

Chaloner nodded. 'Not that it matters now.'

Lester's expression was fierce. 'It *does* matter, Tom. He stole our gunpowder and sold it for personal gain, which ranks with aiding the enemy in my book. He was a traitor.'

'Well, he will not do it again.'

Before Lester could respond, they heard footsteps, and turned to see Clifford swaggering towards them. The politician had donned a handsome blue coat for the occasion, and his ornamental sword hung on the heavy gold sash that was draped across his shoulder. Anyone looking at him might be forgiven for thinking that he had won the engagement single-handed. Certainly, it seemed he was ready to accept the grateful thanks of King and country.

Lester bowed, but only just deeply enough to be polite. 'What arrangements have been made for the prisoners, Sir Thomas?'

A flicker of irritation crossed Clifford's face; he did not want to bother with the hapless wretches in the holds while there was adulation to be had from Harwich's waiting hordes.

'I imagine the church here has a crypt,' he said shortly. 'They can lodge there until I can hire soldiers to escort them to their new home.'

'Which is where?' Chaloner asked.

'The Theological College in Chelsea,' replied Clifford. 'Do you know it? It was once famous for its polemical priests.'

'Chelsea?' blurted Lester, shocked. 'But that is less than three miles from London! Is it wise to house enemy sailors so close to the capital? What if they escape?'

'They will not escape,' retorted Clifford irritably. 'If they were intent on running back to the United Provinces, they would have tried to break out while we were still at sea. But they remained below decks, as meek as mice, so there will be no danger from them.'

'Because they are still shocked and frightened,' argued Lester. 'But they will not stay that way, and once on dry land, they will recover their—'

'*I* am Commissioner for the Care and Treatment of

4

Prisoners of War, not you,' snapped Clifford, nettled. 'So it is for *me* to determine where they go. And I have chosen Chelsea.'

'Are there any other commissioners?' asked Chaloner, in the hope that if so, one of them might prove to be more sensible.

'Three,' replied Clifford shortly. 'And they all agree with me.'

'What about the clerics you mentioned?' pressed Lester, unwilling to concede defeat. 'Do they not mind sharing their home with enemy sailors? Or will you employ them as guards?'

Clifford shot him an impatient glance. 'The College was deemed a failure years ago, and all its fanatics left. The building was empty, so we commandeered it in the government's name.'

At that point, he noticed that Admiral Berkeley was heading for the gangway, so he scurried away without another word, determined to be first ashore – and first to accept the joyous compliments of their grateful countrymen.

Chaloner and Lester leaned against the rail, watching the controlled chaos of disembarkation. The crowds continued to cheer and wave their hats, and the crew, resplendent in their best rigs, acknowledged them with proud smiles.

'Here comes the Admiralty Proctor,' said Lester, nodding to where a portly individual was making his way through the throng. 'Richard Franklin. He will have fresh orders for me, letters for the officers and men, and money for repairs.'

Chaloner glanced at the gaping hole in the ship's side, and then at the jagged wound where a great gun had been blasted off its tracks to career across the deck. 'They will not be cheap.'

'No,' agreed Lester. 'Last time, I was obliged to put to sea with half of it left undone, because he only brought me a fraction of what was needed. To be frank, I suspect he stole some, because the navy office knows how much new masts cost.'

'Or perhaps it was the Treasury that was niggardly,' suggested Chaloner, who knew how the government worked all too well. 'They would rather you fought battles without taking damage, so they can spend our taxes on new clothes for the King instead.'

'They would rather we suffered no injuries either,' said Lester wryly. 'The Sick and Hurt Fund will have to be tripled if all our wounded sailors are to be compensated for their sacrifices.' He pushed away from the rail as the proctor reached the foot of the gangway. 'Franklin will be mobbed by the crew the moment he embarks, so I had better go and protect him. There was plague in the city when we left, and my people are desperate for news of their loved ones.'

When the proctor stepped aboard, Lester bellowed orders that saw the anxious seamen draw back, and then escorted him to the quarterdeck. Once there, Franklin opened his bag of letters, and began calling out names. Chaloner was surprised to hear his own among them, and moved forward to accept a fat package. It was from the Earl, and included a note from his friend Surgeon Wiseman. He moved away from the jostling throng to open it.

Lester joined him a short time later, spitting fury because the money Franklin had brought was wholly insufficient for making *Swiftsure* seaworthy, but he was still expected to return to action within the week. Then he saw Chaloner's ashen face.

'Tom? What is the matter?'

'My wife,' replied Chaloner in a slow, shocked voice. 'She is dead.'

Lester gazed at him in horror. 'Dead? But she cannot be! How?'

'A week ago.' Chaloner's fist closed around the letter. 'Of the plague.'

16 July 1665, Chelsea

Nancy Janaway was terrified. Strange things were happening, and she no longer felt safe. She had tried to tell people about it, but no one would listen – at least, no one in a position to help. That was the trouble with Gorges House. Officially, it was an establishment that catered to ailing gentlewomen. In reality, it was an asylum – a place where the rich deposited their mad female relations – and who cared what lunatics thought?

Eventually, she had plucked up the courage to confide in Dr Parker, the senior physician, but although he had sat with every appearance of interested concern, she knew his mind had been elsewhere. He was of the earnest belief he had been put on Earth to cure insanity, so he had almost certainly been thinking about his next experiment. She doubted he had heard a word she had said, much less taken her seriously.

She grimaced when she recalled how he had ended the discussion – by telling her that she would soon be ready to go home. But she did not want to go home! She felt safe in Gorges, with its tall walls and sturdy gates. Outside was where the shadowy figures lurked, especially on the road that wound north through the marshes. She had lost count of the times that she had seen their sinister shapes from her bedroom window.

As it was stifling indoors, she decided to go and sit in the orchard. The towering walls that surrounded the house and its grounds were partly to keep the residents in, but also to provide them with privacy. Gorges was not like Bedlam, where inmates were regarded as entertainment for the general public. It was a haven of benevolence and compassion, and spectators were never allowed in to gawp. It was expensive to stay there, of course, and Nancy knew she was lucky to have been offered a place – she was not wealthy, but Dr Parker had agreed to treat her free of charge because she was local. She had made great progress under his kindly care, and might have been happy . . . were it not for the shadows.

Yet her fears eventually began to recede, because the orchard was lovely that evening – sweet with the scent of ripening fruit and freshly scythed grass. Bees droned among the summer flowers, and birdsong drifted in from the surrounding fields. She perched on a bench under an ancient apple tree and closed her eyes.

Suddenly, there was a rumpus from Buckingham House next door, which made her start up in alarm, but then she sank back down again, chiding herself for a fool. That particular mansion had been leased to a courtier keen to escape the plague, and wild revels took place there on a daily basis. It was said that the fellow missed the scandalously debauched atmosphere of White Hall, and aimed to recreate it in Chelsea. Sometimes, Nancy watched their antics from her bedroom window with her friend Martha Thrush. They made her laugh, and helped her forget the dark shadows that lurked in the marshes.

She leaned back, gazing up at the fruit-laden branches above her head. Then there was a sharp snap as a twig broke underfoot. She started to turn, a smile on her lips. Who was coming? Martha, perhaps, wanting to sit and chat. Or Mrs Bonney, to tell her that there were freshly baked cakes in the kitchen.

But before she could look, hands fastened around her throat – large ones, which immediately cut off the air to her lungs. She struggled, and tried to cry out, but no sound emerged other than a choking gasp. Terrified, she fought harder, but the fingers were strong, and she could not twist free. She felt herself growing light-headed, and the sounds of the summer evening merged into a meaningless roar. Eventually, she stopped fighting and went limp.

The shadow stared at her for a moment, and seeing she was dead, slipped soundlessly away.

Chapter 1

The Palace of White Hall was eerily deserted. A hot breeze blew a stray broadsheet across the empty expanse of the Great Court and played with a door that had been left ajar, setting up a forlorn echo. The rooms that had so recently been alive with the sound of the King's merry revels were silent and still.

Thomas Chaloner, spy for the Earl of Clarendon, was unsettled by the difference. Three months ago, it had been jam-packed with people, carriages and horses, a bright bustle of lively noise, but then the plague had struck and everything changed. It had started with a few isolated cases, but had spread fast, and parish clerks were now recording nearly two thousand deaths a week, with church bells tolling almost continually for those who had fallen prey to its deadly touch.

Chaloner was unimpressed that the King should have abandoned the city. True, it would be a political disaster if he died – he had failed to produce a legitimate heir, and the next in line to the throne was his unpopular brother James – but his subjects were terrified by the unseen horror that moved among them, and His Majesty's flight had done nothing for morale. They peered through the palace gates to see weeds sprouting between the cobbles and windows nailed shut, and whispered to each other in fear-filled voices that the Court was never coming back.

Yet there was still life in White Hall, because a few servants and officials had been left to keep an eye on the place. They pottered about lethargically, enervated by the heat, and resentful that they should have been the ones chosen to stay. Chaloner's employer was one of them – the Earl had once been Charles II's most valued advisor, but the two men had grown apart since the Restoration, and the King had been delighted with the chance to escape from his prim old mentor's incessant nagging.

But not even he could keep a powerful peer in a plague-infested city for ever, and an invitation, albeit an ungraciously worded one, for the Earl to join him, had arrived the previous evening. There had been great jubilation in Clarendon's household, and preparations to depart had begun immediately, lest the fickle monarch should change his mind.

'I cannot wait to go,' said Thomas Kipps, the Earl's Seal Bearer, as he and Chaloner stood together in the shade of the Great Gate. 'It is like a palace of ghosts here, and I do not mind telling you that I find it disturbing.'

Kipps was a tall, bluff man with a friendly face, who loved the pageantry associated with his post, and always sported the Clarendon livery of blue and gold – although 'gold' was a misnomer as far as Chaloner was concerned, given that the Earl had chosen a rather unattractive mustardy yellow for the colours of his house. Chaloner declined to wear it, and instead favoured plain clothes – dark green hat, coat and breeches, and a white shirt with just enough lace to satisfy the current fashion. No self-respecting spy liked to draw attention to himself, and his attire had been chosen for its anonymity. Yet there were two distinctive things about him: watchful grey eyes, and a refusal to wear a wig – he preferred the convenience of his own brown hair, which did not fall off when he ran, was less prone to lice, and was a good deal cooler in hot weather.

He winced when the bells of nearby St Margaret's church began to toll – three, then a pause followed by sixteen: the plague had claimed a young man. Kipps saw his reaction and clapped a sympathetic hand on his shoulder.

'It is always difficult to lose a loved one, and I am more sorry than I can say that you have been deprived of Hannah. She was . . .'

He trailed off awkwardly, and concealed his discomfort by offering Chaloner some tobacco. Smoking was a much-favoured preventative for the plague, and few Londoners risked leaving home without a pipe. Chaloner took a few strands without enthusiasm; he was still struggling to acquire the habit, and not doing very well with it.

'When will our Earl join the King at Syon House?' he asked, equally keen to talk about something else. He had never been good at analysing his feelings, and his wife's death had left him with a bewildering gamut of them, few of which he understood.

Kipps' expression hardened. 'It is an outrage that he

has been left here for so long. He is Lord Chancellor, one of the most important men in the country! But he will not be going to Syon House, Tom. The King is already bored with it, and plans to move to Hampton Court instead.'

Then that explained the invitation, thought Chaloner. Hampton Court was much larger than Syon House, which meant it would be easier for His Majesty to avoid the Earl's company.

'I was talking to my good friend Sir Philip Warwick yesterday,' Kipps grumbled on, puffing great clouds of smoke that made a mockery of Chaloner's paltry wisps. 'Do you know him? He is Secretary of the Treasury, and a splendid fellow. Well, he is also disgusted that so many of us were left behind to rot.'

'Is he?' Most of Chaloner's attention was on trying to stop his pipe from going out.

'He says it is unreasonable to expect him and his staff to stay here and die. Court posts are meant to be lucrative – a reward for being good Royalists. They are not supposed to be dangerous.'

Chaloner forgot his pipe as the implications of Kipps' words hit him, and he turned to regard the Seal Bearer in disbelief. 'Wait a moment! Are you telling me that the Treasury is still here in London? The King did not take it with him?'

'Syon House has no secure place to put it,' explained Kipps. 'A coal cellar was offered, but that was hardly the thing. So, yes, it is still here – along with all its officials.'

He nodded to the north-east corner of the Great Court, where the Treasury had been housed since the Restoration five years ago. A purpose-built chamber had been created for it, one with extra-thick walls and a door designed to withstand an assault by cannon.

'Is that why the King decided to move to Hampton Court?' asked Chaloner. 'I imagine it has strongrooms aplenty.'

Kipps lowered his voice, although there was no one around to hear. 'It does, and the Treasury will be ferried there next month. Personally, I think it should go now. What if the guards catch the plague in the interim? All thieves would have to do is step over the corpses and take the lot!'

'Yet it will be risky to move it.' Chaloner's pipe had gone out, but he could not be bothered with the rigma-role of relighting it, so he put it in his pocket, where a strand of hot tobacco burned a hole in his favourite breeches. 'Every villain in the country will line its route.'

'They will not know, because the exact date of its removal is being kept secret. It was the Earl's idea to transfer it on the quiet, and he knows what he is doing.'

Chaloner begged to differ. The Earl was appallingly naive about such matters, and if the Treasury's riches were stolen, his enemies would ensure he lost his head for it. His household would be dissolved, and Chaloner, who had fought for Parliament during the wars, had spied for Cromwell's government in the Commonwealth, and hailed from a family of infamously dedicated Roundheads, would be unlikely to find another job in Royalist London.

'Of course, it would be a magnificent haul if robbers did make off with it,' Kipps was saying brightly. 'His Majesty's coffers are unusually full at the moment. Positively bursting, in fact.'

'Because he has not been here to raid them?' Like all

Londoners, Chaloner knew how much of the public purse was squandered on the King's frivolous pleasures.

Kipps shot him a baleful look. 'No, because of all the extra money that has been raised to fight the Dutch. Battles are expensive, you know.'

Chaloner did know, and thought the government had been stupid to declare war on the United Provinces in the first place, given that they were always complaining about a shortage of cash.

'It is not just buying ships, provisions and paying seamen,' Kipps preached on. 'The prisoners we have taken are very costly to house. I was shown the figures in my capacity as Messenger of the Receipt for the Treasury, you see. I was aghast.'

Chaloner was puzzled. 'You have resigned as the Earl's Seal Bearer?'

Kipps shook his head. 'I inveigled myself a second Court post, lest our employer falls from grace. I recommend you do the same, Tom. These are uncertain times, and only a fool does not take precautions against the vagaries of the future.'

'I cannot see him being very pleased about that – he expects total loyalty from his staff.'

'He understands expediency. Besides, being Messenger does not take much of my time. All I have to do is stand around and look important. I could put in a word for you, if you like. There is a vacancy for a Sergeant at Arms.'

'You have that kind of influence?'

'Warwick – who will make the appointment – is a good friend, as I said. Come with me now and I shall introduce you. Then you can decide for yourself whether you would like to apply.'

*

The offices occupied by the Treasury were on either side of the specially constructed strongroom, and Kipps led the way to a small but comfortable chamber with an elaborately carved ceiling. It was cool, and a pleasure to enter after the building heat outside. Three men sat at a table, and all shrank away in alarm when Kipps walked in with a stranger.

'Do not worry,' the Seal Bearer said, raising his hands reassuringly. 'Tom does not have the plague. Since April, he has either been at sea with the Fleet, visiting his family in Buckinghamshire, or stuck in Clarendon House translating letters into Dutch for the Earl.'

Clarendon House was the Earl's home, a recklessly ostentatious structure that had one redeeming feature: it was in Piccadilly, and so some distance from the city and its diseases.

'Thank God,' breathed the first, a thin, sallow man with a soulful face. When he spoke, his teeth clacked together nervously. 'One cannot be too careful these days. And I cannot smoke, because it hurts my throat, so my only protection is London Treacle.'

'An excellent prophylactic, although fearfully expensive,' averred Kipps, then turned to Chaloner. 'This is Sir Philip Warwick, Secretary of the Treasury. Like us, he was left to dice with Death while the rest of the Court jaunted off to Syon House.'

'It is disgraceful,' spat Warwick, returning Chaloner's bow. 'And reckless. After all, who will guard the King's gold if we die of the plague?'

'I do not mind staying,' said the second man, a plump, oleaginous individual with food-stained clothes. 'The Court's departure has left a lot of broken hearts among

16

the female servants – wounds I am more than happy to heal.' He winked lasciviously.

'This is Captain George Cocke,' said Kipps, using the clipped, dismissive tone he reserved for people he did not like. 'He is our accompter, which means he does fancy things with figures.'

Cocke pouted irritably. 'I balance the books. It is not difficult to understand, Kipps, and I fail to grasp why I am obliged to explain it to you *every* time we—'

'And this is Francis Stephens.' Kipps cut across him curtly to indicate the third man. 'Our Sergeant at Arms. We should have two, but the other quit his commission when he learned he would have to stay in London.'

Stephens was a burly fellow with a bad complexion, who immediately launched into a diatribe about the amount of work he was obliged to do now that he was alone. Cocke rolled his eyes and waddled out, and the moment he was out of earshot, Kipps interrupted Stephens' rant.

'There is the fly in the ointment, Tom. If you are appointed, it will put you in the company of *that* loathsome fellow. He is a desperate nuisance with women, and every lass in White Hall will be relieved when the Treasury is transferred to Hampton Court.'

'Bullen Reymes claims it cannot be moved before August,' said Warwick, fanning himself with a newsbook. 'Although it could go tomorrow, if the truth be told. It is only a case of loading up a few carts and appointing some suitable guards.'

Bullen Reymes was an avowed enemy of the Earl, a short, bullet-headed politician with a quick temper and a perpetually angry face. He was Prefect of the Treasury, which meant he was responsible for its security, although

17

the post carried a very meagre salary and few perks. He had been lobbying for a better one for years, on the grounds that he had beggared himself by supporting the Crown during the civil wars. However, as many folk were in a similar position, Reymes' case was neither unusual nor pressing as far as the King was concerned, and his pleas fell on deaf ears.

'Reymes!' sneered Kipps. 'What does *he* know?'

'Not much,' acknowledged Warwick with a wry smile and a sharp click of his incisors. 'However, the King's gold *is* his responsibility, so it will move on his say-so.'

'There he is now,' hissed Stephens suddenly. 'And Sir William Doyley with him.'

He pointed through the open door to where Reymes, quivering with rage as was his wont, was conversing with a man who possessed unusually large eyes. The eyes opened even wider when their owner indulged in a pinch of snuff that made him sneeze. Kipps chuckled spitefully.

'Our Earl arranged for both of them to be appointed Commissioners for the Care and Treatment of Prisoners of War. Reymes is livid.'

'Is he?' Chaloner was bemused. 'Why? I thought he wanted a well-salaried post.'

'He does,' smirked Kipps, 'which is why our Earl's victory is so sweet. Being a commissioner will cost far more than it pays, and will entail a lot of hard work. Doyley is happy to serve his country, but Reymes is outraged.'

'But he cannot refuse the "honour",' added Warwick, 'so now he has *two* undesirable posts.'

'Although being a commissioner is the worst,' grinned Kipps, 'as its disadvantages are threefold: it will keep him away from Court and the centre of power; it will cost him a fortune; and it will be a thankless chore – if he does it well, no one will notice, but if he fails, there will be hell to pay. I certainly should not want it.'

'It is rare for Clarendon to best an enemy,' remarked Stephens, still watching Reymes and Doyley through the door. 'But he succeeded royally with Reymes.'

'Especially as it could not have come at a worse time,' put in Kipps, gleeful on his employer's behalf. 'Reymes had just rented a mansion in Chelsea, and invited lots of courtiers to join him there. It is expensive, and I doubt he would have done it, if he had known he was going to be made a commissioner.'

'He was burgled recently, too,' gossiped Warwick. 'That cannot have helped his finances.'

'So was I,' sighed Stephens. 'These days, thieves assume that *all* wealthy folk have abandoned their London homes for safer pastures, and view every respectable house as fair game. It is dangerous to be in bed at night, especially on the western side of the city.'

'It is a sorry state of affairs,' agreed Kipps. 'The plague has all but eliminated honest trade, so the poor grow desperate. I feel for them personally. Food is expensive, and so are medicines against infection.'

'They can always smoke,' said Stephens. 'Tobacco *is* the best defence against the disease, after all. It says so on the packet, so it must be true.'

'Then keep some close,' advised Kipps. 'One never knows who might carry the sickness. But it is almost eleven o'clock, Tom, and we shall be needed in Clarendon House. Shall we go?'

Out on King Street, Chaloner and Kipps were faced with an important decision: to take a carriage to Piccadilly

19

or walk. By the very nature of their trade, hackneymen were vulnerable to the plague, and fares were often obliged to run for their lives when drivers exhibited signs of ill health. But travelling on foot meant passing those who might be infected, and that was dangerous, too.

'We shall walk,' determined Kipps, when the driver of the coach they hailed began to cough. Chaloner suspected it was because of the dust that hung thick in the air – the result of weeks of dry weather – but the Seal Bearer lit his pipe to ward off the contagion, and indicated that Chaloner was to do the same.

They made their way up King Street, both wilting under the unrelenting glare of the sun, and Chaloner wondered if it was the hottest summer he had ever experienced in England. Crops withered in the fields, streams and brooks ran dry, and even the mighty Thames was reduced to a fraction of its normal size. With no rain to wash away rubbish, London reeked, its ditches choked with accumulated filth. Some folk said it was the rank stench of decay that was responsible for spreading the plague, a notion Chaloner felt might well be true.

It was far too hot for anything other than shirtsleeves, so Chaloner removed his coat and slung it over his shoulder, although Kipps stubbornly refused to follow suit.

'I hate walking about half-naked,' the Seal Bearer confided sheepishly. 'It feels so . . . so *ungentlemanly*. My wife laughs at my fastidiousness, but I cannot help it.'

'Will she travel with you to Hampton Court?' asked Chaloner politely. As Mrs Kipps rarely visited White Hall, he tended to forget she existed.

'Yes, and then she and Martin will take lodgings nearby.' Kipps gave a sweet, loving smile. 'Martin is my son. He was born without all his faculties, but he is a dear, kind boy – gentleness itself. Of course, I do not tell just anyone about him. Courtiers can be cruel, and I could not bear to have anyone mock his slow ways.'

Chaloner was touched by the expression of trust. 'How old is he?'

'Twelve.' Kipps continued to smile. 'I hate spiders, and he checks my room every night to ensure that there are none lurking. How many lads would do that for a silly old sire? Franklin! How are you this fine morning?'

The man he addressed in his hearty, ebullient manner was the portly Admiralty Proctor, who had delivered the letter telling Chaloner that he was a widower for the second time.

'I should not be here,' Franklin growled, raising a pomander to his face on an accompanying waft of sage, comfrey and garlic, herbs said to be effective at neutralising pestilential miasmas. 'I should be in the country, safely away from this terrible pestilence.'

'As should we all,' agreed Kipps. 'Have you been invited to Hampton Court?'

Franklin scowled. 'No – the Privy Council has ordered the Admiralty to stay here. God damn them for selfish rogues! If I die, I shall haunt them for the rest of their miserable lives.'

He stamped away, leaving Chaloner and Kipps to traverse Charing Cross, an open area that was usually full of traffic and pedestrians, but that was now disconcertingly quiet. Eventually, they reached the rural lane called Piccadilly. Not many weeks ago, it had been calf-deep in mud, but now it was bone dry and pounded flat by the feet of all those who had trudged along it to escape the city. It made for easy walking, although the two small carts they passed threw up clouds of dust that caught in their throats and stung their eyes. Chaloner knocked the tobacco from his pipe and put it away. It was hard enough to breathe without making matters worse with smoke.

Londoners hated Clarendon House, and scathingly referred to it as 'Dunkirk House', because its owner had overseen the sale of that port to France at a controversially low price. Many claimed the French had bribed him, and that the Earl had used the money to build himself the palace in question. As Dunkirk was currently being used as a base by Dutch pirates to harry English shipping, it was not uncommon for Clarendon House to be pelted with rotten vegetables – or worse.

That morning, it was a whirl of activity. A line of wagons stood outside, heaped with chests, while servants scurried in all directions, falling over each other in their haste to work as fast as possible. Their efforts were woefully disorganised, and the Earl's wife, Lady Frances Clarendon, was tired, hot and frustrated as she struggled to impose some sort of order on them.

'They have no idea how to load,' she grumbled, as Chaloner and Kipps approached. 'We are supposed to travel to Hampton Court tomorrow, but we shall never be ready at this rate.'

'So soon, My Lady?' asked Kipps in surprise. 'The King will not leave Syon House until the end of next week. You will arrive at Hampton Court long before him.'

Frances smiled seraphically. She was the only member of the Earl's family who Chaloner liked: the sons were haughty, pompous and overbearing, while the one daughter he had met was spoiled and unfriendly. 'Quite – which means we shall have the first choice of rooms.'

Kipps laughed. 'You are very wise. Is the Earl going tomorrow, too?'

'Business will keep him here until Friday, but the rest of us are eager to be away from Piccadilly – not for fear of the plague, but to escape the heat.'

'Hampton Court will be no cooler,' warned Chaloner. His recent journey from Buckinghamshire had told him that the countryside was just as unpleasant as the city.

Frances tapped him lightly on the shoulder with her fan. 'But it will *seem* cooler among all those green trees. And it will not reek of sewers.'

Chaloner could only suppose she had never been there.

'That cart will not do,' declared Kipps, frowning at a wagon that had been stacked with so many heavy articles that even the strongest team of horses would be unlikely to move it.

'No,' agreed Frances. 'So you can oversee its reloading, while Thomas makes your apologies inside. My husband will not mind me commandeering his staff, under the circumstances.'

Chaloner left Kipps to do her bidding, and strode across Clarendon House's ornate portico to a carved door that would not have looked out of place in a basilica. Inside, the house stank of anti-plague herbs. Being wealthy, the Earl could afford a lot of them, and no expense had been spared to protect the family he loved.

Beyond the portico was a large marble hall known as the Great Roome. It was a bleak, unwelcoming space, cold even in the height of summer, and Chaloner stood there for a moment, savouring its chill after the inferno outside. Then he aimed for My Lord's Lobby, where his

23

employer worked when not at White Hall. He knocked on the door, and pushed it open when he heard the call for him to enter.

The Earl of Clarendon sat at an elegant Venetian desk, gouty foot propped on a stool in front of him. He had been slender when he had followed the King into exile after the execution of Charles I, but his girth had expanded exponentially since the Restoration, when high office won him unlimited access to good food and wine. He wore a handsome blond wig with curls that tumbled luxuriously over his shoulders, and his clothes were made from the finest silk.

Chaloner was immediately suspicious when the Earl looked up and smiled. His master was rarely friendly towards him, because he deplored the fact that he was obliged to hire an intelligencer to protect him from his many enemies. Moreover, the fact that Chaloner had fought on the 'wrong' side in the civil wars remained a problem in the Earl's mind, and the spy would have been dismissed without a second thought if there had been a Royalist with similar talents. Fortunately for Chaloner, there was not.

'There you are,' the Earl said genially. 'As you know, we have been invited to join the King at last. My family will go tomorrow, but duty ties me here for another three days, so you can escort me to Hampton Court on Friday. Where is Kipps?'

'Helping to reload a cart, sir.'

'Good. I want my family away from this pestilential city as soon as possible. The King was wrong to leave us here for so long.'

Chaloner was sorry the Earl felt compelled to keep company with someone who did not like him, but it was hardly something he could say, so he did the wise thing and remained silent. After a moment, the smile returned to the Earl's lips, although it was more strained than affable.

'Did you enjoy visiting your brothers and sisters in Buckinghamshire? You were gone a month and only returned five days ago, so I imagine you did.'

'Yes, thank you.' Chaloner wondered where the conversation was going. His answer to the question was sincere, though: his childhood had been a happy one, and the passing years had done nothing to diminish his affection for his siblings, or theirs for him.

The Earl continued to beam, although his eyes were now distinctly uneasy. 'And have you recovered from your . . . er . . . experience?'

'The Battle of Lowestoft, sir? Of course. It was nearly two months ago now.'

'It must have been terrifying.' The Earl shuddered. 'We won a great victory, but at what price? Several thousand Hollanders killed, and another two thousand taken prisoner, not to mention our own dead. And all those cannonballs whizzing about! But I was not asking if you had put that behind you. I meant . . . you know.'

Chaloner regarded him blankly. 'Not really, sir.'

The Earl's voice dropped to an exasperated whisper. 'Your wife, man! Hannah. I told her it was reckless to go to the theatre while the plague grips our city, but she would not listen to me.'

'She would not listen to anyone,' said Chaloner bitterly. He had since been waylaid by any number of courtiers, who wanted him to know that they had advised her to find a safer way to spend her afternoons.

He stared morosely out of the window. He and Hannah

had married before they really knew each other, and it had not taken them long to discover that they should have chosen other partners. Yet he had never wished her gone from his life, and it had been a nasty shock to return from sea to discover her dead and buried in a common pit. The little house they had rented together near Westminster had been shut up by the authorities, although not before the servants had absconded with everything that had been remotely portable, including his beloved viols.

Losing his musical instruments had been a terrible blow, and he was ashamed of himself for being more distressed about them than about his wife. He had tracked the culprits down, but too late – the viols were already on a ship bound for the Province of New York. Had he been a vengeful man, he might have taken comfort from the fact that the servants had paid a heavy toll for their dishonesty – they were dead of the plague themselves, probably caught when they had raided Hannah's bedroom while her body was still in it.

'Losing a wife to the pestilence must be especially painful for you,' said the Earl, adopting an expression of fatherly concern. 'Because the same thing happened to your first spouse.'

Chaloner's first wife, Aletta, had died in Holland, twelve years ago, along with their baby. He wondered why the Earl was pursuing the subject when it was not an easy one for either of them. 'It is a cruel disease, sir.'

'It is,' agreed the Earl softly. 'And although it was not the contagion that took my son Ned last January, I do understand what it is like to lose a loved one. You have my sympathy.'

'Thank you,' said Chaloner, still wary.

'Right,' said the Earl, rubbing his plump hands together in patent relief. 'I can now tell Frances that I have done what she ordered, and enquired after your well-being. You are quite recovered from your misfortunes, and I am free to set you an assignment – although you need not start it until you have escorted me to Hampton Court on Friday.'

'As you wish, sir.' Chaloner was also glad the discussion was over, but wished Frances had not cajoled her husband into expressing a concern he did not feel. 'Does it have anything to do with moving the Treasury from White Hall?'

The Earl looked puzzled for a moment, then waved a dismissive hand. 'No, no. I did suggest that it should be spirited away secretly one night, but I am sure Bullen Reymes can manage that without our help. And if he fails, his head will roll, which I shall not mind at all. He is a vile beast, always intent on doing me harm.'

'But he will say it was your idea,' Chaloner pointed out. 'It—'

'I shall deny it,' interrupted the Earl, although Chaloner seriously doubted that would work. 'Now, it is a beautiful day, so walk with me outside while I tell you what I want you to do.'

It was not a beautiful day as far as Chaloner was concerned. It sizzled as the sun reached its zenith, and there was not so much as a breath of wind. The Earl, who hated the cold, revelled in it. Like a lizard, thought Chaloner uncharitably, watching his master waddle along beside him in fashionable shoes that were painfully tight.

'Hark at that lovely thrush!' the Earl exclaimed, although it was a robin whose piercing song sounded from a distant tree. 'They are my favourite of all birds. They eat slugs, for a start – loathsome creatures that have destroyed my lettuces.'

He pointed to a sorry row of plants that might have fared better had someone bothered to water them. As it was, they sat in parched soil, and wilted. Obliged to stand in the full glare of the sun to inspect them, Chaloner appreciated how they must feel.

'The assignment, sir,' he prompted, keen to receive his orders so he could retreat to the shade.

'I want you to go to Chelsea for me,' said the Earl. 'It is a charming village, quite close, and yet far enough to be safe from the plague. For the moment, at least.'

Chaloner was relieved that the mission did not involve returning to sea. He had had enough of bloodshed, and had no wish to endure a second Lowestoft.

'I have ridden past Chelsea several times,' he said. 'It is full of mansions.'

The Earl nodded. 'Eight or nine very fine houses. One is named Gorges, and is a lunatic asylum for gentle-women. I want you to look into a case of theft there.'

It was a peculiar task, but that was nothing new, and Chaloner began the tortuous business of trying to find out why his employer should want him to explore such a matter. The Earl had a nasty habit of sending him into situations armed with only half a story, which was always annoying and sometimes downright dangerous.

'What is your interest in the place?' he asked. 'Specifically.'

'I am one of its benefactors. I was once obliged to lodge an elderly aunt there, and they treated her with such kindness that I feel compelled to help them in return. She was quite mad, poor soul – threw in her lot with Cromwell and declared herself a Parliamentarian. Well, we had to lock her away for her own good.'

'I see.' Chaloner glanced covertly at him, to assess whether he was being told that *he* was mad for supporting the Commonwealth, but the Earl's expression was distant as he continued.

'She was cured eventually, and now lives in Oxford, where she is unlikely to frolic with republicanism again.'

'What does being a benefactor entail?'

'Donating money, mostly. Dr Parker, the senior physician, has made significant advances in the study of lunacy, and I am proud to support such work.'

Chaloner knew he was being spun a yarn. First, the Earl had never shown any interest in curing insanity before; and second, he was notoriously mean, and did not part with cash readily. As always, he was holding something back.

'You say there has been a theft,' he prompted, hoping the truth would emerge as they talked.

'Several. A number of items have been filched from the residents, who are mostly wealthy, so their possessions are valuable. But worse, someone has been pilfering the funds that *I* have provided. Mrs Bonney, the housekeeper, believes that a total of *thirty pounds* has disappeared!'

He spoke so seriously that Chaloner almost laughed. Thirty pounds should have been nothing to such a rich man. 'Good gracious!'

The Earl narrowed his eyes. 'It is a fortune to Gorges. However, what is worse is the fact that these nasty crimes are distracting Parker from his work – namely healing the songbirds.'

Chaloner regarded him askance. 'Songbirds?'

'Inmates,' explained the Earl testily. 'But I dislike the

word, as it makes them sound like convicts. But songbirds are often caged, as are lunatics, and I consider it a kinder term. Oh, and while you are there, you must also protect these songbirds from harm.'

Chaloner's bemusement intensified. 'What manner of harm?'

'Any harm. It is almost as important as catching the thief.'

The Earl loved money, so Chaloner believed he was eager to find out what was happening to his donations, but he also knew there was yet more to the story. He tried again to tease it out.

'Can you tell me anything else, sir? It will save time, and allow me to work more efficiently.'

'Gorges houses some twenty songbirds,' obliged the Earl. 'It is managed by Mrs Bonney, under a board of governors, of which I am the head. The other board members are Dr Parker and his assistant Dr Franklin, who is brother to the Admiralty Proctor; their accompter George Cocke; Andrew Kole, who advises on investment; and Robert Underhill, who claims to be a gentleman but who looks like a Roundhead.'

Chaloner was not sure what was meant by the last remark, but was sure it was nothing complimentary. 'I met a man named George Cocke this morning – a Treasury official.'

'A fat, oily person with an eye for the ladies?' When Chaloner nodded, the Earl went on, 'Then it is the same man. He is an associate of Bullen Reymes, and sometimes stays in the mansion that Reymes has rented to escape the plague. So does Kole. Scoundrels, all of them!'

Chaloner recalled what Sir Philip Warwick had said about Reymes' houseguests: that they were courtiers.

Cocke was one, by virtue of his Treasury post, but Chaloner had never met anyone at White Hall named Andrew Kole. He said so.

'Kole is a speculator, who *thinks* he bought the Chelsea Theological College from the government,' explained the Earl. 'Unfortunately for him, he misread the deeds and only hired it from us. Thus he was annoyed when we took it away and turned it into a gaol – as you may have heard, it is where we put the prisoners we captured at the Battle of Lowestoft.'

Chaloner nodded, recalling how Captain Lester had thought it was too close to London. 'Kole does not hold you responsible for depriving him of his property, does he?'

The Earl shook his head. 'Personally, I thought it was rather unkind. However, Kole allowed himself to be blinded by greed – the College was ruinous, so he effected a few repairs, and aimed to make a quick profit by renting it out to aristocrats fleeing the plague. Losing it has broken him financially, which is why he is obliged to live on Reymes' charity.'

'And this is the man who tells Gorges how to manage its funds?' asked Chaloner warily. 'One who misinterpreted legal documents and lost everything he owns?'

'He was very successful before the college fiasco, and it is hard to condemn a man for a mistake that I might have made myself – the legal wording *was* very sly.'

'Does he bear the government a grudge?'

'Oh, I imagine so. I certainly would. But you can judge him for yourself, Chaloner. There is a board meeting today, and as I did not want to travel all the way to Chelsea myself, I ordered them to hold it here instead.'

31

'They do not mind?' Chaloner was startled by his employer's selfish attitude to the convenience of others.

The Earl's smile was smug. 'They defer to me as the major benefactor.'

Chaloner was still unhappy with what he had been told – or rather, what he had *not* been told – about the task he had been assigned, and had a lot of questions. 'You decry Kole and Cocke as scoundrels, yet you donate money to a foundation where they have a say in how it is spent. Why—'

'They have very little power,' interrupted the Earl dismissively. 'Because *I* make all the important decisions. Perhaps one of them resents it, and steals for revenge. You will have to find out, but do not worry about offending them – if anyone resigns in a huff, I shall replace him with someone of my own choosing, which will suit me very nicely.'

'I see.'

The Earl was thoughtful for a moment. 'There is something else you can do for me while in Chelsea, too: visit that prison. I am uncomfortable with the notion of a lot of hostile Hollanders so close to London, and I want you to assess whether they pose a risk to national security.'

'Is there any reason to suppose they might?'

'Oh, yes! It is being run by four commissioners, one of whom is the hateful Reymes. The others are Sir William Doyley, who cannot go five minutes without a pinch of snuff; John Evelyn, who lives in Deptford; and Sir Thomas Clifford, who is at sea with the navy.'

Chaloner had seen Doyley take snuff at White Hall that morning, while he knew Clifford from *Swiftsure*. He had never met Evelyn, although he was familiar with the name – the family had made gunpowder for both sides during the civil wars.

'I shall ride to Chelsea today,' he said, thinking that concerns about the gaol were a lot more pressing than a missing thirty pounds. It seemed that Lester had been right to question the decision to use the place.

'No, you will not,' countered the Earl irritably. 'I told you – I want you here until Friday. It is only three days hence anyway, which will make no difference to either matter.'

Chaloner was not so sure, but knew better than to argue. 'Very well, sir.'

'There is one last thing before we go inside: I want you to play some music for a gathering I am obliged to hold tomorrow. I dare not hire professionals, lest they have the plague.'

Chaloner experienced a sharp pang of grief. 'I cannot, sir. My viols were stolen by the servants after Hannah . . . when she was not there to stop them.'

The Earl grimaced. 'Dishonest staff! The bane of any decent establishment. But Kipps told me that you have already bought a replacement.'

'Yes,' acknowledged Chaloner. 'But it is not—'

'Do not worry about disappointing my guests,' interrupted the Earl. 'They are mostly unimportant people, who will not mind amateurs.'

Chaloner resented the implication that amateur equalled mediocre. Indeed, he might have made music his career, if his father had not deemed it an unsuitable occupation for gentlemen. He sometimes wondered what his sire would have thought of his work with the Earl, and suspected he would have been appalled. It was not a happy notion, but much had changed since the wars, and a youngest son with no inheritance was obliged to make a living as best he could.

'I am not ready to play it in public yet,' he said stiffly. 'Viols are like horses – it takes a while to get to know their—'

'Nonsense,' said the Earl briskly. 'I am sure you will do splendidly. But I hear the bell striking the hour, so we must hurry or we shall be late for the meeting.'

The Gorges board of governors was being entertained by Kipps when Chaloner and the Earl arrived. The two medical men were identifiable by their black coats and hats. Parker was long-nosed, thin and restless, while Franklin was younger and plump, with a merry twinkle in his eye that suggested dealing with mad ladies had not deprived him of his sense of humour. Chaloner had the feeling that he would be more pleasant company than his surly brother.

Mrs Bonney could not have been more woefully misnamed, and was one of the least handsome people Chaloner had ever met. She was powerfully built, with hairs sprouting from her chin, ears and nose, and beefy arms that were no doubt useful for restraining awkward patients. Accompter Cocke had homed in on her, apparently in the belief that no female should be exempt from his lecherous attentions, and was flummoxing her with whispered innuendos and sly movements of his sweaty hands.

The last two were Underhill and Kole. The Earl was right about Underhill, Chaloner thought, because the fellow's plain clothes and cropped hair *did* make him look like a Roundhead. Yet his manners and speech were polished, almost excessively so. He was admiring his host's books, taking them from the shelves to run covetous fingers over their bindings.

Kole, by contrast, was all frills and fluff. However, the lace that frothed too extravagantly at his throat was of poor quality, while his sword was cheaply made, and likely to snap at the first riposte. His wig was obviously borrowed, because it did not fit him properly, and the shine on his shoes was due to paint, rather than the gleam of expensive leather.

Was one of them responsible for the thefts, as the Earl had suggested? Chaloner assessed each in turn as Kipps embarked on a lengthy monologue about the city's latest plague measures. The most obvious suspect was Cocke, whose job as accompter would give him access to the money. But any hint of dishonesty would see him dismissed from the Treasury – a post that would earn a lot more than thirty pounds and a few baubles. Surely, he would not take the risk? The same was true of Mrs Bonney and the physicians, who would also have much to lose by indulging in unscrupulous practices. That left Kole and Underhill, and Chaloner decided to concentrate on them first.

'Smoking will *not* keep the plague out of Gorges,' Underhill was declaring with considerable conviction. 'Tobacco is the devil's herb, and will do more harm than good. Do not issue the inmates with pipes, Parker. Give them London Treacle instead.'

'That would be expensive,' remarked the Earl uneasily. 'Who will pay?'

'You, of course,' replied Underhill, and brandished the book he held, the clasp of which was solid gold. 'You have plenty of money.'

'I do not believe that London Treacle is a particularly

efficacious solution, personally,' said Dr Franklin, much to the Earl's obvious relief. 'Time-honoured remedies are always best, and I never leave home without a simple sponge soaked in vinegar.'

'Coffee,' whispered Parker, biting a fingernail and regarding the company with quick, furtive glances. 'It has many admirable properties, as we are discovering at Gorges. I believe the only way to combat the pestilence is by chewing the raw beans.'

He produced a box with a flourish, and offered them round. Everyone took one except Mrs Bonney and Franklin, who claimed they had tried them once and would not make the same mistake twice. Chaloner soon saw their point: the beans were foul, and tasted nothing like when they had been roasted.

'I think I might prefer the plague,' muttered the Earl, snapping his fingers for Kipps to bring him wine to wash away the flavour.

'Of course, we all know that the pestilence is spread by burglars,' declared Cocke. 'They invade the homes of the sick in search of easy loot, then pass the disease to those they meet on their way home.'

'Burglars have been more active recently,' agreed Parker, looking around as if he imagined some might appear in Clarendon House there and then.

'They have, but they are not so stupid as to prey on plague victims,' countered Underhill, his Roundhead features full of scorn. 'They target *empty* homes, ones belonging to the cowards who have fled the city in fear for their lives.'

'Cowards, like government ministers,' said Kole sourly, not looking at the Earl. 'And it serves them right. They rob people with their high taxes and their sly interpretations of the law, so they *should* know what it feels like to lose their most cherished possessions.'

'Time is passing,' said the Earl, eyeing him coolly. 'So let us be about our business. We are all busy people, after all.'

He conducted them into the chilly expanse of the Great Roome, and indicated that they should sit at the table. He took the chair at its head, with Mrs Bonney and the physicians on one side, and everyone else on the other. Chaloner took up station by the window, where he could watch and learn without being obliged to contribute, and Kipps stood by the door.

Cocke laid out pen and paper to make notes of the proceedings, and then he and his fellow board members regarded the Earl expectantly, waiting for him to declare the meeting open – all except Underhill, who was more interested in the books that lined the walls, at which he gazed with open longing.

'Jem, Lil and Una Collier have settled well at the almshouse,' reported Mrs Bonney, when the Earl nodded to say she could begin. 'They will be an asset to us in time.'

'In time?' echoed the Earl, frowning. 'Why not at once? The agreement was to house and feed them in exchange for their labour. Surely they should be an asset immediately?'

'They are still finding their feet,' explained Mrs Bonney. 'They—'

'But they moved in months ago,' argued the Earl. 'They should have found them by now.'

'They hail from Bath, so Chelsea is still new and strange,' said Franklin. 'However, we hired them out to the Theological College this week, and Warden Tooker

37

will pay us for their services. Not much, admittedly, but every little helps, and we are *very* short of funds.'

'What about the thefts?' asked the Earl, ignoring the bald hint that more donations were needed. 'Have you made any headway in tracking down the culprit?'

'Not yet,' replied Parker. 'Although I am inclined to think that an inmate is responsible – not from malice, but from illness.'

The Earl regarded him oddly. 'I thought you took gentlewomen with unbalanced humours. I did not realise that you housed the criminally insane as well. Another Bedlam, in fact.'

'Gorges is a world apart from Bedlam,' flashed Parker indignantly. '*We* treat ailments with kindness and under-standing. And coffee, of course.'

'Coffee?' repeated the Earl uncertainly.

'We believe it can cure madness, sir,' explained Franklin, politely deferential to a major benefactor. 'The bean has many admirable properties, and one is to—'

'These thefts have gone on far too long,' interrupted the Earl, more interested in the money. He pointed at Chaloner. 'So my intelligencer here will investigate on my behalf. He will start his enquiries on Friday, after he has delivered me to Hampton Court.'

There was an immediate clamour of objections: the board was unanimous in its opinion that no such measures were needed.

'It would upset the residents and be counterproductive,' declared Underhill, his shrill voice rising above them all. 'We would rather handle the matter ourselves.'

'I am sure you would,' said the Earl coolly. 'But it has been more than a month since this matter was first reported to me, and you are still no nearer to catching the culprit.'

'These things cannot be rushed,' declared Parker. 'And Underhill is right: your man's presence will distress our patients.'

'It is true,' said Franklin, while Mrs Bonney nodded at his side. 'Some of our ladies are in a very fragile state, and we cannot risk an outsider coming in with a lot of impertinent questions.'

'After all, we do not want their wealthy kin to take them away,' added Underhill slyly. 'It would not only damage their chances of recovery, but also deprive us of much-needed income.'

'Hear, hear,' agreed Kole. 'It is better that we tackle the culprit internally.'

'You have done your best, no doubt,' said the Earl shortly. 'But you have failed, so it is time for me to intervene. And that is my final word on the matter.'

Chaloner listened to the discussion with interest, intrigued that none of the governors wanted him to pry into their world. He had not taken to Underhill, Cocke or Kole, while Parker was jittery and ill at ease. Mrs Bonney and Franklin seemed more sanguine about the prospect of a detective in their midst, but perhaps they were just more adept at hiding their true opinions. He found he was rather looking forward to unearthing the secrets that this mismatched group hoped to hide from him.

'Rather you than me,' said Kipps, once the governors had gone, and he and Chaloner were sitting in the staff parlour on the top floor, which boasted a splendid view of the Earl's scrubby vegetable patches. 'I should not like to go to Chelsea. I am looking forward to Hampton Court.'

'Are you?' Chaloner thought there could be little worse than a lot of courtiers crammed into a palace that, while sizeable, was still considerably smaller than White Hall.

The Seal Bearer smiled dreamily. 'Lady Castlemaine will be there, and I have missed her glorious attributes this last month.'

The King's mistress's thighs represented Heaven on Earth, as far as Kipps was concerned, and he was so enamoured of them that he was willing to overlook the fact that they belonged to one of his employer's most deadly adversaries.

'Have you ever been to Chelsea?' asked Chaloner, thinking there was no harm in starting his enquiries early, and so aiming to learn a little about the village and its residents.

Kipps nodded. 'My wife had a melancholy last year, so I put her in Gorges for a spell. It is a good place – she came home happy, healthy and tranquil of mind.'

Chaloner wondered if he should have taken Hannah there, as then she might not have gone to the theatre when everyone had warned her against it. Was it *his* fault that she was dead? Because he was a poor husband who had failed to notice that she had needed a guiding hand? Should he have tried to secure employment that did not necessitate leaving her alone for months at a time?

'How did you hear about Gorges?' he asked, to stem the tide of guilty thoughts.

'Surgeon Wiseman recommended it. He has a lunatic wife of his own, so knows all the best asylums.' Kipps smiled. 'I admire our Earl for supporting Gorges. The

40

other governors pay what they can, but he supplies the bulk of its funding.'

'I was under the impression that all the inmates were from wealthy families. Do they not pay boarding fees?'

'Of course, but there is still a shortfall. Our Earl ensures that the place runs as it should, and that Parker has enough money for his experiments.'

'And all because an aunt was there in the Commonwealth?' asked Chaloner sceptically.

'A very sad case, by all accounts, but Gorges cured her. Mrs Bonney might be a dragon, but she runs an efficient operation – or she did before the thief struck – while Franklin and Parker are devoted medical men who are gentle with their charges. However, the board could do without Underhill, Cocke and Kole. None are men I like.'

'No?' probed Chaloner. 'Why not?'

'Underhill claims to be a gentleman, but there is something about him that does not quite ring true. And who are his kin? I know none of them.'

'Why would you? He is a Parliamentarian, and your acquaintances tend to be Cavaliers.'

'It is more than that, Tom. There is something . . . something *awry* about him. Meanwhile, Cocke is a scoundrel, as you will have sensed when I introduced you earlier, and you should investigate him first. He will almost certainly transpire to be corrupt.'

'Do you have any particular reason to accuse him?'

'Instinct. He is a rogue, and I shall dance naked in King Street if you discover otherwise. And as for Kole, he is like a keg of gunpowder – he is furious that the government cheated him over the Theological College, and is set to explode.'

41

'Stealing thirty pounds and a few trinkets is exploding?'

Kipps eyed him beadily. 'No, but it could be a start. He is a speculator, which means he takes risks in the hope of huge returns. He wins some and loses others, but this was loss on a massive scale, and he is not the type to take it lying down. I doubt he holds the Earl personally responsible, but you never know. I advise you to watch him very carefully.'

Chaloner nodded his thanks for the warning. 'Why were any of them chosen to serve on the board? I understand Mrs Bonney and the *medici* – they work there – but Underhill, Kole and Cocke seem odd selections.'

'Parker invited Underhill, because they are friends and live together. Meanwhile, Kole was the richest man in the village when he owned the Theological College; now he is the poorest, but Parker said it would be unkind to dismiss him, so he remains. And finally, Cocke offered his accompting services for a very modest sum, so he was accepted with alacrity.'

'Why would he do that?' asked Chaloner suspiciously.

'He said it was to support a worthy cause, although I do not believe him. I think he just wants to get at Gorges' ladies. Our Earl would be delighted if Cocke was the culprit, because Cocke is a crony of his enemy Reymes – as is Kole, for that matter. If you embarrass Reymes by exposing him as a man with corrupt acquaintances, the Earl's gratitude will know no bounds.'

'Well, then,' said Chaloner, 'I had better see what I can do.'

As the Earl had decreed that Chaloner could not travel to Chelsea until Friday – although the Gorges governors would be in London anyway, for the following night's soirée at Clarendon House – Chaloner decided to move his enquiries along by visiting Wiseman, to see what the surgeon could tell him about the asylum.

A glance at the Earl's several expensive clocks told him that Wiseman would be in White Hall, dosing its few remaining staff with anti-plague remedies. The fear of infection was so great that they could not be trusted to physick themselves, as most were of the opinion that the more they swallowed, the safer they would be. They would not be the first to poison themselves with something intended to protect.

He walked along Piccadilly, then turned south at Charing Cross, acutely aware of the subdued, anxious atmosphere that permeated everything and everyone. Folk scurried along with their heads down, as if they imagined that even catching the eye of another person might be enough to bring them low, and bells tolled almost without stopping.

He arrived at White Hall and aimed for the chapel, where he knew Wiseman would be working. The surgeon, like many in his trade, was of the opinion that his remedies were more effective when administered in a holy place. Chaloner had no idea whether it worked or was rank superstition, but he understood why *medici* were eager to leave nothing to chance where the plague was concerned.

Wiseman was an imposing figure – tall, broad and clad in red from head to toe. He had thick auburn locks that tumbled around his shoulders, and even his boots were scarlet. He added to his impressive physique with a regime of lifting heavy stones each morning, so he was enormously strong. Chaloner pitied his patients, suspecting that if he decided that a particular course of treatment was in order, few would be able to fend him off.

Chaloner was not sure why he liked Wiseman, who was arrogant, rude and egotistical. He supposed it was because he had learned how to see beyond the *medicus*'s flaws to his virtues, which included a deep sense of loyalty to those he deemed worthy and an unshakeable sense of justice. At first, he had resisted the surgeon's overtures of friendship, but Wiseman had persisted, and Chaloner was now glad of it. It was Wiseman who had written to tell him about Hannah's death, and who had used his influence to help find where she had been buried.

'There,' Wiseman said, as his last patient gulped down the potion he offered and fled outside to giggle with her cronies. 'I have done all I can, and if they succumb now, it will not be my fault.'

'Have you seen the latest Bill?' asked Chaloner, referring to the official mortality figures that were published each week. Every Londoner knew that the real numbers were actually far higher, but they studied them assiduously anyway, hoping to see some sign that the disease was beginning to loosen its hold.

'More than eighteen hundred dead of the pestilence in seven days,' replied the surgeon grimly. 'There will be even more next week, and cases will continue to rise until winter bites. These terrible visitations are always the same, and we have not seen the worst of this one yet.'

As if to prove him right, the bells of nearby St Margaret's began to ring for a child.

'So there was truth in all those omens?' asked Chaloner, talking more to distract himself from the mournful sound than because he wanted an answer. 'The strange new stars, the oddly shaped clouds, the streams that ran with blood instead of water?'

'I do not know about that, but I can tell you that the weather is not helping. First, there was a bitterly cold winter, then an unusually wet spring, and now this scorching summer. Tens of thousands will die, and the King is wise to take himself to a safe place.'

'But you will stay?'

'Only fools linger in the city now – or folk with nowhere else to go. I shall join the King in Hampton Court in a few days. I have already sent my servants and most valuable possessions on ahead of me, because far too many burglars are at large to risk leaving anything behind. As you should know, given that you were a victim yourself.'

'My house was not stripped bare by burglars, but by the maid and footman that Hannah hired when I was away. They were afraid they would be turned out when I came home, so they aimed to steal enough to tide them over until they could find other employment.'

'And *would* you have turned them out?'

'Yes,' replied Chaloner shortly. Hannah had possessed an unerring capacity to select the most sullen and dishonest rogues available, and there was no reason to suppose that the last pair had been any different from the rest, even though he had never met them.

'Well, there you are then: they were wise to take precautions. They were unlikely to find other employment, given that people are afraid to look at each other these days, let alone hire new minions.'

Disinclined to dwell on the matter, Chaloner changed the subject. 'The Earl wants me to investigate a series of thefts at Gorges House, and Kipps tells me that you know the place.'

'I do. In fact, my wife is there now. It was hardly fair to leave her in Bedlam while its inmates die like flies, so I took her to Gorges instead.'

Most men with incurably insane spouses would have welcomed an opportunity to be rid of them with no trouble to themselves, but Chaloner was not surprised to learn that it was a recourse the surgeon had refused to consider. The hapless Dorothy had been lost to Wiseman for many years, and although his mistress – an imposing lady named Temperance North – had succeeded her in his affections, the surgeon remained scrupulously solicitous of her welfare.

'I plan to visit her on my way to Hampton Court,' Wiseman went on. 'Shall we go together? Dorothy mentioned these thefts in a letter she wrote to me, along with a death – a murder, in fact.'

Chaloner sighed irritably. So he was right: the Earl *had* been holding something back. Would his master never trust him? But why neglect to mention such an important detail when he would learn it the moment he arrived in Chelsea anyway?

'Who died?' he asked, stifling his exasperation.

'Another resident – one Nancy Janaway. Why? Will you investigate that as well?'

'Yes, probably,' grumbled Chaloner. 'They might be connected.'

'Good,' said Wiseman. 'I do not like the notion of her keeping company with killers. She might get ideas, and go on the rampage herself. And when Dorothy goes on the rampage . . . well, all I can say is that you do not want to be within slashing distance.'

'Lord!' muttered Chaloner.

Chapter 2

When he had returned from sea, Chaloner had abandoned the little cottage that he and Hannah had rented together, and taken rooms in Covent Garden instead. They were in a fine house that belonged to Wiseman, who had bought it cheap after its owners had decided to uproot and move to plague-free Suffolk. The surgeon did not live there himself, because he was currently serving as Master of the Company of Barber Surgeons, a post that brought with it free accommodation in Chyrurgeons' Hall. Chaloner occupied the top floor, while the rest of the building was let to a family of apothecaries, who filled it with the sweet aroma of herbs. As they claimed their pomanders were effective against the plague, Chaloner supposed it was as safe a place to be as any.

His lodgings comprised two spacious chambers, one of which commanded a fine view of the market, while the other overlooked a line of poky back yards. Wiseman had lent him furniture and other basic items until he bought his own, but as Chaloner was disinclined to go shopping when it was something he and Hannah would have done together, 'home' was spartan and not particularly comfortable.

The following morning – Wednesday – he sat at his front window, wondering if London had ever been more forlorn. By dawn, the market was usually alive with activity, as traders converged with horses, carts and wares, making the air ring with shouts and the rattle of wheels on cobbles. That day, only a handful of vendors had arrived, and they kept well away from each other, wanting only to sell what they had brought and leave. Traffic was sparse, too. Those in carriages kept the curtains drawn, while pedestrians scurried along with their hats pulled low, lest they were hailed by someone they knew – someone who might carry the plague.

It was a dismal sight, so Chaloner turned his attention to the room, although this was no more uplifting. The only items of a personal nature were a book of poetry that had belonged to his first wife – he had hidden it behind a skirting board, which had saved it from the servants' sticky fingers – and his new viola da gamba, or bass viol, which he did not like nearly as much as the old ones. There was also a letter from Hannah, for which he had Kipps to thank: the Seal Bearer had found it tossed in the garden after the staff had fled, and had kept it safe until his friend had come home.

It had been written while Hannah was in the grip of her final fever, and there was little in it that made sense. His relationship with her had been complicated, fraught with emotions he could not begin to comprehend, but he had believed that she had loved him. The letter made him uncertain, something he was finding unexpectedly difficult to handle. It concluded with:

*The ghost-man wille leade the Peace-Maker and the
Dandey to Stryke the Sicke and the Hurte. I knowe
you wille understand, as I had it from the play-howse.
Beware of smokey half-fisshe and Candels in Battell.*

Chaloner could not imagine why she thought he would
understand such garbled words, and his failure to do so
bothered him profoundly. He had tracked down as many
of her acquaintances as he could find, and asked what
they knew about her determination to visit the theatre
in the face of all reason. None had been able to answer,
although he had learned that the 'play-howse' was the
Duke's Theatre in Lincoln's Inn Fields, where she had
watched *The Indian Queen*. Yet even knowing this had not
helped him fathom her behaviour, and he was eventually
forced to concede that it would just have to remain a
mystery.

Even so, he took the note from the mantelpiece, and
read it for at least the fiftieth time. Should he do what
Wiseman recommended, and throw it away, on the
grounds that she had not been in her right mind? But
it was the only memento he had of her, and he was
loath to part with it.

To take his mind off his inadequacies as a husband,
he sat down with his viol and bowed a series of exercises,
supposing he had better practise if he was to play for
the Earl that evening. Fortunately, his neighbours were
tolerant of the noise, although they had asked for some
more cheerful tunes. Since Hannah's death, he had
tended to favour sombre pieces, feeling jaunty airs were
disrespectful.

Music was his greatest love, and had helped him through all manner of crises. It was helping him now, and he felt the beginnings of relief from the nagging unhappiness that had gripped him ever since he had learned about Hannah's death. He began to play a piece by Michael Praetorius, but the viol did not respond as he would have liked, and he eventually faltered to a stop. What was wrong with him? Was he losing his touch? Or would he play better on a different instrument? Somehow, he suspected it was not the viol that was the problem.

He set it down and picked up Hannah's letter again, thinking about the last time he had seen her. They had quarrelled, because she had spent more money than they had earned for the second week running. Or rather, he had mentioned the matter, and she had responded with a furious tirade about penny-pinching. Her reaction had irked him, because they had suffered problems with debt earlier in the year, and he had hoped she had mended her ways. Then she had aimed a kick at his best viol – an unforgivable offence, as far as he was concerned – and stormed out to carouse with her fun-loving friends at Court.

Had he been a disappointment to her? He had never once told her that he loved her, even though he had known that it was something she had longed to hear. Would it even have been true? It was a question he had asked himself many times, and he still did not know the answer.

Eventually, he pulled his mind away from Hannah, and turned it to work. The Gorges governors would be among the guests that evening, so he would question them about the thefts when they arrived – and about the murder, too.

50

That left the prison and its commissioners. Clifford was at sea, and thus unavailable; Chaloner was disinclined to speak to Reymes, given his hostility towards the Earl, which was likely to be exacerbated when discussing duties he had not wanted in the first place; and Doyley might be similarly hostile, because the two were friends. The fourth and last was John Evelyn, whose home was in Deptford, some five or six miles distant. The Earl had declared Chelsea off limits, but he had said nothing about Deptford, and Chaloner would be back in plenty of time to play at the soirée.

The best horses for hire were from the Crown on Fleet Street, so Chaloner started to walk there. The bell of St Clement Danes tolled as he passed, to mark the demise of a woman and her baby. The first of the day's funerals was already underway, and a sombre procession emerged, aiming for a huge open pit. One mourner coughed, and found himself standing in splendid isolation. Most of the others smoked furiously, while the rest took surreptitious sips from phials. Chaloner pulled his own pipe from his pocket, and regarded it without enthusiasm before shoving it away again.

He reached the inn, where he chose a large bay with white socks, and while it was being saddled, he became aware of a familiar but not very pleasant smell. It came from the nearby Rainbow Coffee House, and he decided that a dish of the beverage might put him in good stead for his journey, despite the obvious risks of entering such a place. As he opened the door, he recalled Parker's contention that the bean could cure insanity, but doubted it was true. If it were, coffee houses would not be famous

51

for the wild and foolish opinions that were regularly brayed in them.

The Rainbow was not comfortable, did not sell good coffee, and most of its clientele was bigoted and unfriendly. Chaloner had no idea why he kept going back there, and supposed it was because it never changed – it had a feeling of permanence that was reassuring when his own life was in a constant state of flux.

As usual, the owner, Thomas Farr, had burnt his beans, so the air was full of greasy brown smoke. It had been allowed to settle on the windows for so long that they were opaque, although this was not necessarily a bad thing. The government's spies liked to monitor coffee houses, and the oily sheen prevented them from peering through the glass and taking note of who was inside.

The Rainbow was notably emptier than usual, although its regulars still gathered for their pre-work tipples. Farr was serving them from a tall jug with a long spout. He had been busy with his sugar-nips – the pincer-like implement that allowed manageable pieces to be clipped from sugarloaves – and bowls of it stood on the table to disguise the taste of his brew. Chaloner never took any, as a silent but futile protest against the hellish conditions for slaves on plantations.

'What news?' called Farr, voicing the traditional coffee-house greeting. 'Although I do not expect much from you or anyone else these days. It is nothing but plague, plague, plague.'

'Perhaps it is God's judgement on us for fighting the Dutch,' said Joseph Thompson, the pious rector of St Dunstan-in-the-West. He shook his head sadly. 'The pestilence walks among us, and what do we do? Make war on another Protestant nation, one that was kind to the King when he was in exile. They deserve better from us.'

'God does not agree, or He would not have let us win the Battle of Lowestoft,' declared Fabian Stedman, who spent so much time in the Rainbow that Chaloner was not sure he was telling the truth when he claimed to be a printer. He was a fervent Royalist, who thought that the King and his Court could do no wrong; he was in a dwindling minority, as people learned that His Majesty fell a long way short of what they had hoped for when the monarchy was restored.

'It must have been an awesome sight,' said Farr, regarding Chaloner enviously. 'I should have liked to have seen it myself, although from a safe distance, naturally. I would not want cannonballs whistling over my head.'

'Or through it,' said Thompson grimly. 'Men died in that encounter, and it is ghoulish to want to be a witness. Is that not so, Chaloner?'

'Nonsense!' cried Stedman, sparing Chaloner the need to reply. 'It was a glorious day – one when God smiled on our brave captains.'

'It was a great victory,' agreed Farr. 'And it taught the Dutch a lesson they will not forget.'

'Really?' asked Thompson archly. 'Then why are they still at sea, preparing for the next engagement? If they had been as badly trounced as you claim, they would be suing for peace.'

'Because they are fools,' replied Stedman stoutly. 'They lost thousands of their sailors, but do not know when to concede defeat. Have you heard that the ones dragged from the sea are now housed in Chelsea? Word is that they are better fed than most of us.'

'Thanks to the commissioners who were appointed to look after them,' said Farr, shaking his head disapprovingly. 'Men who will see that the rascals live in luxury.'

Chaloner had been in enough prisons to know that this was unlikely to be true. However, he was glad the subject had been broached, because it gave him the chance to ask a few questions. The Rainbow was a great place for gossip, and he used it shamelessly for his investigations.

'Do you know any of these commissioners?'

'I know *of* them,' replied Farr promptly. 'Reymes is a vicious brute with more enemies than stars in the sky, although his friend Doyley is as gentle as a lamb. Then Evelyn is a writer, and Clifford is a politician who likes sitting on committees.'

'But you have never met them,' said Thompson disdainfully, and turned to Chaloner. '*I* have, though, so you should listen to my opinions about them, not Farr's.'

'Well, go on then,' said Farr acidly. 'Enlighten us with your superior knowledge.'

Thompson obliged. 'Clifford is ambitious, Reymes is aggressive, Doyley is intelligent, and Evelyn is a saint.' He smiled fondly. 'I plan to visit him at his home in Deptford next week. We were at Oxford together, and I have some seeds to give him.'

'Seeds?' queried Farr warily.

'We share an interest in horticulture,' explained Thompson.

'I am going to Deptford, too,' said Chaloner, thinking that Evelyn might be more willing to talk to him if he arrived with a mutual friend. 'Perhaps we can ride there together. But it must be today, not next week.'

'Why would you want to go there?' asked Farr, with

the rank suspicion of a man who rarely travelled. 'I cannot imagine there will be anything to see, other than fields, woods and bogs.'

'This coffee is terribly strong, Farr,' remarked Stedman, changing the subject with a briskness that was typical at the Rainbow. 'Is it from a different kind of bean?'

'No, I used twice as many as normal,' explained Farr, while Chaloner had one sip and decided to take no more. 'I attended a lecture by a physician from Chelsea yesterday – a Dr Parker, who said that strong coffee will stop us from catching the plague. He is a medical man, so he must be right.'

'From Gorges House?' asked Thompson. 'He told *me* that coffee can cure madness, but said nothing about the plague. Of course, that was before the disease arrived in the city . . .'

'Coffee is a remarkable plant,' averred Farr sagely. 'With many health-giving properties. Take you lot, for example. The reason you are all hale and hearty is because you drink my brews.'

'No, it is because we smoke,' said Stedman, puffing out a great cloud of it. 'That is what will keep us safe.'

'Well, I put *my* trust in the Lord,' said Thompson loftily. He stood and looked at Chaloner. 'If you want to travel today, we should go – before the morning grows any hotter.'

The journey to Deptford took two hours at a comfortable pace, most of it through the fields that provided London with its staples – wheat, barley, oats, fruit and vegetables. The sun had baked the ground so hard that most crops had withered, and the harvest looked set to be poor. The road was busy with people fleeing the city, but the villages along the way did not want anyone stopping in them, lest they carried the sickness, so would-be visitors were encouraged to keep moving.

'I have known all four commissioners for years,' Thompson said, as he and Chaloner left Rotherhithe, where they had tried to water their horses; they had prudently abandoned the attempt when three men appeared with pistols. 'Reymes is very quarrelsome and has clashed with all manner of folk – Evelyn, your Earl, Clifford, Buckingham, the Strangeways family . . .'

'The Strangeways family?'

'A clan of Chelsea fishmongers. I cannot imagine what induced Reymes to begin a feud with them, as they are lowly folk, and sparring with them is undignified. I feel sorry for Evelyn, though. He deserves better than to be thrust into Reymes' abrasive company all the time. So does Doyley, for that matter.'

'Have you ever been to Chelsea?'

Thompson was suddenly furtive, although it had been a perfectly innocuous question. 'I might have gone once or twice. Oh, look at that magnificent oak! I am surprised it has not been chopped down and used for building boats. We are near the royal shipyards, after all.'

He prattled on, not giving Chaloner the chance to ask more, and by the time his monologue had run dry, they had reached Deptford. In stark contrast to London, this was a hive of activity, as its yards churned out new vessels to fight the Dutch. Its people were suspicious of strangers, too, and more than a few touched amulets, spat or glared as Chaloner and Thompson rode past.

'Of course I will introduce you to Evelyn,' said Thompson warmly, when Chaloner casually expressed a desire to meet the man. 'You will like him very much.'

Evelyn's home was called Sayes Court, an undistinguished house encircled by remarkable grounds that boasted terraced walks, an arboretum, a kitchen garden with transparent bee hives, and an orchard with three hundred trees. An army of labourers was at work in them, and as water was pumped from the river, Evelyn's little empire was a bright oasis of green in the dusty yellow-brown of the surrounding countryside.

The man himself was thin, delicate and looked as if too much responsibility had been placed upon his narrow shoulders. He had a pale, tired face, and was comfortably clad in old breeches and a darned white shirt. His hands were ink-stained, and he had clearly been at work when Chaloner and Thompson were shown in.

'I was appointed commissioner in May,' he said, discussing an 'honour' that few would have been pleased to accept. 'It is a great privilege, because I am to serve with Thomas Clifford.'

'Really?' Chaloner was astonished to learn this should be considered a bonus, rather than something to be avoided at all costs.

Evelyn nodded. 'He sits on lots of committees, so knows many influential people.'

'Tell Chaloner about Reymes and Doyley,' prompted Thompson.

Evelyn grimaced. 'Doyley is a fine man, although I cannot stop sneezing when he is near, because of the snuff he loves so much. Reymes is much harder to like. Good manners prevent me from saying more, but you will understand what I mean when you meet him yourself.'

'Why was Chelsea's Theological College chosen as a prison?' asked Chaloner.

'Because it was empty and available – although Andrew Kole will tell you that it was nothing of the kind. He thinks he bought it, you see, and beggared himself repairing the place, ready to rent out. Of course, he is not the only one who thinks the College belongs to him.'

'Ah, you refer to the younger Sutcliffe,' said Thompson, nodding. 'The elder – who was Dean of Exeter Cathedral – paid for most of the building work out of his own pocket. He is dead, but his nephew believes the College should now be his, passed to him with the rest of his uncle's estate. Did you ever meet John Sutcliffe, Evelyn? A more sinister fellow does not exist! Word is that he was an assassin during the wars, and that he thoroughly enjoyed the work.'

'Yes, I heard those tales,' replied Evelyn. 'But then he shifted his interests to the theatre, and I am told that he now prefers Shakespeare to knives.'

They were ranging away from Chaloner's original question, so he brought Evelyn back on track. 'Are you happy with the arrangements that are in place for the Dutch prisoners?'

'Not really,' sighed Evelyn. 'Conditions are cramped, and if plague breaks out . . . well, suffice to say that few will survive. I suggested an exchange – Hollanders swapped for men of our own – but the government feels it is too early in the hostilities.'

'What about security?' pressed Chaloner, more concerned about the danger to London. 'Is it possible for the inmates to escape?'

Evelyn smiled. 'It is possible, but I doubt any will try. Most do not speak English, and would be recaptured immediately. And even if they did manage to evade our patrols, what could they do? Steal a ship and sail back to Holland? That would not be easy!'

'If there are several hundred of them, they could march to London and cause trouble.'

'There are two thousand, actually,' said Evelyn. 'But they would never set their sights on London – they would be too frightened of catching the plague. Good heavens – here come Reymes and Doyley! I am popular today.'

Chaloner watched with interest as the two other commissioners were ushered into Evelyn's parlour. Reymes was all self-important bustle, while Doyley verged on the lethargic; he produced a box of snuff and took a sniff, although it was Evelyn who sneezed.

'We have been to a meeting in Greenwich,' explained Doyley, passing Evelyn a bundle of paper that was liberally adorned with brown smudges; more were on his cuffs, suggesting that snuff-taking was not a very clean business. 'So we took the opportunity to bring you these – the figures for last month's victuals at the prison.'

He turned his large eyes questioningly on Chaloner, indicating that he wanted an introduction. Evelyn obliged, although Reymes flushed red with anger when he learned that he was in company with a member of the hated Earl of Clarendon's staff.

'Satan in Dunkirk House!' Reymes spat. 'It was *his* idea to give us this damned commission, knowing that to refuse would be regarded as an act of insurrection. But it is a terrible post, with meagre pay and no opportunity for advancement.'

'Oh, come, Reymes,' said Evelyn soothingly. 'Think of the good we can do.'

'I do not want to do good,' snapped Reymes. 'I want what I am owed. I gave my all for the King during the wars, and he should compensate me accordingly. It is all very well for you and Doyley – you have wealthy families – but I deserve to be treated more sympathetically.'

Doyley took another pinch of snuff. 'We are proud to do our duty,' he said, shooting his friend a look that warned him to guard his tongue in front of Chaloner and Thompson – men they did not know. 'I should not like anyone to think that we are ungrateful for this opportunity to serve our country.'

Evelyn sneezed a second time, while Reymes sneered his disdain for the remark.

'Chaloner was just asking about prison security,' said Evelyn, dabbing at his nose with a grubby handkerchief before tactfully changing the subject, 'and our ability to keep our charges within its walls. What do you say to that?'

'I say he mind his own business,' flared Reymes. 'I know what Clarendon is doing – he wants his spy to find faults with what we have done. Well, he will be disappointed, because there is nothing amiss with our arrangements.'

It had crossed Chaloner's mind that his employer wanted there to be problems, so he could strike Reymes with the final *coup de grâce*. He hoped all would be in order, though: Doyley and Evelyn seemed decent men, and he had no wish to see them used as pawns in political games.

'That was not why—' he began.

'Of course it was,' snarled Reymes. 'But the prison is our concern, not his, and if he attempts to interfere again, I shall tell the King that he is organising a break-out himself, and aims to topple the government by using freed Dutch seamen.'

'You must harbour a very deep dislike for him,' said Chaloner, astonished by the wild threat – one that not even the Earl's most rabid adversaries would believe.

'I hate him,' declared Reymes uncompromisingly. 'And I wish him all the harm in the world. I shall wish you the same, if you approach me with this business again.'

There was no point in prolonging the interview, so Chaloner took his leave, declining Evelyn's offer of a tour of the garden followed by dinner. Reymes ignored Chaloner until he was out of the room, then released a stream of invective that comprised a lot of bad language and imaginative name-calling. Chaloner listened for a moment, but it was all hot air – the Earl had made an enemy of a man who was powerless to fight back, and who was full of bitter frustration about it.

It was mid-afternoon when Chaloner collected his horse from Evelyn's stable for the return journey. Thompson had decided to stay, eager to see what new arboreal species his friend had acquired since they had last met, and Reymes had business in the village, but Doyley approached with a friendly smile.

'May I ride back to the city with you? It is unsafe to travel alone in these desperate times.'

Chaloner was more than happy to spend time with a commissioner, especially as Doyley transpired to be an erudite and interesting companion. He had been a professional soldier in the Swedish army until his father had died, at which point he had been obliged to return home to manage his inheritance. Later, he had been knighted by the first King Charles, of whom he had been a fervent supporter. He regarded Chaloner appraisingly.

'I imagine you fought for the other side, though.' He

smiled and raised his hand when Chaloner opened his mouth to deny it. 'I knew your uncle – another Thomas Chaloner.'

'Many people did,' said Chaloner, rather bitterly.

His father's brother had signed the old King's death warrant, which had made him a hero under Cromwell's government, but a dangerous dissident in the eyes of the current one. He had been a lively, flamboyant character with a vast circle of friends, and Chaloner was always being accosted by people claiming to have known him. He often found himself wishing that his kinsman had been a little less gregarious.

'He knew how to enjoy himself,' sighed Doyley wistfully. 'Yet you do not seem cast in the same mould. *He* would not have declined an invitation to hobnob with Evelyn.'

'No,' agreed Chaloner, and briskly changed the subject, unwilling to discuss a kinsman who would have been executed as a traitor had he not managed to flee the country first. 'Do you live in Chelsea, or are you obliged to travel there whenever you visit the gaol?'

'My town home is in Hatton Garden, so if I need to be in Chelsea for any length of time, I stay with Reymes, who rents a house there.'

'You do not lodge in the prison? There must be some accommodation for staff and visitors.'

'There is.' Doyley chortled, although it turned into a series of snorts as he inhaled more snuff. 'But I would never consider sleeping there – I might not get out again! It is a secure place, and Warden Tooker manages it very well.'

'So the College was a good choice of building for the purpose?'

'I believe so, and it has fulfilled that function before – Oliver Cromwell kept Scottish rebels in it at one point. It was squalid then, but we shall ensure conditions are better this time. It will cost us a great deal of our own money, of course, but that cannot be helped.'

'So I can report to my Earl that you are satisfied with it?'

'You may. Have you ever been to Chelsea? It is a lovely place – and famous, too, with Dr Parker and his amazing work in curing lunacy.'

'Using coffee, apparently.'

Doyley shrugged. 'It does not matter *why* he is successful, only that his treatments help the afflicted. Of course, it was unfortunate that one of them died.'

'I heard about that. It is said that she was murdered.'

'Strangled,' nodded Doyley with a sigh. 'In the orchard, apparently.'

'How easy is it to gain access to Gorges House?'

'Not very. There is a high wall around it, and its gates are kept locked for obvious reasons – to protect vulnerable residents from prying eyes, and to prevent the others from getting out. A few of them are seriously disturbed.'

'Are any dangerous? In other words, could the victim have been killed by another patient?'

'The governors claim that an intruder did it, but who can blame them? They will lose wealthy clients if it is put about that they accommodate killers.'

'*Do* they accommodate killers?'

Doyley shrugged. 'Well, Dorothy Wiseman is a powerful lady who has hurt others before.'

Chaloner's heart sank. He did not want to investigate a murder where the chief suspect was his friend's wife.

*

For the rest of the journey, Doyley spoke knowledgeably on all manner of subjects, and Chaloner was sorry when they eventually reached the city, as he could have listened for longer. Doyley made his farewells and aimed for the Royal Exchange – emptier than usual, but still active – while Chaloner rode on. It was late afternoon, and the air was parched and still. Dust hung like a miasma, and he wondered if the plague lurked within it. He lit his pipe, although not with much expectation that it would protect him.

He returned the horse to the inn and went home, where he washed and shaved in a bowl of brackish water. Then he donned a clean white shirt, black breeches and grey long-coat, grabbed his viol and set off to Clarendon House. The clocks were just striking six as he walked up the drive.

The soirée was to be in the Chapell Pavilion, a gloriously ornate hall adorned with religious art. Its windows had been thrown open in the hope of catching a breeze, but the sun had been pouring into it all day, so it was like a furnace. Even the Earl, who was unnatural in his appreciation of heat, complained.

'It makes wearing a wig very uncomfortable,' he confided to Chaloner. Then he looked the spy up and down critically. 'Although you seem to have left yours at home.'

'It was stolen,' said Chaloner, supposing some good had come out of the servants' perfidy. He segued to another subject, before the Earl could order him to buy a replacement. 'I travelled to Deptford today, to ask John Evelyn about the prison.'

The Earl eyed him coolly. 'I thought I told you to stay in the city.'

'You told me not to go to Chelsea,' corrected Chaloner, then decided this might be construed as impertinence, so added, 'Your unease about the College worried me, sir, so I decided to waste no time. Three of the four commissioners were there, and they all said they were happy with its security, but I shall assess it for myself on Friday.'

'Reymes is a villain, so leave no stone unturned,' instructed the Earl. 'Do you hear me?'

Chaloner nodded, although he was sorry to learn that the main purpose of the exercise *was* spite, not concern for London's safety. He turned the discussion to Gorges.

'While I am in Chelsea, would you like me to investigate the Gorges murder as well as the thefts?' he asked, purely to let the Earl know that he had found out about it.

But the blood drained from the Earl's face, and when he spoke, it was in a horrified whisper. 'What murder?'

'An inmate,' replied Chaloner, watching him closely. So he had not known, he thought in surprise, which meant it was something else that his master was so assiduously keeping from him.

'Which one?' asked the Earl hoarsely.

'Nancy Janaway. She was strangled.'

'Lord!' gasped the Earl, plainly shocked. 'You *must* catch the culprit. Begin your enquiries at tonight's soirée. All the governors will be here, and you have my permission to ask them whatever you like – including why none of them has bothered to mention the matter to me.'

'Very well, sir.'

'Then come to tell me what they say. However, my family must not know what you are doing. Is that clear? They are aware of the thefts, but the death must be kept from them at all costs. I should never hear the end of it if they find out that I pour my precious money into a place where residents perish in suspicious circumstances.'

'They are still here? I thought they would be in Hampton Court by now.'

'They were delayed, because the carts were too top-heavy to travel. They will go tomorrow, and I shall follow the day after. But I am glad they are here, as it happens – they have agreed to help me entertain my guests this evening.'

'You do not need my viol, then?' Chaloner found himself relieved, which bemused him, as he never usually dodged an opportunity for music. What was wrong with him? Some sort of divine revenge for not caring for Hannah as he should have done?

'You can play jigs for the first hour, but then I want you to concentrate on getting answers.' The Earl eyed him disapprovingly. 'You say your wig was stolen, but what about your livery? I want all my staff in uniform this evening – I cannot have folk thinking that I am too poor to provide my people with suitable attire.'

'The servants took them too, after Hannah—'

'Then you must purchase some more,' said the Earl briskly. 'Meanwhile, you may borrow a blue coat and yellow breeches from me, and my son will lend you a wig. The clothes will be a tight fit, of course, but that cannot be helped.'

The coat and breeches were not tight at all, given the Earl's princely girth. Moreover, both were made of thickly expensive material, while the wig was weighty and made Chaloner's head ache. The Earl regarded him appraisingly when he reappeared, so Chaloner hastened to distract him, lest he ordered some additional article of clothing donned in the name of appearances.

'Who else is coming tonight, sir, besides the Gorges governors?'

'A smattering of merchants, the Treasury men, a few Admiralty clerks and some gentlemen from White Hall. I felt obliged to acknowledge their courage before I abandon the city, too. It was my wife who invited the board, though – they are lowly creatures compared to the others. Oh, and the Rector of Chelsea is coming as well.'

'For any particular reason?'

'He was standing with the governors when my wife extended the invitation, and she says it would have been rude to exclude him. Personally, I think she should have waited until he had gone, because he is not a very nice man, as you will see when you meet him. But my guests are beginning to arrive, so you had better get to your post.'

The 'consort' was to play in an antechamber, decorously out of sight of the guests in the Chapell Pavilion, but close enough so the music would be easily audible and thus fill any awkward silences in the conversation. Lady Clarendon was already there, fussing over the arrangement of chairs, when Chaloner and the Earl walked in.

'Have you ordered enough wine, dear?' she asked her husband. 'You tend to be miserly on these occasions, but it is better to have too much than not enough.'

'I am sure the Court debauchees would agree,' said the Earl sourly. 'However, this is an abstemious household, so no one will be offered more than one cup of claret. Except the musicians, who will have none. They cannot play and drink at the same time anyway.'

Amusement flashed in Frances' eyes. 'Will you have them faint from thirst, then? Let them have what they want – it will calm their nerves. Have you told Thomas who the others will be?'

The Earl obliged. 'Mr Greeting from the King's Private Musick, who happened to mention that he was free tonight; my cousin Brodrick; and my daughter Anne.'

Chaloner's heart sank. Greeting was a talented violist, but Brodrick was mediocre, and Anne was downright embarrassing. He looked to where she was talking in a loud, important voice about the wonders of Hampton Court, declaring that she had not been included in the first wave of refugees from the city because she had been too busy. She was a short, sour-faced woman who considered herself a cut above everyone else because she was married to the King's brother, and was thus set to become queen if His Majesty died without issue.

'She *wishes* it was her decision to stay,' whispered Thomas Greeting, coming to stand next to Chaloner when the Earl and his wife had gone. His post as one of the King's professional musicians allowed him plenty of time to indulge in his favourite pastime: Court gossip. 'But the truth is that she was left behind because she was not wanted.'

'Really? I thought the King liked her.'

'Nobody at Court likes her. And she plays the flute like an ape, although she will tell you that she has the fingers of an angel. Do not disabuse her, though, or she will flay you alive.'

The last member of the consort, Sir Alan Brodrick, was one of the Court's most infamous rakes, which everyone knew except the Earl, who would hear no bad word about him. Brodrick loved good music, which was why he rarely played himself – he knew his own limitations in that regard. He entered the antechamber reluctantly.

'I tried to refuse,' he said defensively, as he sat at the virginals, 'but Clarendon would not listen, so now I am obliged to make an ass of myself in this ridiculously hot uniform. Still, at least none of my friends are here to witness my humiliation. Most have gone to Chelsea.'

'Chelsea?' queried Chaloner. 'Not Hampton Court?'

Brodrick's expression was bitter. 'None of us were invited to Hampton Court – that is reserved for *important* people, apparently. It came as a nasty shock to learn that the King does not value me, after all I have done for him.'

'I feel the same,' agreed Greeting. 'And I said as much to Bullen Reymes, who promptly asked me to join him in Chelsea instead. I leave at first light tomorrow, and I am looking forward to it. It will be excellent fun.'

'Really?' asked Brodrick doubtfully. 'My friends said so, but I assumed they were just putting a brave face on the situation.'

'We shall celebrate as never before,' declared Greeting, and turned to Chaloner. 'Reymes has taken the lease on Buckingham House, which is the largest mansion in Chelsea, and he has extended his hospitality to anyone left behind in White Hall. His revels are the talk of the country, so we shall have a far better time with him than in boring old Hampton Court.'

Try as he might, Chaloner could not imagine the surly Reymes presiding over the kind of rambunctious carousing that would rival that of the King's dissolute favourites.

'Are you sure?' he asked sceptically.

'My friend Hungerford has just spent a week there,' replied Greeting. 'And he told me that the place is one long, continuous party. Indeed, he felt compelled to come back to London for a rest, as it had all but exhausted him.'

'Perhaps I *should* go, then,' said Brodrick, brightening. 'It was good of him to ask me really, given his antipathy towards my cousin. Yet such entertainments must be costly, and he is not a wealthy man. Why is he doing it?'

'He says he lost a lot of friends when the plague last struck, and he wants to spirit as many of us out of town as possible,' explained Greeting, then smirked maliciously. 'Although I suspect his real aim is to curry favour with the King, who must have *some* qualms about leaving us here to die.'

'And hosting us will salve His Majesty's guilty conscience and put him in Reymes' debt,' mused Brodrick. 'Clever.'

'There will be at least thirty of us in Chelsea,' Greeting went on happily, 'so do not worry, Brodrick – you will not want for lively company. But we had better decide what to play before Anne appears and demands a solo.' He shuddered at the prospect.

They selected some suitable pieces, tuned their instruments and began. It was a duet by Couperin with some basic keyboard accompaniment. Chaloner was aware that his playing was mechanical rather than inspired, and saw Greeting regarding him quizzically, clearly wondering what was wrong. Chaloner was tempted to ask if they could swap viols. Surely it was the instrument that was at fault? Then Anne arrived.

'Stop,' she commanded imperiously. 'How dare you start without me.'

'We had not started,' lied Brodrick. 'We were just practising.'

'Well, you should have waited. James? Bring me my flute.'

A strutting child of five or six – the Earl's youngest son – obliged, and there was some consternation when Anne tried to play, only to discover that the brat had shoved a grape inside it. Red juice dribbled down her white dress, resulting in a wail of dismay from her and a gale of malevolent laughter from the boy. Then her mother and other brothers arrived: Henry, aloof and pompous, and Lawrence, acid-tongued and ambitious. Both were in their twenties, and had already embarked on careers in politics and at Court.

'Would you like a cup of wine before you start in earnest?' asked Frances pleasantly. 'You must be terribly hot, sawing away in all those thick clothes.'

'We would, and we are,' replied Brodrick promptly. 'Make mine a large one.'

Frances turned to Lawrence. 'Will you fetch it, dear?'

'I most certainly will not,' declared Lawrence, affronted. 'I am no servant.'

'I told Father that they should have nothing until they had finished performing anyway,' said Henry, giving his kinsman a spiteful glance. 'They may have a drop later, if there is any left.'

'So let us begin,' said Anne, and launched into a piece without telling anyone what she had chosen, so she played a squeaky solo until the other three could work out what they were meant to do. Accompanying her was not easy, as she had no sense of timing, and a habit of replaying the parts she liked while omitting the more difficult ones. Chaloner struggled to keep a straight face, especially when he saw Brodrick's agonised expression.

After a while, he became aware of someone standing in the doorway. It was the oily Cocke, eyes fixed glisteningly on Anne's low-cut bodice. The accompter wore a fine blue coat, but it was entirely devoid of lace, which looked odd in such elevated company. Even Chaloner, who deplored frills, had some on his shirt, while the other guests had deployed yards of it.

'Exquisite,' Cocke simpered when there was a pause – an unscheduled one, as Anne had decided she was not going to perform the next section, and was perusing the page to see where she might like to go next. As Chaloner was sure Cocke's compliment could not pertain to the music, he could only assume he meant her bosom. 'Pray continue. I have always loved Gibbons.'

'That was Dowland,' said Greeting shortly. 'But we shall have Gibbons if you like. Ready, Chaloner? One, two, three!'

He began a piece for two viols. Anne stamped her foot in petulant fury when she realised there was no part for her, but Cocke slithered up and began muttering in her ear. Chaloner fully expected her to clout him for his impudence, and was surprised when she allowed him to take her arm and escort her away. He was even more startled when she smiled, and he supposed the greasy accompter had qualities to which he himself was blind.

'Thank God!' breathed Brodrick, once she was out of earshot. 'I think I might have throttled her if she had carried on much longer. She should not be allowed near a flageolet, let alone a flute.'

*

72

Once Anne had gone, the music improved, although Chaloner still felt his own playing was well below par. He made an excuse to change viols with Greeting, and was disheartened when it made no difference. Then Anne reappeared, Cocke in tow, and announced that she was going to perform a solo. Chaloner left the antechamber abruptly when he saw she was aiming to massacre a piece by Henry Lawes, one of his favourite composers.

'The only way I shall get through this evening is by dulling my mind with drink,' murmured Greeting, who had followed him out. 'I recommend you do likewise.'

He disappeared into the milling throng, leaving Chaloner to loiter in the shadows and assess who had accepted the Earl's hospitality. They were an eclectic assortment, and stood in clusters. The Gorges folk were in one corner, a group of navy clerks and merchants was in another, while the Treasury men were by the window; Doyley was with them, but Chaloner was astonished to see that Bullen Reymes had deigned to enter the home of his sworn enemy. He wondered if there would be trouble. A noisy clot of courtiers hogged the middle of the room – a few who had been charged to mind the palace in the King's absence, but most were the penniless hangers-on who His Majesty thought he would do without in Hampton Court.

'Poor Anne,' said Frances, coming to stand beside him during a particularly squawky section. 'I do not think the King's Private Musick need fear competition from her.'

'No,' agreed Chaloner, glumly thinking that they need not fear competition from him either. Then he realised it was not the most politic of responses, but Frances was already talking about something else.

'I understand you are to investigate these thefts at Gorges,' she went on. 'I am so glad. It is a *good* place, and I was sorry to hear that some unscrupulous villain has been at work there. I am sure the residents will be much happier knowing that you aim to expose the culprit.'

Chaloner was tempted to point out that if the residents were dangerous lunatics, they probably would not care. 'Have you ever visited Gorges?'

'Once. It is a pretty place with a large orchard, although I have heard tales of a spectre that roams at night. Perhaps you would look into that, too, although please do not tell my husband. I should not like to worry him.'

So Chaloner was now under orders from the Earl to keep Nancy's murder from the rest of his family, and under Frances' orders to investigate phantoms without telling the Earl. Yet again, he sensed there was a lot he was not being told about the assignment in Chelsea. He was about to see if he could prise the truth from Frances, when Anne appeared in angry tears because Brodrick had said something to offend. Frances hurried away to smooth ruffled feathers, so Chaloner returned to his observations. The courtiers had grown raucous, which was just as well, as they drowned out the unpleasant sounds that began emanating from the antechamber again. Then Greeting approached.

'Lady Clarendon asked Brodrick so prettily to accompany Anne that he could not refuse,' he reported grimly. 'All I can say is that I am glad it was not me. Are you drunk yet? If not, you should be, as we are likely to be ordered back in there at any moment.'

'Do you know any of these people?' asked Chaloner,

in the hope that the gossiping violist might be able to tell him something useful.

'The courtiers, of course, and the Treasury men. Secretary Warwick is one of the most boring fellows I have ever met, but I suppose he cannot help it, and he is a very worthy person, I am sure. I am surprised Prefect Reymes is here, though, because he hates the Earl. You should watch him, Chaloner – he might do your master harm. Hah! See? Here comes trouble now.'

There was trouble indeed, as the Earl had approached Reymes with a sly smirk. Chaloner edged closer, to hear what was being said.

'How do you like being a commissioner, Reymes?' the Earl asked, all airy innocence.

Reymes scowled. 'I know I have you to thank for that particular burden.'

He spoke with such vicious rage that Chaloner would have denied it had he been the Earl, but Clarendon was not a man to resist a gloat. He inclined his head smugly.

'I thought it would suit your talents.'

Fury and contempt vied for supremacy in Reymes' eyes as he looked around him. 'I never thought *I* would set foot in Dunkirk House. Yet here I am, a fêted guest.'

'Hardly fêted,' said the Earl tightly. He abhorred the nickname for his home, and hearing it never failed to rile him. 'Just one of many petty bureaucrats I felt obliged to entertain. After all, you have so little else in your lives. And none of you have been invited to Hampton Court.'

'Nor were you until two days ago,' Reymes flashed back. 'Your star is fading fast.'

But the Earl had regained his self-control. 'So is yours,

now that you have accepted the post of commissioner. It will be expensive in time and money, and the potential for disaster is great.'

'What do you mean?' demanded Reymes dangerously.

The Earl smiled sweetly. 'The Theological College is in a very parlous state, so you will be faced with constant bills for repairs. But when we are at peace again, and it reverts to the Crown, no one will appreciate what you have done. Instead, you will be held responsible for any damage.'

Reymes' face was so dark that Chaloner hurried forward, afraid that the prefect might whip out his sword and dispatch his tormentor there and then, but Kipps was there before him. The Seal Bearer took Clarendon's arm, and politely but firmly steered him away to meet other guests.

'Ignore him, Bullen,' advised Doyley gently. 'The buildings are not as bad as he claims, because Kole spent a fortune upgrading them.'

'That is true,' agreed Warwick, and clicked his teeth together. 'And if there are any bumps or scratches, you will not need to pay workmen to put all to rights – the prisoners will do it for free.'

At that point, Stephens, the bulky Sergeant at Arms, mooted the possibility of another cup of claret, and the Treasury men moved away together. When they had gone, Kipps joined Chaloner, mopping his face with a silken handkerchief.

'Our master is his own worst enemy sometimes,' he remarked ruefully. 'Why did he have to goad Reymes? I do not like the fellow, but nothing can be gained from jibing him.'

*

Chaloner resumed his surveillance with Kipps at his side. However, he had not been observing for long before Cocke bustled up. The accompter had exchanged Anne for Lady Savage, one of White Hall's most flamboyant characters, a person of indeterminate age with a face that showed the ravages of high living. She was puffing a pipe, claiming in a husky voice that it was to ward off the plague, although everyone knew that she had been a devotee of tobacco for years.

'A fine soirée, Kipps,' Cocke declared. His hand snaked behind his companion, and did something that made her squeal and slap him playfully with her fan. 'You can tell your master so, although you might mention that he should not introduce the cheap wine quite so early in the proceedings. We are still sober enough to tell the difference.'

'This is not one of your drunken orgies,' said Kipps coldly, but Cocke had already waddled away. The Seal Bearer scowled after him. 'I cannot abide that man. He is not even wearing any lace, which is doubtless a deliberate insult to his host. Moreover, I am uncertain of his probity, so when you investigate those Gorges thefts, be sure to question him first.'

'It would be foolish to risk a lucrative Treasury post for a few pounds from Gorges,' said Chaloner. 'So I doubt he is the culprit.'

'Do not be so sure. He thinks everyone else is stupid, and that he can do what he likes without being caught. Well, I am relying on you to prove him wrong. Incidentally, he has *three* posts, not two – he is accompter for the prison, as well as for the Treasury and Gorges. And if he *is* cheating Gorges, we do not want him anywhere near the other two. Oh, God!'

Chaloner jumped in alarm, then relaxed when he realised that Kipps had only seen a spider crawling up the doorpost. He knocked it into his hand and tipped it out of the window. The Seal Bearer gave a wan smile.

'I hate those things . . . their long legs and hairy bodies . . .' He shuddered. 'But let us talk of nicer things. Your playing was lovely, and I wish Martin could have heard it. He adores music. I do not suppose you would consider playing for him one day, would you?'

'I doubt he would be impressed,' said Chaloner gloomily. 'I cannot settle to it at the moment.'

Kipps shot him a sympathetic glance. 'Probably something to do with Hannah, but it will pass, and Martin will not mind a few rough notes. Come tomorrow.'

Chaloner did not want to go, but it would have been churlish to refuse Kipps, who had always treated him kindly. He nodded reluctant assent, and the Seal Bearer smiled his thanks before disappearing to talk to the navy men. Among them was the Admiralty Proctor – Richard Franklin – who was with Dr Franklin from Gorges. Chaloner immediately noted the resemblance between the two. The proctor was complaining about being left behind in plague-ridden London, while the physician was informing him that a sponge dipped in vinegar would keep him from infection. Neither was listening to the other.

'They are brothers,' said Samuel Pepys, a navy clerk with whom Chaloner had a passing acquaintance. He was smoking a pipe, and a bottle of London Treacle poked from his pocket; Pepys was taking no chances. 'Peas in a pod, as you can see.' Then he cleared his throat uncomfortably. 'I mean no disrespect, but would you like the name of a decent tailor?'

Chaloner did not feel equal to explaining why he was wearing clothes that were several sizes too big, so he asked a question of his own instead. 'How much longer will you stay in London?'

Pepys smiled briefly and regretfully. 'I cannot leave – we must keep the Fleet in fighting trim against the Dutch. Our sailors take their turn against the sword; I must not therefore grudge to take mine at the pestilence.'

He began to talk about the other guests at that point, showing himself to be an amusing, if spiteful, observer of human nature. One man who drew his particular attention was Rector Wilkinson of Chelsea, whom he described as 'a man of very scandalous report'. The epithet was apposite, because Wilkinson *did* look like a cleric with radical opinions: he had wild hair, wilder eyes, and his movements were taut and jerky, as if he was constantly on the verge of blurting seditious remarks.

Pepys did not stay with Chaloner long, as there were more important people to impress, so the spy took the opportunity to home in on the Gorges governors.

Underhill was inspecting the Earl's books again, looking more Parliamentarian than ever in his plain but well-cut clothes and severely shorn hair, while Kole looked around resentfully, jealous of the wealth he saw. The speculator was still wearing his flashy clothes, but the paint had chipped on his shoes, and the bright lamplight exposed the darns on his elbows.

Next to them, Mrs Bonney was patently uncomfortable in the splendour of Clarendon House, and twisted her reticule anxiously in her man-sized hands. Meanwhile, Franklin had abandoned his brother, and was arguing furiously with Parker – it seemed that Parker had doctored some of the wine as an experiment to see if it hastened the onset of drunkenness. Franklin's disapproval could be seen in the angry set of his mouth, while Parker was indignant that his assistant should dare criticise his scientific endeavours. Chaloner thought Franklin had the right of it – it was hardly ethical to dose someone else's guests with dubious potions. Both fell silent as he approached.

'I understand that one of your charges was murdered recently,' he said bluntly, aiming to provoke a reaction. He was not disappointed.

'How did you find out?' cried Parker, and clutched his goblet so hard that he broke the stem, while the other governors exchanged glances of dismay. All except Underhill, who looked smug.

'I told you it was a mistake to try and keep it quiet,' he said, all arch vindication. 'And I was right. Now it will look as though we have something to hide.'

'We had to keep quiet for our patients' sake,' argued Mrs Bonney defensively. 'Because what will become of them if the Earl withdraws his support and we are forced to close? It would be too cruel, when so many are on the verge of recovery.'

'Like Dorothy Wiseman?' asked Chaloner artlessly.

'No, not like her,' replied Franklin. 'She will never be well, no matter how much coffee we persuade her to drink.'

'Tell me about Nancy Janaway,' ordered Chaloner. 'Who killed her?'

'We do not know,' said Franklin with a shrug that was half helpless and half bewilderment that such a thing should have happened. 'However, it was not an inmate. Most are gentle ladies who would never hurt a fly, while the others are closely supervised at all times.'

'Besides, Nancy was strangled,' put in Kole. 'And all

our patients are women – they do not have the strength to throttle people.'

Doyley had thought that Mrs Wiseman did, Chaloner recalled. 'A member of staff, then?'

'Of course not!' snarled Parker. 'They are all beyond reproach.'

'We have strong gates and high walls,' said Franklin, more conciliatory. 'But it is not a prison, Mr Chaloner – breaking in would be difficult, but not impossible. The culprit must have come from outside.'

Chaloner was about to ask more when a footman sounded a gong: the Earl wanted to make a speech. He began by thanking everyone for remaining at their posts in the face of looming death, and finished with the promise that they would always be remembered with affection if they were unlucky enough to die. If it was a homily intended to inspire, it failed miserably, and Chaloner suspected it would do more to encourage the listeners to flee than to stay.

Afterwards, polite guests took their leave, while those who did not know they were outstaying their welcome accepted another cup of wine. The latter group included the Gorges governors, commissioners Reymes and Doyley, and Rector Wilkinson, along with a smattering of courtiers who never departed from anywhere as long as there was still drink to be had.

'I wish they would go home,' whispered Frances to Chaloner. 'I want my bed, as tomorrow will be another very busy day for me. Will they take the hint if you start to pack up your viol and blow out the candles?'

Chaloner was about to oblige when there was a dreadful wail. At first, he assumed that Anne had started to play again, and it was indeed she who had issued the noise. He hurried into the Great Roome to see what had happened.

He arrived to find her pressed against the wall, her face as white as snow. She was staring at Underhill, who lay on the stairs, his dour Parliamentarian features slack in death. And around his neck were marks where hands had fastened around it and choked the life out of him.

Chapter 3

The Earl was appalled that murder had been committed in his home, and stared at Underhill's body in mute horror. More practical, Frances ushered her younger children and the sobbing Anne away. She tried to include Henry and Lawrence in her kindly shepherding, but was informed curtly that they would leave when it suited them. Chaloner felt like boxing their ears – he would never have addressed *his* mother in so disrespectful a manner.

'Brats,' muttered Kipps under his breath. 'When I compare them to Martin . . .'

Chaloner ordered the agitated guests back into the Chapell Pavilion, and told them to wait there. Perhaps one had seen something that would allow the culprit to be identified. Or one was the killer. Regardless, they were going nowhere until they had been questioned.

'You must find who did this, Chaloner,' whispered the Earl, ashen-faced. 'And fast. If you fail, my enemies will use it to harm me.'

'Surely not, sir,' said Kipps comfortingly. 'It is not as if Underhill was a baron or a Member of Parliament. His death is an inconvenience, but that is all.'

'He was a guest in my house,' replied the Earl tightly. 'And thus entitled to my protection.'

'This is what comes of trying to win the affection of minions,' said Lawrence. He was the Earl's second son, and wished he had been the first. He addressed his brother smugly. 'I told you that fêting tradesmen, debauchees and clerks would bring us trouble. It was a stupid idea.'

'It was a *good* one,' snapped Henry crossly. 'Our family is unpopular, and we need all the support we can muster, even from lowly sources.'

'Well, you included a killer in your reckless largesse,' Lawrence shot back. 'I bet the villain is Reymes. He has always hated us, and you should not have asked him here.'

Henry scowled at him. 'I had to. We invited all the other Treasury men, and there is no point in deliberately poking a hornets' nest with an insulting exclusion. Besides, I had hoped that rifts would be healed tonight – that he might become a friend.'

'I do not want him as a friend, thank you very much,' said the Earl shortly. 'He is a worm, and I do not wish my name to be associated with his in any respect. I only agreed to have him here so that he could see how far he is beneath me in worldly wealth. Shall I order his arrest, Chaloner?'

'Not yet,' said Chaloner quickly, even as his master turned to issue the command to the waiting servants. 'We should wait until we have solid evidence before—'

'Evidence?' interrupted Lawrence haughtily. 'What foolery is this?'

'Foolery that will prevent you from making a needless mistake,' replied Chaloner. He had never liked Lawrence, and thought him an imbecile of the first order. 'Reymes is a commissioner and the Treasury's prefect. If he is innocent, he will sue, which will cause your father all manner of problems.'

'True,' acknowledged the Earl. 'So you had better start investigating at once, Chaloner. But do not take too long, because I want you in Chelsea as soon as you have delivered me to Hampton Court. Kipps will help you find this vile killer *and* the Gorges thief. Two heads are better than one after all.'

'Me?' gulped the Seal Bearer in alarm. 'But I am no intelligencer! I would not know where to start with such a—'

'I said *help* him,' interrupted the Earl irritably. 'Not take control.'

'But you will need me at Hampton Court,' cried Kipps, dismayed. 'To carry your seal.'

'James can do that,' said the Earl, glancing to where his youngest son had escaped from his mother, and was watching from the top of the stairs. 'It is time he learned some responsibility.'

'Lord!' breathed Kipps, and Chaloner could not tell if he was more appalled by the prospect of hunting felons or his duties being performed by a small child. 'I shall do my best, of course, but are you sure you would not rather appoint someone else, My Lord? Or leave Tom to manage by himself? I imagine he prefers working alone.'

Chaloner did, but Kipps would be a better helpmeet than most. The Seal Bearer had already acknowledged that he did not know what he was doing, which meant he was unlikely to hare off on hunches of his own, and an assistant might prove useful. He nodded acquiescence, although Kipps continued to vacillate between horror and apprehension.

'Good,' said the Earl, and released a gusty sigh. 'Thank God the navy men had gone by the time this terrible crime was committed. They are responsible for keeping the Fleet afloat, and I would have been accused of treason if I had been obliged to arrest one of them.'

'There are only twenty guests left,' noted Henry, glancing into the Chapell Pavilion. 'So it should not be too hard to determine which one of them is the villain.'

'Not necessarily,' argued Chaloner. 'He must be very sure of himself, to strike in so public a place. Such confidence suggests that he might be extremely difficult to—'

'No excuses,' interrupted Lawrence shortly. 'This is important. Our good name is at stake.'

The Earl was already climbing the stairs to his private quarters, so his sons hastened to follow, leaving Chaloner and Kipps alone. Kipps glared after them resentfully, then turned to Chaloner.

'I am sorry you are lumbered with me, Tom, but I shall try not to disappoint. So what do you want me to do first? Confront Reymes? Lawrence is right – the man is so filled with hate that he would certainly kill to harm our Earl.'

'We need more than that to accuse him, so let us see what the body can tell us.'

From the position of the corpse, it appeared that Underhill had been admiring the contents of an ornate Florentine bookcase when he had been attacked, probably from behind. Chaloner placed his own fingers over the bruises on the throat, and discovered that the culprit's hands would have been very slightly larger. A quick examination revealed no other marks on the body, although Chaloner did find three volumes of poetry secreted in Underhill's pockets.

'What are they doing there?' asked Kipps in confusion. Then understanding dawned. 'He was going to *steal* them! What a rogue!'

'For their gold clasps, perhaps,' said Chaloner, assessing each in turn. 'Or their rarity value – serious collectors would pay a fortune for these.'

'Then perhaps *he* is Gorges' thief,' suggested Kipps. 'After all, a man who filches from one house will not baulk at robbing another. But who killed him? Is there anything on his corpse to tell?'

'No – and there must have been forty people here in Clarendon House when he died. The culprit could be any one of them.'

'Twenty,' corrected Kipps. 'Henry counted them, if you recall.'

'I was including guests, servants *and* family.'

'Well, then you can *un*include them,' said Kipps firmly. 'Because none of our people will be responsible. Or do you see young James and Lady Clarendon as stranglers?'

'Not them – their hands are too small.'

At that point, Chaloner realised the same was true of Henry, Lawrence and Anne as well; they had inherited their mother's slight build. Not the family, then. And on reflection, he did not believe that a servant was responsible either. All were acutely aware that their future depended on the Earl staying in power, and it did not take a genius to understand that a murder under his roof would give his enemies fuel with which to damage him.

'Our master is unpopular,' said Kipps, 'and it is not

87

unknown for undesirables to burst in from the street, howling about Dunkirk. Perhaps one of *them* dispatched Underhill. Or perhaps he was killed by a burglar – they have been very active on this side of the city recently.'

'Burglars tend to prefer empty houses, and no one could have thought this was unoccupied, when it blazed with lights and was full of noise. And someone wanting to make a political point about Dunkirk would have left a message behind to explain himself.'

Kipps did not look convinced, but shrugged amiably anyway, unwilling to gainsay Chaloner's greater experience in such matters. 'Very well. So how do we proceed?'

'First, we need to find out who last saw Underhill alive, and next we must learn more about him, and identify anyone who might want him dead.'

'Then we had better make a start,' said Kipps without enthusiasm.

The two men entered the Chapell Pavilion, where they were immediately assailed by a barrage of questions, angry words and accusations. While he listened, Chaloner noticed that the guests had kept to their factions, with the exception of Parker, who paced restlessly at the far end of the room, reaching out trembling fingers every so often to straighten a painting or touch a piece of sculpture.

'Keeping us here like common criminals is an outrage,' declared Reymes furiously, gripping the hilt of his sword. 'Release us at once, or you will be sorry.'

'It is the accepted protocol in such situations, Bullen,' said Doyley quietly. He started to put a calming hand on his friend's shoulder, but was evidently afraid that he might lose it, so he let it drop to his side. 'For our own safety. After all, the killer might still be here.'

There was renewed consternation at this notion, and a second clamour broke out. Eventually, Chaloner raised his hand for silence.

'We have some questions, and the quicker they are answered, the sooner you can go home,' he announced. 'Obviously, the first thing we need to know is: who saw Underhill last?'

'I spoke to him an hour ago,' volunteered Dr Franklin, putting a vinegar-soaked sponge to his nose. Chaloner studied him hard, thinking he seemed oddly unmoved by the death of a fellow governor – unlike the others, whose faces were ashen. 'He said it was too hot in here, so he was going to stand in the Great Roome, where it is cooler.'

'I heard him say that, too,' agreed Mrs Bonney timidly. 'But then Dr Parker announced a plan to dose everyone in Chelsea with quicksilver, to see how many he could render temporarily insane, and my attention was taken by him.'

'It was a joke,' explained Franklin, although he shot an uneasy glance behind him, where his colleague was gazing into the eyes of a marble bust. When Parker leaned forward to deal it a smacking kiss on the lips, Chaloner wondered whether Parker had been at the quicksilver himself.

'I am no man's keeper,' declared Kole haughtily, 'so I did not notice Underhill at all. Indeed, I was not even aware that he was here until someone shouted that he was dead.'

'I think you were,' countered Doyley, eyeing the speculator in distaste. 'Because I saw you talking to him

89

shortly before he left for the Great Roome. Please do not lie. It is hardly helpful.'

'*I* saw you with him as well, Kole,' put in Reymes. 'But not talking – *arguing*.'

'Oh, yes – about the weather,' blustered the speculator. 'I forgot. We were discussing the heat, but it was an unmemorable conversation, which is why it slipped my mind.'

'It was not a "conversation",' countered Reymes, glaring at him. 'It was a quarrel.'

'It was not!' bleated Kole, although his furtive eyes told the truth. 'It was a difference of opinion about clouds. Nothing more. *I* did not kill him.'

Rector Wilkinson released a bark of scornful laughter. 'So you say, but you are the obvious culprit, because you hated him. As did you, you and you.' He stabbed a bony finger at Reymes, Cocke and Parker in turn, then whipped around to address Chaloner. 'Do you want to know why?'

'It might be useful,' replied Chaloner evenly, although the spiteful cant in the cleric's eyes warned him to treat any allegations with extreme caution.

Wilkinson began to speak in a shrill bray that drowned out the startled objections of those he had accused. 'First, Kole: Underhill was cleverer than he, and often made him look stupid. Second, Reymes: he means Clarendon harm, and would certainly kill an innocent man to achieve his objective. Third, Cocke: Underhill suspected him of stealing from Gorges House. And last, Parker: he is a lunatic, whose actions are no longer rational.'

Chaloner suspected that Wilkinson might be right about Parker, who alone made no effort to defend himself. The others were furiously indignant, though, and said so in no uncertain terms, which delighted the rector, who cackled malevolently, relishing the agitation he had caused.

'Was Underhill interested in books?' asked Kipps, cutting across the clamour. Personally, Chaloner would have let it run, in the hope that anger or a guilty conscience would lead to inadvertent revelations.

'He was passionate about them,' replied Franklin cautiously. 'Why?'

'Because he was in the process of stealing some when he was killed,' replied Kipps. 'Which makes us wonder if a fellow governor dispatched him, to spare Gorges embarrassment.'

There was a stunned silence, which was eventually broken by Mrs Bonney. 'No! You must be mistaken. Mr Underhill was not a thief.'

While she was speaking, Parker bounded over and thrust his face so near to Wilkinson's that Chaloner was sure it was going to be punched. The rector restrained himself with obvious effort.

'Underhill was my friend,' the physician said tightly. 'We shared a house for months, and he never showed any inclination to pilfer. You lie, sir.'

'He did not steal from you, because you have nothing worth taking,' retorted Wilkinson unpleasantly. 'Unlike this place, which is full of tempting baubles. Indeed, I would not mind some myself.' He picked up a clock in such a way that Chaloner half expected him to shove it in his pocket and go home with it.

'Perhaps Underhill wanted to read these books to our patients,' suggested Franklin charitably. 'Expanding their minds with knowledge is something we encourage, after all.'

Parker abandoned the rector and addressed Chaloner. 'No, no, no! The killer left a false trail to lead us all astray. He is cunning, you see. I know him well.'

'Do you?' asked Chaloner keenly. 'Then who is he?'

'A man who is as dark as night,' replied Parker with a peculiar grin. 'And who is lithe, hook-nosed and brooding with evil.'

'A name, please, Parker,' said Kipps impatiently. 'Murder is a serious business, especially one that threatens to harm my Earl.'

'Satan,' replied Parker promptly. 'Although he also goes by Beelzebub and Lucifer.'

'How did Underhill make his living?' asked Chaloner, after another startled silence, during which Parker returned to the statue and began to whisper to it. The Gorges folk exchanged uneasy glances and moved closer together, as if to present a united front against whatever might follow.

'He did not have to earn a living – he was a gentleman,' replied Franklin. 'A very learned one. He made a number of interesting and helpful observations on our work.'

'He did,' agreed Mrs Bonney, 'and his demise will be a sad blow to our progress in curing lunacy. I have never met a man who was better read than Mr Underhill.'

'He *was* well read,' acknowledged Doyley, rummaging in his pocket for his snuff. 'I think he was an Oxford man. He never talked about his kin, but I imagine he had a fine home somewhere.'

'Not too fine,' sniggered Wilkinson. 'Or he would not have been lodging with Parker.'

'Dregs,' announced Parker grandly. Everyone looked at him for an explanation, but none came, and it was not long before he turned his attention back to the bust.

92

'How did Underhill spend his time, if he was not obliged to work?' asked Chaloner, choosing to treat Parker's peculiar proclamation as irrelevant.

'By reading, mostly,' replied Franklin. 'No subject was too abstruse for him, and he was rarely without a tome. They were his greatest love.'

Chaloner had seen Underhill twice, and on both occasions he had been admiring the Earl's books. Had someone taken umbrage when he had availed himself of a few? Murder seemed an extreme response to petty theft, but violence always escalated in hot weather, and it appeared that Parker had tampered with the wine. He studied the twenty faces in front of him, thinking that the Gorges people and the Treasury men were certainly high on his list of suspects, as was the spiteful Rector Wilkinson.

'Did any of you dislike Underhill?' asked Kipps. Chaloner regarded him askance, astonished that he should expect that question to be answered honestly. 'Other than Kole.'

'I *did* like him,' objected Kole, licking dry lips. 'He was charming, and I am proud to have known him. In fact, he was my favourite governor, and I shall miss him terribly.'

'Liar,' sneered Cocke. 'You detested each other. Wilkinson is right: Underhill was always exposing your stupidity, which is something no man appreciates.'

'Rubbish!' cried Kole. 'We did enjoy lively exchanges of opinions, but there was nothing antagonistic in our relationship. Unlike yours – he was always catching *you* out in lies and misrepresentations. And, while Wilkinson is wrong about me, he is right about you: Underhill *did* think that you were the Gorges thief.'

Cocke's expression hardened. 'I am a respectable man.'

'Gorges is full of lunatics and liars, while the Treasury is run by rogues,' declared Wilkinson haughtily. 'And the Court is worse than both. Clarendon should hang the lot of you.'

While Kipps struggled to keep the peace by offering the detained guests leftover cake and more wine, Chaloner interviewed each one in turn. When he had finished, Chaloner leaned against a wall, to review both what he had learned from their replies and what he had been able to deduce from his own observations.

Underhill had declared the Chapell Pavilion too hot, and had gone to the Great Roome to cool down, although his real intention had almost certainly been to steal books, probably ones he had identified on his earlier visit. He had been alive when the first wave of guests had taken their leave, because the Great Roome was an open hallway, and a corpse there would have been noticed. Thus all those who had politely departed after the Earl's speech could be eliminated as suspects, which left the twenty who were clamouring at Kipps to be allowed to go home.

Underhill had been throttled, like Nancy Janaway, and as Chaloner doubted there were two active stranglers with connections to Chelsea, he suspected that both lives had been taken by the same hand. Thus Kipps' suggestion of a fanatical outsider invading Clarendon House to kill a guest at random was unlikely.

The remaining courtiers and Treasury men could also be eliminated, because the first group had been involved in a drinking game in which the absence of anyone would have been noted, while the second had been

94

discussing the King's gold, and no one had dared slip away, lest they missed something important. Thus all had alibis in each other. This left Chaloner with eight potential suspects.

First, Kole, whose responses to questions had been incriminating, and who had lied about his interactions with the victim. Next, Cocke, who Underhill had accused of the Gorges thefts, which was certainly a powerful motive to kill. Third, Parker, who professed to be the victim's friend, but whose behaviour was eccentric to say the least. Fourth and fifth, Franklin and Mrs Bonney, who might have learned that Underhill was a thief, and aimed to prevent a scandal and a possible withdrawal of funds – both would want to protect Gorges, given that their livelihoods depended on it. Sixth, Reymes, who would love to see the Earl embarrassed with a crime. But was he reckless enough to do it, knowing that fingers would automatically point in his direction? Chaloner glanced at the angry red face and decided that he was. Seventh, Doyley, whose military past meant he was no stranger to bloodshed, and who, as a man of considerable learning himself, might object to a crime that targeted precious books. And last, the vindictive Wilkinson, who might well strangle someone for warped reasons of his own.

Chaloner was thoughtful. There were motives galore for Underhill's murder, but what about Nancy's? He was tempted to ask about her while he had everyone together, but the guests were restless, frightened and resentful, so it was not a good time. Besides, it would be better to learn more about her first, so as to be armed with hard facts. He nodded to Kipps to say he had finished, and the Seal Bearer announced that everyone was free to go.

The courtiers were the first to depart, doing so in a noisy throng, and sounding much as they did after one of White Hall's infamous debauches. Chaloner wondered what the Earl, lying in his stately chamber above, thought of the hullabaloo. The Treasury men and Doyley were not long in following, although they did so with more decorum; Warwick and Doyley even asked Kipps to thank the Earl for his hospitality, although Reymes thrust past muttering that he wished his host to the devil. The Gorges contingent was last.

'Will you return to Chelsea tonight?' Kipps asked conversationally, as he held open the door.

'Tomorrow,' replied Franklin. 'We shall stay with my brother Richard tonight. He has plenty of room now that his lodgers have fled the city.'

'A visit to London is a rare opportunity to replenish our supplies at the market,' elaborated Mrs Bonney. 'Everything is a good price at the moment, because the plague keeps so many customers away. We plan to stock up on pegs, needles, thread, spades, baskets, plates—'

'And clogs for the fairies in the garden,' interposed Parker.

Cocke laughed nervously. 'Dear old Parker! Always trying to amuse us with jests.'

'*I* shall not go shopping, of course,' declared Kole loftily. 'I shall visit Lincoln's Inn, to locate deeds that prove the government's seizure of my College was illegal.'

Chaloner watched them walk down the torchlit drive. Parker was reeling all over the place, obliging Franklin and Mrs Bonney to hold him up. Had he had too much of the wine he himself had doctored, or was something else amiss?

'I have not decided where I shall be tomorrow,' said

Wilkinson, speaking in a low hiss that made Chaloner jump – he had thought everyone had gone. 'Perhaps here, perhaps there. It depends where the Lord sends me.'

He stalked away, head held high, although his dignity suffered a blow when he stumbled over a pothole. Chaloner took a deep breath to clear his head, but the air was hot and reeked of the city, even from a distance. Kipps came to stand next to him.

'Cocke,' the Seal Bearer declared. '*He* is the culprit. Underhill found out he was a thief, so Cocke wrung his neck. And as the fellow is a desperate lecher, we can conclude that he killed Nancy when she rejected his advances. There, I have solved the case already.'

'Maybe,' said Chaloner. 'Although others also have motives.'

He listed them. When he had finished, Kipps tapped his chin thoughtfully.

'There was a lot of coming and going all night, and I saw every one of your eight leave the Chapell Pavilion at one point or another, although I cannot recall exactly who went where when.'

'Well, try,' instructed Chaloner shortly. 'You do not need me to tell you that this is important.'

Kipps screwed up his face in an expression of intense concentration – one that looked vaguely painful – but eventually, he shook his head. 'I am sorry, Tom. It will not come. But we had better remove the body now. The Earl will not be very pleased if it is still on the stairs when he comes down for his breakfast.'

Chaloner deposited Underhill in the Westminster charnel house, and then walked home to Covent Garden. It was a cloudless night, but there was so much dust in the air that he could not see the stars, while the light cast by the moon was feeble and sickly. He heard the rumble of wheels on cobbles, and knew it was the wagon that collected the plague dead, doing its business in the darkest hours of the night in the hope that the true scale of the problem would not cause panic among the general populace.

He arrived to find a carriage waiting outside his house, and although there was no coat of arms to identify it, he knew exactly to whom it belonged.

Joseph Williamson ran the country's spy network, and was a coldly aloof man who still had much to learn about espionage. He and Chaloner had an uneasy relationship in which neither quite trusted the other, although this was better than the open antagonism that had existed between them when they had first met. The coach door opened, and a hand beckoned Chaloner forward. The coach was lit from within by two large lamps, which must have rendered it unpleasantly stuffy.

'No, do not climb in!' the Spymaster barked, jerking back and thrusting a pomander against his nose. 'You have probably come straight from the charnel house, and I know what horrors lie in there. Keep your distance, if you please.'

He looked older than when Chaloner had last seen him, and there were lines of strain around his eyes. War was a difficult time for any spymaster, with masses of information landing on his desk every day. And it was not just the Dutch who were a problem: the countless rebels and malcontents who had preferred Britain when it was a republic were delighted that the plague had driven the government from the city, and many aimed to turn the situation to their advantage.

'What do you want?' asked Chaloner, more curtly than was wise, given that Williamson was a powerful man with assassins and enforcers at his disposal.

'To know what happened to Underhill. I met an acquaintance earlier, who told me that he has been murdered. It is a damned shame, because he was one of mine.'

'A spy?'

Williamson inclined his head. 'He monitored the Chelsea prison for me. You will appreciate that having two thousand captured Dutchmen so near the capital makes me nervous.'

'Then why did you approve the plan to put them there? You must have had other buildings at your disposal.'

'Actually, we did not – and as devout Anglicans, we cannot do what your friend Oliver Cromwell did, and commandeer churches and cathedrals for the purpose. The Theological College was chosen because it was empty, and we needed something fast.'

'So you think Underhill was dispatched to prevent him from reporting to you?'

'It is a possibility, don't you agree?'

Chaloner was thoughtful. This put an entirely different complexion on the murders, and he could no longer guarantee that the killer was one of the eight suspects he had shortlisted. *He* could have slipped unnoticed into Clarendon House, to dispatch a rival quietly and without fuss, and so could any other intelligencer worth his salt.

'An inmate of Gorges was also strangled,' he said. 'Was she a spy too?'

99

'I am not so desperate that I need to recruit lunatics,' retorted Williamson, then grimaced. 'Although that might change if the government cuts my budget any further. I do not know why the madwoman was killed, although I imagine Clarendon has charged you to find out. Perhaps you will send me a copy of your findings when your investigation is complete?'

'If the Earl agrees. How well did you know Underhill? Was he trustworthy?'

'None of my spies are trustworthy, Chaloner – decent men do not dabble in espionage, as you should know. Present company excluded, of course. And to be honest, his reports were sketchy and uninformative, but I was unable to decide whether he was just not very good at gathering information, or whether he was being deliberately obstructive.'

'Why would he be obstructive? Did you recruit him against his will?'

'On the contrary – he was delighted to be on my payroll. Of course, I was tempted to demand a refund most weeks, as his letters were seldom worth the expense.'

The arrangement with Williamson explained a great deal, thought Chaloner. Underhill was a gentleman, but one who stole books, which suggested he had no or little income to call his own. The money he earned for spying would keep the wolf from the door, but was unlikely to stretch to luxuries like rare tomes. Did that mean he *was* the Gorges thief, stealing to supplement what Williamson paid him?

'Did his reports include anything about Nancy Janaway?'

'He said she was strangled in Gorges' orchard by a spectre.' Williamson saw Chaloner's eyebrows go up and

100

shrugged. 'I am only repeating what he wrote. Apparently, some sort of ghost has been haunting the village, which has gullible residents terrified out of their wits.'

Chaloner did not mention that Lady Clarendon had charged him to look into that particular matter, lest the Spymaster took it upon himself to ask her why. Chaloner knew the Earl would never forgive him if he did something to bring Frances to Williamson's attention.

'Did he tell you anything else about Chelsea?' he asked.

'Yes, something rather worrisome, actually – that the prison is not as secure as he felt it should be. You will have to visit Chelsea to explore these murders, so perhaps I could prevail on you to step inside the gaol, and let me know what you think.'

Chaloner inclined his head, declining to reveal that the Earl had already asked him to do it, then asked, 'Do you know why Clarendon supports Gorges?'

It pained him to put the question, revealing as it did that his knowledge of his employer was lacking, something no good spy liked to admit, but he could not, in all conscience, ignore an opportunity to find out.

Williamson blinked his surprise. 'Because an aunt exhibited Parliamentarian sympathies during the wars, and had to be incarcerated there. Surely he told you?'

Chaloner nodded, but his suspicion that there was more to it remained. 'Is there anything else you can tell me that might speed the investigation along?'

'Nothing – and I would certainly say if there were. I want answers just as badly as you.'

Once Williamson had gone, Chaloner was restless and uneasy, his mind full of questions. He knew wine would

101

help him sleep, but the jug he had bought several days ago had turned sour in the heat, so he started to walk towards Fleet Street and the small lane that led off it named Hercules' Pillars Alley. Halfway along was the building owned by Wiseman's mistress, Temperance North, which housed an exclusive 'gentlemen's club' – a brothel that catered to the very rich, and where decent claret was always available.

He had not seen Temperance since he had returned from sea, partly because the Earl had kept him busy in Clarendon House, but mostly because he had been afraid that she would ask about his feelings regarding Hannah's death, a prospect that unnerved him profoundly. However, he was confident that he could deflect any uncomfortable questions that night by talking about Underhill's murder. And as she and her girls heard a lot of gossip, they might even be able to help him.

He reached the club to find it in darkness, and the porter who usually guarded the door against undesirables – mostly men who could not afford the exorbitant prices Temperance liked to charge – was not at his usual post. A closer inspection revealed that all the window shutters were nailed up.

Panic gripped him. Had the plague struck and Temperance was dead? Then he pulled himself together. Wiseman would not have let such an event pass unre-marked. He walked to the back, and saw a lamp burning in the kitchen.

'We have been closed for weeks now,' said Temperance's helpmeet Maude, once he had been greeted with pleasure and settled with a cup of wine; there had also been solicitous enquiries about his well-being following Hannah's death, but he managed to cut these short by

102

asking after the club. 'Our patrons dare not come, and you can understand why. Fear of the disease drives everyone these days.'

'So where is Temperance?'

Guiltily, Chaloner suspected that Wiseman had already told him, but the surgeon had a penchant for tedious monologues, and Chaloner often stopped listening halfway through. Fortunately for their friendship, Wiseman rarely noticed, although it did mean that Chaloner occasionally missed out on important information.

Maude smiled, revealing smoke-stained teeth. 'In lodgings near Syon House. The girls are with her, and will continue to provide the services our courtly clients desire.'

'The King will move to Hampton Court soon. What will they do then?'

'Why, follow him, of course. What else?'

Maude smoked continuously as she told him her news, filling the small room with a swirling fug. Then she made some coffee, and he had taken a sip before he remembered that her brews were one of the most poisonous beverages in the country – her first husband was said to have died from a single gulp. He forced himself to swallow, unwilling to offend her by spitting it out.

When she ran out of gossip, he told her about Underhill's death, but was disappointed when she had never heard of his eight suspects, and nor was she aware that there was an asylum at Chelsea. However, she did have a tale about Underhill himself.

'He hailed from the Fleet Rookery, which as you know is a den of criminals. He gave himself airs, but the truth is that he was as common as muck.'

Chaloner was not surprised: he had detected something awry in Underhill's manner from the moment they had met. Moreover, there was the way he had been described – as a gentleman, who was thought to own a country estate, although no one knew it or his kin. Had someone uncovered the deception, and killed him for presuming to foist himself on the company of the respectable?

'His is quite a tale,' Maude went on. 'He was out burgling one day, but all his victim owned was books. He took them anyway, but decided to glance through them before selling them on. He enjoyed them so much that he promptly went out and stole some more. The knowledge he gleaned from them soon became prodigious.'

'Knowledge about what?'

'Everything: philosophy, plants, the Bible, animal husbandry, fashion, witchcraft, horse racing. Then he pinched some nice clothes and declared himself a gentleman. Rich people believe him, and offer hospitality on the understanding that he will reciprocate one day. Of course, he never could.'

'So he was a cheat. Was he still a thief?'

'He had no need to steal as long as wealthy hosts saw to his needs. And he was not a fool, to bite the hand that fed him. However, I suspect books would have been irresistible, so I am not surprised to hear you say that he tried to make off with some from Dunkirk House.'

'Do his old rookery associates resent his success?'

'You mean did one march out to Piccadilly and strangle him? No – they are all admiration for his audacity. I am afraid you will have to look elsewhere for your culprit.'

Chaloner was bemused. 'But he dressed in clothes

that made him look like one of Cromwell's more fervent supporters, and his manners were surly. If he aimed to ape gentlemen, why not pretend to be a Cavalier?'

Maude laughed. 'That was the genius of his plan. Everyone is a Royalist these days, and there are hundreds of them in London alone, all penniless and scavenging where they can. But who in their right mind would pretend to be a Roundhead? Well, Underhill did, and it meant no one ever questioned his claims. Simple, but effective.'

Chapter 4

Chaloner fell asleep in the chair after his third cup of wine at Hercules' Pillars Alley, and woke just as dawn was stealing across the rooftops. It was Thursday, which meant he had one more day before the Earl wanted him to travel to Hampton Court and Chelsea, so he decided to make the most of it by learning about Underhill's curious past. He also wanted to speak to Clarendon House's staff, in the hope that one of them might have noticed something to help him solve the murder.

There was no sign of Maude, but bread, cheese and breakfast ale had been left for him on the table, along with a pouch filled with herbs that he supposed was to keep him safe from the plague. It smelled of lavender, rosemary, juniper and sage. He drank the ale, put the pouch in his pocket, wrapped the food in a cloth, and set off towards the place from which Underhill had hailed.

The Fleet Rookery was an area where crime was rife, and the forces of law and order dared not tread. It was the domain of thieves and killers, and visitors were not welcome. Chaloner was aware of unseen eyes watching him as he made his way to Turnagain Lane, but no one tried to stop him. He had been there before and they knew where he was going: to visit a woman named Mother Greene. The residents were afraid of her, believing her to be a witch.

The plague was more in evidence in the rookery, being an overcrowded, insanitary part of the city, and Chaloner was appalled by the number of doors marked with red crosses. Many houses appeared to be abandoned, and he wondered if their occupants were all dead inside. It certainly smelled as though they were – the reek of decay was powerful and all-invasive in the airless alleys.

'Tom!' exclaimed Mother Greene warmly, when she opened her door to his knock. She flung the fragrant contents of a small flask over him, although whether to protect him or herself was impossible to say. 'Come in and tell me what you have been doing these last few weeks.'

Chaloner had always liked her cottage with its exotic aroma of potent plants. There were several mixing bowls on the table, and he supposed she had been making plague remedies, like everyone else with any modicum of expertise in the art of healing.

'*Sal mirabilis*,' she explained, when she saw where he was looking. 'Or "miraculous salts" in common parlance – although not miraculous enough to save most of my customers. Still, they are cheaper than London Treacle, which is beyond the means of all but the wealthiest folk. I heard about your wife, by the way.'

Chaloner opened his mouth to speak, but then was not sure what to say. He did not want to launch into an interrogation about Underhill immediately, because Mother Greene would consider it rude, but he could not bring himself to make small talk about Hannah.

'It is all right,' she said kindly. 'You do not have to

107

tell me about it. Sit by the hearth and enjoy a pipe of tobacco instead. Unless you have brought me breakfast?'

Chaloner handed her the cloth bundle, and watched her eyes light up. The bread was fresh and soft, a far cry from the rough loaves she usually ate, while the cheese was rich and creamy. She hobbled outside, and returned a moment later with a jug of frothing milk, taken fresh from the donkey that was tethered in the yard outside.

'You have bought one of my pouches,' she said, sniffing suddenly, although how she had managed to detect the contents of his pocket through the reek of her other potions was beyond Chaloner. He pulled it out and she nodded her satisfaction. 'Good. It will not keep you safe, of course, as nothing can, but it will mask unpleasant smells as you walk.'

'Is the disease very bad here?'

She nodded soberly. 'You were brave to come. Are you not afraid?'

'I try not to think about it.'

'Which makes you either very wise or very foolish. Why are you here? It must be important to risk such a journey.'

'To ask about a man named Robert Underhill. Did you know him?'

'Why? Is he dead?' When Chaloner inclined his head, she continued: 'Pity. He thought he could live happily for ever by deceiving the rich, but I warned him that it was only a matter of time before he was exposed. How did he meet his end?'

Chaloner told her about the murder and the thefts from Gorges, ending with a question. 'Was he the kind of man to steal from an asylum?'

108

'No,' she replied with total conviction. 'He would not have risked all he had built for thirty pounds and trinkets. He probably accepted the governorship to impress others he aimed to sponge from – your Earl, most likely – so stealing from them would have been counterproductive. He was too shrewd for that.'

'But he *did* steal from Clarendon – three valuable books.'

'Ah, yes.' Mother Greene shook her head slowly. 'Books. He never could resist those – not once he had tasted the knowledge they held. However, it is possible that he intended to take them back once he had finished with them – perhaps when living at Clarendon House at your Earl's invitation and expense.'

'That would never have happened,' said Chaloner. 'Clarendon cannot abide Parliamentarians, and Underhill was definitely not his kind of guest.'

'Well, I suppose we shall never know,' said Mother Greene.

'When did you last see Underhill?'

'A few weeks ago. He told me that he had befriended a medical man in Chelsea, who was delighted to host him in exchange for intelligent conversation.'

'Did he mention arguments with anyone?'

'None, and I was under the impression that he had found himself a pleasant niche, and intended to stay a while.'

Chaloner supposed he had better find out whether Parker had discovered that his houseguest was not all he claimed, and had killed him in a fit of indignation. He listed his other suspects, and was disappointed when Mother Greene shook her head to say she knew none of them, and that no one matching their descriptions had been in her domain. Except one.

'Andrew Kole,' she mused. 'Is he the speculator who bought some big old ruin, spent all his money repairing it, and was broken when the government took it away from him?'

Chaloner nodded. 'He came here?'

'Once. He followed Underhill to my house. It occurred to me that he might have discovered Underhill's game, and aimed to claw back his riches by blackmail. But he would not have won that contest: Underhill would have run circles around him.'

Her words placed Kole firmly at the top of Chaloner's list of suspects.

Feeling the need to discuss the murders, but doubtful that Kipps would provide any useful insights, Chaloner walked to Lincoln's Inn on Chancery Lane. He rapped on the gate, and was aware of being scrutinised very carefully before it was opened. Voice muffled by a protective scarf, the porter informed him that Mr Thurloe, bencher of that great foundation, was in his rooms.

Chaloner walked slowly through the venerable buildings with their ancient, peaceful grounds, until he reached Dial Court, named for the astronomical instrument that graced its centre, a piece of equipment so complex that no one knew how to use it. He climbed the stairs to the first floor, aware of the comfortingly familiar scent of polished wood and old books. It was the one place in London where he felt truly at home, although that was not saying much, given that his current abode contained so little he could call his own.

He knocked softly on the door to Chamber XIII, and opened it to see John Thurloe sitting at a table, writing. Thurloe had been Oliver Cromwell's Spymaster General and Secretary of State, although no one looking at his modest bearing and diffident manner would imagine that he had held the security of a nation in his hands for several years. He had retired from politics at the Restoration, and now lived in quiet obscurity, splitting his time between London and his Oxfordshire estates.

He had fled London when the plague had first erupted, vowing to stay away until the crisis was over. Then one of Cromwell's sons had needed help with an urgent legal matter, so he had come back – he was devoted to the Lord Protector's family, and refused them nothing, even if it meant risking his life. He had solved the problem with his customary efficiency, but then had agreed to stay for a few more days to deal with pressing Inn business – business that involved sitting safely in his chambers and never going out.

'Stay back, Tom!' he gulped in alarm. 'Where have you been today?'

'The Fleet Rookery,' replied Chaloner wickedly, knowing what Thurloe's reaction would be. He was not disappointed: the ex-Spymaster cowered away in horror. Thurloe imagined himself to be in fragile health, and was always swallowing pills and potions in an effort to regain the vigour he had experienced at twenty. The prospect of catching the plague had sent him apoplectic with terror, and Chaloner dreaded to imagine how many 'preventatives' he had devoured to keep the sickness at bay.

'Are you insane?' Thurloe scrabbled frantically for the pouch of herbs that lay next to him. 'It has more victims than any other part of the city! And you come from there to me?'

'Directly,' replied Chaloner. 'After eating breakfast with one of its inhabitants.'

'Then stay away!' cried Thurloe, burying his nose in the little bag. His next words were muffled. 'I would have thought that you, of all people, would know better. Hannah tripped around imagining herself to be immune, and look what happened to her.'

It was a low blow, and Chaloner felt his impishness drain away. 'True,' he acknowledged.

'Had you come an hour later, you would have missed me,' Thurloe went on. 'My coach leaves at eleven.'

'There will not be anyone left in the city soon,' said Chaloner, ignoring Thurloe's command to remain in the hall and going to sit on a stool. 'The Earl will travel to Hampton Court tomorrow, and his family goes today. White Hall is empty except for the Treasury men and a few unlucky servants, and weeds grow in the middle of Fleet Street, because there is so little traffic.'

'Ask the Earl to take you with him,' instructed Thurloe. 'And if he refuses, come to me in Oxfordshire, although you will have to submit to tests to prove that you have not brought the contagion with you. I would never forgive myself if Ann and the children . . .'

'Thank you, but he wants me to visit Chelsea. He is patron of the lunatic asylum there, which has been the victim of thefts. There have also been two murders – an inmate and a member of its board of governors. Robert Underhill.'

'The man who hailed from the gutters, but who read a few books, and declared himself a gentleman? Is that why you went to the Fleet Rookery in the face of all common sense?'

'You know him?'

'He was a "person of interest" during the Common-wealth, because he appeared from nowhere and claimed to be rich. I investigated him thoroughly, but he was just a cheat who aimed to live off the generosity of others. You say he has been murdered?'

'Strangled in Clarendon House, and I have eight suspects among his fellow guests. However, having learned his background – as a fraud *and* a spy for Williamson – I wonder if I should widen my search. Such a career must have earned him enemies.'

'Not his career as an imposter – he always moved on before he was exposed, which is why he remained in business for so long. Did you say he died in Clarendon House? Why was he there?'

Chaloner gave an account of what had happened, then listed those who had had the opportunity and the motive to kill Underhill. Thurloe was one of those rare individuals who could listen without interrupting, and he sat in silence until Chaloner had finished. Then he spent some moments with his eyes closed, pondering. The pouch of herbs lay forgotten on the table.

'You think his murder and Nancy's are connected?' he asked eventually.

'Well, both were throttled.'

'That might be coincidence. It is the method of choice where a bloodless death is required, as I am sure you know. Does one suspect stand out from the others?'

'Andrew Kole – on the basis of his guilty manner when answering questions, the fact that he and Underhill quarrelled, and that he once followed Underhill into the Fleet Rookery. Of course, none of it is real proof . . .'

'I know Kole, too. He "bought" the Theological College, because he thought he could turn it into a quick profit, but he was blinded by greed, and failed to read the contract properly. Indeed, his claim on the place is one of the matters that has kept me in London these last few days, when common sense screams at me to race home.'

'Kole hired *you* to represent him?'

Thurloe raised his eyebrows. 'He could not afford a lawyer from Lincoln's Inn. However, the government can, and we were asked to ensure that its agents had acted correctly when they seized the building. They did, and my assessment will be read to Kole this afternoon. However, I imagine he will continue the fight, even though the law is against him.'

'He did say that he intended to spend the day here, hunting down deeds to prove his case.'

'He will not find any, because they do not exist.' Thurloe stood abruptly. 'I am uncomfortable with you breathing the same air as me, and I shall feel safer outside. Walk with me in the gardens.'

Lincoln's Inn's grounds comprised neatly gravelled paths, small hedges and carefully sculpted shrubs. Mature trees at the far end provided some shade, but the rest suffered the full brunt of the sun. Some kindly soul had filled a shallow bowl with water, and a family of sparrows were bathing in it, flinging up showers of droplets that caught the sunlight as they fell.

'I shall miss this place,' sighed Thurloe. 'I wonder if I will ever see it again.'

Chaloner regarded him in alarm. 'Why should you not? Oxfordshire is not the end of the world, and you have made the journey many times before.'

'These are deadly times, Tom, and it is difficult to know what the future holds for any of us. I may not *want* to return if this terrible pestilence inflicts too many changes on the city I love.'

114

'What does the future hold for the Theological College?' asked Chaloner, unwilling to dwell on the plague. 'For instance, why does Kole persist with his claim, when everyone else seems to accept that he was outmanoeuvred by the government?'

'Desperation, I imagine. When the Dutch war is over and the prisoners have gone, the King has promised the place to the Royal Society. Kole will never have it, despite spending his entire fortune on making it habitable. Of course, he is not alone in thinking it should be his.'

'You mean there are people who support him?'

'No, I mean that there are two other claimants. It was built sixty-odd years ago by Dean Sutcliffe of Exeter Cathedral. He is dead now, but his nephew and chief beneficiary – *John* Sutcliffe – thinks the College belongs to him.'

Chaloner recalled being told as much in Deptford. 'I have heard that the younger Sutcliffe is a very sinister fellow.'

'He is. I was obliged to watch him very carefully during the Commonwealth, because he is a malcontent, dissatisfied with everyone and everything around him. Before he inherited his uncle's estate – such as it was without the College – he made a living as an assassin. He worked for both sides during the wars, and my sources told me that he thoroughly enjoyed the work.'

Rector Thompson had said the same, Chaloner recalled. 'Does he live in Chelsea?'

'In Greenwich. According to my contacts, he has retired from killing, and passes his time by watching plays. Of course, that is difficult now all the theatres have closed.'

'Commissioner Evelyn mentioned his love of dramas,'

said Chaloner, and then wondered if he had walked past the man without knowing it. 'What does he look like?'

'Lean and hungry, with a menacing demeanour.'

Chaloner would have noticed anyone fitting that description. 'Who is the third claimant?'

'Rector Wilkinson, another of your suspects. He was the College's last provost and thinks it should again be filled with polemical divines. He is a vile character – a religious bigot.'

'Bigoted enough to kill?'

'Quite possibly. However, I predict that Underhill's murder will be connected to the prison, and if I were you, I would start my enquiries there.'

'Because he was spying on it for Williamson?'

'Yes, and because he associated with two of its three claimants – you say he had violent disagreements with Kole, while living in Chelsea will have put him in Wilkinson's path.'

'But being a Gorges governor put him in company with *five* of my suspects – Kole, Parker, Franklin, Cocke and Mrs Bonney.'

'True, but thirty pounds and a few baubles are not in the same league as legal ownership of a large and valuable estate. One is far more likely to result in murder than the other.'

'Should I confine my enquiries to Kole and Wilkinson, then?'

'Begin with them, but keep an open mind. And certainly do not limit yourself to those who attended the Earl's soirée. You could have slipped past Clarendon House's guards with ease, and so could other professional spies.'

Chaloner remained uncertain. 'But Underhill was strangled, just like Nancy. How can *she* have a connection to the College? I doubt she was allowed out to form an association with it.'

Thurloe shrugged. 'Perhaps when you solve Underhill's murder, you will solve hers, too.'

'What else can you tell me about the College?'

'It was founded by King James, as a place for clerics to air controversial theological opinions, although it ceased to function as such long before I became Spymaster.' Thurloe hesitated, but then forged on. 'I should be honest with you, Tom. The *real* reason I encourage you to investigate the place is because an informant has recently expressed concerns about it.'

Thurloe had inspired great loyalty among those he had employed during the Commonwealth, and many former spies continued to send him reports and snippets of information, even though he was rarely in a position to use them.

'What did he say, exactly?' asked Chaloner.

'Nothing specific, just that he senses something amiss. There have been odd comings and goings at night, and an air of secrecy surrounds it. It is locked up tight for obvious reasons, but my friend says that security there is too intense.'

'*Can* security be too intense in a prison full of enemy warriors?'

'The gaolers will not talk, even for free ale, while Warden Tooker is entirely the wrong kind of man for such a post. For a start, he was dismissed from Newgate for corruption.'

'I have spoken to three of the four Commissioners for the Care and Treatment of Prisoners of War – Evelyn, Reymes and Doyley – and they seem content with Tooker's rule.'

117

'Probably because they do not know his history.'

Chaloner was thoughtful. 'I doubt Spymaster Williamson is aware of any of this. He said Underhill was a poor intelligencer, who sent him sketchy and unreliable reports.'

'Then enlighten him. Unfortunately, I doubt he can do much to help you, as he needs to channel all his resources into the war. But I had better leave or I shall miss the Oxford coach. Farewell, Tom. God save you from all harm.'

Chaloner trudged along the hot, dusty streets to Piccadilly, lighting his pipe when someone passed him coughing. He arrived to find Clarendon House gripped by the same frenzied activity as the previous day, with loaded carts waiting in the drive, and servants racing about like madmen in an effort to make all ready for departure. Kipps was waiting for him, and so was the Earl.

'Have you solved the murder?' his master demanded. 'You have had plenty of time.'

Sourly, Chaloner wished the Earl would investigate a killing himself, so he would know that it sometimes required more than a day to identify the culprit. He gave a brief report on his findings.

'Perhaps we should leave for Chelsea now,' suggested Kipps, clearly unimpressed with the little Chaloner had managed to glean. 'It would be—'

'And who will escort me to Hampton Court, pray?' interrupted the Earl archly. 'The roads are dangerous at the moment, because so many paupers are living in the woods to escape the plague. I should not like to be ambushed. Besides, a day will make no difference to the prison, while I sent Brodrick to Gorges this morning, to guard the songbirds and begin the process of hunting its thief.'

'Brodrick?' blurted Chaloner, astonished that the Earl should imagine his dissipated cousin capable of either task.

'He will hand the enquiry to you when you arrive, never fear. Incidentally, Williamson wants copies of all your reports, so you had better oblige. I do not want *him* vexed with me.'

With Kipps in tow, Chaloner began the laborious task of interviewing all the staff who had been on duty the previous night. Everything went well for a while, although it was not easy to keep their attention when most were more interested in ensuring that they were not left behind when the ponderous cavalcade got underway. Then Kipps grew bored with the repetitive nature of the exercise, and began asking questions of his own. These led to gossip, none of which was pertinent to their enquiries, but that had him agog with prurient interest. Chaloner grew increasingly exasperated as he struggled to keep the discussions on track.

'That was fun,' Kipps declared when the last 'witness' had gone. They had learned nothing about Underhill, but were now conversant with the fact that Lady Savage drank more wine than any man at Court, that the Earl favoured plain calico drawers, and that Lawrence, married less than two months, was already keeping a mistress. 'Perhaps I should help you more often.'

'Not if I ever want to solve any crimes,' muttered Chaloner.

Kipps beamed, unfazed by the spy's sullen temper. 'It is too late to do more now, so you can come to my house tonight, as planned. You had not forgotten, had you?'

119

He glanced around furtively, to ensure no one was listening. 'Martin is looking forward to it.'

Chaloner had forgotten, and was sorry the prospect of playing did not please him as it should. 'It will be my pleasure,' he lied.

'Good. But first, you had better visit Williamson, and tell him what you have learned so far. Our Earl is right: we do not want him annoyed with us for being uncommunicative.'

He had a point, so Chaloner trudged to Old Palace Yard, where the Spymaster had his lair. Williamson was at his desk when he arrived, windows thrown open in the hope of catching a breeze. Through them, Chaloner could see nearby Westminster Hall, where the blackened heads of traitors were impaled on specially crafted spikes. There were several bloated black flies in the office, and he flapped them away in distaste, not liking to imagine where they might have been first.

'Thank you,' said Williamson, after Chaloner had relayed all that Mother Greene and Thurloe had told him. 'When will you go to Chelsea? Now? You could be there by nightfall.'

'Tomorrow. Did you know Underhill's background when you recruited him?'

A pained expression crossed the Spymaster's face. 'No, although I should have guessed. A gentleman would have provided his services free of charge, but Underhill wanted money. Keep me informed of your progress, Chaloner, but if you use cipher, please do not make your code too elaborate. I am short of cryptographers at the moment, as well as decent spies.'

These were not words to inspire, and Chaloner found himself concerned for his country as he hurried to Covent

120

Garden to collect his viol. He shoved the instrument in a canvas bag rather more roughly than he would have done his old ones, and set off for Kipps' home on Bow Street. While he walked, he began to invent reasons as to why he could not play that night. Sore fingers, perhaps. Or broken strings. Kipps would never know that they had been snapped on purpose.

He knocked on the door, and a maid conducted him to a parlour at the back of the house. The walls were adorned with crudely childish paintings, all of which had been framed like the works of Great Masters, while the floor was a muddled chaos of toys. Kipps was kneeling in the middle of it with a brawny, moon-faced boy and a small, pretty woman. All three were helpless with laughter. It was a touching scene, and Chaloner saw there was more to the Seal Bearer than the affable, slightly ridiculous courtier with a zealous devotion to ceremony and tradition.

'Tom!' Kipps cried, scrambling to his feet. 'You must forgive the mess. We have been trying to teach Martin how to smoke, but he cannot get the hang of it.'

Olivia Kipps came to give him her hand, after which Martin affected a clumsy bow that made both parents burst into spontaneous applause. The boy grinned happily, then spoiled the effect by throwing his arms around their guest in an affectionate hug. Chaloner was taken aback, but Kipps and Olivia did not seem to find it unusual, and both started to talk at the same time, which made it difficult to hear either. It became harder still when Martin joined in, speaking in a slow drawl, which suggested that words did not come easily to him.

After a simple but well-cooked meal, Martin clamoured at Chaloner to play. Chaloner obliged, but although the

121

boy whooped his appreciation, the spy was unimpressed by his own performance. The instrument felt dull, and failed to come alive to his touch as the others had done. Martin did not care, and danced jig after jig, until he was so tired that he could barely stand.

'Thank you, Tom,' said Kipps softly, when Olivia had gone to put the exhausted boy to bed. 'You have given him much pleasure tonight. But you see why I cannot have him at Court. People would mock him, which would break his heart. And mine. I hate to see him hurt.'

Chaloner thought Kipps was wise to keep Martin away from cruel tongues, although he sensed more good in the lad than in the whole of White Hall put together. They sat in companionable silence for a while, smoking and sipping chilled spiced wine.

'Have you thought any more about being the Treasury's second Sergeant at Arms?' Kipps asked eventually. 'You are just the man we need, and I know I could persuade Warwick to take you. The salary is a hundred pounds a year, which would cushion you nicely, were anything to happen to the Earl.'

It was a respectable sum, and Chaloner was touched that Kipps was prepared to sponsor him. He murmured his thanks, and Kipps patted his shoulder in a gruff gesture of friendship, before covering his awkwardness by beginning to talk about the murders.

'Cocke,' he said. '*He* is behind this nastiness – I feel it in my bones. But I am sure you will get to the bottom of it, no matter who it transpires to be. The Earl is wise to place his trust in you.'

Chaloner laughed. 'I hardly think he has done that.'

'Of course he has,' said Kipps earnestly. 'He thinks the world of your abilities, although he would sooner die than tell you so. But it is late, and we should talk about happier things than theft and murder, or we shall give ourselves bad dreams. More wine?'

Chapter 5

It was another sultry night, and Chaloner found himself thinking about Hannah, who would have insisted that the windows be closed against the night air, which she had considered injurious to health. Yet a stuffy room had not kept her safe, and it was with angry defiance that he threw the shutters open as far as they would go. Then he tossed and turned restlessly, but sleep would not come, mostly because his thoughts kept turning to his sudden inability to play the viol.

Eventually, he rose and lit a candle, intending to read until sleep claimed him, but he could not concentrate on Rushworth's *Historical Collections* – a turgid tome that Wiseman had lent him – so he picked up the note that Hannah had written on her deathbed instead.

At first, he had been grateful to Kipps for salvaging it, but now he began to wonder whether he might have been happier without the thing. He stared at it for a long time before eventually dozing off slumped across the table.

When he woke the following day, he felt stiff, sluggish and not at all inclined to traipse to Hampton Court and then Chelsea. He dunked his head in a bucket of cold water, and when that did nothing to sharpen his wits, he went to the Rainbow Coffee House, in the hope that a dose of Farr's best would do the trick – and keep the plague and madness at bay into the bargain.

'What news?' called Farr, flapping his hand to see through the fug that pervaded the place. There was some burned bean involved, but most came from his patrons' tobacco.

Chaloner coughed, and everyone regarded him in alarm. 'Smoke,' he croaked in explanation.

'It will do you good,' averred Farr. 'That and a dish of my coffee.'

'And prayers,' put in Thompson piously. 'The Almighty is always ready to help the godly. Although the best way to avoid infection is to leave the city, of course.'

'Most of my wealthy customers have already gone,' sighed Farr. 'But I have no country acquaintances to visit, so I am doomed to stay here, flirting with Death.'

'*I* cannot go, because I am needed to ring the bells,' declared Stedman importantly. 'No one would know who was dead if I did not toll to mark their passing, and I consider it my patriotic duty to stay.' He glanced at Chaloner. 'Although I suppose *you* will not be here for much longer. Your master's household departed yesterday, and he will follow today.'

'Hampton Court is reputed to be very nice,' said Thompson. 'Although I am reliably informed that its sanitary arrangements leave a lot to be desired.'

'I am not going to Hampton Court,' said Chaloner, deftly steering the discussion towards his enquiries. 'The Earl is sending me to Chelsea.'

'Chelsea?' echoed Farr in distaste. 'Why? I doubt it

is far enough away to be safe, and it will not have the city's attractions – like coffee houses.'

'You are wrong, Farr,' said Thompson superiorly, 'because there are plans afoot to open one near the church.' He smiled at Chaloner. 'Will you visit the Theological College while you are there? I am sure our friend Evelyn will be keen to hear what you think of his prison.'

'Those captured Dutchmen should have been housed somewhere else,' said Stedman severely. 'Chelsea is too close to London.'

Farr sniggered. 'It is worth the risk, just to annoy two very unpleasant people – namely John Sutcliffe and Rector Wilkinson. Both think that particular building belongs to them, and word is that they were furious when the government turned it into a gaol.'

'You know them?' probed Chaloner.

'Oh, yes. They used to come here for coffee. Sutcliffe would insist on quoting Shakespeare, while Wilkinson always tried to drown him out with long tracts from the Bible.'

'There is nothing wrong with long tracts from the Bible,' put in Thompson coolly.

'I do not suppose Andrew Kole accompanied them, did he?' fished Chaloner hopefully. 'He is also of the opinion that the College belongs to him.'

Thompson spoke up when Farr shook his head. 'I met Kole once – in Chelsea, after we had both been to church. We were chatting in the porch, when a fellow named Underhill happened to walk past. Kole exploded with rage and threatened to kill him for spying. Underhill denied doing any such thing, of course.'

'Was Kole serious about dispatching him?' asked Chaloner keenly.

126

'Oh, yes,' replied Thompson. 'There was a look in his eye that I remember from the wars. He was in earnest all right.'

'What were you doing in Chelsea, Thompson?' asked Stedman curiously.

The rector promptly became flustered, and began several sentences that he did not finish. In the end, he released a gusty sigh. 'Very well, I shall tell you the truth, given that keeping it quiet will result in speculation – which is sure to be a good deal more colourful than the sorry reality. I was obliged to place my wife in an asylum there.'

So that was why Thompson had dodged the subject on the road to Deptford, thought Chaloner, recalling the rector's oddly furtive manner when the village had been mentioned.

'In Gorges House?' asked Stedman. 'If so, she was in excellent hands. I have printed several of Dr Parker's pamphlets on madness – the man is a genius.'

'Well, he quite cured her of her malady,' said Thompson. 'Him and prodigious amounts of coffee. Of course, she was not *mad* exactly – just possessed of a deep and debilitating sorrow.'

'Then you were right to send her to Parker,' averred Stedman. 'I can name you a dozen ladies who have benefited from his expertise.'

Chaloner could name two himself – Dorothy Wiseman and Olivia Kipps – and wondered if Gorges' popularity explained why the Earl had offered to support it. If it became fashionable, the chances were that it would also become profitable, and make him some easy money.

'May I speak to Mrs Thompson?' he asked, feeling it

would do no harm to find out about the foundation from a former inmate before visiting it himself.

Thompson smiled warmly. 'Of course. Would now be convenient?'

The rectory of St Dunstan-in-the-West was directly opposite the Rainbow, and was the proud owner of a walled garden. As Thompson had an interest in horticulture, his little arbour had been lovingly watered, and was green and fragrant with flowers. Four plump chickens scratched in the moist soil, while a fifth basked in the sun. There was a herb garden by the back door, where Gertrude Thompson was picking mint. The air was full of its scent, hot and pungent.

'Chaloner wants to know about Gorges,' said Thompson, once their guest had been settled on a bench in the shade, and plied with cakes and fruit cordial.

Gertrude smiled fondly. 'It is a remarkable place – home to a few genuinely disturbed minds, but most are only in need a spell of quiet contemplation. Along with coffee, of course. I take a dish every morning now, and I have never felt better.'

'It is a pity coffee houses exclude women,' interjected Thompson. 'If they were open to the gentler sex, there would be far fewer deranged ladies.'

Chaloner begged to differ. The patrons of the Rainbow were hardly rational, while some men spent their entire lives in such places without ever making a sensible remark.

'What did you think of Parker?' he asked. 'Did you find him . . . unhinged?'

Gertrude blinked her surprise. 'No! There is not a

saner man in all the world. How could he be otherwise? You cannot treat the mentally fragile if you are not wholly cogent yourself.'

'He did not engage in staring contests with marble busts, or make peculiar remarks?'

She laughed. 'Of course not! And nor did Dr Franklin or Mrs Bonney, before you ask. I have never met kinder, gentler people.'

'When did you last see Parker?'

Gertrude considered carefully. 'Before the plague, which means April. However, I assure you, Mr Chaloner, there is nothing of the lunatic about him.'

Chaloner was puzzled. What had caused Parker to change? The constant company of madwomen? 'Did you know Nancy Janaway?' he asked. 'She was murdered.'

Gertrude nodded sadly. 'My friend Martha Thrush wrote to me about it. She even begged me to take Joseph to Chelsea, to catch the killer on her behalf.'

Chaloner regarded Thompson in surprise. 'Do you have talents in that direction, then?'

Thompson shook his head. 'But Martha was desperate for help from any quarter. Well, who can blame her? It cannot be easy to live in a house where someone has been unlawfully slain.'

'Poor Nancy,' sighed Gertrude. 'She had been stricken with a melancholy, but she was almost better. It is a wicked shame that her life was snatched away just as she had recovered.'

'Who at Gorges might have killed her?' asked Chaloner. 'A fellow resident? A servant? One of the governors?'

'It is an establishment for gentlewomen,' said Gertrude reproachfully, 'and the dangerous ones are kept under very strict supervision. Meanwhile, the servants are

129

beyond reproach, and why would a governor take against poor Nancy?'

'Did you meet the governors?'

'All except the Earl of Clarendon, who gives money but does not visit himself. Mrs Bonney, Dr Parker and Dr Franklin are angels, but I did not care for the others. Mr Cocke is a lecher, Mr Kole has a nasty temper, and there is something very distasteful about Mr Underhill, as if he is pretending to be something he is not.'

She was perceptive, and Chaloner's interest in her opinions quickened. 'Underhill was murdered last night, and Kole and Cocke are on my list of suspects.'

'They should be. Both are selfish, and I never did understand why they agreed to serve as governors, when it costs them time and money.'

'Oh, I can answer that,' put in Thompson. 'To get themselves into Clarendon's company. Doubtless they hope he will do them favours in the future.'

'Gorges has a thief,' said Chaloner. 'Does either strike you as the kind of man to steal?'

'Yes, but I doubt either would risk it,' replied Gertrude. 'Mr Cocke works at the prison and the Treasury, as well as Gorges, and any hint of dishonesty would see him dismissed from all three, leaving him penniless. And Mr Kole will never reclaim "his" college if he is branded a felon.'

'When you were at Gorges, were you confined to your room, or did you go out?'

'It was not a gaol, Mr Chaloner. We could leave any time we wanted. We often strolled to the market, went for walks, or attended church.'

'Then you met Rector Wilkinson?'

Gertrude pulled a face. 'He is more interested in

130

squabbling about religion than in practising Christian virtues. He is not a very nice person. Yet Martha tells me that his house is always full of visitors these days, although I cannot imagine why.'

'Personally, I suspect he is gathering like-minded fanatics with a view to reopening the College,' said Thompson. 'I hope he does not succeed.'

'There is one other odd thing about Chelsea,' said Gertrude. 'It has a spectre, a ghost that glides around frightening people. I saw it myself when I visited Martha and Nancy a month ago – a sinister apparition in a long coat. It may have been my imagination, but I think I saw burning eyes.'

'It *was* your imagination,' said Thompson firmly. 'There is no such thing as ghosts. Except the Holy Ghost, of course, but that is not the same thing at all.'

'Well, this was certainly not holy,' averred Gertrude. She turned to Chaloner. 'You are friends with Surgeon Wiseman, are you not? His wife is at Gorges. Ask him your questions.'

It was a good idea, and Chaloner promised to act on it.

It was nearly nine o'clock when Chaloner arrived at Clarendon House – the hour when the Earl had said that he would be ready to leave for Hampton Court. Unfortunately, the Dutch ambassador appeared at the same time with urgent business, which he claimed was likely to keep the Lord Chancellor busy until mid-afternoon at the earliest. Kipps was disgusted.

'While we kick our heels here, Cocke will be destroying the evidence that will allow us to charge him with murder and theft,' he said crossly. 'He may even evade justice.'

'Cocke may not be the culprit,' warned Chaloner. 'Indeed, the case is stronger against Kole.'

'Of course it is Cocke! The man is a rogue.'

Chaloner regarded Kipps thoughtfully. 'What makes you so keen to see him in trouble?'

'Nothing,' replied the Seal Bearer, but in a way that made Chaloner sure he was lying.

'I will likely find out anyway, and if it affects our investigation, you should tell me now.'

An expression of intense pain suffused Kipps' amiable face. 'He made me do something of which I am deeply ashamed. Even now, I can hardly bear to think of it . . .'

Chaloner's interest was piqued. 'What?'

Kipps would not meet his eyes. 'Cocke saw me once with Martin. He asked if the boy was mine, but I was so afraid that Martin would become the object of ridicule if I introduced them that I said he was a servant's child. He made me deny kinship to my own son!'

'Did he believe you?' Chaloner seriously doubted that the bluff Kipps could successfully deceive a worldly individual like Cocke.

'He laughed slyly, and a couple of weeks later, he asked me for money. I refused, so he took to following me. I keep rooms here in Clarendon House, and you are the only one who knows about Bow Street, so I was able to avoid going home. Yet I sense he has not given up . . .'

It was unpleasant, and said nothing good about the accompter, but it was hardly grounds on which to accuse him of murder. As gently as he could, Chaloner said so, finishing with, 'He will not harm Martin, though, I promise. I will speak to him, and he will not trouble you or the lad again.'

132

'Thank you,' said Kipps gratefully. 'And in return, we can include Kole as a suspect, if you like – although only on condition that you remove that spider over there. It has been watching me since dawn, and is getting ready to make its move. It sees my wig as an excellent place for a web.'

As he had time to kill, Chaloner decided to follow Gertrude Thompson's advice and visit Wiseman. He did not take Kipps with him, because the two men did not like each other: the Seal Bearer found Wiseman's penchant for red clothes risible, while the surgeon had scant time for Kipps' love of pomp and ceremony.

Chyrurgeons' Hall was in Monkwell Street, just to the north of the old city wall. It comprised not only lecture halls, a refectory and accommodation blocks for its members, but also the peculiarly shaped Anatomy Theatre. Chaloner was relieved to find that particular building abandoned that day, dreading to imagine what a dissection would be like in the heat. As it was, he detected a whiff of something unpleasant in the air, a combination of decay and the spirits used to preserve interesting specimens for teaching purposes.

The Master's lodgings were above the main hall, and were Wiseman's for a year. His colleagues had not wanted to elect him, but he had been the only senior member who had not yet had a crack at the post, so they had had no choice. Unfortunately, his bombastic and insensitive reforms were earning him more enemies than ever, and Chaloner was acutely aware of unfriendly glances as he was conducted across the yard by the porter.

Chaloner climbed the stairs to find that the surgeon had only just risen, having spent much of the night with a patient. He was in the midst of his daily stone-lifting routine, which gave him the powerful muscles needed to subdue frightened clients and reset broken bones. Chaloner felt tired just watching him: the day was far too oppressive for such vigorous exertions.

'Have some breakfast,' the surgeon panted. 'Raw beef and stewed lettuce, items guaranteed to aid digestion and promote good health.'

The meat had attracted flies, while the amorphous mass of greenery had been cooked to within an inch of its life, so Chaloner declined. He did not normally pass up food, given that he was invariably uncertain when his next meal would be, but Wiseman's offerings were more than he could stomach that morning. To avoid a confrontation if the surgeon insisted, Chaloner told him about Underhill's murder.

'Then I must go to Chelsea at once,' the surgeon declared, dropping the stone in a corner. The thud it made as it landed was testament to its great weight. 'I cannot have Dorothy at the mercy of some lunatic strangler. It is my duty to look after her, given that she is unable to do it herself.'

'Yes,' agreed Chaloner, guilty thoughts of Hannah's last illness filling his mind.

Wiseman misread him. 'You are thinking of Temperance, and how convenient it would be for us if Dorothy died. Yet although I love Temperance, I shall never marry her. We are happy as we are, and I refuse to make the same mistake that you did with Hannah – hurling yourself into a union with scant thought for the consequences.'

'My marriage was not a mistake,' objected Chaloner, offended.

'Of course not,' said Wiseman scathingly, and changed the subject before Chaloner could argue. 'When are you going to Chelsea? Perhaps we could ride there together.'

'Today, as soon as I have delivered the Earl to Hampton Court.'

'Hampton Court,' echoed Wiseman with relish. 'I shall definitely travel with you then, so I can bag a decent room before the rabble arrives. And *then* we shall go to Chelsea.'

'Kipps will be helping me—'

'That buffoon!' spat Wiseman. 'Well, all I can say is that I hope he does not hamper your investigation. I cannot have Dorothy put at risk because of his stupidity.'

There was no point defending Kipps – Wiseman tended to be intractable once he had made up his mind about someone, and Chaloner knew better than to challenge him. 'How well do you know the Gorges governors?' he asked instead.

'Parker's medical views have merit, but there is nothing remotely interesting about Mrs Bonney or Franklin. They are both worthy people, I am sure, but as dull as ditchwater. And as for Kole and Cocke . . . well, they are beneath my dignity to notice.'

Chaloner was beginning to remember why so many people found Wiseman objectionable. 'You said Dorothy wrote to you about the thefts and Nancy's murder. Do you still have the letter?'

Wiseman poked about in the chaos of paper that comprised his desk, but it was not long before he conceded defeat with an apologetic shrug. With a sigh, Chaloner saw he had wasted his time, and that he had achieved nothing from the visit except acquiring a second travelling companion who would quarrel with the first.

'Is Parker sane?' he asked, as Wiseman walked with him down the stairs to the yard.

Wiseman regarded him askance. 'Of course he is sane! Do you think I would entrust Dorothy to a lunatic? Whatever prompts you to put such a question?'

'I have met him twice, and he acted peculiarly on both occasions. Unless you consider kissing statues normal?'

'He was probably jesting with you. He has a very wry sense of humour.'

Chaloner suspected that Wiseman would revise his opinion once he reached Chelsea and saw Parker for himself. 'Why did you choose Gorges for Dorothy?'

'Because it is the best place in the country. She has been mad for nigh on two decades – she exhibited the first signs just a few weeks after our marriage. Yet I have high hopes that Parker will effect a complete cure.'

Uncharitably, Chaloner wondered if it was life with the surgeon that had driven the hapless woman out of her wits. He was about to ask if Wiseman had met Nancy Janaway, when they were intercepted by two of the surgeon's colleagues. Lawrence Loe and Ralph Foliard were portly, arrogant individuals in horsehair wigs.

'The Company's annual feast,' began Loe. 'You promised to tell us today whether you plan to cancel it or to proceed as normal.'

'I am too busy to think about it at the moment,' said Wiseman, dismissively enough to be offensive. 'Chaloner is here on Court business, which is a lot more important than yet another opportunity for you two to gorge.'

'I beg to differ,' said Foliard stiffly, 'because this decision will affect all of London. If we gather in one place, we may catch the plague and die, thus leaving no qualified surgeons to deal with the crisis. But if we postpone it, everyone will think we are afraid, which will damage morale.'

'But I *am* afraid,' declared Wiseman. 'Only fools are not.'

'In other words, he wants to call it off,' muttered Foliard to Loe. 'Although why he could not have just said so politely is beyond me.'

'Did I hear you discussing Parker just now?' asked Loe. 'You should not treat with him, Wiseman. He claims to cure madness with coffee, but everyone knows that insanity is caused by worms in the brain, and the only remedy is to open the skull and pick them out.'

'He considers exercise beneficial, too,' added Foliard with a scornful snigger, 'and has hired two dancing masters to help his patients jig about.'

'How do you know?' demanded Wiseman, belligerent because *he* deemed exercise beneficial as well, and he resented the sneer in the remark.

'Because we have just bled the pair of them – bleeding is a good protection against the plague, as you know,' replied Loe. 'They are staying in the Greyhound tavern on Holborn, and will return to Chelsea tomorrow. They also told us there was a murder at Gorges – a strangling. I hope your wife was not responsible.'

'Dorothy is not a strangler,' said Wiseman. 'She is more of a stabber.'

As neither Loe nor Foliard knew how to respond to this particular nugget of information, Wiseman swept past them and went on his way, pulling Chaloner with him. The surgeon mopped his face with a piece of cloth that was ominously smeared with blood, almost certainly not his own.

137

'This heat will make the plague rage ever more fiercely,' he said sombrely. 'We are wise to leave the city.'

'What about your patients?' asked Chaloner. 'Will you abandon them in their hour of need?'

'The important ones have already fled, and there is nothing I can do for the rest, so they may as well save their money. Have you invested in any useless pre-ventatives?'

Chaloner showed Wiseman his pipe.

'Smoking will not protect you,' the surgeon declared, snatching the offending item from Chaloner's hand and hurling it over the wall. 'Try eating the tobacco instead.'

Chaloner took a few strands and put them in his mouth, wincing at the bitter taste and the burning sensation that followed. Wiseman continued to dispense medical advice.

'Of course, the only thing that will *really* keep you safe is staying away from plague victims altogether. And if you are careless enough to let someone cough on you, rinse out your mouth immediately with vinegar. Hah! Here is Dorothy's letter! It was in my pocket all along.'

Chaloner took it from him. It was penned in a firm, neat cursive, but the margins were thick with peculiar symbols and random squiggles. He regarded Wiseman questioningly.

'She is a lunatic,' shrugged the surgeon. 'They are not noted for their coherent communiqués. Yet she does have spells of lucidity. Unfortunately, they are usually followed by interludes of distressing violence. All sharp implements must be hidden, or she will have them in you.'

Again, Chaloner sincerely hoped he would not discover that Dorothy had made an end of Nancy in one of her savage moods. He turned his attention to

138

the letter, suddenly and painfully reminded of the one Hannah had written with its nonsensical rambling about peacemakers and dandies. He pushed that one from his mind and concentrated on Dorothy's.

My Fyne Rich'd
The Batman stalks the sorrie arbor and hee has Eyes in the Neare Gardenn. The Property of My Absentt One has been cruellie slaine and J knowe nott howe to Comforte his Sadde Soule. There are theeves in Gorgess with Goldenn Eares and Fingers, and a Jyme that Singeth, and they put great storre in my coffin. Come soone, My Beloved Onne.
Dorothy.

He looked at Wiseman in mystification. 'How in God's name did you deduce from this nonsensical ramble that Nancy was murdered?'

'Because I know my wife. Her "Absent One" is a Chelsea bell-founder named Thomas Janaway, who used to visit, but who comes no longer. The explanation as to why is in the following clause: the "property" is Janaway's wife Nancy, who is "cruelly slain".'

'If you say so.'

'I do. Janaway always paid his respects to Dorothy when he came to see Nancy, even when she was not in a position to appreciate it.'

'Why would he do that?' asked Chaloner suspiciously.

'Some folk are just imbued with natural charity, Chaloner,' replied Wiseman, who was not known for this himself. 'And I think he was genuinely fond of her, although the affection could not have been reciprocated,

139

of course. She barely knows herself, let alone anyone else.'

Chaloner tapped the letter. 'It sounds as though she knows Janaway to me.'

The Greyhound was a large coaching inn on one of London's busiest thoroughfares. It had been a friendly, noisy place, where patrons mingled freely and exchanged information about their journeys. That day it was silent, and its few customers sat in uneasy clusters, eyeing with suspicion anyone who went too close. Others declined to enter at all, and stood outside with masks over their faces.

Chaloner stepped into the tavern's cool interior with relief, glad to be out of the sun, and reached for his pipe before remembering that Wiseman had thrown it away. He took a plug of tobacco from his pouch instead, and shoved it in his mouth. The taste was foul, but he persisted manfully, supposing it was better than buboes.

He knew without asking which two patrons were Gorges' dancing masters. They sat by a window wearing outrageously foppish clothes, while French face-paints gave their cheeks an exaggerated whiteness and turned their lips into scarlet slashes. Their wigs were so thickly powdered that dust floated in the sunlight around their heads. However, a closer inspection revealed that their eye-catching attire was threadbare, and their shoes were scuffed and in need of new heels.

They were naturally nervous to be approached by a stranger, although they agreed to talk when Chaloner explained that he had been charged by the Earl of Clarendon to probe the unfortunate happenings at

Gorges. They introduced themselves as Jeffrey Bannister and James Hart, and were difficult to tell apart, although Hart was the more feminine and acid-tongued of the two.

'You chew tobacco, I see,' Hart said. 'Good. It means you are safe from infection. The government should make it compulsory.'

'I prefer London Treacle,' said Bannister, waving a bottle. 'Although it is terribly expensive.'

'Very,' agreed Chaloner. 'Far in excess of what dancing masters are normally able to afford.'

'We earned good salaries in our last posts,' explained Hart. 'We were saving to buy a private carriage, but what use will that be if we are dead? It is better to spend it on surgeons and London Treacle. *And* we elected to stay here at the Greyhound, rather than a cheaper but more crowded inn.'

'It might have been safer still to stay in Chelsea,' Chaloner pointed out.

'Yes,' acknowledged Bannister. 'But we are owed money for past lessons, so we thought we had better collect it before our clients either die or leave the city for good. We considered forgetting the debt, but we did the work, so we should collect our dues, lest word spreads that we are easily cheated. And where would that leave us in the future?'

Chaloner brought the discussion around to the thefts.

'It was a great shock when Mrs Bonney announced the news,' averred Hart. 'I had believed Gorges to be a decent establishment, or I would not have taken a post there.'

'Nor would I,' agreed Bannister. 'We have the very best references. First, we were in Paris, and then in Bath, which, as you will know, are the top places in the world for dancing.'

Chaloner knew no such thing, but was willing to believe them. 'Were you at Gorges when Nancy Janaway was strangled?'

Hart's hand went to his own throat. 'Yes, and it was a terrible thing. I saw her walking towards the orchard, but I did not imagine for a moment that it would be the last thing she did.'

'Who found her?'

'A lunatic named Dorothy Wiseman, who is allowed out for a stroll some evenings, if she is in a mellow mood. At first, it was assumed that she did it, but her keeper assures us that she did not leave Dorothy for a moment. Thus Dorothy is innocent.'

Chaloner was relieved to hear it. 'So who did kill Nancy?'

'We think it was a governor,' whispered Bannister, looking around carefully, to ensure no one was listening. 'Andrew Kole was lurking around the orchard on that particular day. I saw him myself, but when I asked what he was doing, he refused to say.'

'He considers himself too grand to answer questions put by the likes of us,' added Hart. 'But he certainly heads *our* list of suspects.'

'So you have no idea what he was doing?'

'None at all,' replied Hart. 'But it *might* have had something to do with the thefts. He strikes me as a dishonest sort of fellow. Do you not agree, Jeffrey?'

'Oh, yes. He is dirty, too, because he likes gardening. At least, I have seen him several times in the rectory, rooting around by the compost heaps. It is hardly genteel.'

142

'He is not like poor Underhill, who was a *true* gentleman,' said Bannister. 'I am deeply sorry that he is no longer with us. Strangled in Dunkirk House!'

'Do you think Nancy and Underhill were killed by the same person?' asked Chaloner.

'Well, Kole was in both places when the victims died,' replied Hart. 'So . . .'

'I have been told that a spectre lurks in Chelsea. Have you seen it?'

'No, thank the good Lord,' said Hart with a shudder. 'Although there is no doubt that it exists – half of Chelsea has had one kind of encounter or another with the thing.'

'It is the heatwave, you see,' elaborated Bannister. 'It drives folk out for cooling walks at the witching hour. This horrid weather has a lot to answer for – exacerbating the plague *and* encouraging ghosts out of their graves to frighten decent folk.'

It was noon when Chaloner left the Greyhound. The brightness was dazzling after the gloom, with the sun reflecting off the baked mud of the street in a glare that made him squint. Then the heat hit him like a blast from a furnace, and he felt sweat begin to prick his back. He crossed the road, where there were patches of shade, although most were occupied by panting dogs or irritable cats.

He had not gone far when he passed a doctor in full plague costume – mask, gloves, long canvas coat, brimmed hat, and a stick that allowed the *medicus* to examine patients without using his hands. The mask was made from leather, fastened to the head by straps, and comprised the familiar bird-like features – a long 'beak' stuffed with straw and protective herbs, and glass eye-holes. Chaloner could see nothing of the wearer's face, but there was something familiar about his gait. When he heard 'coffee grounds' muttered as their paths crossed, Chaloner was left in no doubt: it was Parker.

He was loath to accost the physician directly, lest Parker had been in contact with plague victims and carried the infection with him. However, he was curious as to why the man should be undertaking such duties when he was supposed to be a specialist in ailments of the mind. He watched him for a moment. Parker continued walking until someone stepped out of a doorway to intercept him. It was Accompter Cocke, fat and sweaty in his unkempt clothes. They exchanged a few words, then went their separate ways.

At that point, Chaloner saw he was not the only one monitoring the Gorges governors. Wilkinson was slinking after Cocke, his blazing eyes fixed determinedly on his quarry. Chaloner joined the end of the procession, and trailed them to the Fleet River, where Cocke disappeared inside the Rose, a seedy tavern known for cheap ale and prostitutes. Wilkinson remained outside, so Chaloner decided to tackle him there. The rector jumped in alarm at the voice so close to his ear.

'I am visiting kin,' he declared furtively. 'My father, who is a hundred and six.'

'He lives in the Rose?' asked Chaloner. That particular tavern catered to heavy drinkers and philanderers, and he doubted those would be high priorities for an elderly man.

'Nearby. However, I do not see him very often, lest familiarity causes him to change his will. We do not

144

always see eye to eye, you see, so the less I visit, the less likely he is to disinherit me.'

'Do you see eye to eye with Cocke?' asked Chaloner, wondering if Kipps was not the only one the oily accompter had attempted to blackmail – the rector certainly seemed like the kind of man to harbour dark secrets.

Wilkinson eyed him angrily. 'Cocke is a rogue, and I cannot imagine how he contrived to get himself jobs in Gorges and the Treasury.'

'And the prison,' said Chaloner, aiming to provoke. 'A building you think belongs to you.'

'It *does* belong to me, and anyone who thinks otherwise is a fool. Now bugger off.'

Chaloner retreated, but not far. He watched the rector take up position behind a water butt, to wait for Cocke to reappear. But Wilkinson was far too impatient for surveillance, and the barrel was in the sun. He stayed at his post for no more than ten minutes, before leaping up and storming inside. Chaloner followed, taking care to stay in the shadows, which was not difficult in so dark and seedy a building.

'What are you doing here, Cocke?' Wilkinson was demanding belligerently. 'Do you not have work to do in Chelsea?'

'Not today,' replied Cocke evenly, and if he was surprised by the priest's angry appearance, he did not show it. 'Now go away, please. I want to enjoy a quiet drink and the latest *Newes*.'

He picked up the government newsbook that lay on the table in front of him, and began to flick through it. Furious at the abrupt dismissal, Wilkinson slapped it down.

'I will go when you tell me the nature of your business in London,' he snarled.

Cocke raised laconic eyebrows. 'Very well, if it will see me left in peace. First, I helped Mrs Bonney and Franklin purchase supplies for Gorges, then I decided to treat myself to some new lace, lest we are invited to Dunkirk House again. I felt naked last night, while the rest of you frothed and fluttered. Well, I shall not be found lacking again. Here. What do you think?'

He pulled a packet from his pocket and fingered its contents admiringly. The wrapping was so clean that Chaloner was sure he was telling the truth about buying it that day, and Cocke's appreciation of its quality was obviously genuine. Of course, that did not mean it was all the accompter had done after leaving his friends, and Wilkinson obviously thought the same, because he continued to bombard him with questions. Cocke refused to say more, and the discussion ended with the rector storming out in exasperation.

'You can come out now, Chaloner,' Cocke called, which startled the spy, because few people were able to detect him when he wanted to stay hidden. 'The lunatic cleric will not be back.'

Chaloner emerged from his hiding place and sat opposite him. 'Why is he so interested in your activities?'

Cocke shrugged. 'He is a very peculiar man, as you would know if you spent any time with him. In fact, you should ask *him* about the thefts and Underhill's murder.'

'On what grounds do you accuse him?'

'How about his erratic behaviour and violent character? You saw the ferocity of his passions just now. Can

146

you not see him exploding with rage and throttling someone?'

Chaloner could. However, he could also see Cocke doing it – the accompter was, after all, a man who had used a child's misfortune in an attempt to extort money from a loving and protective father.

'Where were you when Nancy Janaway was murdered?' he asked, ice in his voice.

Cocke gave one of his greasy smiles. 'It is difficult to say, given that no one can be sure exactly when she perished, but I was probably at the prison, sorting out its finances.'

Chaloner knew instinctively that questioning Cocke further would be a waste of time, because the accompter was going to have an answer to everything, and was far too slippery to be caught out in inconsistencies. He stood, and leaned forward to speak in his most intimidating manner.

'Do not pester Kipps for money again. It would be most unwise.'

He had the satisfaction of seeing fear flicker in Cocke's eyes, although it was momentary, and the accompter was quickly on the offensive again. 'But he is a fellow with secrets, and he is Messenger of the Receipt to the Treasury. If he poses a risk to its security—'

'He does not,' said Chaloner in the same quietly menacing voice. 'So leave him alone.'

Supposing he had better see whether the Earl was ready to travel, Chaloner hurried back to Piccadilly. He forced himself to gnaw on another plug of tobacco while he traversed Charing Cross, as virtually everyone he passed seemed to be coughing or sneezing. He arrived at

147

Clarendon House, only to be informed by Frances that the Earl had gone to White Hall.

'I thought you would be in Hampton Court by now,' he said, surprised to see her.

'The rest of the family have gone, but I decided to wait for my husband. And I wanted a word with you anyway. About Gorges.'

She was obviously upset, which told him that her concerns went deeper than the thefts or the spectre she had mentioned at the soirée.

'How may I be of service, My Lady?' he asked kindly.

'I have just found out about Nancy Janaway,' Frances blurted. 'That she was strangled, like Mr Underhill. I want to know if both were killed by the same culprit. One who was here, in my home.'

'It seems likely,' replied Chaloner. 'But the Earl will be vexed if he learns that you have found out about Nancy. He wanted to keep it quiet. Who told you?'

Her expression softened. 'He does his best to protect us, but it does not always work, and servants gossip. You *must* find the culprit, Thomas. Unsolved murders, both here and in a foundation we support, will damage us at Court. Our enemies . . .'

'I will do my best,' he promised.

She smiled wanly. 'Thank you. Your loyalty is much appreciated.'

Keen to find out if the Earl intended to delay his departure until the following day, Chaloner headed for White Hall, taking a shortcut through St James's Park. There was not a soul in sight, and even the birds seemed to have disappeared. All was silent, and he began to feel oddly lonely. Thurloe would be on his way to Oxfordshire;

148

Temperance, Wiseman and Kipps would soon be lodged in and around Hampton Court; and his only other friend, Captain Lester, was away on HMS *Swiftsure*.

He could see the roofs of Tothill Street across the dusty expanse of brown grass, which made him think of Hannah – they had lived there before her profligacy had forced them to make economies. It would have been pleasant to stop at the house they had rented for a cool drink and a few moments of her company. Then it occurred to him that their conversation would have revolved around how she had spent that week's pay, and he was assailed with an emotion that felt suspiciously like relief that he would no longer have to worry about it. Guilt followed, and he found himself trotting very briskly, as if he could outrun his unhappy reflections.

He arrived at the palace, sweating and breathless, at the same time as a sleek carriage adorned with the crest of the Company of Goldsmiths. The vehicle was waved inside by the soldiers on the Great Gate, after which it clattered across the cobbles towards the Treasury strong-room. Chaloner walked in that direction only because it was shadier than the more direct route, and he felt he had been broiled quite long enough on his hike through the park.

A dozen men emerged to greet the coach. Prefect Reymes was in charge, barking orders at the guards, who were led by Secretary Warwick and Sergeant at Arms Stephens. Kipps stood with them, doing nothing other than look official, while Cocke, red-faced from the wine he had downed at the Rose, loitered with a ream of documents. At a nod from Reymes, two soldiers began hauling sacks from the carriage, while the remainder took up defensive stances, muskets at the ready.

'It is all right,' called Kipps, when several weapons swivelled around to lock on to Chaloner as he walked towards them. 'He is a friend.'

Warwick and Stephens nodded amiable greetings, but Reymes pointedly turned his back on the spy. It was a deliberate insult, but Chaloner was too hot to care. Meanwhile, Cocke scowled, as if to say that the threats issued in the tavern earlier had not been forgotten. Chaloner gazed back, equally cool, noting with interest that the newsbook poking from the accompter's pocket had PROPERTIE OF THE ROSE: DO NOT REMOVE inked across the top.

Reymes spat something inaudible, and stamped inside the strongroom to bark orders at the labouring men. Chaloner glanced through the door after him, and was astonished to see that the chamber was virtually empty. There were several dozen small metal chests, a pile of ingots and a modestly sized jewel box. And that was all.

'Is that it?' he asked of Kipps incredulously. 'I thought you said it was unusually full at the moment.'

The Seal Bearer chuckled. 'It is. You see, the Treasury's wealth is stored as gold, mostly guineas, which takes up far less room than common coinage. Just one of those little boxes holds enough to buy a palace and more.'

'Which is why we need reliable men to keep it safe,' said Warwick, with a businesslike clack of his teeth. 'And I understand that you are interested in being our second Sergeant at Arms. Others have applied, of course, but I want someone with military experience, and you come highly recommended by Kipps. Thus you are exactly the kind of fellow we need.'

'You are in, Tom,' murmured Kipps, pleased. 'I told

you I could do it. Now all you have to do is submit a formal request, and the post will be yours.'

Chaloner thanked him, although with some misgivings. He had never been very interested in money, and the thought of spending his life safeguarding the stuff did not fill him with enthusiasm. Yet a hundred pounds a year was a handsome salary, and would certainly keep the wolf from the door, should the Earl no longer need him.

'What is happening?' he asked, nodding towards the coach.

'Donations for the war,' explained Kipps. 'From the goldsmiths. It is very kind of them.'

'Well, they *should* pay,' said Cocke sullenly. 'This conflict was started for their benefit – so they can get richer by wresting the best sea-routes from the Dutch.'

'It will go to Hampton Court next month, along with the rest of the King's gold,' confided Warwick, ignoring him. 'I cannot wait! Not only is it dangerous to be here, with the plague only streets away, but we are vulnerable with the palace so empty. Thank God the Earl wanted it moved, or Reymes would have kept us here until every last one of us was dead.'

'Reymes,' spat Kipps in disgust. 'He is not fit to be prefect.'

'He is not,' agreed Warwick. 'And when we get to Hampton Court, I am telling the King that he is patently unsuited to the task. Hopefully, someone better will be appointed in his place.'

'Good,' said Kipps. 'It is difficult to work with a man who is incompetent *and* rude.'

Chaloner noticed that although Warwick, Kipps and Stephens were happy to chat, the eyes of all three constantly scanned the yard, alert for trouble. Cocke, on the other hand, only watched the sacks disappear inside the strongroom with greedy fascination. Then Stephens spoke.

'I have remembered something that might help you solve Underhill's murder, Chaloner. I meant to tell you yesterday, but business here kept me too busy. It happened at Clarendon House, when Underhill and Kole were discussing the recent spate of burglaries. Kole said he hoped *he* would not be the next victim, and Underhill scoffed at him, saying that no self-respecting robber would bother with paupers. Kole was livid.'

'At the notion that thieves would be uninterested in him?' Chaloner was puzzled.

'At the fact that Underhill brayed that he was broke,' explained Stephens. 'As a speculator, Kole needs the confidence of investors. Everyone knows that his fortunes took a blow when the government seized the College, but it is not general knowledge that he is completely destitute.'

'Perhaps you are right, Tom,' whispered Kipps. 'Cocke is not the killer – *Kole* is. After all, you heard what Parker said: that the culprit is lithe, hook-nosed and brooding with evil. It is a description that fits Kole much better than Cocke. Except the bit about evil, of course.'

'Parker also named Satan,' recalled Chaloner. 'So I am not sure we can trust his testimony.'

'Perhaps,' said Kipps, 'but we shall bear it in mind anyway.'

Chaloner was thirsty after his trek across the park, so before going to see the Earl, he went to the Spares Gallery, an unofficial refectory for minor courtiers. It had earned its name by being a repository for unwanted pieces of art, and servants still ensured that food and drink were left there for those whose work kept them in the palace. The ale jug was empty, so Chaloner went to the adjoining pantry to fill it. As the pantry was cooler than the main room, he stayed there to drink, but he had taken no more than two or three gulps when Reymes and Doyley arrived.

'The Treasury has not been this rich since Cromwell was in power,' said Reymes, seeing the Spares Gallery was deserted, and recklessly assuming that the pantry was empty, too. 'The goldsmiths have been very generous.'

'I hope Warwick remembers to remind the King that their donation is for the war,' said Doyley worriedly. 'They will never forgive him if it he spends it on his next party.'

It was not an unreasonable concern, given the amount the Court was reputed to squander on its pleasures, but Reymes waved it away with a careless flick of his hand.

'Why does Satan's spawn still lurk in Dunkirk House?' he asked. 'He should leave for Hampton Court before Charles changes his mind and tells him not to come.'

'Do not call Clarendon names,' said Doyley irritably. 'It is not genteel.'

'"It is not genteel",' mocked Reymes, and scowled as he poured himself a large cup of claret. 'What is not genteel is Clarendon foisting this damned Commission on us. It is costing us a fortune, and we will never see a penny of it back.'

'It is our patriotic duty to—'

'It is *my* patriotic duty to retrieve what I lost in the wars, which I cannot do as long as I am lumbered with

153

the care of these wretched prisoners. Perhaps we should let them escape. Then we will be released from our obligations.'

'Do not jest about such matters! There are those who might think you are in earnest.'

Chaloner strongly suspected that Reymes *was* in earnest, but before the prefect could reply, there was a clatter of footsteps, and Warwick and Stephens entered, both complaining about the heat. Chaloner considered emerging from the pantry to join them, purely for the delight of letting Reymes know that his intemperate words had been overheard, but then decided to continue listening instead: Reymes and Doyley were two of his suspects for killing Underhill, after all. The foursome discussed the goldsmiths' generosity for a while, citing figures so vast that Chaloner felt his head reel. Then the conversation turned to the plague.

'It draws closer to White Hall with every passing day,' said Doyley grimly.

'It does, and I wish we did not have to wait a month before moving the Treasury,' said Stephens, casting a significant and very disapproving glance in Reymes' direction. 'We should whisk it away tonight. It would be far safer in Hampton Court.'

'Rubbish!' countered Reymes. 'Besides, you cannot "whisk it away" like a load of onions. Appropriate security arrangements must be in place, or thieves will descend on it like locusts.'

'Only if they knew it was coming,' argued Warwick. 'We could do it in secret.'

'Fool!' sneered Reymes. 'Nothing is secret in White Hall – our plans would be common knowledge within the hour.'

'How?' asked Warwick with quiet reason. 'The palace is deserted.'

'It is not deserted,' averred Reymes. 'It is crawling with servants, who have nothing to do but eavesdrop and gossip. Ergo, the Treasury is going nowhere until August.'

'But we might be dead by August,' said Stephens angrily. 'Who will guard it then?'

'You will just have to be careful. Besides, the plague might abate in the interim, so perhaps we shall be spared the exercise altogether.'

'Unlikely – Surgeon Wiseman believes it will rage until winter bites,' said Warwick. 'So Stephens is right: keeping it here is reckless.'

'Who is prefect – you or me?' demanded Reymes. 'I repeat: it stays until August. If you do not like it, resign, and I shall ask the King to appoint someone who does *not* question my judgement.'

There followed a short, tense silence, broken only by an agitated clicking from Warwick's teeth. It was Doyley who ended it, and Chaloner was under the impression that he had disliked being obliged to witness the Treasury men's quarrel.

'Chelsea is a charming village,' he said with a bright smile. 'I am so glad my duties as commissioner take me there on a regular basis. Its streets are nice and clean, and the river does not smell nearly so badly of sewage.'

'I am amazed by your choice of guests, Reymes,' said Stephens. His clipped, sullen tone indicated he was livid that his concerns had been so summarily dismissed. 'Surely you could have found more refined companions?'

'I selected them for their liveliness,' replied Reymes stiffly. 'Which makes a pleasant change from the doom

155

and gloom around here. I said as much to Wilkinson after church last night.'

'Church?' queried Warwick. 'On a Thursday? Is that some peculiar Chelsea custom?'

'A special service for the plague,' explained Reymes. 'The whole village turned out, including my guests, the residents and staff of the asylum, and even Warden Tooker and a few guards from the prison. Doyley and Cocke attended, too.'

Doyley gave a short laugh. 'Wilkinson does not often see a full building, but it was packed to the gills last night.'

'It was wretchedly hot, though,' grumbled Reymes. 'If he holds another, I am not going.'

The four of them wandered out at that point, so Chaloner escaped and hurried to the Earl's offices. These overlooked the Privy Gardens, usually a bright explosion of flowers and neatly manicured hedges, but now unkempt patches of weeds and desiccated shrubs.

'There you are,' said the Earl, when Chaloner knocked at the door. The window shutters had been thrown open to allow the sun to stream in, and Chaloner felt himself wilt. 'Good. You have had ample time to discover who killed Underhill now. Who was it?'

'I cannot be sure until I go to Chelsea, sir,' replied Chaloner, smothering his annoyance at his employer's unreasonable expectations. 'But Kole is currently at the top of my list of suspects.'

'He must have acted in revenge for the government seizing his college,' said the Earl angrily. 'Even though I had nothing to do with it. Damn the fellow!'

At that moment, there was an urgent pounding of feet in the hall outside, and Kipps burst in.

'A letter has just arrived for you, sir. From Chelsea.

The messenger does not know who it is from, but he says it is important, and that you should read it immediately.'

The Earl's face was pale as he tore open the missive, and a gamut of expressions crossed his portly features: relief, disappointment and finally anger. His eyes were accusing as he looked up.

'You are wrong to accuse Kole, Chaloner, because he is dead himself. He was found in Buckingham House this morning – strangled, just like Underhill and the woman from Gorges.'

Chapter 6

It was evening before the Earl announced that he and Frances were ready to travel to Hampton Court. Wiseman joined the cavalcade, although as Surgeon to the Person, he insisted on a place in a coach. Chaloner and Kipps were allocated two elderly nags, the best horses having been bagged by Henry, Lawrence and their retainers the day before. Chaloner was exasperated by their selfishness, which would put him and Kipps at a distinct disadvantage if robbers did attack, and an ambush was certainly possible, given that much of the journey would be in the dark.

It was a long and uncomfortable ride, fraught with false alarms from the jittery guards. The Earl complained about the pain of his gout if the cavalcade got up any speed, obliging them to move at a perilously stately pace. Chaloner spent the whole time on tenterhooks, knowing that most of their escort would prove next to useless in the event of trouble. The full moon in a cloudless sky was a mixed blessing: it allowed them to see where they were going, but lit them up like a beacon, showing any would-be robbers what a splendid prize they would make with their sumptuous coaches and liveried retainers.

But eventually, the lights of the great palace loomed out of the blackness, and he heaved a sigh of relief. The Earl and Frances promptly hurried away to see what quarters their offspring had managed to bag, while the gregarious Kipps went to exchange news with friends in the hall. Wiseman, cognisant of the dignity that went with his exalted post, demanded and was given a room near the royal apartments.

Naturally solitary, Chaloner found an empty stable loft and passed what was left of the night in an uneasy slumber, during which his dreams teemed with high-waymen, strangled corpses and Hannah. He awoke confused, disorientated and not in a particularly good mood. His mouth felt dry and sour from all the tobacco he had eaten the previous day, and he had a crick in his neck. He lay in the straw for a while, thinking about the letter that the Earl had received about Kole.

Mysteriously and annoyingly, the Earl had refused to say who had sent it, and nor would he let Chaloner read it for himself. Chaloner had tried to reason with him, but his employer had obstinately declined to relent. This peculiar and inexplicable behaviour told Chaloner yet again that there was more to the Earl's interest in the asylum than making charitable donations.

So who had sent it? A member of staff or a governor, who had agreed to act as the Earl's spy on the inside? An inmate? Chaloner knew he would find out sooner or later, which made the Earl's determination to be secretive even more exasperating. He pushed his irritation to the back of his mind, and pondered what few facts the Earl had consented to share.

159

According to the informant, Kole had last been seen at midnight, and his body had been found at six the following morning. Chaloner thought about his suspects for Underhill's murder – down from eight names to seven now that Kole had become a victim. The conversation he had overheard in the Spares Gallery told him that all had been in Chelsea the evening before the murder, attending the special service in Wilkinson's church.

Of course, his list would almost certainly expand once he started to investigate. First, it should probably include the so-called spectre – it would not be the first time a killer had pretended to be a ghost in the expectation that no one would look too closely at his crimes. Then he should not forget the fact that Kole had been lodging with a lot of unruly courtiers; it was entirely possible that there had been a falling out, and that one had dispatched him over some petty dispute. And finally, there was Underhill's association with Spymaster Williamson, which would certainly have made him enemies had the information leaked out.

He ate a breakfast of bread and pickled herrings, then waited impatiently until Kipps and Wiseman deigned to appear. If either noticed his bad temper as they rode through the parched countryside, they did not remark on it. Kipps was full of the gossip he had heard the night before, while Wiseman was more interested in bragging about the quality of the quarters he had been allocated. However, it was not long before the discussion turned acerbic. Kipps soon tired of Wiseman's hubris, while the surgeon's sharper mind yearned for more intelligent conversation.

'Did you learn anything last night that might help

with our enquiries, Kipps?' asked Chaloner, when an initially harmless debate about peas looked set to become violent.

'Only that everyone is amazed Cocke was appointed prison accompter, because he is so untrustworthy,' replied the Seal Bearer. 'And they think the Earl is rash to suggest transferring the King's gold to Hampton Court, when a fool like Reymes is in charge of its safety.'

'And how is that pertinent to the murders, pray?' asked Wiseman sneeringly.

'It is background information on two leading suspects,' retorted Kipps crisply. 'Which Tom tells me is an important part of any investigation.'

Wiseman was not about to admit that the Seal Bearer might have a point, so he turned to another subject. 'What is wrong with you today, Chaloner? You look very green around the gills.'

'From the tobacco you suggested I eat,' said Chaloner, resisting a sudden urge to spit, as he was sure that neither of his companions would approve. 'My tongue tingles and my throat hurts.'

'You *ate* it?' asked Wiseman. 'That was reckless – it is poisonous.'

Chaloner regarded him in alarm. 'Poisonous?'

'Oh, yes. I never touch the stuff myself, and I strongly suspect that any virtues it might possess are far outweighed by its dangers.'

'But you told me to do it!'

'Did I? Well, I read a paper by the learned men of the Royal Society last night, which proves beyond all doubt that tobacco juices are lethal. They performed experiments and . . .' He trailed off when he saw Chaloner's dark expression. 'But perhaps we had better

161

not discuss those. How much longer do you think this heat will last? I am heartily sick of it.'

Irritably, Chaloner tossed the remainder of the pouch away, and vowed to have no more to do with the plant ever again. Assuming he survived his current encounter with it, of course.

It was much easier travelling by day than by night, and they made good time, so Wiseman was able to announce that it was ten o'clock exactly when they reached the outskirts of Chelsea. He waved a new-fangled invention called a 'pocket watch' at his companions.

'The King gave me this for my birth-day,' he bragged, directing his remark at Kipps, to whom such favours mattered. 'What did he give you for yours?'

'I have ridden past this village several times,' said Chaloner quickly, to avert yet another sparring match. 'But there has never been enough time to explore it.'

'You will not have time to explore it now,' said Kipps, looking away from Wiseman, who was dangling the watch provocatively. 'You will arrest Cocke for killing Nancy, Underhill and Kole, and then we shall return to Hampton Court. The Earl needs us, and I have no inclination to linger here in present company.'

'I shall not tarry either,' declared Wiseman haughtily. 'I shall wait just long enough to ensure that Dorothy is safe – a day or two at most – and then I will leave, too.'

'But hopefully not with us,' muttered Kipps.

Chelsea stood on the banks of the Thames, and comprised a collection of red-roofed houses set amid trees. At its centre was All Saints' Church, an ancient building topped by an oddly modern cupola. The river front was punctuated by attractive piers, and the boats tethered there were fishing smacks and pleasure craft, rather than the filthy lumbering barges that plied their trade in the city.

The village boasted an inordinate number of stately homes – at least eight, with smaller mansions interspersed among them. Even the labourers' cottages were smart, with none of the impoverished hovels that usually characterised rural settlements. It had two wide, well-maintained roads running from east to west, linked by a patchwork of lanes. To the north lay the marshes, although these had suffered from the drought, and were now reduced to patches of parched mud.

'This is known locally as the *King's* Road,' said Wiseman, gesturing to the track along which they rode. 'Because Charles has plans to make it his personal highway to Hampton Court. Of course, he will have to fill in some of these potholes first, because otherwise, he runs the risk of falling in one and never being seen again. Some are huge.'

The first building of substance they passed was the rectory, a structure that had been built to last. It had enormously thick walls and a stone roof, which lent it an air of stocky permanence. Its window shutters were in excellent repair, and its front door was reinforced with iron. Chaloner supposed that Wilkinson maintained its fortress-like qualities in case his radical religious views led to an attack. By contrast, its grounds were unkempt. What had once been neat vegetable plots were seas of waving grasses, while the orchard was choked with brambles. Flies droned in the still, sweltering air, and there was something desolate and slightly sinister about the place.

They rode along one of its boundary walls until they reached a crossroads. The centre of the village lay to the south, down a spacious street named Church Lane. They turned down it, with the rectory wall still on their left, and saw the entrance to a palace on their right. This was Buckingham House, Chelsea's largest and most prestigious residence, which stood at the end of a sweeping, beech-lined drive. Chaloner recalled that it was currently leased to Reymes, and was where Greeting and Brodrick intended to carouse with other Court debauchees.

'And Gorges is behind it,' said Wiseman, pointing towards a smaller but prettier mansion that could just be seen through the trees.

But Chaloner was looking in the opposite direction. From his elevated position on the horse, he could see over the rectory wall to where Wilkinson was on all fours by a compost heap. The man might have gone undetected, were it not for the fact that he was wearing formal religious vestments, including a scarlet cope. It was such an odd sight that Chaloner reined in to stare. Kipps and Wiseman did likewise.

'Hah! Got the bastard!' Wilkinson leapt up, clutching something in his hand. He scowled when he saw he was the object of scrutiny. 'Are you three *spying* on me?'

'Of course not,' replied Kipps indignantly. 'However, you cannot grub about in the dirt in full ecclesiastical regalia and expect not to be noticed.'

'What a man does in his garden is his own affair,' declared Wilkinson. 'So bugger off.'

'We are here to investigate the murders of Nancy Janaway, Robert Underhill and Andrew Kole,' announced Kipps importantly. 'We shall want to talk to you at some point.'

'I am sorry they are dead,' said Wilkinson, his harsh features softening into a reflective expression, 'because it means the end of them for ever. I know some fools believe in eternal life, but I cannot be doing with all that twaddle.'

Chaloner blinked his astonishment. 'And this from an Anglican cleric?'

Wilkinson eyed him in disdain. 'Oh, you are one of those tedious traditionalists, are you? And people wonder why I yearn to revive the Theological College! I want to discuss religion with like-minded radicals, not dreary conformists.'

'Lord!' muttered Wiseman. 'The Church does not usually let its ministers go around spouting that sort of remark. Why has he not been extruded?'

'Probably because his bishop is too busy with the plague,' said Kipps, and called a question to the scowling cleric. 'How well did you know Underhill and Kole?'

'Liars and cheats, both of them,' snarled Wilkinson. 'And Nancy Janaway was a whore. All women are, which is why I shall never marry.'

Chaloner regarded him with distaste, and went on an offensive of his own. 'Why were you following George Cocke yesterday?'

Wilkinson's eyes narrowed. 'So you *are* spying on me! I should have guessed when you appeared from nowhere at the Rose, and started asking impertinent questions about my father.'

'Actually, I asked about Cocke,' corrected Chaloner, 'who you were tailing. Why?'

Wilkinson scowled at him. 'If you must know, I was trying to ensure that he did not enter an area where the pestilence rages, and thus bring the sickness to Chelsea. I did it for the common good. Not that my actions are any of *your* business.'

165

Chaloner was unconvinced. 'But it was Parker who wore the plague costume, not Cocke. Therefore Parker was the one more likely to venture into dangerous territory.'

'Wrong!' declared Wilkinson. 'Parker donned those clothes to protect himself, not to traipse into rookeries. Franklin and Mrs Bonney did the same, while even those ridiculous dancing masters shied away from strangers and booked themselves into a decent inn. But Cocke wandered where he pleased without so much as a pomander. I do not care if he kills himself, but I will not have him endangering me. Or my congregation,' he added as an afterthought.

'But you followed him into the Rose,' Chaloner pointed out. 'A tavern frequented by rookery folk. You might have caught the plague there yourself – and brought it back to Chelsea.'

'Impossible! I swallowed a whole bottle of London Treacle to protect myself. However, that stuff is expensive, so it is not something I can afford to do every day.' Wilkinson glared at him. 'Now go away. And if you ever spy on me again, I shall blow off your head with my pistols.'

'Pistols?' asked Chaloner, beginning to suspect the rector was out of his wits. 'Those are unusual items for a priest to own.'

'I am an unusual priest.' Wilkinson opened his hand to reveal what he had caught – a butterfly, which he had crushed until its wings were mangled and its body a gooey mess. 'I hate these things. They are stupid creations with their pathetic fluttering.'

'Lord!' breathed Wiseman a second time. 'If *he* is the kind of clergyman his Theological College produced, then perhaps it is just as well it was closed down.'

*

Chaloner and his companions were about to ride on when a hackney carriage turned into the lane behind them. It rolled to a standstill outside the entrance to Buckingham House, and three men alighted: Reymes, Doyley and Cocke, their faces and clothes pale with dust from the journey.

'I insist, Bullen,' Doyley was saying to Reymes. 'I shall enjoy your hospitality here, so the least I can do is pay your share of the coach fare.'

Reymes inclined his head in thanks, and Doyley counted the coins into the driver's hand. They turned expectantly to Cocke, but the accompter had busied himself with the bags, and was pretending not to notice. With a resigned sigh, Doyley paid for him as well, and Chaloner saw a flash of greedy triumph in Cocke's eyes.

'I hope you do not plan to relax here too long, Reymes,' called Kipps provocatively. 'Your place is in White Hall with the King's gold.'

'I know it is,' said Reymes tightly. 'But I am compelled to be in Chelsea on prison business – which means that if anything *does* happen to the Treasury, it will be Clarendon's fault for making me a commissioner.'

'The Treasury is perfectly safe,' said Doyley. He sounded tired, as if he had repeated these words rather too often. 'Warwick and Stephens are competent fellows. Besides, you plan to visit the city most days, so do not tease poor Kipps with these implications that the gold is at risk. It is not.'

Cocke finished fussing with the luggage, and came to speak to Reymes. 'Shall I take my usual room in Buckingham House, or do you have somewhere else for me this time?'

Reymes smiled vengefully: the accompter's shabby

167

antics over the coach fare were about to cost him dear. 'Several more courtiers arrived yesterday, so there is only one room free – and that is for Doyley. You will have to find other lodgings.'

'There is no need for that,' called Wilkinson, coming to rest his elbows on his garden wall like a gossiping fishwife. 'Doyley can stay with me.'

Doyley eyed the bleak rectory without enthusiasm. 'You mean in there?'

'Yes, of course.' Wilkinson pulled a disagreeable face. 'If life was fair, I would be provost of a thriving Theological College, and you would have three good servants to tend your needs. But life is *not* fair, so you will have to make do with rather less.'

'What a splendid solution,' said Cocke quickly. 'Thank you, Wilkinson. I am sure Doyley will be very comfortable with you while I stay in Buckingham House.'

'It is settled then,' said Wilkinson. 'Come along, Doyley. I do not have all day.'

He disappeared into his overgrown garden, while Reymes glowered after him, furious that his ploy to punish the accompter's meanness should have been so neatly subverted. Meanwhile, Doyley regarded the forbidding rectory with trepidation, and Cocke smirked his triumph.

'It is only for a night or two,' the accompter said gloatingly. 'I am sure you will manage.'

'I am glad we met,' said Chaloner, nudging his horse forward, so it was between Cocke and Reymes, who was looking decidedly dangerous. 'We have been ordered to investigate the murder of Kole. He died in your house and—'

'Ordered by Clarendon?' demanded Reymes, bristling

with new anger. 'Well, you can piss off. No minion of his is going to set foot on *my* property.'

'Clarendon is Lord Chancellor of England, Bullen,' Doyley reminded him quietly. 'He has the power to authorise such an enquiry, and you have nothing to hide. Let his men do their work.'

Reymes glowered. 'Very well. However, I was in bed when Kole died, and all my guests have alibis in each other, so his lackeys will have to look elsewhere for a culprit.'

'Can Mrs Reymes confirm your story?' asked Kipps sweetly.

Reymes scowled. 'There is no Mrs Reymes, as you know perfectly well. I sleep alone.'

'Forgive me,' drawled Kipps. 'I had forgotten that England's women have so far managed to resist your . . . charms.'

'Few can resist mine,' put in Cocke with a leer.

'We shall need to speak to everyone who was in Buckingham House when Kole died,' said Chaloner, ignoring him and continuing to address Reymes. 'May we do it now?'

'You may not. Prison matters will keep me occupied all morning, and I do not want you poking about here without me. You may come this afternoon, on condition that you treat my visitors with respect. One rude word, and I shall throw you out myself – by force if necessary.'

'He did not mean that,' said Doyley, as Reymes stamped away. 'It has been a tiring few days, what with work for the Treasury *and* the Commission, and this hot weather is a trial. He will be perfectly amiable after a cup of cool wine.'

Chaloner seriously doubted it, and Reymes' unsteady temper had put him at the very top of the list for all three murders. He glanced at Cocke, who was haggling with two children over the paltry sum they were to be paid for carrying his luggage inside Buckingham House, and decided that the accompter's name was second.

As they rode on, Kipps and Wiseman began an ill-natured debate about the best place to stay, and Chaloner supposed his mind must have wandered when they had agreed to share lodgings. He would have vetoed the notion had he been paying attention, because he had no wish to keep company with two men who would constantly be at each other's throats.

'I always stay in the Goat in Boots,' Kipps was declaring. 'It has excellent stables.'

'Yes, but *I* am not a horse,' argued Wiseman. 'We shall go to the White Hart, where the food is more palatable. The Goat always smells of fish.'

'The Swan,' said Chaloner firmly. Thurloe had recommended it as clean, quiet and run by a landlord who knew the village and its inhabitants like the back of his hand – and who was always willing to share his knowledge for a coin or two. It was also conveniently close to the prison.

'Very well,' conceded Wiseman. 'Although it is farther from Gorges than I would like. Still, I suppose the walk will do me good.'

'It will,' said Kipps, looking pointedly at Wiseman's bulk. 'But it had better not be full of spiders. Lord, I am hungry! We left so early this morning that I did not have time for breakfast.'

'I have some strips of meat, which I dried in the

170

Anatomy Theatre,' said Wiseman. 'I could probably spare a couple, if you were desperate.'

'How kind,' said Kipps with a moue of revulsion. 'But I think I can last a few more minutes.'

Church Lane was named for All Saints', which stood at its far end, and looked far too small to accommodate everyone who lived there. Moreover, its graveyard was tiny, and already crammed with memorials. If the plague came, space would be a problem.

The lane widened outside it, forming a large square that ran down to the river. A weekly market was held there on Mondays, but something was happening that Saturday, too – a summer fair. Girls skipped around a maypole, trestle tables were loaded with cakes and garden produce, and there was a sense of happy frivolity – a marked contrast to the sombre, frightened atmosphere in London. A trio of musicians played a medley of popular songs with more enthusiasm than talent, and young people were dancing. The scent of hot baked apples was in the air, mingled with the aroma of burning wood and roasting meat.

Chaloner and his companions were stopped by two soldiers and a crone before they reached the festivities. The men were armed with muskets, which they trained on the visitors, while the woman hobbled forward.

'Have you come from London?' she demanded sharply.

'Yes, but we do not have the plague,' stated Wiseman. 'I am the King's surgeon, and thus the most eminent medical man in the country. I would know if we were infected. And we are not.'

Chaloner would have treated such arrogance with the scepticism it deserved, but the men exchanged impressed glances and lowered their weapons. The crone was more

171

cautious, and peered at each of the three in turn, although she soon nodded to say that they had passed muster.

'You would be surprised at the cheek of some folk,' she confided. 'They come here, direct from the city, and act as though we should be pleased to see them. Well, we are not.'

'Other than the courtiers at Buckingham House,' added one of the men. 'We like them. They keep the entire village amused with their antics.'

'They do,' chuckled the crone. 'And all in the front garden, too! If I did that sort of thing, I would use the back, out of sight.'

'I think they like an audience,' explained the man. 'Although they do perform at odd times – sometimes late at night, then in the middle of the day . . .'

'You would not catch *me* out late at night,' growled the second soldier. 'I would be afraid of meeting the spectre. I saw it once, and that was enough for me.'

'The spectre?' queried Chaloner innocently.

The fellow glanced around, and lowered his voice. 'The ghost that murdered Nancy and Mr Kole, and that steals from Gorges. It probably killed Mr Underhill, too, although that was in London, and we had not known that it likes to travel.'

'It probably uses a headless horse,' put in the crone sagely.

'Any number of us have seen it,' the man went on, 'but it is like mist – here one moment and gone the next.'

'Can you describe it?' asked Chaloner.

'It looks like a spectre,' replied the soldier, regarding Chaloner as though he was short of wits. 'A dark, evil figure in a long coat.'

172

'What is its name?' Kipps shrugged at the trio's immediate puzzlement. 'Even phantoms have names. How would they address each other otherwise?'

'I am sure they have their ways,' said the crone darkly. 'But we just call it "the spectre". Or sometimes "the stranger", as it has not been here very long. Just since the end of June.'

'That is when the College became a prison,' remarked Chaloner.

'I suppose it is,' acknowledged the crone. 'Although that must be coincidence, because none of the Dutchmen have died, so it is not *their* tortured souls who haunt our streets.'

'True,' agreed the first man. 'My brother works in that gaol, and he would have told me if there had been a death. Besides, he says it is shut up tighter than the Tower of London at night, and that even a ghost would have trouble getting out.'

'Lord, this is gloomy talk!' exclaimed the crone. 'Let us dwell on happier things.' She waved a gnarled hand in an expansive gesture. 'There is ale in the church, and you look as though you could do with some refreshment. Stop there first, and then enjoy the festivities.'

Although Chaloner felt he should start interviewing people at once, the prospect of a drink was too tempting to ignore. He paid a boy to mind the horses, and followed Kipps and Wiseman through the porch. His head ached from squinting against the sun, and it was good to relax for a moment in the cool fustiness of the ancient building.

His companions made a beeline for the ale, but Chaloner explored first – a habit from the wars, when only fools did not assess avenues of escape before venturing too far inside places they did not know. The church was dark and intimate, with thick walls and narrow windows that kept out the heat. It was full of tombs, commemorating such wealthy parishioners as Lord Dacre, the Duchess of Northumberland and Sir Arthur Gorges. He went to inspect them more closely, and when Kipps came to give him a flagon of ale, he was standing by one dedicated to Sir Thomas More, which was carved with a lengthy inscription composed by the martyr himself.

'What beautiful Latin,' he said, sure Kipps with his love of ceremonial precision would agree. '*At societ tumulus, societ nos, obsecro cœlum Sic Mors, non potuit quod dare vita, dabit.*'

'I do not like Moors,' said Kipps. 'Not after what they did in Tangier last year.'

Chaloner regarded him askance. '*Mors*, not Moors. He is talking about him and his wife being united in Heaven, and death granting what life had denied.'

'You have grown morose since losing Hannah,' observed Kipps critically. 'And it is not healthy. The best thing you can do is find yourself another woman.'

Chaloner blinked his astonishment at the advice, but by the time he had found his tongue, Kipps was back with the ale-selling ladies, where he and Wiseman were engaged in a competition to impress – both were susceptible to a pretty face. Chaloner shook off the Seal Bearer's remarks, and returned to the monuments.

One was new and dedicated to the memory of a John Unckles, draper. Its inscription informed the reader that Unckles had been the beloved husband of Eleanore, and would be deeply missed by all who knew him. Chaloner stared at it, wondering if he should erect one to Hannah.

She would have wanted it, he was sure, and the gaudier and more expensive the better.

'Did you know John Unckles?' came a voice at his side.

He turned to see a woman, who was almost as tall as he, with flowing black hair and dark eyes. Her face was rosy from the sun, and large, capable hands suggested she was used to physical labour. He felt an immediate attraction towards her, although he was not proud of it – not when he had just been pondering how to honour his dead wife.

'You stared at the tablet for so long that I was sure you must be paying your respects,' she went on. 'John knew so many people, and they all liked him. I am Eleanore, his wife.'

'He lived in Chelsea?' asked Chaloner, more for something to say than for information.

Eleanore nodded. 'He died last year, and I miss him still. He was a lovely person.'

Chaloner supposed he should be making similar remarks about Hannah, although they would not be true. She had been fun-loving and generous, but her sour morning temper and careless profligacy meant 'lovely' was not a word he would ever use to describe her. Idly, he wondered if her facile friends from Court would eulogise over her in a year's time. One or two had approached him on his return from sea to express regret at her passing, but none had mentioned her since.

'You seem sad,' Eleanore said. 'Are you thinking of someone you have loved?'

'My wife. She died a few weeks ago.'

'Time helps,' said Eleanore kindly. 'I did not think I would live when John . . .'

Chaloner was far more comfortable discussing her bereavement than his own. He pointed at the memorial. 'He was thirty-five.' His own age, he thought. 'It is young to die.'

'He worked at the College, and accidentally cut himself with a pair of scissors. He died from poisoned blood a few days later.'

'Why did the College need a draper?' asked Chaloner curiously.

'Mr Kole decided that it would be cheaper to buy curtains than repair rotting shutters, so he hired John to sew him some. But the building has been turned into a prison for Dutchmen now, so John would have lost the work anyway – the windows have bars, not drapery.'

'Do the villagers mind it being put to such a use?'

'Oh, yes! Most think that a mass escape will see us all slaughtered in our beds. Yet their fears are groundless, because the Hollanders are too cowed to think of breaking out.'

'How do you know?'

'I have a job in the kitchens, and I see them every day. But never mind the gaol. What do you think of our village? I hope you did not come via Church Lane. If you did, you probably saw Rector Wilkinson rooting around in his compost.'

'We did. In full Eucharistic regalia.'

Eleanore rolled her eyes. 'He is nearly always the first thing visitors see, and it gives us a bad name. I suppose you noticed Buckingham House, too. It is quiet at the moment, but you will know when its occupants wake up.'

'Are they very disruptive, then?'

'Terribly – we have never seen anything like it. We

176

had heard about the wild debaucheries at White Hall, of course, but we never expected to witness them in action.'

'Lord!' muttered Chaloner, wondering what Reymes thought he was doing by inflicting such unseemly spectacles on the good people of Chelsea.

Eleanore smiled, revealing small white teeth. 'But we do not mind. They keep us entertained for hours, and all for free.'

Chaloner found himself warming to Eleanore Unckles, which was unusual, as he tended to be wary when making new friends. He pushed his investigation to the back of his mind, and listened to her talk just for the sheer pleasure of it, learning that her husband had left her a small cottage near Buckingham House, but very little else. She took him outside and pointed it out – a pretty place with roses around the door, a thatched roof, and herbs in the garden.

'I like it here,' she said, smiling in a way that made his stomach flutter. 'Perhaps you will, too. How long will you be staying?'

'A few days,' he replied, surprising himself by hoping it would be longer. 'The Earl of Clarendon wants me to investigate three deaths and explore a series of thefts.'

She shuddered. 'No one has ever been murdered here before, and we all want the culprit safely locked away. I hope you find him.'

'Did you know any of the victims?'

'Of course – this is a small village. Mr Underhill was a close friend of the Countess of Derby, a woman whom Dr Parker admires for her experiments with plague water. He arrived a few months ago, and was promptly appointed as one of Gorges' governors.'

177

Clever Underhill, thought Chaloner, to research his victims' caprices before making his move. And the Countess had died the previous year, so was not in a position to confirm or deny an acquaintance with the man, allowing him to claim anything he liked. Eleanore chattered on.

'Meanwhile, Mr Kole moved here when he bought the College. Or rather, when he *thought* he bought the College – the government says he only rented it. When he was made homeless, he went to live in Buckingham House instead.'

'Why there?'

'Because Mr Reymes let him have a room cheap. He did not have much money left once the government had made its move. Of course, nor did Mr Sutcliffe.'

'Mr Sutcliffe?' fished Chaloner.

'The nephew of the cleric who built the College. He claims his uncle left it to him in his will, although the lawyers disagree. He was an assassin during the wars, which is why he loves the theatre, of course – plays allow him to forget all the blood he has spilled.'

'I see. And where does *he* live now?' Chaloner knew the answer to that, because Thurloe had told him, but there was no harm in having it confirmed.

'Greenwich, apparently. He stormed away when the government told him he would never have the College, and I have not seen him in weeks.'

'Did you know Nancy Janaway? I understand her husband is a bell-founder.'

'He will know nothing useful,' said Eleanore. 'He is distracted by grief, and you will have no sense from him, poor man. If you want to know about Nancy, ask me.'

'You were friends?'

'Very close friends. However, I cannot imagine why anyone should hurt her – she was a dear, sweet, kind girl. Would you like to see Mr Kole's body, by the way? It is over here.'

Eleanore did not wait for an answer, but led the way to the Lady Chapel, where the speculator lay in a cheap coffin. Kole was dressed in the same clothes he had worn in London, complete with painted shoes and darned coat. Clearly, the government's antics had brought him very low indeed.

'What have we here?' came a booming voice from behind them. It was Wiseman, who had a professional interest in corpses, and dissected a lot of them at Chyrurgeons' Hall.

'Mr Kole,' supplied Eleanore helpfully. 'The man who was murdered the night before last.'

'Strangled,' Wiseman announced, after an examination that had Chaloner stepping hastily in front of Eleanore, to prevent her from seeing something that might give her nightmares. 'By a person with the same-sized hands as the rogue who throttled Underhill.'

'How do you know?' asked Chaloner warily. 'You never saw Underhill's body.'

'Oh, yes, I did – it was in the Westminster charnel house, so I took the liberty of a peek.' Wiseman turned back to his subject, and continued to speak as though he was addressing a hall full of students, rather than two people in a quiet church. 'It is clear to me that both were attacked from behind, which is unusual. Most stranglers approach from the front.'

'You may be right,' said Eleanore thoughtfully. 'His body had fallen forward, you see . . .'

'Of course I am right,' declared Wiseman. 'I am never

anything else. But how do you know how his body fell? Did you see it in situ?'

Eleanore nodded. 'When I heard the news, I ran straight to Buckingham House.'

'Why?' asked Chaloner, thinking that it was a ghoulish thing to admit.

'Because I knew that Mr Reymes would want Mr Underhill's room scrubbed out as soon as possible, ready for his next guest – I clean for him, you see – but when I arrived, the body was still there. Once the servants had carried it away, I looked to see if there was anything that might identify the killer, but there was nothing.'

'You should have left it alone,' admonished Wiseman. 'You are neither a professional investigator nor a surgeon, and you might have destroyed vital clues.'

'I did not, because there was nothing to destroy,' Eleanore assured him earnestly, and turned back to Chaloner. 'I parcelled up Mr Kole's belongings and sent them to his kin in Kent. Mr Reymes was very grateful, and gave me a shilling.'

'You should watch her, Chaloner,' murmured Wiseman when she had gone. 'There is something not quite right there. Rushing to the room of a murder victim and packing up his bits and pieces is a very odd thing to do. Do you not agree?'

Chaloner supposed he did.

The encounter with Eleanore had bemused Chaloner. Had she really tidied out Kole's room so it could be used for more guests? It was certainly possible – he had heard for himself that Buckingham House was full. And why had she discouraged him from speaking to Nancy's husband? Because she knew what grief was like, and aimed to protect a man whose feelings would be raw? If so, it raised her in his estimation.

'Here is the Swan,' said Wiseman, cutting into his contemplations. 'Good. I am ravenous.'

The Swan was a rambling place on the riverbank. It had something of a holiday atmosphere about it, with patrons rejecting the stuffiness of indoors to spill outside, hoping to catch a cooling breeze. They had taken their ale with them, and sat or lounged under the spreading oaks at the water's edge. Wavelets rippled lightly on a pebbly shore, and children splashed happily in the shallows.

Chaloner, Kipps and Wiseman were allocated a large chamber on the first floor. Its windows were open, and swallows dipped in and out, stealing feathers from the mattresses for their nests. The travellers deposited their saddlebags and walked back downstairs, where Kipps went to check on the horses, and Wiseman called for ale and the best food in the house. Chaloner sat at a table and absently scanned an old newsbook.

'Liver pudding or boiled eels?' asked the landlord. His name was Smith and he, like his wife and three children, was enormously fat. All five were hard at work, struggling to cope with the flurry of custom created by the fair.

'Neither, thank you,' said Chaloner, thinking he had never been offered less appealing fare, not even in France. 'Is there anything else?'

'No,' replied Smith shortly. 'So take it or leave it.'

'The liver is an admirable organ,' declared Wiseman authoritatively. 'I have several pickled in Chyrurgeons' Hall, including one that belonged to my brother-in-law.'

Smith regarded him warily. 'Is he dead, then?'

'Oh, yes,' said Wiseman. 'But his liver was not nearly

181

as interesting as his brain. Have you ever cooked *brain* pudding? Its propensity to liquefy will make for a most interesting texture.'

'I got liver or eels,' repeated Smith, evidently deciding to stick to what he knew. 'And nothing else. Except for a lettuce, but I am saving that for tomorrow.'

'We shall have the liver then,' determined Wiseman. 'Assuming it is of suitable quality?'

'Oh, it will be,' vowed Smith. It sounded like a threat.

He bustled away, and appeared moments later with an overly generous lump that reclined imposingly on a pewter tray. The garnish was a sprig of parsley that looked lost on it.

'Crikey,' murmured Chaloner, regarding it askance.

'My mother makes these,' said Wiseman, taking one of his surgical knives and slashing at it rather wildly. 'Lamb guts stuffed with grated offal, suet, bread, cream, raisins and rose water.'

'Are they edible?' Chaloner supposed he should not be surprised to learn that the surgeon had a mother, although he could not imagine what she might be like. Alarming visions of a scarlet-clad woman of similar proportions to her son filled his mind.

'Generally, although she has a tendency to over-boil them. This, however, has barely seen hot water, because it is still pink inside. Landlord! I am not in the habit of devouring raw entrails. Bring us the eels instead.'

'You eat that or go without,' retorted Smith. 'I got better things to do than run after patrons.'

While Wiseman blinked his astonishment at their host's uncivil rejoinder, Chaloner wondered what had possessed Thurloe to recommend the place. 'How long have you been here?' he asked.

182

'Six weeks,' came the belligerent reply. 'Why?'

Chaloner supposed he would have to inform the ex-Spymaster that the new management was rather less accommodating than the old, and that Thurloe should avoid the Swan if he ever needed a berth in Chelsea. Meanwhile, Wiseman was glaring at Smith.

'We should have gone to the White Hart. The food there is not served raw.'

'Go, then,' shrugged Smith. 'See if I care.'

He strutted away, leaving Wiseman gaping in shock a second time. Chaloner laughed – it was not often that anyone confounded the surgeon. Seeing the pudding was all they were going to get, he took a tentative bite, but all he could taste was nutmeg. He pared the cooked bits from the outside, and ate enough to blunt his hunger, hoping there would be something better for supper.

Kipps arrived from the stables, and showed himself to be an indifferent judge of victuals by devouring a sizeable slice of the pudding and declaring it food fit for a king. When he had finished, Chaloner suggested that they begin their enquiries, but the landlord returned with a dish of shredded lettuce, which he slapped on the table.

'Here,' he said grudgingly. 'You may have this.'

'May we indeed?' murmured Wiseman. 'And what has prompted this change of heart, pray?'

'Ellie Unckles,' explained Smith. 'She just told me that you are here to catch Nancy's killer. You should have said, because then I would have given you this straight away. Nancy was a good lass, and I would like to see her murderer caught.'

'Did you know her well?' asked Chaloner.

'Well enough to know that she did not deserve to be slaughtered.'

'Few people do,' said Chaloner soberly. 'So why do you think she was killed?'

Smith shrugged. 'She was a sweet girl – not like Kole and Underhill, who were rogues. Between you and me, I thought Kole was the strangler, but now he is a victim himself. I believed he was the spectre, see – hiding his mean face under a long coat with a hood.'

'The spectre is a person?' probed Kipps. 'I thought it was a ghost.'

'There are fools who will tell you so, but I saw it with my own eyes, and it looked earthly enough to me. But as the villain is not Kole, I got other suspects. The first is Sutcliffe.'

'The dead Dean of Exeter Cathedral?' asked Kipps in a hushed voice.

Smith regarded him contemptuously. 'His nephew, who is alive and vexed that the government seized the Theological College. He is a sinister devil, and certainly the kind to wander about at night, frightening the gullible.'

'I was told that he had moved away from Chelsea,' fished Chaloner.

'He did – to Greenwich – but I can still see him thinking that it is amusing to terrify stupid people. He is that kind of man. Of course, I have never actually *met* him . . .'

'And your other suspects?' Chaloner was not sure why he asked, given that Smith's theories were based solely on hearsay and prejudice.

'The prisoners.' Smith spat, narrowly missing the liver pudding. 'They are foreigners, and I do not hold with those. One might have sneaked out to kill and steal.'

'I understood that security is tight at the College,' said Chaloner.

Smith sniffed. 'Some of the rogues will have money, and anything is possible for a price.'

'I hope he is wrong,' said Kipps worriedly, when Smith had gone. 'There are two thousand prisoners in that place, and it will not be easy to identify which one escaped to go a-strangling.'

When they had finished eating, Chaloner stood, aiming to visit the College before any more of the day was lost, but before he could reach the door, three men walked in: an elderly one with bandy legs, a burly fellow in his forties and a youth of twenty. All had unusually long chins and short noses, and it was clear that they were three generations of the same line.

'Who are you?' demanded the oldest. 'Spymaster Williamson and his sprats?'

'Certainly not!' declared Wiseman indignantly. 'I am Surgeon to the Person, while Chaloner and Kipps are the Lord Chancellor's emissaries.'

'Oh,' said the old man, clearly unimpressed. 'I expected Williamson. Here we are with a shoal of Dutchmen on our doorstep, and we have three Chelsea residents slaughtered. Clearly, the Hollanders are to blame, so Williamson should be here, making sure it does not happen again.'

'What makes you so sure that a Dutchman is responsible?' asked Chaloner.

'Who else would it be?' demanded the oldster truculently. 'I do not care about Underhill and Kole, but Nancy was a nice lass. Although not very good at gutting cod.'

'Perhaps Williamson is busy devising ways to win the Dutch war,' suggested the son. 'Which *is* important, because I am sick of the villains raiding our fishing grounds.'

185

'True,' agreed his sire. He fixed Chaloner, Kipps and Wiseman with a beady eye. 'And do not say the Battle of Lowestoft will make them think twice about trespassing in our waters again. The scum will be after our herring before you can say "eel pie and oysters".'

The youth released a bored sigh. 'Then perhaps you should be at sea stopping them, Grandfather. You will do a better job than those admirals, most of whom have never set foot on a ship before. Then I could compose an ode about your courage and daring.'

'I would rather you wrote about fish,' said the old man. 'What is the use of having a poet in the family, if he does not extol things that matter?'

'And what can be more important than fish?' agreed his son.

The young man assumed an expression of weary patience. 'I *have* written about fish – endless ditties about turbot, pike and halibut. The problem is that no one other than you two wants to read them, and I need to broaden my horizons if I am to become famous. Do you think we should introduce ourselves to these fellows, by the way? They may not know who we are.'

'Unlikely,' said the old man. '*Everyone* knows that I am John Strangeways, and I am eighty.'

'And that I am his son Giles,' added the middle-aged man. 'While Wadham here is the heir to our fishmongery, and a poet fit to challenge the best wits at Court.'

Strangeways addressed the visitors. 'We have been in the fish business for seven generations, which is impressive when you consider how far Chelsea is from the sea. And if you want to know why we do not move to Wapping, well, then I shall tell you: it is because of Bullen Reymes.'

186

'I do not follow,' said Chaloner, although Rector Thompson had mentioned Reymes' feud with a family named Strangeways.

'Bullen Reymes,' repeated the old man loudly, as if the lack of understanding lay with Chaloner's hearing. 'He is a shark – a dangerous predator, no use to man nor beast.'

'Our mortal enemy,' elaborated Giles. 'He should never have been made a commissioner *or* Treasury prefect, because he is mean, vicious and sly. And he looks like a monkfish.'

'A monkfish?' Chaloner was beginning to be overwhelmed by the piscine references.

'The ugliest of marine creatures,' explained Strangeways. 'In fact, we are here to suggest that if the murderer is not a Dutchman, then you should charge Reymes with the crime. He will commit any sin or vice in an effort to make himself rich. He is a terrible man. A shark, as I said.'

'Or a monkfish,' added Giles.

All the while, Wadham had been eyeing Wiseman with open interest. 'You say you are a surgeon, so will you give me your professional opinion on something? My father believes that smoking and drinking will protect me from the plague, and urges me to do both. I enjoy neither, but I will persist if they will keep me safe. What do you think?'

'He thinks I am right,' said Giles, pulling out a pipe with the biggest bowl Chaloner had ever seen. 'How could he not, when it is *obvious* that smoke and wine keep a man healthy?'

'Raw mackerel,' countered Strangeways. 'Rubbed on the chest every morning. That has kept *me* safe from

187

innumerable sicknesses, and it will do the same with the plague. However, it has not helped the pains in my knee. Do you have a cure for that, Surgeon?'

'Of course,' replied Wiseman loftily. 'But I am expensive, so I doubt you can afford it.'

'Oh, yes, I can,' declared Strangeways, and tossed a purse on the table, where it landed with a substantial thud. 'Name your price.'

Wiseman did, and Chaloner felt his jaw drop. Strangeways nodded careless agreement and handed over the money as though it was nothing. Wiseman pocketed the coins and knelt on the floor, indicating that Strangeways was to sit on the bench in front of him. Giles watched intently, to ensure his sire was not cheated, but he need not have worried. Wiseman was nothing if not flamboyant, and proceeded to conduct an examination that would have made even the most demanding of patients feel he was getting his money's worth.

While they were busy, Chaloner cornered Wadham, to see what the youngster had to say about his family's quarrel with Reymes. Unfortunately, Wadham was more interested in talking about himself.

'I hate fishmongery,' he confided. 'All I want is to be a poet.'

'Can you not do both?' Chaloner's great-grandfather had written some very good verses, all composed while following a successful career in politics.

'It is difficult to concentrate when I am surrounded by people who blather about cod and pilchards all the time. And they make unreasonable demands. Have you ever written an ode to a plaice? It is not easy, I can tell you.'

'Tell me about Reymes,' ordered Chaloner, before Wadham could ask him to try it. 'And why your family dislikes him.'

'He arranged for laws to be passed that restricted our fishing rights – out of sheer malice. You should ensure *you* do not earn his enmity or your life will be a misery. He is a horrible man.'

'One capable of murder?'

'Oh, yes. He probably killed those people just to strike at the Earl of Clarendon, whom he hates.' The lad smirked. 'We are going to open a coffee house near Buckingham House soon. Those places reek, and ours will cause him much inconvenience.'

'And you accuse him of spite,' muttered Chaloner, regarding the lad wonderingly.

'That is not our only motive,' said Wadham, turning defensive in the face of Chaloner's disapproval. 'We are also doing it because Dr Parker says that coffee will protect the whole village from madness and the plague. Hah, look! There is the man himself.'

He pointed through the window, to where the physician was walking in an oddly erratic manner towards the river, stopping every so often to talk to himself. When he began to dance after a passing chicken, Chaloner was even more sure the man had lost his reason. Moments later, Franklin appeared and began speaking in a low voice, after which Parker allowed himself to be led away.

'Did you know the three murder victims?' asked Chaloner, turning back to Wadham.

'Of course.' Wadham glanced around furtively and lowered his voice. 'I love being out on summer evenings, searching for my Muse, and I often saw Underhill sneaking around the prison. It occurred to me that he was a spy, but I suspect he was just nosy. He liked to read, you see.'

'I am not sure I understand the connection.'

'Well, people who read are naturally curious, are they not? I saw the spectre, too, although I certainly did not follow *that* to find out what it was doing! Landlord Smith probably told you that it is either a Dutchman or Sutcliffe, but he is wrong – it is definitely supernatural. When I saw the thing, I ran away.'

'But you followed Underhill?'

Wadham nodded. 'Several times, although he did no more than gaze at the prison, as if he was waiting for something to happen. Nothing ever did. I saw Kole out and about, too. He was in the habit of peeping through other people's windows at night.'

'Why?'

'To watch women while they undressed. I challenged him the first time I saw what he was doing, and he *claimed* that he had lost a key in the bushes. The second time, it was a dropped coin. I did not bother asking again.'

Chaloner recalled what Hart and Bannister had said – that Kole had loitered in Gorges' orchard. Had that been to ogle the inmates through their bedroom windows? Yet the dancing masters had also spotted Kole by Rector Wilkinson's compost heaps, and those were unlikely to have been frequented by naked ladies.

'Shall I tell you who I really hate?' asked Wadham, and forged on without waiting for an answer. 'George Cocke. He is a rogue of the first order, and I would not trust him with a button.'

'Why do you call him a rogue?'

'Because he is a sot, who likes whores, drinking and

cards. Ask anyone. Yet his shabby attire shows that he is not a wealthy man, so how does he pay for these vices?'

'By spending his three incomes on them,' suggested Chaloner. There was also the possibility that Cocke earned money from blackmail, as he had tried to do with Kipps, although Chaloner did not mention that to the boy, and turned the discussion back to the victims. 'You said you followed Underhill and Kole on occasion. What about Nancy?'

'That would have been difficult,' replied Wadham. 'She was in the asylum, and although she was free to leave whenever she liked, she never did.'

'What was she like?'

Wadham smiled. 'A pretty lass. I cannot imagine why she married the bell-founder, who is as ugly as sin. Cocke made a play for her, of course, but I do not know if she considered his advances welcome or an imposition. I was busy with a girl of my own at the time.'

Chaloner was thoughtful. It would not be the first time that a jealous husband had dispatched an unfaithful wife, and had then been obliged to kill others to keep his actions quiet. Perhaps Eleanore had been wrong to warn him against tackling Janaway.

'Come, Wadham,' called Strangeways. He wore a satisfied grin and the biggest bandage Chaloner had ever seen: Wiseman had excelled himself. 'The prison is expecting a delivery of fish from us this afternoon, and we do not want our Dutch friends to starve.'

'Do we not?' asked Wadham, puzzled. 'I thought you said we did.'

Chapter 7

'I suppose we should begin with the College,' said Kipps, as he and Chaloner left the Swan. 'Two thousand foreign sailors so close to the city makes me very uneasy, and we should assess whether they pose a risk.'

Chaloner had harboured a passionate dislike of gaols ever since he had been imprisoned for spying in France, and did not relish the thought of stepping inside another. He flailed around for an excuse to put it off, although he knew he was a coward for doing so, especially as Thurloe had thought it was where answers would be found.

'We should learn more about the victims first,' he hedged.

'But they and the prison might be connected,' argued Kipps. 'After all, we know that Underhill was monitoring the place for Spymaster Williamson.'

'True,' acknowledged Chaloner. 'But tomorrow will be soon enough.'

'You know best,' said Kipps, although his doubtful expression belied the words. 'So what *shall* we do? Speak to Nancy's husband? Wilkinson called her a whore, so perhaps Underhill and Kole were her clients, and Janaway killed them for it. Of course, Janaway was not in Clarendon House when Underhill died . . .'

'How do you know? We did not see him, but the guards are shamefully lax, and it is not impossible to sneak past them.'

'Right,' said Kipps, surging purposefully to his feet. 'Then let us be at him.'

Chaloner stood more slowly, uncomfortably aware that he was about to flout Eleanore's request for the bell-founder to be left alone. But Kipps was right – Janaway was an obvious route forward, and their first duty was to the investigation, not a woman they barely knew.

They learned from Landlord Smith that Janaway's workshop was on the eastern fringes of the village, past the disturbingly named Bloody Bridge. They walked slowly, the heat sapping their energy. Chaloner boiled in shirtsleeves and loose breeches, and failed to understand how Kipps could bear his stylishly close-fitting long-coat and the lace that cascaded down his front.

They trudged up Church Lane, and turned right along the King's Road, which took them past the rectory's main gate again. Chaloner glanced along its weed-infested path, and caught a flash of movement in an upstairs window. Two men were peering out at him, although both ducked back when they realised they had been spotted. Neither of them were Doyley.

Kipps saw them, too, and waved cheerfully, although there was no response from the house. 'Londoners are using even the remotest ties of kinship to escape the plague,' he remarked. 'They must be refugees from the city, fleeing for their lives. And who can blame them?'

'Yet Wilkinson is not a compassionate man,' remarked

Chaloner. 'I do not see him offering a safe haven to the desperate. Perhaps it was his servants.'

But Gertrude Thompson had been told that the rector received lots of visitors, so perhaps he possessed a kindness that he preferred to conceal, although surely it was peculiar to keep guests in the attic? Or had he imprisoned them there? Chaloner supposed he would have to find out.

They walked on. The bell-foundry was the last building before the King's Road became a grassy track, and comprised a large workshop, raised in stone to avoid mishaps from flying sparks, and several sheds in which bells and dome-shaped casts were stored. It reeked of grease and hot metal. The whole place was deserted, although a cooling furnace indicated that it had been active not long before, as did a lot of hurriedly downed tools.

'So where is he?' asked Kipps, looking around in annoyance. 'Did he know we were coming? There is a half-eaten apple on that bench, as if someone was obliged to abandon it all of a sudden.'

Had Eleanore warned Janaway that he might be questioned? Chaloner hoped not. He had instinctively felt he could trust her, and it perturbed him to think that he might have been wrong.

There was a house adjoining the workshop, so he knocked on the door. When there was no answer, he shoved it open, and entered a home that had once been well maintained, but that now showed signs of neglect – Nancy had been a good housewife, but her widower had let things slide. There was nothing of interest inside, except a pile of charcoal sketches depicting a young woman. She had a pretty, gentle face, and he supposed

194

that Janaway had drawn them, so as not to forget what his dead wife had looked like. Chaloner stared at them and thought perhaps he should do the same with Hannah.

'We should go,' said Kipps. 'There is nothing here, and Reymes is expecting us at Buckingham House. Let us hope he is a good host, because I would kill for a cool ale.'

Buckingham House was mostly Tudor, but had recently been graced with oriel windows, an ornate baroque porch and a clock tower capped with an onion dome. It was three storeys high, and had dozens of rooms. It was reached by a long, tree-lined drive, which opened up into a spacious courtyard containing statues and an elaborately carved fountain.

'Most of the revels take place out here, apparently,' remarked Kipps, looking around with interest. 'Which is rash, given that it is in full view of Church Lane. The villagers love to come and watch at the gates, then gossip about what they have seen in the taverns. I asked Reymes why he did not keep his guests' antics indoors, out of sight, and he said it would be too hot.'

'It must cost a fortune to rent,' said Chaloner, gazing up at the noble façade. 'Yet he says he spent all his money supporting the King during the wars. So how does he pay for it?'

'How indeed?' agreed Kipps. 'He makes no secret of his determination to claw back all he lost, yet he squanders a fortune on hosting courtiers he does not even like.'

'How do you know he does not like them?'

'Well, think about who he invited: Alan Brodrick, cousin of his most bitter enemy; Greeting, gossip and malcontent; Sir Edward Hungerford, rakehell and not the kind of fellow Reymes finds amusing. Shall I continue?'

'Perhaps he did not lose as much during the wars as he would have everyone believe.'

'He has been saying for years that the conflict all but broke him, and there is no reason to doubt it. However, he is Prefect of the Treasury . . .'

'I think the rest of you would notice if he was using the King's gold to fund his social life.'

'Not necessarily – not when Cocke is the only remaining accompter. That sly fellow would certainly aid and abet theft in exchange for a cut. You are wise to question Reymes' finances.'

Suddenly, the front door burst open and two servants appeared with a table. They were followed by a handful of musicians, although Greeting was the only one Chaloner recognised. The performers arranged themselves into a rough consort and began to play, loudly and with an appalling lack of skill – Greeting had to be drunk, thought Chaloner, or he would have refused to be part of it.

More servants arrived with jugs and cups, and then a party was underway. The courtiers poured from the house, their shrill voices competing with the music, and Chaloner was amazed by how quickly the atmosphere turned debauched. Almost immediately, villagers began to gather at the gates, clearly expecting to witness something scandalous.

Chaloner saw that Kipps was right to remark on Reymes' odd choice of company, as none were the kind of people he would have expected the commissioner to befriend. Edward Hungerford, Richard Newport and

Henry Savile were libertines; Lady Savage was renowned for unrestrained drinking; and Betty Becke was infamously bawdy. All were wild, even by White Hall standards – wastrels and debauchees, who lived off the public purse, but gave nothing in return.

Brodrick was there, face flushed from wine, while Cocke stood next to him, one plump arm around the shoulders of a giggling girl – Reymes' hospitality evidently extended to providing professional prostitutes as well. Chaloner waited until Cocke had disappeared with his woman, then approached Brodrick, hoping a report from the Earl's cousin would save him some time.

'Well?' he asked briskly. 'What have you learned?'

Brodrick regarded him blankly. 'Learned about what?'

'The Gorges thefts. The Earl charged you to start investigating.'

Brodrick waved a dismissive hand. 'I have not had time – Reymes keeps us far too busy. I popped in once or twice to make sure the songbirds were safe, but you can take over that duty now. I have never been comfortable in asylums. And do not say it is for fear they may not let me out again – it is because illness of any kind distresses me.'

While glad that Brodrick had not done any harm by blundering about amateurishly, Chaloner was unimpressed that he had absolutely nothing to impart. Then Reymes spotted them, and put paid to further conversation by stamping over.

'Have you timed your arrival to coincide with the distribution of fine wine,' he asked sourly, 'or is it coincidence that you came now?'

'Coincidence,' replied Chaloner coldly, disliking the

inference that he was a scrounger, like the courtiers who frolicked around them.

'Although I should not refuse a cup, should it be offered,' put in Kipps amiably.

Brodrick beamed tipsily. 'I did not believe Greeting when he told me of the delights on offer here, but you do us proud, Reymes. Who needs Hampton Court? Chelsea is much better!'

'It would be better still if Lady Castlemaine were here,' sighed Kipps. 'Thoughts of her thighs have given me comfort through the very darkest of times. My wife's are quite respectable, of course, but what I would not give for a glimpse of the Lady's.'

Brodrick laughed gaily. 'Then your wish may be granted, because she *is* here. She was not invited to Hampton Court either, as the King is vexed over her public conversion to Catholicism.'

'I do not see why,' muttered Reymes. 'The Catholic Church will have gained nothing, while the Anglican Church will have lost nothing.'

At that point, the lady in question emerged from the house. In deference to the heat, she was very scantily clad, which allowed her to flaunt the exquisite lines of her body: an impressive physique for anyone, but especially a mother of four. The gentle rounding of her stomach suggested she had not been out of royal favour for long, and it seemed that the King could soon expect a fifth child in the royal nursery. Male courtiers raced to her side, and the atmosphere turned louder and more raucous than ever. The other women rolled their eyes, and set about reclaiming some of the attention.

'Kole,' said Chaloner to Reymes, eager to complete

his enquiries and leave, 'would it be possible to see his room and the place where he died?'

'For God's sake, Tom,' said Kipps in a strangled voice, and Chaloner glanced around to see the Seal Bearer's eyes fixed unblinkingly on the Lady's legs. 'Can you not relax even for a moment? Here is the Eighth Wonder of the World, and you want to talk about murder?'

'I shall show you myself, Chaloner,' said Reymes, ignoring him. 'Then I can be sure that you will do no mischief. Follow me.'

Chaloner was glad to be away from the merry debauchery, although Kipps dragged his feet. They entered the house, where Reymes led them through a ballroom with enormous windows and gilt-edged mirrors. Its splendour was marred by the wine stains on the floor and the marks on the walls, probably from lobbed food.

'I gather there was an event here last night?' asked Chaloner drily.

'There are events most nights,' replied Reymes. 'Indeed, we are having one tomorrow. It goes against the grain to invite Clarendon's lackeys, but I suppose you can come, if you want.'

'Yes, please,' said Kipps, although Chaloner was disinclined to accept, not just for the grudging nature of the invitation, but because he had no desire to spend time with Reymes or his guests.

'To business,' said the commissioner brusquely. 'I found Kole at six o'clock yesterday morning, lying in that rose garden over there. He was last seen alive at midnight – by Greeting, Brodrick and others. Ergo, he died at some point in between. My guests were carousing most

199

of the night, but I went to bed. I was tired after sitting through Wilkinson's plague service.'

'So who killed him?' asked Chaloner. 'Do you have any ideas?'

Reymes scowled. 'I thought that was what you were here to find out.'

'It is,' replied Chaloner evenly. 'But if you have suspicions, now is the time to air them.'

'I do not. As I told you earlier, all my guests have alibis in each other.'

'It is not looking good for you, Reymes,' said Kipps, uncharacteristically belligerent. 'A man dies in your garden, and you are the only one who cannot account for his whereabouts.'

There was a moment when Chaloner thought the Seal Bearer was going to be punched, but Reymes managed to rein in his temper and even attempt a smile, which did not sit well on his perpetually angry features and served to make him look devious.

'I suppose the culprit *might* be among the courtiers,' he conceded, obviously unwilling to shoulder the role of sole suspect. 'I do not know them well enough to say whether they are the kind of folk to slaughter each other.'

'Then why did you invite them into your home?' pounced Chaloner.

'Because they all hate Clarendon,' flared Reymes, anger rising again. 'With the exception of Brodrick, whom I asked because he is a lively soul who will entertain the others.'

Chaloner did not believe him. Even the embittered commissioner would not squander a fortune on people with whom he shared nothing but a common dislike of one man.

200

'How did Kole seem before you retired?' he asked. 'Did you notice anything unusual?'

'No. I went to my room before the festivities began, so I did not notice Kole or anyone else.'

'You did not wait to join in? Not even for a little while?'

'I am not in a position to frolic into the small hours,' replied Reymes sourly. 'The prison generates a lot of work, and I am obliged to be at my desk at first light. Which is why Clarendon foisted it on me, of course.'

'Where is Kole's room? Upstairs?'

'Yes, but a woman from the village has already cleaned it and sent all his belongings to Kent. There is nothing there to help you now. And Cocke has moved in anyway.'

'You could not have kept it vacant for a few hours?' asked Kipps in distaste. 'To show some respect for the dead?'

Reymes shrugged. 'She had finished before I realised what she was doing. It was presumptuous of her, I suppose, but it saved me the bother of thinking about it, so I did not complain. Indeed, I gave her a shilling for using her initiative.'

Chaloner insisted on seeing the room anyway, so Reymes led the way up the stairs, albeit with ill grace. Kole had been allocated a small but pleasant chamber on the second floor, and Reymes opened the door to an unholy mess. Cocke's greasy clothes were strewn everywhere, and the place smelled of sweat and dirty feet.

Chaloner explored it carefully anyway, ignoring Reymes' gusty sighs of impatience, but Eleanore had been thorough. The only thing of interest was a faint sooty footprint in the hearth, which was too small to have been made by either her or Cocke, and told

Chaloner that someone else – Kole, perhaps – had been doing something up the chimney.

He peered up the shaft, and saw a ledge on which a little package rested. Aware that Reymes was watching, and unwilling to have his find confiscated before he could examine it, Chaloner dislodged the desiccated corpse of a pigeon, which was caught higher up. When Reymes and Kipps recoiled in disgust, he slipped the bundle inside his shirt unnoticed.

When they returned to the garden, Chaloner's spirits sank. Even in the short time he had been in the house, the courtiers had grown more drunk and less inhibited. The villagers at the gates stood in a fascinated semicircle, and he wondered why Reymes should want them to witness White Hall at play. Did he aim to expose its failings to the world, and lead a revolt against the government?

'A word, Ned,' called Kipps, as Sir Edward Hungerford reeled past. Hungerford was an especially hedonistic courtier, who was in the process of squandering what had once been a princely inheritance. 'Were you here when Kole was murdered?'

Hungerford peered at him through bloodshot eyes. 'Kipps? I thought you had followed Clarendon to Hampton Court – although you will have a better time here, I warrant. I have never known such rambunctious entertainment.'

'Kole,' prompted Kipps. 'Did you see anything that might let us catch his killer?'

'Do not bother about him,' slurred Hungerford. 'All he ever did was moan about Parliament seizing his assets. Well, if he wanted to live in a country with an honest government, he should have moved abroad. I am told he was murdered, but I knew nothing of it until Lady Castlemaine told me at noon today. I was rather the worse for wear, I am afraid.'

He lurched away before he could be asked anything else.

'I have a bad feeling that everyone else will say much the same,' said Chaloner, disgusted and disheartened. 'But we shall have to speak to them anyway, just to be sure. What a waste of time!'

'I will do it,' offered Kipps, gazing longingly at the Lady, who was reclining on a bench surrounded by drooling men. 'While you visit Gorges. Call it a division of labour.'

It was not a very fair one, and when Kipps went to collect a cup of wine before entering the fray, Chaloner knew who would be doing the lion's share of the work in Chelsea.

Once away from Buckingham House, Chaloner opened the bundle from the chimney. It contained sketches of women, all engaged in activities they would never have pursued in front of an audience – Kole had spied on them, and had been so gloatingly proud of his 'artwork' that he had signed each piece with his name. Chaloner felt soiled just looking at them, and dumped the lot in the nearest midden, feeling it was the best place for such nastiness. There was one item of interest among them, however: a short message in cipher. The writer had used the simplest of numerical codes, one with which Chaloner was so familiar that he could translate it in his head:

Sir,

I have nothinge to Reporte other than that you shoulde sende your own Spyes to the College. The matter is beyond me. A Spectre roames Chelsey, but no one knows its name, altho there are those who saye it is John Sutcliffe, nephew of the olde Deane. Yett I saw it once, and it trodd light, like a Womann. Reymes spends a Fortune on his Gests, and begrudges them nought, altho they are an Ungratefull hord. Koale the Spekulator is bitter with Rage about his Losses, but he is a feeble Mann with more Talke than Action. If anyone tells you that I stole Mrs Bonny's plate and solde it in the Fleet Rookerie, they are lyinge.
Your Most Humble Servant,
R U

Chaloner regarded it thoughtfully. Clearly, it was one of Robert Underhill's reports to Spymaster Williamson, so why was it in Kole's room? Kole had known that Underhill was a spy, because Rector Thompson had heard them arguing about it, and Mother Green had watched him trail Underhill in the Fleet Rookery, clearly in the hope of proving that there was something untoward about his quarry. Had he intercepted the message because he feared he had been mentioned in it, and if so, had he managed to decode what was written? It was absurdly easy for Chaloner, but he was a professional intelligencer: Kole might have been stumped. And what was this about the spectre being a woman? Could it be true?

Chaloner was still pondering when he reached the gates of Gorges House, a pretty building with mullioned windows and a wealth of Elizabethan chimneys. It was charmingly asymmetrical, and the flowers in its garden gave it a welcoming appearance. A number of 'songbirds' were out, some reading under a tree, others busy with hoes among the vegetable plots, while a few sang. It was a peaceful scene, despite the racket from its less restrained neighbours – until a gale of wild laughter reminded him that not all its occupants were sane.

He was about to ring the bell when a figure emerged from the house. It was Parker in his plague costume. His movements were jerky and agitated as he approached a woman from behind. She gave a shrill cry of fright when she turned to see him there. Most residents looked on with amusement, but a few panicked and began running every which way, colliding with each other as they went. Parker promptly joined in.

Then Franklin appeared and tried to lay hold of him, but Parker was too quick for his slower, fatter colleague, and they careered around the garden in increasingly frantic circles. The chase ended when Mrs Bonney brought Parker down with an impressive flying tackle. The two effete dancing masters, Bannister and Hart, watched the ensuing struggle with troubled faces, and Chaloner knew how they felt: like his, their livelihoods depended on the ability of another person to carry out his duties.

Chaloner shouted to attract attention, but it was Wiseman who came to speak to him – the staff were occupied with bundling Parker out of sight and calming those inmates who had been unsettled by the sight of a plague doctor dashing about.

'You will not be allowed in today, Chaloner, so do not bother asking. Gorges is closed.'

'Then why are you in there?' asked Chaloner archly.

'First, because I am a *medicus*; and second, because

my wife lives here. You, however, will be told to return tomorrow. They are having trouble with Parker, you see.'

'So I noticed. What is wrong with him?'

'Mrs Bonney says it is nothing, but he seems deranged to me.'

'How is Dorothy?'

'I think she has improved, but I shall know more when I discuss her case with the nurses tomorrow. Do not waste your time here, Chaloner. Go and catch your murderer instead.'

Chaloner now had two choices: return to Buckingham House and help Kipps to interview the drunken courtiers, or examine the prison. Neither option appealed, and he wondered if he could visit Eleanore instead, on the pretext of learning more about Nancy Janaway. But conscience prevailed, and he set off reluctantly towards the gaol.

Unlike Chelsea's other mansions, which faced the river, the Theological College had been built towards the road, allowing the Thames to form a pretty backdrop to it. It was enormous, comprising buildings set around two quadrangles. The first boasted a gatehouse at the front, turrets on all four corners, and its cobbled yard was so vast that the buildings in its middle – kitchens, stables, pantries and even a brewery – barely took up any space at all. The second was tiny, but was concealed behind high, featureless walls, and nothing of it was visible from the outside.

As Chaloner approached, he saw that all the windows had been fitted with bars, while the gatehouse had been fortified. He wondered if the Royal Society would still want the place when the war was over and the prisoners had been sent home. Pushing away the desire to leave his inspection for another day, he took a deep breath and jangled the bell that was hanging outside. After what felt like an age, a grille snapped open and eyes peered out.

'I come on behalf of the Earl of Clarendon and Spymaster Williamson,' he announced with as much authority as he could muster. 'They want me to assess the situation here.'

He was aware of being studied, and wished he had thought to dress for the occasion. Shirtsleeves, riding breeches and an old felt hat might be comfortable for wandering about in the sun, but they were hardly garments to impress. Fortunately, the Earl had provided him with a writ of authority before he had left – a gloriously impressive document, embossed with the Clarendon seal, and trailing blue and gold ribbons. He pulled it out and held it up for inspection.

There was a muttered conversation, after which the wicket gate opened to reveal two men. One was small, thin and wore an old-fashioned cloak and a tall hat that reminded Chaloner of a woodcut he had once seen of Guy Fawkes – as did the decidedly villainous expression on the fellow's face. The second was a hulking brute with scarred knuckles and ears that had received too many punches.

'I am Warden Tooker,' said the small man. 'And this is Chief Gaoler Samm, who has forty men under his command, so you can tell your masters that they need not fear trouble. A sparrow could not escape without our permission.'

'Good,' said Chaloner, thinking that here was the person who Thurloe claimed had been dismissed from

Newgate for corrupt practices. 'But I need to see for myself.'

'Do you?' Tooker exchanged a glance with his henchman. 'Are you alone?'

'No,' replied Chaloner, lest the intention was to shove him in a cell in the hope that he and his visit would be forgotten by those who had sent him.

'Then who is with you?' demanded Samm, looking around as if he imagined helpmeets might materialise from the bushes.

'Associates,' replied Chaloner shortly. 'Who are waiting for me to report back to them.'

Tooker made an expansive gesture with his hand. 'Then you had better come in.'

Chaloner stepped through the door with considerable reluctance, shuddering when it boomed shut behind him. It set up echoes that reverberated across the yard, and his stomach lurched painfully. How much longer would his experiences in France haunt him? And given that he reacted the same way every time he set foot in a place with cells, should he look for a different occupation? The post of Sergeant at Arms for the Treasury suddenly seemed very attractive.

Beyond the mighty gatehouse was the main yard, where several hundred prisoners trudged in a shuffling circle. They were well enough clad for the height of summer, but Chaloner wondered what would happen when winter bit. Most were cowed, dejected and frightened, exactly as they had been immediately after the Battle of Lowestoft, when they had been fished from the sea.

'We let them out for an hour each day,' Tooker explained. 'They enjoy the sunshine and a stroll does them good. We do not want them dying on us, after all.

However, this only applies to the obedient ones. We keep the trouble-makers in the Garden Court, and those never leave their cells.'

At that point, Chaloner's eye lit on a knot of a score or so men who lounged in a shady corner, apparently exempt from tramping about in the blazing sun. They were better dressed and sleeker than their fellows, and their leader was a squat, barrel-shaped lout with missing teeth. At a gesture from Tooker, the fellow slouched forward. A second prisoner followed, one who wore the garb of a Dutch sea-captain, although his coat and breeches were shabby.

Tooker indicated the bulky man first. 'This is John Spring, the Hollanders' spokesman.' Then he nodded to the second. 'And Jacob Oudart, their highest-ranking officer.'

'Are you from the government?' asked Spring in English that revealed him to be from Newcastle or thereabouts. 'Come to see how we are kept? Well, we are very comfortable, thank you. We want for nothing, and our gaolers are stern but fair.'

Bemused, Chaloner addressed him in Dutch. 'Surely the prisoners would rather have a spokesman from their own country? It seems inappropriate for an Englishman to represent their interests.'

'I Holland,' declared Spring in the same language, although his thick accent belied the claim. 'They happy with me.' He reverted to the vernacular. 'Now bugger off.'

'That is a curious response towards someone who has come to enquire after your welfare,' remarked Chaloner coolly. 'Why are you so keen to have me gone?'

Tooker was standing behind Chaloner, but the spy

knew he was making frantic gestures, warning Spring to watch his tongue. Oudart stepped forward quickly.

'We do not want you gone,' he said in aristocratic Dutch; his smile was strained, and he had a sallow, sickly look about him. 'Our manners are brittle only because we so desperately want to go home. You have no idea what it is like to be gaoled on foreign soil.'

Chaloner knew only too well. 'Which ship are you from?'

'*Stad Utrecht*,' replied Oudart. 'I was captured when *Royal Charles* sent a fire-ship against me at the Battle of Lowestoft. Which was rather ungentlemanly, if you want the truth.'

Chaloner recalled that part of the action vividly. In the chaos and panic at the end of the engagement, four Dutch ships had collided with each other and become hopelessly entangled. The Duke of York had ordered a fire-ship set loose among them, after which one had exploded, two had sunk and one had managed to escape. Fewer than a hundred survivors had been plucked from the wreckage-strewn water afterwards, and Chaloner was not surprised that Oudart was bitter.

He abandoned the pair, and went to waylay some of the exercising masses, much to Tooker's obvious annoyance, but learned little other than that none spoke much English, which was why Spring had managed to get himself appointed their leader – along with the fact that he had twenty beefy shipmates to back his bid for power. Technically, the honour should have gone to Oudart, but there was some suggestion that poor seamanship had contributed to the disaster with *Stad Utrecht*, and the captain was thus unpopular.

'Spring keeps good order among the inmates,' said

Tooker, coming to take Chaloner's arm and direct him away from the shuffling mariners, 'whereas Oudart was a liability with his ineffectual orders and unpredictable moods. In return for Spring's help, we afford him and his friends a little more freedom than the rest.'

'What kind of freedom?' asked Chaloner. 'Are they allowed outside the prison walls?'

'Do not be ridiculous! But they are permitted to sit while the others walk, and they are given better rations. It is working very well. Watch.'

He nodded to Samm, who rang a gong. Immediately, Spring and his minions began to direct the other prisoners back to their cells; most went willingly, glad to be out of the heat. Spring looked as though he would reclaim his spot in the shady corner, but Samm signalled urgently, and the spokesman slouched indoors after the others.

With Tooker at his side, directing a stream of information into his ear that was both irrelevant and annoying, Chaloner was given a guided tour of the College, although there were too many locked doors for him to see much. He was shown two rooms where inmates sat demurely on folded blankets. Both cells were clean, with water provided for washing. Then he was taken to the refectory, where a few Dutchmen were weaving reed baskets. Afterwards, he was presented with the sales ledgers from the work, Tooker boasting that every penny of profit was reinvested in prisoner welfare.

To see if he was telling the truth, Chaloner sat at a table and began to check the figures for himself. The warden was visibly alarmed, although in the reflection of the window Chaloner saw Samm give his employer a reassuring nod.

Chaloner took his time over the books, refusing to

211

be influenced by the increasingly restless shuffles and sighs from behind him. Eventually, Tooker could stand it no more. He summoned another guard, and ordered him to mind Chaloner, while he and Samm went to do something more useful. When they had gone, Chaloner took the opportunity to question the guard, who was a middle-aged fellow with a blunt, weather-burnt face. His name was Curtis Akers, and he almost fell over himself in his eagerness to cooperate.

'I *was* a farmer, but it has been so hot and dry this summer that all my crops failed, so I was forced to apply for a post here. I cannot say I like it, though.'

'Does it pay well?'

'Adequately.' Akers lowered his voice. 'Clarendon and Williamson are wise to be concerned, because something here *is* amiss, although I am not experienced enough at gaoling to know what. But I do not like Spring – the way he lords it over the others. Then there is the Garden Court . . .'

'You mean the smaller yard behind this one?' It had not featured in the guided tour, because Tooker claimed it would be reckless to open it up without good reason.

Akers nodded. 'Only Samm and a few of his favourites are allowed inside, on the grounds that its prisoners are too dangerous for the rest of us to manage. But if that were true, then surely we would all be needed to keep them in line?'

'That is a good point. So you have never been in?'

'Not once.' Akers glanced uneasily over his shoulder before continuing. 'But it *does* contain prisoners, because supplies are regularly delivered to them. Perhaps they are Dutch admirals, who need to be kept apart from the others for their own safety – it was partly officers' incompetence that allowed us to win the Battle of Lowestoft, after all. However, they never come out for walks.'

'How big is the Garden Court?'

'Not very. My wife tells me it is pretty, though, with flower beds and trees. She was a cook-maid when it was full of angry divines, but she does not approve of me working here now.'

'Why not?' Chaloner was pleased that Akers was answering his questions, although there was something suspicious about the man's eagerness to betray his employers' secrets. He decided to treat everything Akers told him with caution.

'She is afraid that the cramped conditions will breed the plague, which will then kill us gaolers as well as prisoners – and infect our families as well. Such an eventuality will not bother Samm and Tooker, though. They never married, because no woman would have them.'

'What are you saying, Akers?' growled a voice from behind them. It was Samm.

'He is complaining that his crops were poor this year,' supplied Chaloner, when Akers only stared at the gaoler like a frightened rabbit. 'My family are farmers, and they tell me the same.'

Samm did not look convinced, and dismissed Akers with a scowl. Then he turned to Chaloner. 'Have you finished now? If so, Mr Tooker will see you in his office.'

Chaloner shut the ledger. Someone with a good head for figures might be able to spot irregularities, but the matter was beyond him. However, he was sure about one thing: that everything he had been shown that day had been carefully prepared in advance, ready to present

213

to nuisance callers. He stood, deciding it was time he explored on his own terms.

'I will talk to Tooker as soon as I have seen the Garden Court.'

'No,' said Samm shortly. 'It contains dangerous prisoners, and we do not even let most of the gaolers in there. The only way we will open those doors is if you produce an official warrant.'

Chaloner brandished the Lord Chancellor's writ. 'I have one here.'

'One that names the Garden Court specifically,' countered Samm, refusing to look at it. 'Now follow me, if you please.'

As making a fuss would serve no useful purpose, Chaloner trailed across the now-deserted yard to the gate-house, where Tooker occupied a pleasant suite on the first floor – rooms with wood-panelled walls, silk rugs and leaded-glass windows. The warden sat at a desk that was piled importantly high with papers, although Chaloner, adept at reading upside-down, saw that one was a receipt for lavender water, while another was a draft letter to a tailor. Eyeing Tooker's peculiar attire, Chaloner thought it was time he transferred his custom elsewhere.

'Spring did not show himself in a good light today,' said Tooker with an oily smile. 'He appeared bullying and insolent. He is neither, and our system works very well. I hope your report will reflect that.'

'He is a curious choice for spokesman,' said Chaloner. 'He is not even Dutch.'

'Yes and no. He was master of a British merchant ship, which was captured by Hollandish pirates. He was then offered a choice: join the Dutch navy or execution. He and his shipmates chose to serve on *Stad Utrecht*.'

214

'So he is here from misfortune, not treachery,' put in Samm. 'And he is proving himself loyal to the country of his birth by agreeing to interpret for us. He is so conscientious and reliable that Warden Tooker has promised to recommend him for *our* navy when he is released.'

'The Garden Court,' said Chaloner, not pointing out that it still did not make Spring a better candidate for the post than a Dutchman – and he was sure that there would be one among the two thousand who knew enough English for the task. 'Do you really want me to apply for a warrant to inspect it? I doubt Clarendon or Williamson will approve of their time being wasted. Indeed, they may even recommend your dismissal. As might I, in my report.'

The pair exchanged a quick, uneasy glance.

'But there is nothing to see, other than more of what you have already examined,' objected Tooker. 'Men locked in cells. The only difference is that these are dangerous, and I am unwilling to take needless risks with them. Not without a specific warrant.'

His expression was determined, and Chaloner knew there was no point pressing the issue. Instead, he asked about numbers and security protocols. The glib replies did more to raise his concerns than quell them, and he decided that Akers was right: there *was* something odd going on. But what? Clearly, he needed to explore alone, to open the doors that had been closed to him, and see what lay behind them for himself.

While prisons were usually difficult to leave, they tended to be fairly easy to enter, on the premise that no one in his right mind would want to do it. Therefore, it did not take Chaloner long to devise a plan that would allow him to sneak back inside. There was a risk that if he was caught he might not be allowed out again, but it was one he felt obliged to take.

Strangeways had mentioned a delivery of fish to the College that afternoon, so Chaloner walked to the river-bank. Two boats were moored there. The old man and Giles were supervising the transfer of their wares to three waiting carts, while Wadham perched on a bollard, pen in hand as he stared contemplatively across the water. Every so often, his father and grandfather stole proud glances in his direction.

Eventually, the holds were empty and the heavily laden carts trundled off towards the prison. Chaloner followed, pleased when he saw that a combination of locals and visiting fishermen had been hired to offload the goods at the other end. They did not know each other, so it would be simplicity itself to infiltrate them.

He hid his hat and sword behind a hedge, and turned his shirt inside out to hide the lace. He had no face-paints for a disguise, but there was plenty of dust around, and a few judiciously applied smudges completed his transition from clean-cut official to grubby ruffian. No one took any notice as he strode forward and grabbed a crate. Samm was overseeing operations at the gate, but Chaloner kept the box between his face and the chief gaoler, and strolled through it unchallenged.

Once inside, he followed the labourer in front of him to the kitchen, and deposited his crate. Then, when no one was looking, he ducked through a door he had noticed earlier, which led to a yard that was used for storing rubbish. The place hummed with flies, and the stench was enough to make him gag.

He settled down to wait for nightfall, although it was

not long before he wished he had chosen somewhere else to do it. The refuse festered in the heat, and every one of the countless flies that lived there seemed determined to walk on his face. He watched the shadows lengthen, then the sun set in a glorious blaze of red. The sounds of dusk began – guards talking in a desultory manner as food was distributed, the clatter of plates, someone singing a hymn before bed.

Only when silence reigned did he make his move. He opened the door, and his mission almost came to a premature end when he ran into a gaoler. The fellow opened his mouth to shout, but Chaloner knocked him senseless with a punch, bound and gagged him with strips torn from the man's own shirt, and hid him under a mound of vegetable parings in the yard.

He went to the Garden Court first, keeping to the deepest shadows. A guard stood sentry outside, but it was not difficult to distract him with a stone lobbed into some nearby bushes. Unfortunately, the door was barred from the inside, and try as he might, Chaloner could not open it. Frustrated, he hunted for another way in, but all the windows overlooking the Garden Court had not only been fitted with bars, but had been boarded over to prevent anyone from looking through them.

Eventually, he was forced to concede defeat, and supposed he would have to apply for a warrant after all. Then he explored the rest of the College, where he was disgusted, but not surprised, to discover that conditions for the prisoners were wretched – the two clean chambers he had been shown earlier were indeed a deliberate deception. He also learned that their dinner had comprised root vegetables and an inadequate amount of fish, but as fuel was deemed an expensive luxury, the inmates had been obliged to eat them raw.

There was a different story in the rooms allocated to Spring, Oudart and their cronies, however. These were spacious, freshly painted and each occupant had a proper bed. They also had lamps, which allowed them to spend their evenings drinking, dicing and playing cards. Fish had not featured in their evening meal – they had enjoyed roasted meat and fresh bread. Moreover, the doors to their cells had been left open, so they could come and go as they pleased.

A spell eavesdropping in the corridor outside allowed Chaloner to deduce that everyone was English with the exception of Oudart, who had a chamber to himself and was clearly not part of their coterie. He sat alone, staring at the wall with haunted eyes. Chaloner felt a surge of pity for the man. First, he had lost his ship and most of his crew, then he had suffered the humiliation of capture, and now he was Tooker's puppet – the tame Dutch officer trotted out to persuade inquisitive visitors that all was well.

Suddenly, there was a clatter of footsteps, and Chaloner had only just ducked into the shadows when Tooker and Samm arrived. As it was hardly normal for wardens to visit their charges after dark, he eased forward to listen to what was being said. Unfortunately, he had only just reached a good vantage point when two things happened at once. First, there were more footsteps as a guard approached from his right; and second, two of Spring's men emerged from the cell to his left. Chaloner was trapped in between them, and was going to be caught.

There was only one thing he could do. He strode

briskly towards the guard, keeping his head down and relying on the fact that the corridor was very dimly illuminated.

'Where are you going?' asked the gaoler, as Chaloner marched past him.

'Errand for Tooker,' replied Chaloner, not stopping.

There was a moment when he thought the bluff had worked, but their voices had alerted Samm, who came to see what was happening.

'Stop!' he commanded. 'You are not—'

Chaloner raced for the yard. Behind him, Samm bellowed for his men, who appeared with inconvenient speed. Chaloner knocked one down with a punch, and slashed at two more with his dagger, but he was running out of options. He tore towards the kitchen, with the wild notion of barricading himself inside until Kipps could be summoned to negotiate his release.

He faltered in confusion when he flung open the door to see someone standing at the table in the middle. It was Eleanore. She wore an old leather apron, and was holding a paring knife. Her face was wet with tears, and the whole room reeked of onions. He sagged. There was not enough time to subdue her *and* secure doors and windows. It was over.

'In here,' she hissed, moving away from the table and indicating an adjoining pantry. 'Quick!'

Every fibre of his being thrumming with tension, Chaloner watched her open a trapdoor that led to a cellar. He baulked at climbing through it, but his pursuers' footsteps were hammering closer, so he took a tentative step forward. Exasperated, she shoved him hard. He staggered down several stairs, and then was plunged into darkness as the door was dropped back into place.

Chapter 8

The cellar was pitch-black at first, but as his eyes grew accustomed to the lack of light, Chaloner saw a faint rectangle where the door did not quite fit. He eased towards it and peered through the crack, relieved when he felt a slight breeze waft against his cheek. At least he would not suffocate. However, he suspected he would not be there for long: Eleanore would tell Samm where she had so cleverly trapped him, and he would be dragged out for questioning.

The gap allowed him to see the table where she stood – and where she was quickly joined by two other women and a man, who entered the kitchen at a run, and promptly contrived to look industrious. One was rubbing sleep from her eyes, while the other two were unsteady on their feet from ale. The older woman elbowed Eleanore away from her diced onions, so that when Samm burst in seconds later, it appeared as though she, not Eleanore, had done all the work.

'Did a man just come in here?' demanded Samm. He looked dangerous, shadows accentuating his pugilistic features.

'Yes,' replied Eleanore. Chaloner braced himself, but she pointed to the fellow who stood next to her at the table. 'Jem Collier did.'

'Coming back from the latrine,' explained Jem in a West Country drawl so strong that it was barely comprehensible. He was a bulky individual with close-cropped hair and a rascally grin. 'I just come in. Before that, I was in here, working. You can see how many onions I chopped – more than enough for tomorrow. Ask my wife.'

'It's true,' agreed the older woman. She also spoke with the distinctive burr of the west. 'And Una and me ain't been nowhere neither. We've been in here, slaving away.'

She was short, fat and entirely bereft of teeth, so it was difficult to judge her age. Her clothes were of good quality but filthy, and she had not bothered to mend the hole in her sleeve or her unravelling hem. Her skin was pasty, and her hair had been subject to a careless application of dye, so was a peculiar shade of orange.

Una, clearly their daughter, was a younger, slimmer version of her dam, but with more teeth, albeit ones that were already spotted with decay. A bulge under her apron suggested there would soon be a third generation of Colliers. She had been pouting when she had entered the kitchen, and her expression had not changed since.

'We work our fingers to the bone here,' she told Samm sulkily. 'From dawn to dusk.'

'We do,' nodded her mother. 'We've been here all afternoon, chopping and slicing, without so much as a minute to slip off for a pipe.'

Even if Chaloner had not seen them arrive, he would have known they were lying. The single onion they had managed to process between them was in ugly lumps, a marked contrast to the neat mound prepared by Eleanore. Moreover, their eyes were dry, whereas Eleanore was still blinking tears. Like many of their ilk, they assumed a stupidity equal to their own in their dealings with others, which led them to imagine that lies would be believed if delivered with sufficient verve.

'Did a stranger come in here or not?' demanded Samm impatiently.

'Not that we saw,' replied the woman. 'Why? Has one of the prisoners escaped?'

Samm ignored the question and began to search, looking under benches and peering behind sacks of grain. Chaloner tensed when the gaoler poked his head into the pantry, and looked behind him, trying to see if there was anywhere to hide, but it was too dark to tell. He started to ease down the stairs anyway, groping his way in the pitch-black. The door rattled as Samm grabbed the handle.

'I assure you, no one is down there.' Eleanore's voice held a hint of mockery. 'How could there be? It is barred from the outside.'

'So?' asked Jem, puzzled. Then he released a hoot of understanding. 'Hah! It means the cellar must be empty, as no one can lock a door from the *outside* when they are *inside*.'

He laughed loudly, clearly delighted with his incisive analysis, while his wife clapped her hands in appreciation.

Samm slipped the bolt, grasped the handle and pulled. Light flooded into the cellar, and Chaloner tried to move more quickly down steps that were uneven and slick with moisture.

'No one came in,' said Eleanore, so crossly that Samm

turned to look at her, giving Chaloner vital moments to cloak himself in darkness. 'I would have seen. But what has happened? I hope none of the prisoners *has* escaped. I should not like to think that you are poking around in empty cellars, while some unprincipled Hollander rampages about.'

'It was an intruder,' said Samm shortly, slamming the trapdoor and returning to the kitchen. Heart still thumping, Chaloner clambered back up the stairs, and put his eye to the crack again.

'An intruder?' echoed Eleanore. 'Is it anything to do with—'

'You ask too many questions,' snapped Samm. 'And you will desist if you know what is good for you. This is a gaol for dangerous foreigners, and the less you know, the safer you will be.'

It was peculiar logic, and Eleanore obviously thought so, too. 'Why can knowing about the prisoners be—'

'Enough!' barked Samm. 'Why do you come here anyway? Reymes pays you handsomely to clean Buckingham House, so you cannot need the money.' He glanced at the Colliers, who were still persisting in their attempts to look busy. 'And I doubt it is for the company.'

'Here,' objected the woman, offended. 'What do you mean by that? We happen to be very *good* company. Just ask Mrs Bonney at the asylum – she thinks the world of us.'

Samm regarded her in distaste. 'Then she is a fool. But your lazy tricks will not work here, Lil Collier. I know your sort.'

He treated the family to a final glower, then left to rejoin the hunt outside. Lamps bobbed past the door as guards dashed this way and that, and there was a lot of

223

agitated shouting. He issued a stream of orders that made the lanterns jig even more urgently, and Chaloner watched them in despair. How long would they search? Until the intruder was caught? Grimly, he realised it would be a lot harder to leave the prison now that he had been seen.

As soon as Samm had gone, Lil tossed her knife onto the table and aimed for the bench by the hearth. Jem did likewise, tamping his pipe with tobacco and stretching his legs out in front of him with a sigh of contentment. Una started to join them, but Lil had something to say about that.

'What do you think *you're* doing?' she demanded. 'Chop them onions.'

'You do it,' pouted Una. 'I got backache.'

'I'm the one with backache,' growled Lil, as if it was an ailment that could only afflict one person at a time. 'I'm ill, me. I need to sit for a while, and have a smoke to calm my nerves. I'll have a bit of ale, too, so you can get me some before you start the onions.'

She accepted the pipe that Jem had lit for her, and leaned back comfortably. Eleanore shot a warning glance towards the trapdoor, cautioning Chaloner to stay put. He tried to calm his rising agitation: the Colliers were clearly settling in for a lengthy breather, and he felt trapped and vulnerable in the cellar.

'Do the onions, Una,' ordered Jem, when the girl perched on the table and began to pick at a broken fingernail. 'Your mother needs to sit down, and they won't do themselves. And Ellie here won't be no help. She prefers to ask questions than to work.'

Eleanore shot him a contemptuous look but did not

argue, while Una removed herself from the table and contemplated the waiting vegetables with a face as black as thunder. Her parents ignored her sullen temper, and Chaloner had the sense that friction in the family was the norm. Doubtless there would be even more of it when the baby arrived.

'Yet you can't blame Ellie for asking questions about this place, Jem,' said Lil, looking around in distaste. 'I sensed there was something odd about it the moment I set foot inside, and I ain't never wrong about that sort of thing.'

A sudden barrage of shouts from outside suggested that the guards had discovered something significant. Chaloner supposed they had found the man he had knocked out and left in the fly-infested yard.

'They say it was once called Controversy College,' said Jem, and to prove he was the brains of the family, he added, 'That means the men who came here argued a lot.'

'Same as now, then,' mused Lil. 'Nothing has changed.'

'Perhaps it should be called Controversy Gaol,' quipped Jem, and laughed uproariously.

'That Buckingham House crowd is odd, too,' said Lil, when she could make herself heard. 'It's all noise and merrymaking without stop. I like a good time myself, as you know, but those courtiers . . . well, they're unnatural.'

'They sang bawdy songs all last night,' put in Una. 'They knew some I ain't never heard, which makes you wonder about the company they keep. Did you know they brought whores from Southwark to keep them entertained?'

'They should have recruited local lasses,' said Lil

disapprovingly. 'I could have done with the business, and so could you.'

Chaloner suspected that Reymes' guests would have opted for an early night if the likes of Una and Lil had been on offer. He moved slightly, so he could see Jem's face, but the man did not react to the notion that his wife was ready to sell her favours.

'I don't like that rectory neither,' Jem was saying, purse-lipped. 'Wilkinson . . . well, all I can say is that they never had *his* ilk in Bath. I asked him to pray for your bad back, Lil, and do you know what he said? That I was to bugger off!'

'You leave my back alone,' ordered Lil, aggrieved. 'I like it just the way it is.'

Chaloner was sure she did, lest a cure affected her status as family invalid. Meanwhile, Eleanore's attention was fixed on Jem.

'What is it that you do not like about the rectory?' she asked. 'Have you seen something odd happening there?'

'Yes, I have,' declared Jem importantly. 'Namely lights in the attic – in the dead of night, when decent folk should be asleep. I tell you, that vicar is a funny devil.'

'He is, but he had nothing to do with throttling your sister, Ellie,' said Lil kindly. 'Churchmen don't go around strangling people, not even the strange ones.'

Chaloner listened in astonishment. Nancy was Eleanore's *sister*? He grimaced his exasperation. Why had she not told him? There had been no need for subterfuge, and how was he supposed to get to the bottom of the matter when the victim's kin declined to cooperate?

'Things are afoot in Chelsea that you know nothing about, Ellie,' Jem was stating with authority. 'If you don't want to follow Nancy to the grave, you would be wise to leave well alone.'

'You would,' agreed Lil, then heaved herself to her feet. 'I need to go home and lie down, Jem, but first we'll stop at the Swan for a drop to drink. I have a terrible thirst on me tonight.'

'We can't, Lil. Landlord Smith will want to be paid what we owe, so we'd better go to the White Hart instead. Our credit is still good there.'

'But the ale is better at the Swan,' said Lil. 'And that Smith *will* serve me – unless he wants his name blackened around the village.'

'Or I could put a curse on him,' offered Una brightly.

'You stay here and finish them onions,' said Lil, waddling towards the door. 'I'd help, but my back is bothering me something cruel.'

'On my own?' cried Una, as Jem began to follow. 'But that ain't fair!'

'It ain't fair that I got a bad back,' countered Lil loftily. 'You don't know how lucky you are, girl. Now get chopping, while I go for a drink to dull the pain.'

'I'm *not* lucky,' pouted Una when her parents had gone. 'I'm put upon, that's what I am. She lounges about all day, pretending to be ill, while I do all the work. I hate both of them, and I wish they were dead. In fact, maybe I'll put a curse on *them*. I can do it, you know. I watched old Mother Hitching, and I know how it's done.'

'Best not,' counselled Eleanore. 'Go and meet your friends instead. I will finish up here.'

Una did not need to be told twice. She tore off her apron, and was through the door almost before Eleanore had finished speaking. Chaloner waited to be let out, but Eleanore merely picked up a knife and turned back to the table. He shoved impotently against the door, alarm rising in a flood. Did she mean to keep him there permanently?

Eleanore's caution was not misplaced: within moments two armed gaolers marched in and began a systematic hunt of the kitchens. They worked with professional detachment, and Chaloner knew they would search the basement. He groped his way back down the steps, and fumbled in his pocket for the tinderbox and candle stub he always carried. He flinched at the noise the flint made as it struck, and was glad it took no more than two cracks before the candle was lit.

The cellar was huge, and comprised a number of rooms stretching off into the distance. Some had been used to store fruit, flour and other foodstuffs, while others held broken furniture, mouldy bales of straw and logs. One contained a musty pile of coal and some old sacks, so Chaloner blew out the candle and burrowed beneath them, struggling not to cough. It was not long before he heard the trapdoor open, and the guards descended the stairs.

He waited, taut with tension as they drew closer. Then a lantern flickered in his doorway, and the pair began to prod about with sticks – one jab grazed down his leg. He braced himself to leap up and fight, although as his sword was stowed with his hat in the ditch outside the gatehouse, it would be an unequal contest at best.

'I might come and get some of this later,' murmured one, picking up a lump of coal. 'For the winter. The government taxed it so high last year that we could only afford a fire every other day.'

The remark signalled their exit from that room, and

Chaloner allowed himself to breathe again as they moved to the next one. Eventually, they finished altogether, and he heard the trapdoor close behind them. He struggled out from under the sacks, and groped his way back to the stairs, arriving just in time to hear Samm inform Eleanore that it was dangerous for her to be in the College unaccompanied, so he would escort her home.

'Thank you,' she replied graciously, while Chaloner's stomach lurched anew. Would she leave him there all night? 'I will call you when my work here is done.'

Chaloner expected Samm to tell her that she would go at his convenience, not hers, but the gaoler only inclined his head and left. Eleanore waited until the door had closed behind him, and hurried to the pantry. The moment she unfastened the bolt, Chaloner darted out in relief.

'You should not have broken in,' she whispered. 'Tooker and Samm will kill you if they think you are spying.'

'So I gathered,' said Chaloner drily.

'And you should have no need to skulk, anyway,' she went on. 'Not if you are telling the truth about carrying the authority of the Lord Chancellor and the Spymaster General. Those should be enough to see your questions answered.'

'Only if what is happening here is legal,' Chaloner pointed out. 'I tried asking politely, but Tooker declined to cooperate. And he is not the only one who tried to lead me astray – you should have told me that Nancy was your sister.'

Eleanore met his gaze evenly. 'It is difficult to know who to trust, and Nancy was important to me – which is why I have been investigating her death myself. I took

229

jobs here and in Buckingham House, hoping to learn something important. I tried to get one in Gorges, too, but Mrs Bonney said she did not need me, because she has the Colliers.'

Chaloner was desperate to leave the prison and its secrets – Eleanore included – but the yard was still full of bobbing lanterns, which meant he was going nowhere just yet. He took up station by the window, ready to hide again if anyone approached.

'I understand why you think Buckingham House might hold answers,' he said, aiming to distract himself from his rising agitation by seeing what he could learn from her. 'It is next to Gorges, and one of its guests might have seen or heard something to help. But why here?'

Eleanore leaned against the table, her eyes distant. 'Chelsea was a quiet backwater until a few weeks ago, but then curious things started happening at four different locations – here, Buckingham House, Gorges and the rectory.'

'What manner of "curious things"?'

'Odd comings and goings, an influx of strangers, three murders and a roaming spectre.'

'What have you discovered about them?'

'Nothing,' she admitted reluctantly. 'At least, nothing yet. But there are connections . . .'

'Connections?'

'Between this place and Gorges, for a start. Parker and Franklin physick the inmates of both; Mr Cocke manages the accounts of both; and the Colliers skivvy in both.'

Chaloner recalled what had been reported about the Colliers when the board of governors had met in

230

Clarendon House – that they had been living at Gorges' expense for several months, but were not yet the asset that had been anticipated. Having seen them, he understood why they had failed to live up to expectations.

'How did they win themselves such an easy existence?' he asked. 'And why award it to a family from Bath? Were there no deserving locals who wanted the posts?'

'Not really – this is a wealthy village. And Jem and Lil came with excellent references from their previous employers. Mrs Bonney showed me the letters.'

'Has she never heard of forgery?'

'That was my first thought, but the testimonials were beautifully written on expensive paper. The Colliers could never have produced anything so fine.'

'Perhaps not, but they could pay someone to do it for them.'

'They could,' acknowledged Eleanore, 'but they are incapable of distinguishing between high-quality documents and cheap imitations, and will assume that others are, too. They would have chosen a less expensive option – and you and I would not be having this conversation.'

'Perhaps,' acknowledged Chaloner. 'Yet I cannot imagine anyone praising that family. Their testimonials *must* be false.'

'Or penned by someone who wanted them to take employment on the far side of the country,' she countered wryly. 'To be well and truly rid of them.'

It was a good point. 'Regardless, they are clearly undeserving of Gorges' charity, so why does Mrs Bonney not send them packing?'

'Because no one at Gorges has caught them shirking yet, although I think Dr Parker has come close. I know the truth, but no one takes any notice of a poor widow.'

231

Chaloner regarded her askance. 'Why would anyone take their word over yours?'

Eleanore winced. 'I suffered a terrible melancholy after John's death. I am recovered now, but people remember that I was not in my right mind for a while.' She smiled wanly. 'It must run in the family, because Nancy had one, too.'

'Is that why she was in Gorges?' Chaloner was still uncomfortably aware that the hunt outside was showing no signs of abating.

Eleanore nodded. 'For her, it was the sadness of losing a baby. But she was almost cured, thanks to Dr Parker and his coffee.'

'Whose baby?' asked Chaloner, recalling what Wilkinson had claimed about Nancy.

Shock flared in Eleanore's eyes and her jaw dropped. 'Why, her husband's, of course. What a terrible thing to ask! Nancy would never have entertained another man. And *he* did not kill her, lest you think to suggest it.'

'So you have told me already, but I still need to speak to him. I tried yesterday, but his bell-foundry was mysteriously abandoned. Did you warn him that I might visit?'

'I told him that you had come to find Nancy's killer, but I did not recommend that he should disappear. Perhaps the spectre did – our resident ghost has been very active of late.'

'Ah, yes, the spectre. Some folk tell me that it is Sutcliffe, while others claim it is a woman, on account of its light tread. What do you think?'

Eleanore considered the question carefully. 'Not a woman – none of us have the time for that sort of nonsense. It could be Mr Sutcliffe, though – it is the right height and build. But why would he do such a thing, especially as he no longer lives here?'

Chaloner had no answer, so he turned to another subject. 'Have you ever been inside the Garden Court?'

'Not since Mr Tooker installed some dangerous prisoners there. I saw a list of their names in his office once. None looked Dutch, so I suppose they are captured mercenaries, like Spring.'

'Can you remember any of these names?'

'Just three: John Lisle, Will Say and William Cawley.'

Chaloner's stomach somersaulted. 'Are you sure?'

'Yes, why? Do you know them?'

'No,' lied Chaloner. He reached for the door handle. 'But I need to see this list for myself – tonight, if possible. Where was it exactly?'

Eleanore blinked. 'You mean to look for it *now*? Are you insane? You will be caught!'

'We shall see.'

The search had moved to the Garden Court, although sentries had been posted at the door, which meant it was impossible for Chaloner to take advantage of the fact that it was unlocked. It did, however, allow him to slip out of the kitchen and steal towards the gatehouse. Meanwhile, Eleanore called for Samm to take her home, and once the chief gaoler had gone, the frenetic atmosphere eased considerably. Better yet, Samm's absence meant that Tooker was obliged to supervise the hunt himself, leaving his quarters unattended, which enabled Chaloner to sneak inside them with no trouble whatsoever.

He started with the paper-loaded desk, which held so much inconsequential nonsense that he supposed Tooker had amassed it for the sole purpose of convincing visitors that he was busier than was the case. He searched the rest of the office quickly, then repeated the operation in a bedroom that reeked of cheap perfume and tobacco. The only other chamber in the warden's suite was a pantry, which held an eclectic array of salt-stained goods – the prisoners' belongings, which had either been confiscated or exchanged for favours. Unfortunately, there was no sign of the list.

He returned to the office, and stared at the desk. Then he smiled – there was an inconsistency between the size of the drawers on the outside and the space available on the inside. He set to work, and it was not many moments before he identified the one with the false bottom. He lifted it out to reveal a veritable treasure trove of documents and records.

On top lay a book listing all the bribes – money and goods – that had been taken from the prisoners, along with their estimated value; each entry had been initialled by Samm. There were also papers detailing 'expenses' paid to some of the staff, along with a bill of sale for firearms, although the latter was far in excess of what should have been needed for guarding prisoners, no matter how dangerous they were alleged to be. Most were covered in dirty fingermarks, making Chaloner wonder what Tooker had been doing with them.

Finally, he found what he was looking for – a list of names, although someone had been careless with a flame, because the bottom of it had been burned off. There were ten on the undamaged part, and he estimated there had been two more below, making a dozen in all. As Eleanore had said, it began with Lisle, Say and Cawley.

One advantage of having a regicide uncle meant that Chaloner knew the identities of all those who had played a role in the old king's trial and execution, and six of the men on Tooker's list had done just that. Say and Cawley had signed the death warrant; Lisle had sat on the tribunal; Andrew Broughton and John Phelps had prepared the relevant paperwork; and Ned Dendy had been the court's Sergeant at Arms. All were thought to have fled to Switzerland at the Restoration, to escape the Royalists' bloody revenge.

The last four comprised two infamous rabble-rousers and a pair of controversial clerics. The newsbooks had carried stories about them the previous year; all were said to have sailed to New England, where the laws against radical religion and politics were less rigid.

Chaloner stared at the paper in his hand. Were these men being held secretly, so their supporters would not storm the prison to set them free? It would certainly explain why security was so intense, and claiming that they were unruly Dutchmen was an excellent ruse.

So what was going to happen to them? More public executions would create martyrs, so that was unlikely. Would they be locked up quietly for the rest of their lives? Slyly murdered, so that no one would ever know their fate? Or was the list an invention – a collection of names intended to frighten away the curious? After all, how could so many formidable dissidents have been arrested without the tale leaking out?

Still, he was sure about one thing: Spymaster Williamson did not know what was happening, because if he had, he would not have asked Chaloner to pry there – he would have ordered him to stay well away and mind his own business. So who *did* know? Members of the government? The King? One of the country's many power-hungry barons?

Suddenly, footsteps sounded on the stairs. Chaloner shoved all the papers and the ledger inside his shirt, closed the secret drawer, and retreated to the pantry. Moments later, the door clanked and Tooker bustled in. The warden removed his Guy Fawkes hat and cloak, flopped into a chair and began to tamp his pipe. His hands were filthy, and Chaloner cringed at the notion that documents Tooker had touched were now nestled against his own bare skin.

Tooker leaned back in his chair, gave a weary sigh and closed his eyes. He was alone, and it was too good an opportunity to pass up, so Chaloner slipped out of his hiding place, sneaked up behind him and grabbed him around the neck. Tooker struggled in alarm, although he desisted when he felt the prick of steel against his throat.

'Oh, God!' he croaked in terror. 'It is an inmate, come to murder me.'

Chaloner saw no reason to disabuse him. It would be a lot more convenient if Tooker never found out that the Lord Chancellor's spy was the invader his men were so feverishly seeking. He whispered, to prevent the warden from recognising his voice, and effected a strong Dutch accent for good measure.

'The prisoners in the Garden Court are not my fellow countrymen. What are they—'

'Do not ask me about them!' gulped Tooker. 'They are dangerous, and I fear for my life on a daily basis. But I can tell you no more – the government does not confide in me. I am just under orders to house them until further notice.'

'So they are guests of your government?'

'Of course! Who else would want people locked up? Please let me go. I am a—'

'Something odd is happening in this prison. Certain comings and goings . . .'

'You mean the whores?' bleated Tooker. 'Yes, I let a few in every so often. It is irregular, I know, but better that than dealing with lust-crazed inmates. I did the same in Newgate, and we never had any trouble. Tell me your name, and I shall arrange for one to visit you as well.'

Chaloner was sure he would – along with Samm and a sharp knife. 'Do you supply them to the occupants of the Garden Court?'

Tooker managed to shake his head. 'It would be too risky. I told you: they are dangerous.'

'You *do* know who they are,' stated Chaloner, pressing his blade harder against Tooker's throat. 'So I want their names and why they—'

'I do not!' objected Tooker. 'The government has always recommended that I remain in ignorance, and who am I to question the advice of powerful men?'

'I think I shall kill you,' whispered Chaloner, as menacingly as he could. 'You are corrupt and devious, and you make yourself rich at our expense.'

'No!' squeaked Tooker, struggling frantically. 'Please! I am an honest man.'

Chaloner pulled the ledger from his shirt with one hand, while keeping a firm grip on his captive with the other. 'This says otherwise.'

'I have never seen that before,' squawked Tooker. 'What is it?'

'Evidence that you accept bribes from us in exchange for favours. And that you pay your men to keep their mouths shut and ask no questions.'

'Oh, *bribes*.' Tooker sounded relieved. 'All wardens

take those, so it is expected of us. Samm keeps a record, does he? I did not know. And of course I pay my gaolers not to babble. We cannot have them blathering about our security arrangements to all and sundry. But tell me what *you* want, and I will give it to you, no questions asked. Just list your demands.'

At that moment, Chaloner heard the guards through the open window, asking each other where the warden had gone. Unless he wanted to be caught with a dagger pressed to Tooker's throat, it was time to leave. He hauled Tooker to the pantry, bundled him inside and locked the door.

'Stay there and keep quiet,' he ordered. 'One squeak, and you will never be safe again.'

There was silence from within. Suspecting it would not last long, Chaloner donned Tooker's hat and cloak, and ran down the stairs. Outside, the search was still underway, although it was less urgent, as the gaolers began to suspect that their quarry was no longer there.

Chaloner strode towards the gate, keeping his head down to conceal his face. The gaoler on duty snapped to attention, then politely ushered 'Warden Tooker' through the wicket door, wishing him goodnight as he did so.

Chapter 9

The next morning dawned hot and clear. Chaloner rose as soon as light began to streak the eastern sky, leaving Kipps and Wiseman snoring fit to raise the dead, and went downstairs, where Smith was serving breakfast ale and sweet buns dappled with currants. Chaloner refused the buns – they were obscenely sticky, as several wasps had discovered to their cost – and was brought a slab of old bread and runny cheese instead. These were slapped down so irritably that he wondered why Smith had opted to pursue a career in the hospitality business.

While he ate, he dashed off letters to the Earl and Williamson, outlining his findings and asking each for a warrant to explore the Garden Court. He paid Smith's eldest son a shilling to deliver them with all possible haste, but Williamson received piles of urgent correspondence every day, while the Earl had an annoying habit of ignoring messages from his staff, so Chaloner had no great expectation of a speedy response from either.

Then he sat back and reviewed all he had learned to date, aware that he still had far more questions than answers. However, he was sure about one thing: Eleanore was right – everything did revolve around the four locations she had mentioned.

First, the College. *Were* there dissidents in the Garden Court, and was Tooker telling the truth when he said that the government was involved? Was it significant that three suspects for the murders – Commissioners Reymes and Doyley, and its accompter Cocke – had connections to the place? Chaloner drummed his fingers on the table, recalling that Thurloe, whose opinion he trusted, had told him to concentrate his enquiries there. Moreover, Underhill had begged Williamson to send his own spies to the prison, because he sensed that something was amiss. Unfortunately, there was nothing Chaloner could do until he had his warrant, so the gaol would have to wait.

Second, Buckingham House. Kole had been murdered in it, and two suspects – Reymes and Cocke – lodged there. Why had Reymes invited so many debauchees to stay with him? Chaloner did not believe for a moment that it was to keep them safe from the plague, as the commissioner was alleged to have claimed; or that it was to curry favour with the King, as Greeting had suggested. After all, why would His Majesty care about the welfare of courtiers he had so readily abandoned? However, Reymes was holding a soirée that evening, so Chaloner decided to join it, and see what might be learned by watching the guests at play.

Third, the rectory. Wilkinson was not a pleasant man, yet several witnesses had mentioned an unusual number of visitors. Was Kipps right, and they were just folk fleeing the plague? But if their presence was innocent, why had they ducked out of sight when he had seen them at the window? He made a mental note to ask

Doyley when he next saw him – if there was anything odd going on, the commissioner would know, because he was staying there.

And last, Gorges. Nancy had been strangled in its orchard, Underhill and Kole had been on its board of governors, and four suspects – Parker, Franklin, Mrs Bonney and Cocke – continued to serve in that capacity. Dorothy had written to Wiseman about peculiar happenings there, but could her testimony be trusted? And who was the thief? Had *he* – or she – killed Nancy, Underhill and Kole, perhaps to protect himself from exposure? Chaloner decided to visit the asylum that morning, to see what more he could find out about it and its occupants.

He looked up as Kipps and Wiseman approached his table. Kipps was immaculate in lacy livery, spotless shoes and smart coat, but Wiseman had decided that it was too hot for formal clothes, so he had donned a flowing red robe that made him look like the proprietor of a Turkish brothel.

'Eleanore Unckles was asking after you yesterday,' said the surgeon disapprovingly. 'She wanted to know if you were telling the truth when you claimed to be in Clarendon's employ. I told her to mind her own business.'

'Did you?' Chaloner was surprised – Wiseman was not usually rude to pretty ladies, although less attractive ones could expect to be treated with the same rank disdain as most men.

Wiseman shrugged. 'Her questions made me suspicious. Why did she want to know?'

'*I* talked to her,' said Kipps, which Chaloner suspected had been solely because Wiseman had given her short shrift. 'She is a handsome lass, although I doubt her thighs can compete with Lady Castlemaine's. But whose could?'

'Temperance's,' declared Wiseman loyally. 'And Dorothy's were not bad when she was in a position to keep them trim.'

'You mean Temperance North?' blurted Kipps in astonishment.

'Yes,' said Wiseman shortly. 'She is an angel beneath all those face-paints.'

Sensibly, Kipps chose not to comment, and turned back to Chaloner instead. 'Eleanore is a comely woman, Tom. You should make a move on her – she likes you.'

'She is pretending,' said Wiseman harshly, dashing Chaloner's brief surge of pleasure. 'In the hope that you will tell her your business here. Do not fall for it, Chaloner. She is a very dangerous woman.'

'Dangerous?' scoffed Kipps. 'What nonsense is this?'

Wiseman regarded him pityingly. 'She set out to charm us in the hope of gleaning information about our business here. Well, all I can say is that I hope you did not tell her anything that puts Chaloner in danger. You, I do not care about.' He turned his back on the startled Seal Bearer. 'Stay away from her, Chaloner. She is not what she appears.'

'And this from the man who courts Temperance North,' muttered Kipps, although he had the sense to speak too softly for the surgeon to hear. He smiled at Chaloner. 'Take her, Tom. You will not be disappointed.'

'I cannot,' said Chaloner, unwilling to have Kipps *or* Wiseman breathing down his neck if he did, and so aiming to throw them off the scent. 'I am still in mourning.'

Kipps winked. 'I will not tell. Of course, I cannot speak for Wiseman . . .'

'I do not gossip about other men's stupid indiscretions,' declared Wiseman. 'However, while it is good to get back on a horse after a fall, I strongly advise you to choose another mare.'

Chaloner did not want to discuss it any longer. 'Did you learn anything about Nancy when you were at Gorges yesterday?' he asked the surgeon.

Wiseman eyed him lugubriously. 'I am here to protect my wife, not to act as your assistant. That is Kipps' prerogative, although he returned very late last night, reeking of wine, so I cannot imagine he did much that was useful.'

'Then you imagine wrong,' snapped Kipps, even his amiable disposition beginning to sour under the surgeon's abrasive assault. 'Because I gathered a great deal of interesting intelligence.'

'Such as what?' asked Wiseman sceptically.

'Well, for a start, someone visited Kole in his room on the night of his death. The person was wearing a long hooded coat, which was remembered because the weather is too hot for such a garment. It was probably the spectre – *inside* Buckingham House.'

'The spectre!' spat Wiseman. 'It will be a person under that ghostly attire.'

'Who saw it?' Chaloner asked Kipps.

'Lady Castlemaine. It took a while to wheedle it out of her, but I succeeded in the end.'

Wiseman snorted derisively. 'I hardly think she is a reliable witness. Moreover, she hates Clarendon, so is unlikely to help his minion. She was aiming to lead you astray, and will be laughing at the ease with which she has succeeded. You should have let *me* interrogate her.'

'She likes me,' said Kipps coolly. 'Indeed, she has

offered me a post in her household, should the Earl's fortunes continue to wane. I might accept.'

'You would be jumping from the frying pan into the fire,' scoffed Wiseman. 'Clarendon does teeter on the edge of oblivion, but she is not far behind. Why do you think she is here, not with the royal favourites at Hampton Court?'

'That will change when she presents the King with another bastard in December.' Kipps addressed Chaloner again. 'We *can* believe her, Tom – she has no reason to lie. And you should be grateful for my labours, because she would not have confided in you.'

That was true: the Lady had scant time for Chaloner. 'Did you learn anything else?'

'No, because everyone was drunk. But I shall try again today, and if there is anything to discover from the residents of Buckingham House, I shall have it out of them, never fear.'

'Do not hold your breath, Chaloner,' muttered Wiseman disparagingly.

As it was Sunday, everyone was obliged to go to church – those who refused were likely to be accused of nonconformism. Usually, most villagers walked to nearby Kensington, the rector of which was more congenial than their own, but a rumour that the plague was there meant no one was willing to risk the journey that day. As a consequence, All Saints' was bursting at the seams, and as it was not big enough to accommodate the locals, let alone visitors, there was a good deal of bad-tempered jostling, muttering and shuffling when interlopers inadvertently sat in regulars' pews.

Chaloner stood at the back, which allowed him to

observe his suspects. Reymes and Doyley were in the south aisle, Reymes dozing and Doyley trying to take a pinch of snuff without anyone noticing. They sat next to Cocke, who was ogling a young woman with a baby, his lust so flagrant that Chaloner wondered if there was something wrong with him.

The staff from Gorges were opposite, accompanying those residents who were deemed fit enough to go out. Dorothy was not among them, and Parker was also absent. Franklin and Mrs Bonney seemed tired, nervous and ill at ease, and it was clear that neither had slept well.

The Strangeways clan were in the pew behind Reymes, grandfather and son glowering at the back of his head, although the drowsing commissioner remained blissfully unaware of their simmering hatred. He jerked awake when Wadham poked a prayer book into his nape, which made the youth grin and do it again. He was preparing for a third prod when Reymes whipped around and tore the tome from him with such fury that Wadham blanched and did not move again until the service was over.

The Buckingham House contingent had claimed the best seats at the front, yawning, sighing and clearly resentful of the early rise. Brodrick, Greeting and Hungerford looked seedy, as did Ladies Castlemaine and Savage, although pretty Betty Becke had taken pains with her appearance, and was the recipient of many admiring glances, much to the dismay of Chelsea wives and sweethearts.

'Beloved in Christ,' came an almighty bellow from the narthex, which had everyone leaping in alarm. It was Wilkinson, clad in an elaborate cope that was usually reserved for Feast Days. He wielded an enormous thurible that belched clouds of pungent smoke, an unusual sight in a country that was violently adverse to any hint of popery. 'We are gathered here in the sight of God, so wake yourselves up, you idle buggers.'

He began to stride down the aisle, swinging the thurible around with such reckless abandon that the people he passed were obliged to duck or risk being brained. Incense billowed so thickly that several congregants began to gasp for breath. The visitors watched in open-mouthed astonishment, scarcely able to believe their eyes, although the flat expressions of the regulars suggested that this was nothing out of the ordinary. A ragtag choir followed him in, massacring a processional anthem by Gibbons. Chaloner cast a longing glance towards the door.

Wilkinson reached the altar, and curtly ordered his singers to 'stop caterwauling'. Then he raced through the sacred words at a bewildering lick, omitting large sections and informing his bemused congregation that if they wanted to hear the readings for that week, they would have to look them up for themselves.

'You cannot have Communion either,' he announced belligerently. 'I forgot to bring the bread, and there is only a tiny dribble of wine left – and I am having that.'

He downed it, gave an insincere blessing, and was off back down the aisle so fast that his choir did not realise he had left until it was too late to follow. Some tried, running full pelt, but most did not bother, and stayed to chat with each other in the chancel. Then Wilkinson stood in the porch and demanded donations 'for the poor' as his parishioners filed past him.

'Good God!' breathed Wiseman, stunned by the performance. 'I am no great believer in an overabundance of ceremony, but even I like a bit more than that.'

'It is said that odd things happen in his rectory,' muttered Kipps. 'But with a man like him living there, how could it be otherwise? The fellow is a lunatic!'

Chaloner managed to escape without parting with any money – he did not usually dodge the collection plate, but he was damned if he was going to give his hard-earned pay to the maverick Rector of Chelsea – and stood under a graveyard yew to watch his suspects emerge. Unfortunately, there seemed to be a conspiracy to distract him, as first he was joined by Wiseman and Kipps, then Akers from the gaol, and finally the landlord of the Swan.

'I heard there was trouble at the College last night,' Smith reported, looking hopefully at Akers for more information. 'The spectre broke in.'

'Really?' drawled Wiseman, while Chaloner supposed that was one way for Tooker to avoid telling anyone that he had been held at knife-point by one of his prisoners. 'I thought gaols tended to suffer from the opposite problem – people breaking out.'

'He went there to prowl,' elaborated Smith. 'Then he escaped by impersonating the warden. Tooker is badly shaken by the incident, and will apply for additional pay to alleviate the stress he has suffered.'

'Was it you, Mr Chaloner?' asked Akers, when the landlord had gone to gossip to someone else. 'If so, you are lucky to be alive. Samm is not a gentle man, and if you had been caught—'

'Of course it was not him,' said Kipps impatiently. 'He was asleep all night, as both Wiseman and I can attest. Besides, why would he invade the prison? We have a writ from the Lord Chancellor that allows us to enter legally.'

247

Akers nodded, but his eyes did not leave Chaloner's face. 'Security has doubled, so the culprit will not succeed again.' He looked away, then recoiled in alarm. 'Lord! Tooker is looking right at me, wondering why I am talking to you. I should have kept my distance, fool that I am.'

He scuttled away, head down and contriving to look so suspicious that anyone watching might have been forgiven for assuming that no prison secret had been left unrevealed. However, no one was, and Chaloner was fairly sure that Tooker was not even aware that Akers had been there. The warden seemed to sense that he was the object of scrutiny now, though, because he turned suddenly, and stalked towards Chaloner, Samm in tow.

'Did you hear what happened last night?' he asked. 'My prison was raided by the spectre. It assaulted me in my office, purporting to be a Dutch captive, and damn nearly killed me before making its escape.'

'That is worrisome,' said Chaloner. 'Because it means your security is seriously flawed. You had better show us the Garden Court before—'

'No,' interrupted Tooker sharply. 'We have our orders – the Garden Court is out of bounds to visitors, no matter who they are. As Samm told you yesterday, you must apply for a special warrant before we can let you in. I am sorry, but those are the rules, and they are for the safety of us all.'

'But we will not be found lacking again,' said Samm tightly. 'The next villain who tries to invade us will be shot on sight.'

'Are you sure it was the spectre?' asked Chaloner innocently. 'Not an inmate who is dissatisfied with your rule? Spring, perhaps, aiming to win himself even more freedoms?'

'It was the spectre,' said Tooker firmly, although his eyes were furtive. 'It was—'

Suddenly, there was a screech of furious indignation, and everyone turned to see Betty Becke, the Earl of Sandwich's vivacious mistress, glaring angrily at Cocke.

'My hand was hanging by my side when her posterior backed into it,' the accompter explained with a shrug. 'It is crowded here, and she was jostled. Chelsea needs a bigger church.'

'It does, so tell the government to give me back my Theological College,' called Wilkinson from the porch. 'Then we can hold services in its hall.'

'It is more useful as a prison,' countered Cocke. He turned back to Betty before the cleric could take issue. 'But come, my dear. We cannot allow a little misunderstanding to sour our friendship. We were getting along so well together.'

'We were,' she acknowledged stiffly. 'But I do not approve of lewd antics on holy ground. I have standards, you know.'

If she did, Chaloner thought, they must be very low ones.

'Then come to my room and tell me about them,' coaxed Cocke. 'I keep my London Treacle there, and I shall give you a jar if you do. It is blessed in St Paul's Cathedral by the canons themselves, so is the most effective anti-plague potion ever created.'

Betty made no objection when he ushered her away, although there was another squeal the moment they were through the lychgate. Chaloner turned to Kipps.

'We should visit Janaway again.'

249

'He is probably here,' said Kipps, looking around hopefully. 'Although as neither of us knows what he looks like . . . Hah! There is Eleanore – we shall ask her. I would sooner not traipse all the way out to the bell-foundry again, if it can be avoided.'

Chaloner was pleased when Eleanore murmured that she was glad he was safe. He smiled, but then a sudden image of Hannah flooded his mind – except it was not Hannah, because he could not remember the exact colour of her eyes. The realisation troubled him profoundly, and he decided he had better sketch her as soon as he had a free moment, as Janaway had done with his Nancy.

'We need to speak to your brother-in-law,' said Kipps affably. 'Which one is he?'

Eleanore regarded them reproachfully. 'I thought we had agreed to leave him be. Poor grieving man! He knows nothing, as I have told you already.'

'But he is a witness,' explained Kipps. 'We *have* to interview him, I am afraid.'

'I do not see why,' persisted Eleanore. 'He knows nothing, and talking to you will only upset him – even hearing Nancy's name reduces him to tears. Besides, he was not in church and he will not be in his cottage, so you are unlikely to find him today.'

She smiled prettily at Chaloner before moving away. His eyes were drawn to her hips as she went, but he was not too distracted to note that she continued past her own house and turned right at the top of Church Lane.

'She is going to warn him again,' said Wiseman, narrowing his eyes. 'Sly beggar!'

'Nonsense,' argued Kipps. 'She is just going for a walk.'

250

'In this heat?' drawled Wiseman. 'What an ass you are.'

'You are the ass,' flared Kipps. 'Look – she has just met another lady, and they are strolling along arm in arm, chatting together. There is nothing suspicious about her not going straight home.'

'So you say,' growled Wiseman. 'But I beg to differ.'

'I cannot abide Kipps,' declared Wiseman, as he and Chaloner strode along Church Lane towards Gorges. The Seal Bearer had gone to resume his interviews in Buckingham House. 'I wish you had not brought him with you.'

'It was the Earl's idea,' said Chaloner, hoping this would be enough to stem the surgeon's tirade. For some unaccountable reason, Wiseman respected Clarendon.

The ploy did not work. 'Kipps is a numb-witted fool, and you should disregard any intelligence he provides. Moreover, he carries a sword, but I have never seen him use it, although he says he fought in the wars. I, however, am rather good in a skirmish.'

Chaloner was startled by the claim. 'Are you?'

The surgeon flexed the muscles in his arm. 'Any adversary will know about *my* punches, believe me. And I have plenty of experience with knives.'

'Yes, but on patients and corpses. It is not the same as someone who wants to stab you back.'

Wiseman shot him a disdainful glance. 'Of course it is. A good many of my clients try to fend me off, while there have been several instances where a cadaver has—'

'No,' said Chaloner hastily. 'Save that sort of tale for tonight's soirée in Buckingham House. I am sure Reymes' prurient courtiers will provide an eager audience.'

Wiseman sniffed, offended to have been interrupted, and they walked on in silence. Chaloner breathed in deeply of air that was scented with hot earth and the scorched crops in the surrounding fields. Then a bird sang from a distant tree, and he suddenly understood why Chelsea was so oddly quiet – there were no funeral bells.

They reached the junction of Church Lane and the King's Road, where Chaloner paused for a moment to look towards the Bloody Bridge, but there was no smoke coming from Janaway's forge, and he was disinclined to walk there if the bell-founder was out. He was about to turn towards Gorges when he saw Strangeways and his kin inspecting the house opposite.

'What do you think?' called the old man. 'Would a coffee house fare well here? The garden backs on to Buckingham House, which will be convenient.'

'Convenient for what?' asked Wiseman. 'Reymes' guests to avail themselves of your wares?'

'For tossing our coffee grounds into his garden,' explained Strangeways gleefully. 'And if he does not complain of the reek, we shall deploy fish entrails and tobacco ash as well.'

'Tobacco is a very healthy substance,' averred Giles. He was puffing on his enormous pipe, producing such great clouds of smoke that Chaloner wondered if London should hire him to stand on street corners and fumigate the air. 'Anyone who does not use it is a fool.'

'It will not save you from the plague,' warned Wiseman. 'The only way to avoid infection is to find an underground cave and hide in it until all danger is past.'

'Yes, but that is not very practical,' said Strangeways.

'And what about our fish? They do not leap into boats and sell themselves, you know. Moreover, empty houses attract burglars.'

'As dozens of Londoners are learning,' agreed Giles. 'The plague is a boon for thieves, when so many homes lie empty because their occupants either are dead or fled.'

'Dead or fled,' mused Wadham. 'That is a fine rhyme. Perhaps I shall use it in a scurrilous ditty about Bullen Reymes.'

'Oh, yes,' said Strangeways eagerly. 'And what a wealth of apt words are at your disposal for him – maims, stains, drains, no brains, pains.'

'There he is,' said Wadham, pointing. 'Inflicting his nasty opinions on poor Doyley again.'

'He is coming towards us,' hissed Strangeways. 'Do you have your sword, Giles?'

'I hope you do not intend to stab him,' cautioned Wiseman. 'He is a servant of the Crown – a commissioner and the Treasury's prefect. You cannot go about dispatching royal officials just because they are ignorant scoundrels.'

Strangeways was still cackling his delight at the surgeon's opinion of his enemy when Reymes arrived, all stormy indignation. Doyley was frantically plucking at his sleeve in an effort to divert him, but the commissioner shrugged him off angrily.

'If you lot turn this cottage into a coffee house, I shall burn it down,' he declared hotly. 'You cannot put it here. The villagers do not want it.'

'Actually, they do, Bullen,' murmured Doyley. 'Your guests have shown them what life is like in the city, and they want to be fashionable, too.'

'Then they are fools!' snarled Reymes. 'Empty-headed sheep!'

'I hear your prison was invaded last night,' said Chaloner, grabbing the opportunity to ask its commissioners more questions about the place. 'Did you—'

'We *will* find the culprit,' vowed Reymes, looking hard at Chaloner before treating the Strangeways men to a similarly accusing glare. 'And he will not do it again.'

'It was the spectre,' said Doyley worriedly. 'Or so Tooker claims.'

'I heard a troubling rumour about the Garden Court yesterday,' Chaloner forged on. 'One that says its inmates are not Dutchmen, but dangerous radicals – regicides, no less.'

'Who in God's name told you that?' demanded Reymes irritably. 'Give me the gossip's name and I shall cut out his tongue. What a recklessly foolish thing to say!'

'So it is not true?'

'Of course it is not true!' snapped Reymes. 'Chelsea is a prison for Dutchmen: radicals are in the Tower, where they belong. Christ! How could anyone be so stupid as to start such a tale? The last thing we need is a lot of insurgents coming to demand the release of cronies who are not here.'

'It would be a waste of our resources,' agreed Doyley.

'You are not competent to oversee that gaol, Reymes,' Strangeways sneered. 'You should resign and let Doyley do it all. He is much better at it than you.'

'No, I am not,' objected Doyley in alarm, no doubt imagining the additional expense that would fall on three commissioners rather than four. 'Reymes is essential.'

'More is the pity,' growled Reymes sourly.

Chaloner remembered what else he needed to ask,

and turned to Doyley. 'You must find the rectory very crowded, filled as it is with Wilkinson's other guests.'

Doyley frowned. 'There are no other guests – just me.'

'I saw faces at his attic window,' pressed Chaloner.

'His servants,' explained Doyley. 'He has more than a single man with no family usually requires, but he is not a fellow who conforms to expectations, as you may have noticed.'

Chaloner had, but was about to ask more about the rector anyway, when raised voices stopped him: Reymes and Strangeways were engaged in a furious quarrel about the proposed coffee house. Doyley hastened to quell the burgeoning spat by begging Reymes to accompany him to the prison. However, when Reymes eventually allowed himself to be tugged away, it was not to the gaol that they went – Wilkinson was calling to them from his garden.

'Come and try this,' he was saying, brandishing a decanter. 'It is grass wine. My maid tells me it tastes foul, but I want a second opinion before I pour it down the drain.'

'I am glad *I* am not a commissioner,' said Wiseman fervently, watching the pair walk reluctantly through the gate. 'It is a post that carries rather too many undesirable duties.'

A short while later, Wiseman hammered on Gorges' gate until someone came to unlock it, then sailed towards the front door, which he opened without knocking, bawling for Mrs Bonney as he did so. Chaloner followed, immediately impressed by the house's bright, cheerful atmosphere. The walls were painted yellow or pink, the windows were thrown open to let in the light, and the artwork had been chosen for its uplifting colours and subjects.

Music emanated from one room, which drew him towards it, and he entered to see Hart playing a viol, while Bannister danced with a girl. Hart was surprisingly good, and when Chaloner saw a second instrument by the window, he was tempted to join in. Then it occurred to him that his performance might be indifferent, and he had no wish to embarrass himself in front of strangers, so he just stood and watched instead.

The dancing masters were clad in the same shabby attire that they had worn in London, although Hart had added a small gold earring to his ensemble, and Bannister wore a discreet diamond ring. Their shoes were scuffed, though, and Chaloner thought they should have invested their pay on more practical items.

'You see us at work,' said Hart with a smile, as the last note had faded and the dancers stepped apart. 'What do you make of her?'

'I think she is a fine instrument,' said Chaloner approvingly. 'Venetian?'

'Actually, I meant young Martha Thrush,' said Hart, wagging a mock-admonishing finger at him. 'Is she not very light on her feet, and the most elegant mover you ever saw?'

Martha was a plump girl of fourteen or so, who had not been elegant at all. There was something about her eyes that was familiar, although Chaloner was sure he had never met her.

'This is Mr Chaloner, who works for the Earl of Clarendon,' Bannister informed her. 'We met him in London a few days ago.'

256

The girl curtseyed politely. 'Are you here to find who strangled Nancy?'

'Martha is recovering from the shock of losing a brother,' explained Hart, before Chaloner could reply. 'She is making very good progress, and will soon leave us, alas. We shall miss her.'

'Nancy's room was next to mine.' All Martha's attention was on Chaloner. 'We were friends, and I can answer any questions you might have about her. She was as gentle a soul as you could ever hope to meet, and I cannot imagine why anyone would harm her.'

'Tell me about the thefts,' said Chaloner, deciding to accept her offer. 'Was she a victim?'

Martha nodded. 'She lost a pendant, although it was only made of tin, so was of no great value. I was deprived of a ring, but the villain ignored my jewelled reticule, which is worth six times as much. He took a watch from Dr Franklin, too, which near broke the poor man's heart, as it had belonged to his father. And Mrs Bonney was relieved of a nice plate.'

Chaloner thought about Underhill's report to Williamson, in which he had vigorously denied stealing the plate, although he plainly thought he was going to be accused. *Had* he been the culprit? He asked Martha the question.

'No,' she replied with utter conviction. 'Because there has been another theft since Mr Underhill died – Mrs Young's silver thimble. Personally, I would have taken her silk shawl, which cost a fortune, but the culprit is stupid.'

'So who are your suspects?' Chaloner asked. 'Another resident?'

'I do not have any suspects,' said Martha helplessly.

257

'No one here would steal – not the staff, and not the patients either. Unless it is the spectre. The villagers say that *it* killed Nancy . . .'

'Well, it has been out and about of late,' said Hart with a shudder. 'It has been spotted by any number of people, although not by me, thank God. Parker says it is Satan.'

'I saw it once,' said Martha unhappily. 'It seemed to be floating, and explains why Dorothy always calls it the batman.'

'Perhaps it floated in here then,' suggested Bannister, looking around uneasily. 'It is a very clever rogue, because it only ever steals when we are busy. Yesterday, for example: Mrs Young's thimble disappeared when Hart and I were hosting a singing competition. And Martha lost her ring during an afternoon of musical entertainment.'

Martha smiled wanly. 'Which means we all have alibis. Of course, there is also money missing. Thirty pounds, according to Mrs Bonney.'

'Martha Thrush,' came a booming voice. It was Wiseman, his bulk filling the doorway. 'You seem familiar. Are you any relation to the Thrushes of Southwark? They are patients of mine, a family of tanners. They all have big red noses.'

'No,' stammered Martha. 'None of my family have big noses, red or any other colour.'

'Pity,' said Wiseman. 'They owe me money from their last consultation, and you could have paid on their behalf. I shall never have it if they catch the plague, so time is of the essence.'

'Jeffrey and I tried to collect outstanding fees, too,' sighed Hart. 'In London. But it was simply too dangerous, so we decided to leave it until the plague is over.'

'Although I doubt the rogues will remember the debt,' said Bannister gloomily. 'They will have forgotten us, as is the way with most rich folk.'

Wiseman agreed, and the three of them began an indignant discussion on the matter, each eager to relate tales of wealthy clients' fiscal transgressions. While they outraged each other with their experiences, Chaloner went to Hart's viol. He sat on the chair and bowed a scale. Its tone was rich and mellow, so he began to play a dance, although he was painfully aware that his performance was mechanical and wholly devoid of expression.

'That is nice,' came Martha's shy voice at his side. 'But I think the strings need replacing.'

'You like music?' Chaloner was unwilling to admit that the problem might lie with him.

Martha nodded. 'Dr Franklin says that it is the best medicine available, and thinks that everyone should learn an instrument. Will you join me in a duet?'

'All right,' said Chaloner reluctantly, hoping he would not disgrace himself.

'It will have to be an easy one, though,' she said apologetically. 'Dowland?'

She began a soulful piece he had never much liked, which she did with a fierce concentration and a good many mistakes. He noticed that she had unusually large hands, and wondered why her tutors had not suggested the harpsichord or the virginals instead, where a large span was useful.

'Come now!' cried Hart, his shrill voice cutting through a particularly painful section. 'Why these dismal airs?'

'Because it was my brother's favourite song,' said Martha with a flash of defiance.

'Then he was a sad soul, and it is a pity he was not

happier,' said Hart firmly, removing the bow from her and setting it down. 'Shall we continue our dancing lesson now?'

Out in the hall, Mrs Bonney and Dr Franklin were waiting for Chaloner. Both looked tired, harried and anxious, and made no attempt to hide the fact that they resented his arrival – they would have preferred to deal with Gorges' problems themselves.

'You must be gentle when you speak to our patients, Chaloner,' warned the physician sternly. 'Some are in very delicate health, and we cannot have them distressed.'

'I told you: he will be the soul of discretion,' promised Wiseman. 'Now where is Parker? I want to talk to him about Dorothy.'

'He is unavailable,' said Franklin, exchanging a quick and very furtive look with Mrs Bonney. 'He is . . . running an important trial with coffee grounds.'

The cagily worded reply caused understanding to blossom in Chaloner's mind. 'Has he been experimenting on himself?'

'Of *course!*' exclaimed Wiseman. 'You are a genius, Chaloner! That would explain the eccentric behaviour in a normally rational man, along with the shaking hands, the restlessness and the irritability. What has he been doing, Franklin? Drinking large quantities of coffee?'

There was a moment when Chaloner thought that Franklin would deny it, but then the physician gave a resigned sigh.

'Yes, and eating raw beans. We have tried to stop him, but he is so excited about the possibility of a permanent cure that he will not listen.'

'I never experiment on myself,' declared Wiseman fervently. 'That is what patients are for.'

'He does that, too,' confided Mrs Bonney unhappily. 'But he is a fine *medicus*, and has healed many ladies who have been deemed past medical help by his colleagues, so we turn a blind eye.'

'I hope he has not been practising on Dorothy,' said Wiseman dangerously. 'Bannister and Hart have just informed me that she is an abysmal dancer, but she was once very light on her feet, so if Parker has done something to change her . . .'

'She might have been nimble years ago, Wiseman,' said Franklin kindly, 'but she is older now. Even if she were not deranged, she would have trouble gambolling about as she did in her youth.'

'What do you mean?' demanded Wiseman indignantly. 'She is still in her prime, just like me.'

After a short and rather awkward silence, Mrs Bonney offered Chaloner a tour of the premises, to which the surgeon tagged along uninvited. Gorges was a large house in the shape of an irregular E, with Dutch gables and Tudor chimneys. Most of the upstairs rooms were small, which suited a foundation that cared for twenty patients, and allowed a privacy impractical in other asylums. Downstairs, there was a large refectory, the ballroom, and a clean, airy kitchen. The gardens were prettily organised, and were visible through most of the windows.

Parker and Franklin lived in the village, but the rest of the staff had been allocated rooms on site. These ranged from the pleasant garret occupied by Bannister and Hart, which had been decorated with homemade cushions – although an expensive French clock and a

261

jewelled box were hints that they would have pampered themselves more if they had earned better pay – to the lofts above the stables, where the nursing staff slept. Mrs Bonney had a small but cosy chamber at the back of the house, placed so she could rise quickly if there was a problem during the night.

Suddenly, the peace was broken by the sound of clashing cymbals, followed by the bray of a trumpet and a lot of loud laughter. Chaloner assumed it was the inmates, but was curtly informed that Gorges' guests were more genteel, and that the racket emanated from nearby Buckingham House.

'Courtiers,' said Mrs Bonney darkly. 'Here to escape the plague.'

'What did you think of Underhill and Kole?' asked Chaloner. 'Were they good governors?'

'Yes, on the whole,' she replied. 'Mr Underhill was always reading, so was able to converse on many subjects, which was a delight to our more learned patients.' She lowered her voice. 'But he swore horribly when he thought no one was listening – like a street urchin. It made me wonder if he was telling the truth when he claimed to be heir to a large country estate.'

'I see,' said Chaloner, thinking it was not his place to enlighten her.

'Mr Kole was an odd fellow, though,' she went on. 'He liked to visit us at night, and once I caught him peering through the residents' keyholes.'

'Not Dorothy's, I hope,' said Wiseman, ready to be angry.

'No – the younger ones,' replied Mrs Bonney. 'Martha and Nancy. He said he was just checking they were safely inside, but there was something about the way his eyes glistened . . . it made me uncomfortable, to be frank, so I told him not to do it again.'

It was distasteful, and Chaloner was glad he had destroyed the sketches he had found.

'He was very short of money after losing the College,' she continued. 'So I am afraid he was my first suspect when things started to disappear. However, I actually had my eyes on him when my plate went missing *and* when Dr Franklin lost his father's watch. Thus I can tell you with absolute certainty that he was not the thief.'

'What about Underhill?' asked Chaloner.

'He was away in London for several of the thefts, so no. Besides, Mrs Young's thimble disappeared yesterday, by which time both he and Mr Kole were dead.'

While they had been speaking, Mrs Bonney had been opening doors, to show Chaloner the residents' rooms. All were clean, neat and cheerful. Then they reached the top floor, where the more serious cases were kept, including those who required constant supervision.

'Such as Dorothy,' said Mrs Bonney. 'A nurse sits with her day and night.'

'They are genuinely insane, rather than temporarily unwell?' asked Chaloner. When Mrs Bonney nodded, he asked, 'Then could one have escaped to strangle Nancy, Underhill and Kole?'

'No,' the housekeeper replied firmly. 'We are very careful about security. And even if one had contrived to get out, she would not have gone to Clarendon House, throttled Underhill and then come back again. They might be mad, but they are not stupid.'

Dorothy Wiseman's room contained a bed, a table and two chairs, all of which had been bolted to the floor, and a robust iron-bound chest that was too heavy for her to lift and toss about. There was a large window with stone mullions, which afforded splendid views of Gorges' orchard and the grounds of Buckingham House. A burly nurse nodded a greeting, then took the opportunity to slip into the corridor to smoke.

Dorothy herself was wearing a long white shift. Her feet were bare, and her thick hair tumbled around her shoulders in a raven mat, although attempts had been made to brush it. She was still a striking woman, and Chaloner was sorry that she had been reduced to such circumstances – and sorry that Wiseman should have lost his beloved spouse to an insidious brain-rot.

She regarded her husband blankly, before dropping to all fours and crawling into a corner, where she began to chew a wooden doll. The gnawing grew more frenzied as Wiseman approached, but ended abruptly when she gave the figurine a savage twist that ripped its head from its body. She flung both bits at the chest, where Chaloner saw that several other toys had suffered a similar fate.

'The batman, the batman,' she chanted. 'Lights and trouble. Oil and water.'

'She seems much better,' declared Wiseman, while Chaloner wondered how this poor creature had managed to write the letter he had seen. 'I told you dancing lessons would help.'

'She is calmer, certainly,' acknowledged Mrs Bonney carefully. 'However, I am not sure I would say she is *better*.'

'Rubbish.' Wiseman held out his hand. 'Come, love. Show us how well you can jig.'

He hauled Dorothy to her feet and began a gavotte that brought a smile to her ravaged features, at which point she began to cavort wildly. To Chaloner, her movements were uncoordinated and awkward, but Wiseman, whose lumbering was almost as bad, grinned in delight.

'There,' he said, when she eventually pulled away and went to stare out of the window. 'She has the tread of a fairy, just like me. The King himself has remarked on my lightness of foot.'

'Has he?' asked Mrs Bonney doubtfully, while Chaloner struggled not to smirk.

'Now, dearest,' said Wiseman, turning back to Dorothy. 'Tell Chaloner about the woman who died. You called Nancy the "property of your absent one", because she was wife to Tom Janaway, who has not visited you since.'

'The batman, the batman,' raved Dorothy. 'He stalks, he watches. Look!'

She pointed to the wall behind Chaloner, who turned to see that an inexpertly executed painting of an anatomy lesson had been daubed there. A man in red stood over a flayed corpse, hands raised as he pontificated to a group of mesmerised disciples. The entrails had been drawn in loving detail, as had the teacher, but the artist had evidently run out of steam by the time he had come to the audience, because they had been very carelessly depicted.

'A little something I created for her,' explained Wiseman modestly. 'To remind her of me. She always liked my drawings, and this represents some of my best work.'

Chaloner regarded him aghast. 'But the other patients have pictures of flowers and birds. I cannot imagine a grisly image like this will soothe a troubled mind.'

'Nonsense,' declared Wiseman, although Mrs Bonney shot the spy a grateful look. 'Who is the *medicus* here, you or me?'

Chaloner knew it was an argument he would not win, so he did not waste his time trying. He examined the painting more closely, and saw that one of the admiring spectators had been given a distinctly sinister leer.

'Who is that?' he asked.

Wiseman shrugged. 'Dorothy added him herself. He must be a member of staff.'

'No, he is not,' countered Mrs Bonney. 'I would never employ anyone who looks like him – he would frighten the residents.'

'He flies in the garden,' jabbered Dorothy, stabbing a bony finger through the window. 'And Death walks at his side.'

'She means the spectre,' whispered Mrs Bonney. 'She has seen it several times.'

Chaloner regarded the image thoughtfully. 'Could this be John Sutcliffe?'

'The nephew of the old Dean?' Mrs Bonney peered at it. 'It might, I suppose, although it is not a very flattering portrait of the poor man. I always considered him rather handsome.'

'Look,' hissed Dorothy, pointing again. 'Down in the garden.'

Chaloner went to stand next to her. Directly below was a sculpture of Neptune. Someone had given him a halo of daisies, and his customary trident had been replaced with a long feather, both of which rendered his noble pose faintly ridiculous.

'I did not want her looking at an implement with sharp prongs every day,' explained Wiseman. 'So I ordered it adapted. Now, we had better—'

He stopped speaking abruptly when Dorothy wheeled away, her eyes fixed on Chaloner. The spy was momentarily bemused, but then realised that her mad gaze was glued on the dagger in his belt. He shifted positions, so she could not see it, at which point she made a lunge for Wiseman's hat, in which was a large decorative pin. She had grabbed the ornament before the surgeon could stop her. An expression of savage glee filled her face as she cradled her winnings to her bosom.

'Oh, no!' gulped Mrs Bonney. 'Everyone out! *Now!*'

She was away in a flash, leaving Chaloner and Wiseman alone with a woman whose crazed grin suggested that she intended to do some serious harm.

'Dorothy!' barked Wiseman. 'Put that down at—'

The rest of the sentence was lost in Dorothy's howl as she swooped towards him. Wiseman was a powerful man, but even he was hard-pressed to keep the flailing point away from his eyes. Chaloner rushed to his assistance, and it took the combined strength of both to prise it from her fingers. All the while Dorothy wailed and screeched so loudly that Chaloner felt his ears ring.

'Hold her tightly,' called Mrs Bonney from the safety of the door. 'The nurse is fetching a soporific from Dr Franklin.'

The medicine arrived very fast, but even that short interlude allowed Dorothy to bite, scratch, kick, punch and butt. It was akin to holding a wild animal, a task rendered even more difficult as neither man had any desire to hurt her. It was not easy to make her drink Franklin's potion, either, and more ended up on them than inside her. Then, as suddenly as she had run amok, Dorothy relaxed. She smiled sweetly, so that Chaloner had a glimpse of the woman she might have been.

'Forgive me, Richard,' she said softly. 'It is the batman's fault. I shall sleep now.'

267

She closed her eyes, and after a few moments, her breathing grew slow and even.

'Lord!' muttered Chaloner, once they were outside and the door was locked again. He looked at Franklin. 'What do you usually do when she has this kind of episode?'

'Summon a lot of help,' replied the physician frankly. 'But they do not happen very often, because we keep sharp implements away from her – it is the sight of naked steel that puts her in a frenzy. Perhaps her marriage to a surgeon-anatomist is what pushed her over the edge.'

'Nonsense,' declared Wiseman indignantly.

While Wiseman discussed Dorothy's care with Franklin, Chaloner spoke to her keeper. It was tempting to believe that Dorothy – or someone like her – was the killer, especially as Underhill's report had raised the possibility that the spectre might be a woman, but it quickly became clear that this was impossible. All the less stable inmates were under constant and very strict supervision.

'They *have* to be,' the nurse assured Chaloner earnestly, 'or people would never send their wealthy kinswomen to be cured here, and Gorges would founder.'

It was a good point, and the more he spoke to her, the more certain Chaloner became that she was a reliable and conscientious worker, who would never risk her livelihood or her charges' well-being by letting them escape. He would have to look elsewhere for his culprit.

'Would you like to see my room?' He turned to see young Martha standing behind him. She pointed to the chamber next to Dorothy's. 'It is there. Nancy's is at the end – her things are still in it, because Mrs Bonney says it would be disrespectful to move them just yet.'

'Why up here?' asked Chaloner. 'With the mad . . . with the ladies who need to be locked in?'

'Because you can see for miles,' smiled Martha. 'Come and look.'

She opened the door to a room that was flooded with sunshine. It should have been sweltering, but the windows were open, and it was high enough to catch a breeze. It was decorated with pretty paintings and French furniture, and Chaloner saw an elegant walnut cabinet identical to the one in Clarendon House – which meant it was expensive. Thus Martha was no ordinary patient, and definitely not related to the tanners of Southwark.

When she felt he had complimented her domain and its knick-knacks with sufficient enthusiasm, Martha led the way to Nancy's chamber, which was smaller and more basic, as was appropriate for someone who had boarded free of charge. It was on the corner, so had two sets of windows, rather than the single ones in the others. The first boasted a splendid view north, all the way to the marshes, while the second – like Dorothy's and Martha's – overlooked Gorges' garden, Buckingham House and the rectory, where the distant figure of Wilkinson could be seen tending his compost.

Martha giggled when she saw where Chaloner was looking. 'He is obsessed by those middens – he is a very peculiar man. Perhaps *he* should be in Gorges.'

Chaloner did not think she would enjoy his company if he were. 'Did Nancy spend much time up here?'

Martha nodded. 'She and I looked out of her windows for hours together. Mrs Bonney did not approve, because Mr Reymes' guests can be very uninhibited. We had to pretend to be reading when she came to see what we were doing, but watching their antics was great fun.'

269

'Do you still watch?'

Martha's eyes filled with tears. 'I cannot bear to – not on my own. I would not understand what they were doing anyway, as she was the one who explained things. She was married, you see.'

'Christ!' muttered Chaloner, thinking it small wonder that White Hall's courtiers had such a dismal reputation among the general populace, if it required that sort of qualification to work out what was happening. 'The dancing masters said you will go home soon.'

She gave a wan smile. 'I still miss Edward terribly, but Dr Franklin tells me that means he was a fine brother and worthy of my love, which is a good thing, not a bad. Have you ever lost anyone who meant the world to you?'

Hannah had not meant the world to Chaloner, nor, if he was brutally honest with himself, had his first wife, although the child occupied a place in his heart that would never be filled by anyone else. However, he was not about to reveal such intimate thoughts to a vulnerable teenager, so he asked about life at Gorges instead.

'It can be very noisy at night,' she confided. 'Not just because of the parties at Buckingham House, but there is a horrible family living in the almshouse at the bottom of the garden – Lil, Jem and Una Collier. They often make unseemly rackets with their raucous laughter and drunkenness.'

Then her eyes narrowed – the clan in question had just walked into their garden. Lil and Jem slumped on the bench, and a flap of Lil's imperious hand sent Una slouching inside, presumably to fetch refreshments.

'They might be the Gorges thieves,' suggested

Chaloner. 'They are well placed to break in here when the staff and residents are busy.'

'That is what I thought, but they were in the garden when my ring was stolen. Mr Hart was bored playing the viol while Mr Bannister sang, and admitted to spending the whole time gazing idly out of the window. He says they were there all afternoon.'

'Working?' asked Chaloner doubtfully.

'Of course not. I saw them myself once or twice, and they were lying in the sun. They have an alibi for Mrs Young's thimble, too. It went missing during our singing competition, but they were polishing the hall floor at the time. Mr Bannister, who was nearest the door, said they grunted and grumbled without cease, and quite spoiled his enjoyment of the occasion.'

'I imagine so.'

Martha lowered her voice. 'It is not pleasant, knowing there are thieves and murderers at large. In fact, I am tempted to borrow Mrs Bonney's gun to protect myself. What do you think?'

'Mrs Bonney has a firearm?' asked Chaloner uneasily, thinking it was not the sort of thing that should ever be stored in an asylum.

'Yes, in case the Dutch prisoners ever escape, and come to ravage her.'

Chaloner doubted the bewhiskered Mrs Bonney would attract much amorous attention from the Dutch, and decided to confiscate the weapon before there was a mishap. 'Will you tell me more about Nancy?'

'She was gentle, kind and good, especially to Dorothy. I have tried to emulate her, but I do not have her patience. Or her courage. Dorothy can be wild when she is in one of her moods.'

'Dorothy,' mused Chaloner. 'She mentioned a "batman" . . .'

'Her name for the spectre, as I told you earlier. She painted it on the wall of her room, and she has captured its evil face perfectly – the way it looms broodingly from under its hood.'

Chaloner regarded her sceptically. 'How close were you to this figure when you saw it?'

Martha smiled shyly. 'My father gave me a Dutch telescope, so Nancy, Dorothy and I did not need to be close – we could see it quite well from a safe distance.'

She went to the walnut chest and removed a polished wooden tube with brass fitments. They were popular devices with sea-captains, although Chaloner had never seen one used on land. He put it to his eye, and was rewarded with a superb view of Wilkinson plying a trowel. Then he trained it on Buckingham House, and saw Kipps leaning fawningly over a recumbent Lady Castlemaine. He grimaced. So much for the Seal Bearer's offer to question other witnesses about Kole.

He was about to hand the instrument back when he saw a flicker of movement in Gorges' orchard. Hart and Bannister were chatting to Cocke, while Jem Collier sneaked through the trees towards them with the obvious intention of eavesdropping. They heard him long before he came close, and moved away. Jem reached the spot where they had been standing, and bent to retrieve something from the ground. Chaloner could not see what it was, but Jem shoved it in his pocket.

'Perhaps you should put this away until you leave,' said Chaloner, snapping the glass shut and starting to hand it back to her. 'Lest you see something you wish you had not.'

'I have not used it since Nancy died,' confided Martha. 'Would you like it? It might help you to catch her killer, and I should like to feel I am contributing, even if only in a small way.'

'Perhaps there is a *small* improvement in Dorothy,' Franklin was saying kindly to Wiseman, when Chaloner returned to the corridor. Mrs Bonney was nodding sympathetically. 'But it is best to be realistic, and I am afraid she will never regain her sanity.'

Wiseman glared at him. 'That is not what Parker told me. Can you not feed her more coffee, and see what that might do?'

'It will make her more agitated,' explained Franklin patiently. 'Coffee is a remarkable substance, but it cannot cure *all* forms of lunacy. If Parker said it would mend your wife, then I am afraid he spoke prematurely.'

Wiseman launched into another subject to mask his disappointment. 'I cannot say I approve of the family you have installed in the almshouse. They are not people I want near my wife.'

'The Colliers?' asked Mrs Bonney, startled. 'But they are fine, upstanding folk. Look at the references from their previous employers. No one could ask for more.'

She produced a sheaf of letters from about her ample person. Chaloner inspected them when Wiseman had finished, and was impressed by the fulsome praise lavished on the trio. Mr Dere from Bristol thought they were the most charming individuals he had ever encountered, while Monsieur le Raille from Cheltenham considered them conscientious, honest and virtuous. They had also worked for Sir Edward Hungerford, who had been delighted with the service he had received. As Eleanore had said, the testimonials were on good paper, and very well written.

'Are you sure these are genuine?' he asked.

'I wondered the same,' admitted Franklin. 'But I doubt Lil and Jem know any high-class counterfeiters, so we are obliged to give them the benefit of the doubt. However, they have changed since arriving here – all they do now is eat, sleep and grumble. Parker has been feeding them coffee in the hope that they will revert to their former industrious selves, but it has not worked yet.'

'Well, just keep them away from Dorothy,' instructed Wiseman belligerently.

Afterwards, Chaloner went to explore the asylum's grounds, still pondering the Colliers' references, and thinking that Franklin – and Eleanore – was right to question their authenticity. Of course, they were not the only documents of which he was suspicious.

'Are you sure it was Dorothy who wrote you that letter?' he asked of Wiseman, who had accompanied him. 'Because I cannot see her sitting down quietly with pen and ink.'

'Well, she did,' replied the surgeon curtly. 'She used to write to me a great deal, and it is not something one forgets. Besides, you read it – it was scarcely rational. Of course it was her.'

Chaloner remained dubious, but was disinclined to argue. Then they reached the almshouse, which was a pretty place set among mature trees. It had suffered under the Colliers' occupancy, though. Discarded clothes, half-eaten food and other rubbish had been left lying around outside, and what had once been a well-kept kitchen garden had been allowed to run riot. Dirty streaks trailed down the walls, and the door was chipped and stained.

Lil had not moved from the bench since Chaloner had seen her from Nancy's window, although she had been joined by Jem and Una. All three were smoking in an attitude of slovenly relaxation, despite the fact that it was a time when most honest people were at work. Chaloner took the opportunity to put a few questions about the murders.

'No, we never saw nothing,' Lil replied. 'We work our fingers to the bone for the honour of living here. And me with a bad back, too.'

'You do not leave most of the labour to Eleanore Unckles?' asked Chaloner coolly.

'Her!' sniffed Lil disparagingly. 'She takes bread out of good folks' mouths by offering her services at that prison. She don't need the money, and I got a brother who would like that job.'

'You are lucky to have her,' said Chaloner. 'It saves you from doing anything yourselves.'

Lil shot him a very nasty look. 'You watch your mouth, mister, or I'll put a spell on you. I'm a witch, see, and my curses *work.*'

'Unlike you, then,' muttered Chaloner.

'Witchery is illegal, madam,' said Wiseman icily. 'You cannot—'

'I do what I please, when I please,' declared Lil haughtily. 'And you ain't—'

'The Gorges thefts,' interrupted Chaloner, before she and the surgeon could begin a spat that might last some time. 'What do you know about those?'

'They got nothing to do with us,' replied Jem promptly. 'The spectre done it. I saw it creeping about when all the lunatics were with their dancing masters.'

A sly expression crossed Lil's face. 'I saw it, too, and

275

it looked like a woman. You might want to look in Ellie Unckles' house for hooded coats. She wants to know who killed her sister, see, and will stop at nothing to find out.'

'I saw you in the orchard not long ago,' said Chaloner to Jem, not gracing the accusation with a reply. 'Trying to spy on Cocke, Hart and Bannister. What did you pick up from the ground? Something they dropped?'

'I never picked up nothing,' declared Jem. 'I must have been buckling my shoe.'

Before Chaloner could challenge him, Lil sighed gustily. 'All this annoying talk means I got to lie down – it's made my back ache something wicked. Now go away.'

'I have cured hundreds of bad backs in my time,' said Wiseman, more menacingly than was appropriate for a medical practitioner and a potential client. 'Even the most infirm of beggars rise and walk when they see *me* coming. I am sure I can do something for you.'

'No,' gulped Lil in alarm. 'I got my own cures, thank you. Anyway, I don't hold with men poking about where they ain't got no business.'

'Cure me instead, then,' suggested Una slyly, patting her bulging stomach.

'Not that!' exclaimed Wiseman, shocked. 'It is dangerous. Besides, I am a surgeon, which means I *save* lives. I do not take them.'

'How about a few coins instead, then?' asked Jem hopefully. 'For a poor family, who ain't got no food, other than the scraps what the lunatics don't want.'

'Yes,' said Lil, greed lighting her eyes. 'A bit of money won't go amiss, and there ain't no one more deserving than us. Come on, I know you got some spare.'

Neither Chaloner nor Wiseman obliged, and foul

language followed them until they were out of earshot.

'Scavengers!' spat Wiseman. 'Mrs Bonney is a fool for keeping them on, and I suspect you need look no further for the Gorges thieves. Shall we break into their house and see?'

Chaloner laughed. 'You want to go a-burgling with me?'

'Actually, I thought you could do it while I wait outside or better yet, fetch Kipps to stand guard. He is more suited to such lowly antics than me. Well? What do you say?'

'Perhaps later,' replied Chaloner. 'After Reymes' soirée.'

In the orchard, Chaloner stared for several minutes at the tree under which Nancy had died, but it had been too long ago for any clues still to be there. All he learned was that it would be easy to scale the surrounding wall, and that Gorges was not as secure as everyone claimed. Moreover, the tree was invisible from the house, so he was not surprised that there had been no witnesses to the crime.

He returned to the Swan, to change into better clothes for his evening at Buckingham House, then took pen and paper from his bag. He sat at the table, closed his eyes, and tried to recall the details of Hannah's face. The picture that came immediately to mind was the peculiar 'Portuguese' hairstyle she had favoured for a few months, which involved two large waves on either side of her head. This had been abandoned when she had overheard someone say that she looked like a bat.

He began to sketch. A few quick lines caught the determined jut of her chin, but the hair looked ludicrous, so he screwed up the paper and started again. This time he captured her nose perfectly, but there was something

277

amiss with the eyes. He scrunched that up, too, and started a third. He yielded to the urge to ink in the batwings again, but the eyes . . .

He stared at the image, wishing he had been with her when she had died, then thought again about her last letter. What had she meant by her odd advice about peacemakers and dandies? Was it something to do with the libertines at Court – some of whom he would see that evening? Or by peacemakers did she mean the doves on the Privy Council, who had argued against war with the Dutch – men like the Earl? Or was Wiseman right, and it was all a nonsensical rant brought on by fever?

'Oh, dear,' said the surgeon, peering over his shoulder. 'The eyes are wrong, and that hair makes her look like a bat. Are you ready? Kipps is pacing like a caged lion downstairs, desperate to get back to Lady Castlemaine's thighs. I hope you are not expecting too much help for your investigation, because you will not get it from that dim-wit.'

They arrived at Buckingham House to find most of the courtiers in the ballroom, attempting to drink all the wine before the other guests arrived. The light was fading, so lamps had been lit, but they made the room airless and stuffy, and Chaloner was not the only one who pulled uncomfortably at his finery, wishing he could dispense with some of it.

Reymes was the centre of attention until Lady Castlemaine appeared, at which point he was abandoned without a backward glance. She suggested some games, and it was not long before the atmosphere turned raucous, much to the delight of the villagers congregating at the gate. A group of eccentrically clad musicians began to play, but their repertoire comprised nothing but rough jigs and drinking songs, which did little to raise the tone of the evening.

'No, I shall *not* be playing later,' replied Greeting shortly, when Chaloner posed the question. He cast a disparaging glance at the performers. 'Reymes hired that rabble from the Goat in Boots, and I would sooner die than join them.'

The violist sauntered away to play cards with Brodrick and Hungerford, and Chaloner looked around at the rest of the company. Reymes had been open-handed with his invitations, and his guests included locals as well as visitors. Doyley stood by a window with Rector Wilkinson, who was in the midst of a rant, if the furiously wagging finger was anything to go by. The staff of Gorges were nearby, watching the courtiers' increasingly wild antics with open disapproval. When Wiseman went to exchange greetings with them, Chaloner joined him.

'It was sweet of Reymes to ask us here,' whispered Franklin, 'but I would rather be with my patients. There is so much to do now that Parker is . . .'

'I doubt you will be missed if you slip away,' said Wiseman. 'Nor will I, difficult though that is to imagine, so I shall go with you. Reymes is already serving cheap wine on the grounds that most of his guests have reached the point where they cannot tell the difference. And I refuse to drink it.'

When they had gone, Chaloner wandered into the garden, and was surprised to see the Colliers there, awkward but defiant in their Sunday best. They hovered tentatively on the fringes of the gathering, but gradually grew bolder, and eventually reached the wine, which they proceeded to down as though there were no tomorrow.

279

'What a horde,' spat Reymes. He was standing by an open door, and made no effort to lower his voice. 'Fishmongers, rakehells, mad-doctors, Clarendon's spies, fanatics and almshouse scum.'

'You invited them, Bullen,' retorted Doyley, who had managed to escape from Wilkinson, and was recovering from the experience with a generous pinch of snuff. 'They are your friends.'

'They certainly are not! Most came without any invitation from me. The Colliers, for example. I would throw them out, but there would be a fuss, and I do not have the energy for it. I did include Clarendon's men in a moment of weakness, though – I feel sorry for them, nailing their pennants to such a mast. That pompous bastard will drag them—'

He broke off as Cocke staggered past with Ladies Castlemaine and Savage, jostling him roughly. None of the three stopped to apologise. A wave of noise drowned him out when he began speaking a second time – the musicians had embarked on a popular tavern song and the Colliers were singing along.

'That does it,' Reymes snarled. 'If anyone asks, say the sun has given me a headache, and I have gone to lie down. I am sure the party will carry on quite merrily without me.'

He stalked away, and Chaloner noticed that none of his courtly guests bothered to acknowledge him as he passed. Why did he squander his money on people who did not afford him even the most basic of courtesies? It was clear that he was not one of their set, and his hospitality would never be reciprocated. When he had gone, Chaloner went to join Doyley.

'Lord!' gulped the commissioner, starting guiltily when

280

he realised that Chaloner would have heard every word of the conversation. 'I hope you do not think that I share Bullen's opinions. I *like* Clarendon – he is one of the few high-ranking officials in this country with a modicum of decency.'

Then Cocke reeled towards them, having exchanged his two ladies for a pair of prostitutes. 'Which of these fine lasses will you have, Doyley?' he bawled with a leer. 'Or will you be a gentleman, and concede them both to me? They will probably have a lot more fun.'

Doyley's lips pursed in distaste. 'You are a Treasury accompter, Cocke. Such low behaviour is hardly commensurate with your post in society.'

'Bugger society,' slurred Cocke. He peered at Chaloner through bloodshot eyes, then wagged a dirty finger. 'Clarendon's spy, here to catch thieves and killers. Well, you will fail, and your fall will be as hard and painful as your master's.'

'Are you threatening me?' asked Chaloner, dropping one hand to the hilt of his sword, but Cocke was already staggering away, and did not reply.

Chaloner forced himself to stay at Buckingham House all evening, asking questions about the prison, the murders, the spectre and the Gorges thefts, but he did not expect useful answers and nor did he get them. Eventually, he conceded defeat and went in search of the Colliers. Lil and Jem had passed out behind the rose beds, both clutching empty wine jugs, while Una had been snared by the insatiable Cocke. Chaloner collected Kipps, walked to the almshouse, and searched it from top to bottom while the Seal Bearer stood guard outside.

The cottage was filthy and reeked of unwashed clothes,

spilled food and rancid fat. Unfortunately, the unpleasant business of rifling through the Colliers' belongings revealed nothing pertinent to his enquiries – no hidden stashes of money, stolen property or evidence that they had forged their character references. The only thing of interest was a note in a tobacco pouch, which was in Latin and dappled with the same dirty fingerprints as on the documents in Tooker's office. Chaloner translated it quickly: *the elephants will arrive at dawn on Wednesday, 2nd day of Aug.*

He regarded it in puzzlement. He seriously doubted if a consignment of large mammals would appear in two and a half days' time, so 'elephants' was plainly a euphemism for something else. But what? Cannon? There had been a bill of sale for guns in Tooker's office, although for small arms, not artillery. But what was the message doing in the Colliers' possession? All Chaloner could think was that it was the item Jem had found in the orchard, and that the man had indeed been lying when he had denied it. Unfortunately, he doubted the family knew Latin, so quizzing them about its meaning was not going to get him very far.

'Was it very terrible?' asked Kipps sympathetically, watching him rinse his hands in a bucket of rainwater outside. 'I am not sure *I* could have brought myself to go in. The life of a spy is not for me, Tom, so you can rest assured that I shall not be competing for your position. I would rather live on my pay from the Treasury, and never see the Lady's thighs again.'

'All I found was this,' said Chaloner, handing him the note. 'Which is a pity, as it would have been a tidy solution for that rabble to be the thieves.'

'How can they be the culprits?' asked Kipps, handing

the message back with a shrug to say he had no insights to offer. 'They have alibis for at least two of the crimes. Yet I cannot say I like them, innocent or not. Lil grew bold with drink earlier, and called the Lady a fat whore. The Lady gave her a piece of her mind that made her ears turn red.'

Chaloner laughed, then led the way to the King's Road. There, in the moonlight, they met Wiseman, who told them that he had spent a pleasant and interesting evening with Franklin, discussing surgery and madness. As it was late, and even Kipps conceded that he had had enough courtly revels for one day, they decided to return to the Swan together.

They were about to turn down Church Lane when low voices made Chaloner pause and indicate with an urgent flap of his hand that Wiseman and Kipps should keep quiet. The sound was coming from the rectory, so he crept along the King's Road, his friends at his heels, and peered down its drive. Wilkinson was there, standing next to a heavily loaded cart and holding a lantern that illuminated several men removing wooden boxes from the back of it. He issued a warning hiss when he realised they were being watched, and his companions melted away so abruptly that Chaloner wondered if they had been there at all. Kipps hailed him amiably.

'Would you like us to fetch some lads from the village to help you with that, Rector? There is a cluster of them outside Buckingham House, watching the courtiers at play. I am sure they will not object to a little honest labour in return for a few pennies.'

'Bugger off,' snapped Wilkinson. 'Mind your own business.'

'It is all right, Wilkinson,' came a soft voice, and Doyley

stepped out of the shadows. His eyes were bigger than ever in the moonlight, like a nocturnal animal's. 'We have nothing to fear from these gentlemen.'

Wilkinson glared at him. 'But you said to trust no one.'

'And I was right.' Doyley indicated that Kipps, Chaloner and Wiseman should approach. 'But these three will understand. Cocke, you can come out now, too.'

The accompter lurched from behind a bush. He was unsteady on his feet, and one cheek was smeared with Una's face-paints. Doyley murmured more orders, and others also emerged to resume their labours. They had the look of old soldiers about them, and wore a uniform that comprised brown coats and breeches. They worked in silence, their movements brisk and efficient.

'We are stockpiling food,' explained Doyley, patting one box as it was toted past him. 'In case the plague comes. Flour, salted fish, peas and beans.'

'You will not cure it with those,' said Kipps, frowning his bemusement.

Doyley smiled. 'No, but houses will be shut up for forty days, just as they are in London, which means the parish must supply the needs of those inside – the sick will not stay put if they are hungry. Yet no one will trade with a village that has the pestilence, so we are laying in emergency rations. Reymes and I are doing the same thing at the prison.'

'That is wise and laudable,' said Wiseman. 'But why the secrecy?'

'To avoid panic,' explained Doyley. 'People are already uneasy, and seeing such precautions will exacerbate their fears.'

'Which means that you three must keep your mouths

shut,' put in Wilkinson unpleasantly. 'I have better things to do than provide comfort to frightened rustics.'

'Why are you involved, Doyley?' asked Kipps. 'I understand you working for the prison – you are one of its commissioners – but why help the village?'

'Because our gaolers live here,' replied Doyley. 'And they will not remain at their posts if their loved ones are locked up with nothing to eat. Ergo, it is in our interests to ensure that Chelsea is prepared. Would you like to see the result of our efforts so far?'

'No!' snarled Wilkinson. 'I do not want them in my house, thank you very much.'

Doyley was crestfallen. 'But I should *like* them to see. I would show them the Garden Court, but Tooker would not approve. Why not let me boast a little here?'

'The Garden Court?' pounced Chaloner. 'Is *that* why it is locked up so tight?'

Doyley smiled enigmatically. 'I am afraid I cannot possibly comment.'

'We thought it was full of dangerous radicals,' laughed Kipps. 'Regicides and the like. Are you saying it is actually stuffed with food?'

'My lips are sealed,' said Doyley, although one eyelid dropped in a conspiratorial wink. He turned to Wilkinson. 'Are you sure you will not reconsider? It will only take a moment.'

'Oh, all right, if you must, but do not take all night. I am tired and I want my bed.'

Chaloner had no desire to inspect mounds of provisions, but Wiseman and Kipps were already following Doyley into the house, so he trailed after them. Wilkinson stamped along at his heels, rather closer than was comfortable, while Cocke tottered at the rear.

The rectory was huge, far in excess of what an unmarried country priest might need. There was a dancing hall, a library, and a maze of parlours, pantries and sitting rooms. The food was piled in its private chapel, although the current incumbent evidently spent very little time there, because it was thick with cobwebs, and the hinges on its door were rusty with disuse.

'This will not keep you going for long,' remarked Wiseman, when Doyley proudly indicated his sacks of flour. 'A week at most, if there is a serious outbreak.'

'Give us a chance,' said Doyley, stung. 'We have only been working for a few days. The prison, on the other hand, is much further forward.'

'Why use this house?' asked Kipps, looking around in distaste. 'It is not very clean.'

'For several reasons,' replied Doyley, ignoring Wilkinson's immediate growl of indignation. 'First, because it has thick stone walls, a good roof and window shutters that lock – which may be important if there is a shortage of food, and we need to defend it. Second, because there is plenty of space. And third, because it is cool, unlike the other houses in Chelsea, which are sweltering.'

'Which means our perishables will last longer,' added Wilkinson, lest they had not understood. 'Have you seen enough now? If so, perhaps you would leave.'

Doyley tutted chidingly at him, then began to list all the foodstuffs they intended to store. Bored, Chaloner tried to slip away, aiming to explore with a view to answering questions about the murders, but Wilkinson was having none of it. Chaloner had taken no more than two or three steps when the rector materialised in front of him, daring him to take another.

'The men we saw outside,' Kipps was saying. 'Who are they?'

Doyley smiled. 'I call them our "brown-coats", on account of the clothes we give them to wear. They hail from Bullen's country estate, which is safer than hiring Chelsea men, who might gossip to their friends and families. They will lodge in the attics for as long as we need them, then go home.'

'The villagers believe I entertain lots of secret visitors,' sniggered Wilkinson, while Chaloner supposed it had been the 'brown-coats' he had seen in the upstairs window, ducking away when they realised they had been spotted. 'But they are only Reymes' minions.'

'I am sorry I lied to you about them earlier, Chaloner,' said Doyley. 'But you broached the subject in front of the Strangeways clan, and Bullen tells me that they cannot be trusted.'

'I applaud your efforts, Doyley,' said Wiseman, turning to leave, 'but do not rest on your laurels just yet. You have a long way to go before you are in a position to help the village in any meaningful way.'

'I know,' said Doyley, a little defensively. 'But at least we have made a start.'

Chaloner tried once more to escape and explore the rectory on his own, but Wilkinson stuck to him like glue until he and his companions were outside, at which point the door was slammed closed and locked. Cocke left at the same time, carrying a lantern to light their way. He walked with them to Church Lane, but when they reached the entrance to Buckingham House he stopped and began to speak in an urgent whisper, glancing around furtively as he did so.

'Parker,' he hissed, and Chaloner recoiled at the stench of wine on his breath. 'I have never liked him, and he has been acting very oddly of late.'

'He has,' agreed Wiseman. 'As a result of swallowing too much coffee. I shall advise him against such foolery when I next see him. I would have said something today, but—'

'It is more than that,' breathed Cocke. 'I think *he* is the Chelsea Strangler. After all, who better than a physician to know how to kill? He dons the coat from his plague costume, and wanders about the village, frightening people. They call him the spectre.'

'Why would he do such a thing?' asked Kipps, regarding Cocke with open dislike.

The accompter leaned towards him, and lowered his voice even further. 'He murdered Underhill for being a spy – I heard them arguing about it. And he dispatched Kole for ogling his patients . . .'

'And I suppose he murdered Nancy, too,' said Kipps, his voice thick with disbelief.

Cocke shrugged. 'Well, she lived in *his* asylum. If you do not believe me, search his house for incriminating documents. He wrote *everything* down.'

'We shall consider it,' said Kipps, still eyeing him with distaste. 'Of course, we have also been told that the spectre is an assassin named John Sutcliffe.'

'Sutcliffe is not the spectre,' said Cocke dismissively. 'He left Chelsea when the government seized the College. He does not even visit London any more, not after what happened during the last performance of *The Indian Queen*.'

'And what was that?' asked Chaloner, recalling with a pang that Hannah had gone to watch that particular drama.

'One of the actors fell down stone-dead of the plague. Right on the stage.'

'Actually, that is true,' said Wiseman. 'It was the incident that convinced the City Fathers to close the theatres. Of course, I had been telling them for weeks that encouraging folk to gather in confined spaces was a stupid risk, but they did not listen.'

'Sutcliffe was there?' asked Chaloner of Cocke. 'How do you know? Did he tell you so? Or were you in the audience as well?'

'I hold three important posts – I do not have time to waste in play-houses,' replied Cocke haughtily. 'And I barely know Sutcliffe. But Franklin does, and I had the tale from him.'

'Lying swine,' muttered Kipps, after the accompter had tottered inside Buckingham House. '*He* is the culprit, as I have told you before, and he accuses Parker to protect himself. Well, I am not waking an eminent physician up at this hour of the night on *his* say-so.'

'For once you are right,' said Wiseman. 'Tomorrow will be soon enough to explore these nasty allegations. Parker is a colleague, so I shall come with you, but the claims will be false. He is a *medicus*, and we do not go around strangling people.'

Chaloner was not so sure, given Parker's coffee-induced eccentricity, but he had no objection to leaving the matter until morning. He was tired after several nights of interrupted sleep, and had no wish to initiate what would certainly be a trying confrontation there and then.

'It will give me great pleasure to arrest Cocke,' Kipps was saying gleefully. 'That will teach him to try to blackmail me about Mart—'

'About what?' asked Wiseman keenly, when the Seal Bearer stopped mid-word.

Chaloner watched a battle rage within Kipps. Would he deny his son a second time, or declare Martin's existence at the risk of ridicule?

'A person very dear to me,' he replied eventually. 'Whom Cocke aims to hurt.'

'Some folk have no decency,' said Wiseman, making Kipps glance sharply at him for the unexpected compassion in his voice. 'As I have learned with Dorothy. The best thing you can do is treat them with the contempt they deserve by ignoring them. I, of course, can enjoy a more satisfying form of vengeance – by inventing painful, inconvenient and embarrassing remedies.'

'Cocke is the guilty party.' Kipps returned to his accusations to mask his confusion at the surgeon's kindly advice. 'His post at Gorges allowed him to murder Nancy and to steal; he was in Clarendon House when Underhill died; and his friendship with Reymes let him strangle Kole in Buckingham House. There. It is simple. Our fat accompter has connections everywhere.'

When they reached the Swan, a shadow flitted across the road, wearing a long coat with a hood. Chaloner was after it in a trice, but although he ran hard, the apparition had too great a start, and the night was very dark. It was not long before he was forced to concede defeat. However, he had learned one thing from the encounter: this ghost panted when it ran, so it was definitely not supernatural.

Chapter 10

It was far too hot to sleep properly that night, and Chaloner did not like to imagine what conditions would be like in London, particularly for those shut inside their houses with the plague. Eventually he rose, uncomfortably assailed by the sense that some plot was rushing towards its conclusion, and that unless he found answers soon, more people would die. The note he had found in the Colliers' house had mentioned elephants arriving the day after tomorrow, so was that what everything was spiralling towards? Was it something he should try to prevent? But how, when he did not know what it entailed?

He left the Swan and padded stealthily through the village, hoping the spectre would make another appearance, when he might have better luck catching him – or her – but the streets were empty, and not so much as a mouse disturbed their stillness.

As he passed Parker's home, he pondered Cocke's allegations. Kipps and Wiseman had dismissed them as nonsense, but could the accompter actually be right? The house was dark, and he considered waking the physician up and demanding answers at once, but then

291

thought better of it. It would be daybreak soon, so he might as well wait and do it with Kipps and Wiseman – the physician might be more willing to cooperate if a fellow *medicus* was present.

After a while, he went to the prison, and assessed the walls that surrounded the Garden Court. He could not climb them without a rope and grappling hook, and even then, he suspected that the overjetting coping with its array of vicious spikes would defeat him. So what was *really* inside? Food supplies or dangerous dissidents?

He retraced his steps to see that lights still burned in the rectory, and two brown-coats were visible at an attic window. Then he saw someone else out and about: a boy delivering the latest government newsbook to subscribers. Copies were taken to Gorges, Wilkinson and Parker, but Reymes and his guests evidently had no interest in current affairs, because the lad bypassed Buckingham House, and the last copy went to the Strangeways' fledgling coffee house.

Shortly after, a whole host of folk emerged to sidle through the pre-dawn gloom. First, Cocke slunk along in a very suspicious manner, and Chaloner would have followed him, had he not spotted Eleanore. He pursued her instead, all the way to the College. She knocked on the gate and was admitted, presumably to prepare the prisoners' breakfast. Then he spied Akers, who shot into some bushes all of a sudden, although not because he had seen Chaloner – moments later, Reymes scuttled in from the east, a direction that meant he had been out by the bell-foundry. Perhaps he had friends that way, thought Chaloner, although four in the morning was an odd time for visiting.

It was market day, so carts were beginning to arrive

from the surrounding countryside, too, converging on the open space at the end of Church Lane. Most vendors arranged their wares on tables or blankets on the ground, but the Strangeways had a purpose-built stall with specially fitted slabs, which allowed them to display their fish in neat rows. Father, son and grandson were there, hot and breathless, which was odd, given that their apprentices were doing all the work. All three wore the same clothes that they had donned for Buckingham House the previous night, and Wadham was yawning. Clearly, none had been to bed.

When he reached the Swan, Chaloner woke Kipps and Wiseman. It was only just light, but the sense that something bad was in the offing persisted, and he was keen to speak to Parker as soon as possible.

'You are not going anywhere without breakfast,' said Wiseman, as he donned his scarlet breeches. 'No, do not glower at me. You are unhealthily pale this morning, so I recommend six raw eggs with chopped liver, and a plate of lightly steamed rhubarb.'

Fortunately for Chaloner, such fare was not on offer, and Smith slapped down a dish of cold oatmeal and three pears. It did not take them long to eat, and Chaloner aimed for the door while the other two were still chewing.

Wiseman muttered venomously that the rush had deprived him of his morning stone-lifting routine, but Kipps hummed happily, declaring that his dreams had been most pleasant. They had been of Martin, his lucrative post as Messenger of the Receipt, his many good friends like Warwick, Stephens, Betty Becke, Hungerford and Chaloner – a remark intended to wound Wiseman, whose list was considerably shorter – and Lady Castlemaine's thighs.

293

He was still waxing lyrical about the latter when they arrived at Parker's house. There was no answer to Wiseman's knock, so the surgeon rapped again, then gave the handle a good shake, only to find the door was open.

'Something is wrong,' he said, frowning. 'What affluent *medicus* leaves his house unlocked when there are thieves about?'

'Wait!' hissed Kipps, as Wiseman began to enter. 'What if he is using his privy stool? I should not like anyone bursting in on *me* at an hour when a man tends to be at personal business.'

Wiseman ignored him, but had only taken two or three steps inside before faltering to a stop. Chaloner followed and saw someone lying on the kitchen floor. The window shutters were closed, so it was dim inside, but he could still see that the person was wearing a plague costume.

He lit a lamp and Wiseman removed the mask to reveal Parker's thin, long-nosed face. The physician's eyes were closed in death.

While Wiseman examined the body, Chaloner explored the house, noting a dish of coffee grounds on the table, along with a spoon. Marks showed where some had been scooped out and eaten, indicating that he had chosen to ignore any warnings about its dangers.

'Strangled,' reported Wiseman eventually. 'Someone crept up from behind, and grabbed him around the neck.'

'Just like Underhill and Kole,' mused Kipps soberly. 'And Nancy, probably, although we shall never know for certain, given that she is in her grave. And do not suggest exhuming her, Wiseman. Not in this heat. It would be injurious to our health.'

'Nonsense,' declared Wiseman. 'I have dissected corpses in far less desirable conditions than these, and shall look upon the exercise as a challenge.'

'That will not be necessary,' said Chaloner hastily. 'I think we can safely assume that there is only one strangler. Nancy, Underhill, Kole and now Parker were murdered by the same person, of that I am sure. Is there anything on the body to identify the culprit?'

'The bruises suggest a man, rather than a woman – unless she has unusually large hands.'

There were several ladies in Chelsea who did, thought Chaloner – Mrs Bonney, Martha Thrush and Eleanore, to name but three. Yet he could not see any of them as vicious killers who slunk up slyly behind their victims to choke the life out of them.

While Kipps and Wiseman waited in the garden, he embarked on a painstaking survey of the scene of the crime. A bowl lay broken on the floor, while a chair stood at an odd angle, proof that Parker had struggled when he had been attacked. A torn fingernail showed where he had clawed at his throat in his effort to breathe, and Chaloner shuddered at the notion of being throttled while wearing a mask that must have been suffocating anyway.

He frowned, wondering why the physician had chosen to dress so elaborately – and unnecessarily – on such a hot night. Did it mean that Parker *was* the spectre as Cocke had claimed? He thought of his own encounter with the figure, and supposed it might have been the physician he had chased. But why would Parker engage in such antics? He glanced at the coffee grounds on the

295

table. Were those the answer – Parker's reckless experiments had caused him to lose his reason?

Pen and ink sat next to the dish, suggesting that Parker had been writing when he had been attacked – and Cocke had mentioned that the physician noted everything down – but there was no paper. Had the killer made off with it? If so, what had been written? An explanation of what was happening in Chelsea? An elucidation of what was meant by elephants? A record of his experiments? Or just some lunatic tirade that would make no sense to anyone?

As Chaloner stared at the table, he realised there was a small drawer at one end, inserted so neatly that it was all but invisible to the casual observer. He opened it, and smiled his satisfaction when he saw it was full of documents, with the latest copy of *The Newes* lying on top. The newsbook had been delivered before dawn, and as Chaloner doubted the killer had bothered to put it away, he had to assume that Parker had done it, which meant the physician had still been alive two hours ago.

He sat at the table to study what he had found. There were several documents outlining more of Parker's medical theories, and Chaloner was unimpressed to learn that the physician had taken some serious risks with the patients under his care. He had treated an elderly couple from the almshouse – the Colliers' predecessors – for 'excessive gloom', but a miscalculation in the medicines he had prescribed had killed them. There was no hint of remorse in the notes, just the detached observation that he should have chosen younger subjects. Chaloner showed them to Wiseman.

'All *medici* experiment,' shrugged the surgeon. 'How

296

else will we know if our cures work? However, he should not have used folk who were frail. That was irresponsible.'

Chaloner pawed through the remainder of the pile. Near the top was a letter to the Earl, informing him that Cocke was stealing Gorges' money.

'I *told* you so!' crowed Kipps, coming to peer over his shoulder. 'Cocke must have strangled Parker to prevent him from telling anyone else. His hands are certainly big enough.'

'But first, he accused Parker of the crimes that he himself committed,' said Wiseman. 'What a rogue!'

'Then why did Cocke tell us to come here?' asked Chaloner, unconvinced. 'Parker was almost certainly alive when he suggested we visit – he would have told us that it was Cocke who was guilty.'

'Because Cocke knew we would not act until today,' replied Kipps. 'Indeed, I imagine we are here far earlier than he expected, and he is lucky he had time to carry out his evil work. I suggest we visit Buckingham House immediately, and arrest him before he throttles anyone else.'

Chaloner was not sure what to think, but agreed that another word with Cocke was certainly in order. However, before they tackled him, he wanted to study Parker's papers more carefully. They carried Parker's body to the church, then returned to the Swan, where Landlord Smith was plying his other guests with more of his eccentric fare. This time it was pea pottage, which was hot, stodgy and wholly unsuitable for a sweltering summer's day.

'You say you were up and about before we visited Parker, Tom,' said Kipps, poking at the green sludge without enthusiasm. 'Did you see anyone else?'

297

'Lots of people.' Chaloner spoke absently because he was reading a report on Nancy, which revealed that she would have recovered far more quickly at home than in Gorges, but Parker had wanted to observe her progress without the trouble of traipsing all the way out to the bell-foundry every time she drank her coffee. 'First, the boy who delivered *The Newes*, who was—'

'He should not have wasted his time,' interrupted Wiseman, who was perusing the Swan's copy in some disgust. 'Because the only news is that the Countess of Ossory is safely delivered of a son, and that God has preserved Guildford in a happy condition of health.'

'Then I saw Cocke.' Chaloner could have added that he had seen Eleanore, too, but was disinclined to explain his decision to follow her, rather than the man who was a suspect for murder. Guilt gnawed at him. Would Parker still be alive if he had?

'Hah!' exclaimed Kipps. 'There is the final nail in his coffin – a reliable witness who saw him slinking to the scene of his crime. Or was he creeping away from it?'

'Then Reymes appeared from somewhere east of the village,' Chaloner went on. 'The Strangeways men were oddly out of breath when they arrived at the market. Akers was also sneaking around, and I confess I am wary of his willingness to betray his employers' secrets.'

'And do not forget the spectre,' put in Kipps, abandoning the pottage and coming to help Chaloner with the documents. 'We saw him ourselves last night, and I thought then that it was unlikely to be Parker.'

'Did you?' asked Wiseman doubtfully. 'Why?'

'Because there was something wrong with Parker's limbs – he always moved jerkily, and he could never have outrun Tom. The culprit is Cocke, as I told you from the start. And if I am wrong, then my name is Oliver Cromwell.'

'I would not claim *that* if I were you,' said Wiseman snidely. 'Someone might behead you.'

'I am sure you could sew it back on again,' Kipps flashed back. 'You are always telling us that there is little beyond your medical skills.'

'We had better go to Buckingham House,' said Chaloner, standing abruptly. Parker's papers had told him little of relevance, and he had wasted valuable time by studying them. 'I want to search Cocke's room before questioning him. If we find whatever Parker was writing before he was killed, it might be enough to force a confession.'

'*This* should be enough,' said Kipps, waving the letter that Parker had intended to send to the Earl about the accompter. 'What more do you want?'

'Cocke will claim that Parker was not in his right mind when he wrote that,' explained Chaloner. 'Which will be difficult to deny. We need something better.'

'I suppose so,' conceded Kipps reluctantly. 'But Reymes will not want Cocke accused, lest it reflects badly on him – Cocke is a guest in his house *and* serves with him at the Treasury and the prison. He may refuse to let us paw through Cocke's things.'

'And I am disinclined to fight with him over it,' said Chaloner. 'So how do you feel about creating a diversion while I sneak up there alone?'

'I can do that,' declared Wiseman. 'I shall offer to bleed all his guests.'

'Yes, that will certainly clear the place, said Kipps acidly.

Wiseman glared at him. 'I shall say it will protect

them against the plague, and they will all be eager to accept. Courtiers love watching me work, especially if I produce the occasional spray of blood. They consider it fine entertainment. Which it is, of course.'

The air was hot and still as the three men walked to Buckingham House, and even the wildlife seemed enervated. Chaloner, who liked birds, was sorry to see a dead swallow in the dust of the road, while the sparrows in the churchyard were dull-eyed and lethargic. The ones in Eleanore's garden were different, however. She had put out bowls of water, and they were busy with birds of many different species, drinking and bathing.

Chaloner stopped to talk to her, blithely oblivious of Kipps' knowing grin or Wiseman's scowl of disapproval. She wore a simple dress of blue linen with an embroidered apron over the top, and Chaloner suddenly had a vision of coming home to her pretty cottage of an evening, to be greeted with home-cooked stews and fresh bread. The image startled him. What was he thinking? He barely knew the woman, yet here he was contemplating a cosy future with her!

'I saw you out very early this morning.' He spoke brusquely, because he did not understand the conflicting emotions that raged inside him.

'Going to the prison, probably,' she replied. 'Preparing food is a never-ending grind.' Then she shot him a smile that did nothing to calm his agitated passions. 'Would you like to dine with me later? We could take bread and cheese to the riverbank, and I know a shady spot where we will not be disturbed.'

Chaloner knew he should decline. He could not afford to be distracted by a dalliance, and it was too soon after

Hannah, anyway. On the other hand, he had been working hard on the Earl's behalf, and relaxing for an hour or two would do him good – make him more ready to confront the trouble he sensed was brewing. He found himself nodding acceptance. 'When?'

'This afternoon. Where are you going now? To the rectory?'

'To Buckingham House. Why do you ask?'

'Because there was a lot of activity in Wilkinson's home last night, and I thought you would be going there to investigate.'

'Have you been watching him?' he asked uneasily, disliking the notion of any villager doing something to antagonise the unpredictable cleric.

She nodded. 'From eight o'clock until the small hours. Then I had to leave to prepare my herbs for the market. After that, I went to the prison. It was a busy night.'

'If you did not sleep, you must be tired.'

'Yes, but Nancy was my beloved sister. Catching her killer is important to me.'

'I understand that,' said Chaloner, 'but please do not spy on the rectory again. You are right to suspect that something odd is unfolding there, and it is dangerous to—'

'I can look after myself,' Eleanore interrupted, with a flash of determination that made him admire her all the more. 'I know Chelsea, but you do not. It is *you* who needs to be careful.'

'I am always careful.'

'Are you indeed? Then why were you almost caught when you broke into the prison?' She waved away the response he started to make, although the truth was that he had no good answer to give her. 'Incidentally, I saw

301

the spectre on my way home from the rectory. The last time we discussed him, you told me that it might be John Sutcliffe. Well, you are right – it *is*.'

'How do you know?' he asked warily. 'Did you see his face?'

'No, because it was hidden under his hood, but what better candidate to be a ruthless killer? After all, he *was* an assassin during the wars.'

'Was this apparition light on its feet?'

She stared at him in confusion for a moment, then gave a light laugh. 'You still think it is a woman! Well, you are wrong. It is Sutcliffe, as you will learn when you catch him.'

Chaloner would not have wanted to be jabbed with Wiseman's dirty old fleams, but the courtiers at Buckingham House were delighted by the dual prospect of protection from the plague and the opportunity to watch their fellows undergo a grisly procedure. Ever flamboyant, Wiseman put on a show that had them clustering around with ghoulish fascination, and when he felt his audience losing attention, he had a number of tricks designed to bring them back into his thrall.

'Where is Cocke?' asked Kipps, when the accompter failed to appear with the others.

'I have not seen him since last night,' replied Brodrick, 'when he tried to teach Lady Savage how to play the viol, an exercise that had anyone with ears running for cover.'

'He was very patient,' said the person in question, smiling enigmatically. 'I might entertain you with some airs later today.'

'Christ!' groaned Brodrick, hand to his head.

302

'I have not seen him today either,' said Reymes, scowling as usual. 'But Doyley tells me that he was in the rectory until two o'clock this morning, so I imagine he is still in bed.'

'You know?' asked Kipps, lowering his voice to address the commissioner without being overheard. 'About the stockpiled food?'

'Of course I know,' snapped Reymes irritably. 'It was my idea to amass supplies for the prison, and Doyley suggested that we do the same for the village. He is right: we will be in trouble if our gaolers refuse to come to work because they need to hunt down victuals for kin who are shut inside their houses with suspicious fevers.'

'You were out very early this morning,' remarked Chaloner. 'I saw you by the—'

'I had a headache, so I went for a walk,' interrupted Reymes curtly. 'Not that it is any of your concern. And what were *you* doing, wandering about in the dark anyway?'

Wiseman chose that moment to produce a spurt of blood from Hungerford that had everyone darting for cover, so Chaloner slipped away during the ensuing commotion, supposing he would have to search the room with Cocke in situ if the accompter was still asleep.

The house was virtually deserted as he tiptoed through it, with only the occasional servant moving about his chores. Chaloner listened outside Cocke's door for a moment, and when he heard nothing but silence, he opened it and stepped inside.

The room was empty, so he closed the door, and conducted a brisk but thorough inspection. It did not take long, as the accompter had brought very little with him other than clothes, which were strewn around in a very slovenly fashion, and explained why he always looked so seedy. There was also a box of jewellery, although none of it matched what had been reported stolen from Gorges.

As Cocke was an unimaginative man, Chaloner soon found the bundle of papers that was 'hidden' under the mattress. He unwrapped it to discover a number of interesting items.

First, there were chits signed by Mrs Bonney for Gorges' expenses, which had been entered into a ledger at a slightly higher rate; the difference between the two figures was recorded in a column on the right, under the bald heading of 'personal profit'. No single entry amounted to much, but they combined to make for a tidy sum. Wryly, Chaloner saw he owed Kipps an apology for not listening to his suspicions.

Second, there was a message in cipher, scrawled in an untidy hand. Unlike the code Underhill had used, this one was complex, and Chaloner knew it would take time to translate. Fortunately, he would not have to try, because Cocke would tell him what it said once he was in custody.

Third, and most intriguing, was a list of names. Ten were the same as those on the one Chaloner had taken from Tooker's office, plus the regicide John Dove and the Fifth Monarchist Evan Price, who must have been on the burnt bit at the bottom. He stared at it. Did it mean rebels *were* incarcerated in Chelsea? If so, it would make sense for Cocke to be in on the secret, because he would have to earmark funds for their care. Chaloner wondered if the commissioners knew, too. Or was the whole thing a ruse, designed to conceal the fact that the Garden Court was full of food?

He was about to leave when the door was flung open and Reymes stood there, face dark with anger. Wiseman was behind him looking sheepish, while Kipps was rolling his eyes.

'I am sorry, Chaloner,' murmured the surgeon. 'I was so pleased with my work that I said I wished you were there to see it, which drew attention to the fact that you were missing . . .'

'You have no right to invade my house and pry,' yelled Reymes. 'It is a serious violation of trust, although no surprise from a man who works for Clarendon.' He all but spat the name.

'I explained why it had to be done,' said Kipps sharply. 'Cocke is a thief and a murderer. Would you have us ignore his crimes, just because you are protective of your guests?'

'You should have asked me first.' Reymes shoved a gold coin in Wiseman's hand. 'That is for bleeding my guests, so now we are even. Now leave – all of you.'

'A guinea?' cried Wiseman, regarding it indignantly. 'But I usually charge twice as much. I have to cover the cost of my spoiled clothes, you know.'

'Then you should learn to be more careful,' retorted Reymes. 'And you only relieved three people of their blood, so you cannot expect more.'

Chaloner brandished the papers he had found. 'These prove that Cocke has been cheating Gorges, while here is a list of dangerous dissidents who are incarcerated in *your* prison.'

Reymes snatched them from him, almost tearing one, but Chaloner could read nothing in the commissioner's face as he scanned them quickly.

'They are a nonsense,' he declared. 'This ledger will

be some prank of Cocke's, while these men are *not* in my gaol. How could they be? It would be impossible to keep such a matter quiet, and the whole village would know about it.'

'Would they?' asked Chaloner coolly. 'How, when Tooker and Samm refuse to let anyone inside the Garden Court?'

Reymes lowered his voice to an angry hiss. 'Doyley explained all this to you last night, although he had no right – it is meant to be a secret. Besides, just think about what you are saying: if the Garden Court *was* full of dissidents, how could Tooker and Samm manage them all alone? The answer is that they could not – troops would be needed.'

He had a point, although Chaloner declined to acknowledge it, and remained confused and uncertain about the whole business. He snatched the documents back when the commissioner made a move that revealed an intention to tear them into pieces.

'Where is Cocke?' he asked, shoving them inside his shirt, out of harm's way. 'We still need to question him.'

'I have already told you: I have not seen him today. Try Gorges or the prison. Personally, I do not think he should hold three posts concurrently. It means he does none of them well.'

'Like you, then,' muttered Kipps. 'The Earl was right to make you a commissioner. It will expose your incompetence, and you will lose the Treasury prefectship as well. And good riddance!'

Chaloner, Kipps and Wiseman arrived at Gorges House to find some residents in tears, others sitting in stunned silence, and a dreadful yowling from the top floor.

'That is Dorothy,' cried Wiseman, and ran to the stairs.

Mrs Bonney hurried from the ballroom, where she and Franklin had been struggling to calm a distressed patient with help from Hart and Bannister. The housekeeper's face was pale, and it was clear that she had been crying herself.

'Poor Dr Parker,' she whispered. 'Strangled! And him on the verge of curing madness, too. Our residents are distraught, and we have had to dose several with soporifics.'

Chaloner told her about the ledger, and watched her jaw drop in horror.

'Mr *Cocke* is the thief?' She lowered her voice when several inmates looked in her direction. 'Come to my parlour – this is not a discussion that should be held in public. Martha? Bring us some chocolate from the kitchen.'

Chaloner started to say it was unnecessary – he could not waste time on lengthy explanations when he should be looking for Cocke, and he did not like chocolate, a bitter, oily drink that should never have been imported to civilised nations. But Martha was already speeding away, and he sensed the girl was glad to have something useful to do.

He forced himself to sit still while Kipps furnished Mrs Bonney with a garrulous account of their discoveries and suspicions, feeling the Seal Bearer deserved the chance to gloat about being right. She studied the incriminating ledger in dismay.

'But I paid *three* pounds for the new blankets, and he recorded four! What was he thinking?'

'That Gorges represented an easy way to make money,' replied Kipps briskly.

'Did he steal from the residents as well?' asked Mrs Bonney in a small voice. 'I suppose he must have done. He probably thought they were too lunatic to notice, which was stupid, as there is very little wrong with most of them.'

Martha arrived at that point with a jug and dishes, and Chaloner braced himself to be repelled, but the mixture was surprisingly palatable, perhaps because she had added so much sugar.

'We use a lot of chocolate,' said Mrs Bonney with a wan smile, although it was clear that most of her mind was on Cocke's betrayal. 'Dr Parker believes . . . *believed* it has great medicinal virtue, although it is not as good as coffee, of course. Pour our guests some more, Martha.'

Martha obliged, although she was not very deft at managing the cumbersome jug with its long spout, and more went on the floor than in the bowls. Her ineptitude told Chaloner that she was unfamiliar with basic household tasks, which explained why she had added more sugar than most people would see in a year.

'How is Wiseman's wife?' Kipps was asking. 'She sounded a little . . . disorderly.'

'She was fond of Dr Parker,' explained Mrs Bonney. 'She does not see many people on a regular basis, so tends to form attachments to those who spend time with her.'

'Like Mr Janaway,' put in Martha. 'Although he has not been since Nancy . . . You should talk to Dorothy about Nancy's death, Mr Chaloner. She sometimes notices things that the rest of us miss.'

'Foolish girl,' said Mrs Bonney, albeit kindly. 'Dorothy spends her whole life in another world, and knows nothing about what happened that horrible day.'

'But she can see the orchard from her window,' persisted Martha. 'Not the place where Nancy died, of course, but all around it. And she spends hours looking out. She *might* have seen something. Please talk to her, Mr Chaloner. I will come with you – to interpret what she says.'

'There is no need,' said Kipps. 'Because we have identified the killer. It is the same as the thief – namely George Cocke.'

Martha's hands flew to her mouth in horror. 'No! Are you sure?'

'We are,' replied Kipps firmly, although Chaloner shot him an irritable glance. It was not clear at all that the thief and the strangler were one and the same, and he was inclined to keep looking for the killer. 'I do not suppose you have seen him today, have you?'

'Yes, running full pelt towards the orchard,' replied Martha. 'It was very early – before it was fully light.'

'Was he alone?' Chaloner supposed she had seen the accompter after he had slunk along the King's Road in the dark.

'I think so. At least, I did not see anyone else.'

'He must have spotted us entering Parker's lair,' muttered Kipps in Chaloner's ear. 'And fled to avoid the noose. Damn! He will disappear now, and never face justice.'

Chaloner took his leave of Mrs Bonney, and strode to the orchard. Perhaps Cocke had left something there to indicate where he might have gone, although he acknowledged that this was unlikely. He reached the apple tree where Nancy had died, and looked around, hands on hips, frowning when he saw a pale bump in the grass. He hurried towards it, and then swore under his breath when he recognised the plump features and sightless eyes.

It was Cocke, and he had been strangled.

Chapter 11

Chaloner and a downcast Kipps searched the rest of
Gorges' grounds, while Wiseman examined Cocke's body,
but no one had much to report when they had finished.
The killer had left no clues as to his identity, and Mrs
Bonney and Franklin, both white-faced with horror at
what was happening in their haven of peace, assured them
that no patients could have witnessed anything to help.

'Nancy, Martha and Dorothy are the only ones with
windows overlooking this part of the garden,' whispered
Mrs Bonney in a shocked voice. 'But Martha has already
told you what she saw, while I doubt you will have any
sense from Dorothy. And Nancy is . . .'

'Does this mean Cocke was not the killer after all?'
asked Franklin. He was so wan that Wiseman indicated
he should sit, lest he fainted.

'It seems likely,' replied Kipps glumly, while Chaloner
wished he had confronted Parker the previous night,
because then the strangler's latest two victims might still
be alive. He sincerely hoped that the coded note from
Cocke's room would provide some useful clues, as he
had scant other leads to follow.

'That spectre is to blame,' said Mrs Bonney bitterly. 'What can it have against Gorges? It has now claimed one resident and four governors, which makes me wonder who will be next.'

'Neither of you,' said Kipps encouragingly. 'Not if you are sane and innocent of dabbling in murky waters. You see, Underhill was a spy, Kole a voyeur, Cocke a rogue, and Nancy and Parker unhinged. You are none of these things, so you have nothing to fear.'

Mrs Bonney did not look convinced, and Chaloner did not blame her. Did the victims' association with Gorges mean that Eleanore's list of four suspicious places could be narrowed down to one, and that it was the asylum that was at the centre of whatever was unfolding?

'Perhaps Dr Parker was right to claim that the spectre is Satan,' Mrs Bonney was saying in a fearful voice, 'because these murders are acts of great evil.'

'It is more likely to be a person,' said Kipps practically. 'John Sutcliffe, for example.' He turned to Franklin. 'And Cocke told us that the two of you are *very* good friends.'

The accompter had said no such thing, but Chaloner was content to let the lie go, in the hope that it would shake loose some new information. Franklin rubbed an unsteady hand across his eyes.

'Not friends – acquaintances. He helped us to stage a couple of plays for the ladies, although that was before the government vexed him by seizing the Theological College. I have not seen him since – I think he said he was going to live in Greenwich.'

'Which was a shame,' put in Mrs Bonney. 'Our residents loved his visits.'

'Our residents,' gulped Franklin, regarding her in renewed alarm. 'We have only just calmed them after

312

the news about Parker. How will they react when we tell them that Cocke is dead, too?'

While he hurried away to do his duty, Chaloner stared at the accompter's corpse. Had Parker killed Cocke for his accusing words, then returned home only to be strangled himself? But by whom? Or had Parker been attacked first, and Cocke had witnessed the crime, so had been dispatched to ensure his silence?

'I cannot believe I was wrong.' Kipps sounded thoroughly disgusted. 'I was *sure* Cocke was the villain. Indeed, I was so vocal about my dislike of the fellow that you will doubtless be wondering whether *I* made an end of him.'

'Fortunately for you, I know you did not.' Wiseman pointed to Cocke's neck. 'The bruises are much closer together on him than the other victims, which means *his* killer had small hands – yours are too big. Moreover, he was attacked from the front, but the others were grabbed from behind.'

Chaloner frowned. 'What are you saying? That we have *two* stranglers on the loose now? That is highly unlikely!'

'Perhaps so,' said Wiseman haughtily. 'But it is true nonetheless.'

'These small hands,' began Kipps tentatively. 'Does it mean Cocke was killed by a woman?'

Mrs Bonney promptly put her own paws behind her back, out of sight, although it was patently obvious that they were far too large to have throttled the accompter.

'No, it means he was killed by someone slighter in build than whoever dispatched Underhill, Kole and Parker,' corrected Wiseman pedantically. 'And there is something else, too: either Cocke or his attacker dropped a newsbook this morning.'

313

Chaloner had also noticed it lying in the grass nearby. 'It is Gorges' copy of *The Newes*, which means that Cocke was killed at roughly the same time as Parker. I imagine it came from Cocke, who was in the habit of stealing newsbooks – he filched one from the Rose tavern in London, too.'

Kipps looked pleased. 'So being murdered does not make him innocent of theft?' When Chaloner nodded, he went on: 'Then perhaps he was the *real* strangler as well, but someone saw him kill Parker, so gave him a taste of his own medicine.'

'That is possible,' acknowledged Wiseman pompously.

'I think Cocke knew he was in danger,' said Chaloner. 'He was uneasy when he spoke to us last night, and Martha saw him running "full pelt" towards the orchard this morning. She did not see anyone chasing him, but the view from her room is obscured by trees, so that means nothing.'

'But who would want to kill Cocke?' asked Kipps. 'Other than a lot of ladies who were offended by his unmannerly groping? And me, of course. Hah, I know – Wilkinson! *He* may have followed Cocke when we left the rectory last night, and decided to dispatch him after he saw him muttering to us outside Buckingham House.'

'That is a wild conclusion to draw from the available evidence,' said Wiseman scathingly.

'Not necessarily,' countered Chaloner. 'It would not be the first time that Wilkinson has trailed Cocke – I saw him doing it myself, back in London.'

Kipps shot the surgeon a smug glance. 'So Wilkinson might have intended Cocke harm in the city, but was thwarted there, so he has been biding his time ever since.'

314

'But he is a priest,' gasped Mrs Bonney. 'They do not dispatch their parishioners!'

While that was doubtless true for most clerics, Chaloner was far from certain it applied to the eccentric rector. He bent to retrieve something else from the grass. It was a chisel, but one that was unusually shaped. He had never seen anything quite like it, but Mrs Bonney was able to explain.

'It is a bell-founder's tool, used to score the inside of the bell to get the right note.'

'So *Janaway* killed Cocke,' surmised Kipps. 'He is a bell-founder – and he knows this place from when he came to visit his wife.'

'The chisel probably *does* belong to him,' acknowledged Mrs Bonney unhappily, 'but he might have dropped it weeks ago. He and Nancy spent a lot of time here, walking and talking.'

'He cannot have dropped it weeks ago,' declared Kipps triumphantly. 'Because if he had, it would be rusty.'

'Rust requires rain or dew,' stated Wiseman. 'Both of which have been in short supply since June. Besides, it *is* rusty – there are brown spots all over it.'

'Only very small ones,' argued Kipps.

'Regardless,' said Wiseman, growing impatient, 'it is impossible to tell how long it has been here in the grass.'

'Rubbish!' cried Kipps, equally exasperated. 'Any fool can see it was lost last night. Is that not so, Tom?'

Chaloner was inclined to think Wiseman had the right of it, but was unwilling to take sides. However, he decided to interview Janaway that day anyway, regardless of Eleanore's objections, and was about to say so, when Mrs Bonney produced a pistol. Her hands were unsteady, so she was a danger to them all, herself included, and

315

Chaloner wished he had remembered to confiscate it when Martha had first mentioned its existence.

'What are you doing with that?' he asked, stepping smartly out of her line of fire.

'Protecting the patients,' she replied, waving it in a way that had Chaloner and Kipps ducking away in alarm. Wiseman did not move, but only because he did not know how deadly such weapons could be in inexperienced hands. 'A killer stalks, and I must defend them with any means at my disposal. Although I am not sure how useful this will be against Satan . . .'

Chaloner disarmed her before she could do any harm. Then he aimed at a nearby tree and fired, to empty the dag of its charge. It pulled savagely to the left, telling him that she would have been more likely to kill an innocent than an assailant with such an unreliable piece.

Mrs Bonney was tearful as she clapped her large hands over her ears. 'I have never been comfortable with those things, but Dr Parker ordered me to buy one in London last week. He said a house of vulnerable ladies will be the first port of call for desperate Dutchmen, should the unthinkable happen and they escape.'

Chaloner did not like guns either, but he tucked hers in his belt, determined that she should not have it back. Then he sent her to fetch Hart and Bannister.

'I saw them talking to Cocke here yesterday,' he explained to Kipps and Wiseman while they waited for her to return, 'while Jem Collier tried to eavesdrop. Perhaps Cocke said something then that might help us catch his killer.'

The dancing masters appeared eventually, all fluttering hands and nervous glances, with Mrs Bonney harrying

316

them from behind like a sheepdog. Franklin was with them, pale, agitated and braced for more revelations that would harm the place he had worked so hard to build.

'Is he really *dead*?' asked Bannister in a whisper, eyeing Cocke's corpse warily. 'He looks as though he is asleep.'

'He is dead,' averred Kipps. 'And you were seen here with him yesterday.'

'About an increase in our salaries,' explained Hart. He shot an apologetic glance towards Mrs Bonney and Franklin. 'We like working here, but the pay is derisory. Cocke agreed to look at the figures, to see if Gorges could stand a small rise, which he would then recommend to the board.'

'His death is a serious blow to our expectations,' said Bannister bitterly. 'So *we* did not kill him – we wanted him alive.'

'Did you drop anything while you were here yesterday?' asked Chaloner. 'I saw Jem pick something up from the ground after you left.'

The pair immediately began checking the contents of their pockets, but it was not long before they shook their heads. Hart still had his pot of wig powder, while Bannister had the handkerchief that had been embroidered by his mother, which they claimed were all they ever carried. Which meant it was Cocke who had dropped whatever Jem had stooped to retrieve – almost certainly the note about elephants. Unfortunately, the deduction did not help now that Cocke was unavailable to answer questions.

'So what shall we do next?' asked Kipps, when the Gorges people had carried Cocke's body away, the powerful Mrs Bonney toting the bulk of the load.

'First, we need to question Janaway about the chisel,' replied Chaloner. 'Then we had better visit the prison, to determine once and for all if the Garden Court houses rebels or food.'

And if neither of those yielded answers, he would try to decode the message he had found under Cocke's mattress, and then re-interview Jem – perhaps a knife at the throat would encourage the man to reveal why he had tried to eavesdrop on the accompter.

'If it holds inmates as dangerous as Tooker claims,' said Kipps, 'then perhaps one escaped to go a-strangling, and *he* is this mysterious spectre – as Landlord Smith suggested.'

'I suspect that even Tooker would draw the line at letting his charges come and go at will,' said Wiseman archly. 'Personally, I think that Underhill and Lil are right: the spectre is a woman, one who is tall, strong, skilled at strangling, and fit enough to outrun Chaloner. Eleanore claims it is Sutcliffe, but perhaps that is a lie – a ruse to divert attention away from herself.'

'Yet Sutcliffe *was* an assassin . . .' Kipps was thoughtful. 'I think I shall write to Warwick and Stephens in White Hall today, and ask if they know anything about the man.'

'Why would they?' asked Wiseman. 'Or are your cronies the type to take pleasure in the company of professional killers?'

'They are Treasury officials, and so beyond reproach,' flashed Kipps. 'But they might have come across him on a visit to the theatre, and it is worth a shot. Or do you have a better idea?'

'I could probably think of plenty,' retorted Wiseman, 'were I to try.'

'Then please do,' said Chaloner curtly. 'This is important. No one wandering about at night in disguise can be innocent, so the sooner we question this spectre, the better.'

'I do not have time to do your job for you,' said Wiseman indignantly, although Chaloner suspected that the surgeon had quickly racked his brains and realised that ingenious schemes to save the day were not as easy to contrive as he had thought. 'Franklin is clearly unequal to dealing with Gorges now that Parker is dead, so my duties lie here.'

'So we shall not have your company today?' said Kipps. 'What a pity.'

Unlike the previous time they had visited, the foundry was noisy, as several apprentices and a master laboured over cauldrons of molten metal. However, it was not bells that were being cast, but cannon – four of them in various stages of completion.

'I hope those are not for the prison,' said Chaloner to the man in charge.

The master jumped at the voice so close behind him. He was a large, thickset fellow with a flowing yellow beard, which was a reckless fashion for someone who worked with hot materials.

'Of course not,' he snapped. 'These are for the Dutch war.'

'Thomas Janaway?' asked Kipps, and when the man nodded warily, added, 'We are the Earl of Clarendon's envoys, here to ask you about George Cocke.'

'I barely know him,' replied the bell-founder. 'He is a governor, so I used to nod to him when I visited Nancy in Gorges.' His eyes filled with tears. 'I put her there,

319

because Parker said he could make her better, but I should have looked after her myself. Then she would still be with me.'

'Does this belong to you?' Chaloner showed him the chisel.

Janaway snatched it from him and cradled it to his bosom. 'It is one I gave her, because she wanted to carve my initials in a tree in Gorges' orchard. Where did you find it? I thought it was lost for ever.'

Chaloner did not try to take it back, instinctively sensing that the bell-founder was telling the truth, and that the thing had been lost long before Cocke had died.

'What did Nancy think of Cocke?' asked Kipps.

'She probably liked him,' replied Janaway miserably. 'She liked everyone. Can we talk about something else? Remembering her is painful, especially as her killer still walks free.'

'He does not,' said Kipps grandly. 'It was Cocke, but now he is strangled, too.'

Janaway gaped at him, while Chaloner surreptitiously studied the bell-founder's hands, quickly concluding that he had not killed Cocke because they were too big. However, they were not too big to fit the marks on the throats of Underhill, Parker, Kole and perhaps Nancy. And he, unlike Kipps, did not believe Cocke was the killer, and was inclined to suspect that the culprit was still at large.

'I loved Nancy,' whispered Janaway brokenly, when Chaloner asked him to tell them about her. 'She was the light of my life, and I made her stay at home as much as I could, to keep her safe.'

320

Chaloner frowned. Such devotion was stifling, so perhaps Wilkinson was right, and Nancy – pretty, kind, friendly and loved by all – *had* sought comfort in the arms of other men.

'There are rumours that she strayed from her marital vows,' he began. 'And—'

Although he had anticipated an angry response, Chaloner was unprepared for the speed of Janaway's. There was a blur of movement, and fingers fastened around his neck.

'She had no lover,' the bell-founder howled. 'And I will *kill* anyone who suggests otherwise.'

Chaloner was in no real danger – the dagger in his sleeve was already in his hand – but Kipps did not know it, and surged to his rescue, charging forward with his head down and butting into Janaway so hard that the bell-founder was sent flying. Janaway started to clamber to his feet to resume the assault, screeching his fury all the while, but his apprentices were there to restrain him.

'He is grieving,' shouted one defensively. 'And your questions are offensive.'

'Besides,' added another, 'what decent man would *not* react with rage at the suggestion that his dead wife was a harlot?'

'We are only trying to get at the truth,' said Kipps coolly, brushing himself down.

'You think that because Cocke had an eye for ladies, he seduced Mrs Janaway,' shouted the first. 'But she would not have had him, and he was not a man for rape, so do not look here for her killer. Our master is innocent.'

'However, Chelsea is currently home to a lot of powerful men,' said the second. 'All of whom have dark secrets – secrets they would kill to protect. Investigate *them*, not him.'

Chaloner left the bell-foundry not sure what to believe. Janaway was obviously unstable, and might well have throttled his wife in a fit of jealous pique. Yet Eleanore did not believe him guilty, or she would not have tried to shield him from painful interviews. Or did she know that Janaway was violent, and it was the Lord Chancellor's emissaries she was trying to protect? That possibility pleased Chaloner more than he would have imagined.

'I have been thinking,' said Kipps, breaking into his ruminations. 'We need to explore the Garden Court, but Tooker will not let us in without an official warrant . . .'

'I have sent requests to the Earl and Williamson, but these things take time.'

'They do – if you go through official channels. However, I always carry a blank page stamped with the Earl's seal and a fair approximation of his signature. All we have to do is fill in the details, and we shall have our "warrant" today.'

Chaloner gaped at him. 'You possess the wherewithal to issue writs in our employer's name? Without his knowledge?'

'You never know when one might come in useful, and I am always cognisant of his interests.'

Chaloner was stunned. 'How do you get his seal? He keeps it on a chain around his neck.'

Kipps smiled complacently. 'And I am his Seal *Bearer*

– he gives it to me all the time. Shall we return to the Swan now, and set about forging what we need?'

They passed the market on their way back, which was now a busy jumble of animal pens, carts and people. None of the cattle or poultry wanted to be there, and voiced their objections in a cacophony of irritable grunts, honks, clucks and bleats, competing against the cries of traders with things to sell. The heat was causing tempers to fray, and Chaloner did not think he had ever seen a more fractious gathering.

Eleanore was there, presiding over a table bearing herbs from her garden. She nodded at Chaloner when he waved, but did not smile, and he wondered if she already knew that he had ignored her injunction to leave Janaway in peace.

The Strangeways' fish were by far the most popular items on sale, and their apprentices served a long and restless queue. The old man oversaw the operation with a critical eye, while Giles stood behind him smoking. Wadham sat on a trough, struggling to affect an artistic pose, although his Muse did not seem to be cooperating, and the paper on his knees was blank. He was yawning hugely, and his eyes were bloodshot.

'Herring,' declared Strangeways, when he saw Chaloner and Kipps. 'The finest in the world, and only available from me. How many will you have?'

'Six,' replied Kipps genially. 'I have always liked herring.'

'You did not sleep in your own beds last night,' said Chaloner, more interested in the investigation than in his stomach. He raised his hand when the old man drew breath to deny it. 'You are still wearing the finery you donned for Reymes' party, while Wadham is half asleep.

What were you doing that necessitated being up all night?'

Strangeways regarded him coolly. 'We were attending to business.'

'What business?' Chaloner scowled when the fish-monger exchanged a sly glance with Giles, and lies were clearly in the offing. 'It is treason to interfere with an official investigation – which is what you will be doing if you refuse to cooperate.'

It was untrue, but he doubted the fishmongers would guess he was bluffing.

Strangeways sighed irritably. 'If you must know, we were trying to get our coffee-roaster going, because the breeze would have taken the stench directly through Reymes' bedroom window. But there is more to preparing beans than meets the eye, and by the time we had worked out what to do, the wind had changed. So we decided not to bother.'

'It would have blown the reek towards the rectory instead,' explained Giles. 'And we have nothing against Wilkinson. He is an odd sort, but he cannot help that.'

'I am not so sure,' said Wadham, abandoning his poetry as he stood to stretch. 'Is it true that Cocke is the latest victim of the Chelsea Strangler?'

'Perhaps,' replied Chaloner cagily. 'Why?'

'Because I saw Cocke hurrying past the rectory while we were trying to get our fire lit, and Wilkinson was in his garden – which was a peculiar place to be in the dark. Cocke stopped, and the two of them exchanged words, ones that did not sound very friendly.'

'Do not tell tales, Wadham,' said his father sharply. 'There is no need to make an enemy of Wilkinson – not when we already have our hands full with Reymes.'

'I am not telling tales, I am reporting the truth,' countered Wadham. 'Besides, I have never liked Wilkinson. He spends his whole life aiming to cause trouble by voicing opinions that will offend. It would not surprise me if *he* was the strangler.'

'Enough,' snapped his grandfather sharply. He turned back to Kipps. 'Now, how many fish was it? Ten or a dozen?'

The affable Kipps was putty in his hands, and left the stall with fifteen herring and six mackerel in a parcel under his arm. Chaloner used the bartering time to think about Wilkinson. The rector had followed Cocke in London, and now it seemed that the two of them had exchanged unfriendly words shortly before Cocke's murder. He decided to speak to Wilkinson when he and Kipps had finished at the prison. Perhaps the rector's fingers would be a match for the marks on Cocke's throat.

'What were those rogues saying about me?' came a growl from behind him. It was Reymes, with Doyley at his heels. 'Regardless, it is not true.'

'They told us that you are as honest as the day is long,' replied Kipps wickedly. 'So if it is a falsehood, it means you are just another corrupt official, and Clarendon is right to tell folk that you should not be trusted with a lucrative post in government.'

Reymes glowered. 'Strangeways would never compliment me, so do not play the fool, Kipps. Was he telling you about his filthy coffee house? If it opens, I shall burn it down.'

'He does not mean it,' said Doyley tiredly, as his fellow commissioner stalked away. He put a pinch of snuff on the back of his hand, but was jostled by a scampering child before he could inhale it, so it flew all over Kipps instead. 'He is just overwrought because of the heat. I cannot believe the news about Cocke, by the way.'

'What news?' asked Kipps. 'That he was murdered, or that he was a thief?'

'Both,' replied Doyley unhappily. 'But especially the dishonesty. He was the Commission's accompter, and I am terrified of what we might uncover when we begin to delve into his ledgers.'

'You should be,' said Kipps, brushing the snuff from his coat. 'He was cheating Gorges, so I imagine he was cheating you, too. That selfish rogue – defrauding prisoners and lunatics! Not to mention his efforts to extort money from me over Mart—over something personal.'

'Parker's death will also affect us adversely,' said Doyley dolefully. 'Franklin cannot manage alone, so we shall have to recruit a second *medicus* from elsewhere, which is sure to cost a fortune. Perhaps Reymes is right: this Commission *is* a wretched way to serve our country.'

He walked away, shoulders slumped dejectedly.

Back at the Swan, Kipps produced a sheet of parchment that bore nothing but a disconcertingly authentic likeness of the Earl's signature and an imprint of his seal. Chaloner began to write, hoping his master would never learn what they had done. Seals were sacrosanct, and while he had abused many during his long career in espionage, he had never taken such liberties with an employer's.

Using the elaborately cursive script he always employed when forging official documents, he drafted an order giving him and Kipps the authority to explore the Garden Court. Refusal to comply would be considered an act of treason, and anyone opposing the warrant could expect a sojourn in the Tower. While Kipps got busy with some decorative ribbons, Chaloner locked the papers he had removed from Cocke's mattress in a chest, along with the ones from Parker's house. He would tackle the cipher as soon as they had finished at the prison.

'There,' said Kipps in satisfaction, holding out his handiwork for Chaloner to inspect.

The seal and its fluttering appendages were impressive, although Chaloner would have been suspicious of the fact that the signature and text were in different inks. However, Tooker was not an intelligencer, so hopefully, he would not notice the discrepancy. He nodded his approval, and Kipps suggested donning clothes more suitable for an official invasion. It was a good idea, even though the day was far too hot for formal long-coats, wigs and frilly shirts.

Finally, resplendent in their courtly finery, the two of them set off towards the College, each alone with his thoughts. Chaloner was still pondering whether Janaway was the large-handed killer, while Kipps fretted over a stain on his best breeches, which he felt marred his otherwise pristine appearance.

Akers was on gate duty, and ushered them inside almost eagerly. As they were conducted towards Tooker's office, Chaloner saw Spring watching from the shady corner of the courtyard, his cronies ranged around him. All oozed sullen defiance.

Akers opened the gatehouse door, and began to lead the way up the stairs. However, when they reached the landing, he stopped and glanced around furtively, to make sure they were alone.

'You are right to come with your warrant,' he whispered,

'because something bad will happen here soon. There have been several deliveries of goods to the Garden Court, but we have not been permitted to inspect them. And there is an *atmosphere*.'

'What kind of atmosphere?' asked Chaloner.

'One that the Dutchmen sense, because they are suddenly very rebellious, and we had trouble encouraging them back into their cells after their exercise today. Tooker, Samm and their favourites know what is afoot, of course, but the rest of us gaolers are in woeful ignorance.'

'The deliveries you mentioned are only supplies of food,' explained Kipps. 'Some is being stockpiled here, lest the plague comes. The commissioners told us.'

'We *have* laid in emergency rations for such an eventuality, but those are in the cellars under the kitchen. These went to the Garden Court – and they were the wrong size and shape to be edibles anyway. I wondered if they might be weapons. Muskets perhaps.'

'Why would Tooker allow that?' asked Kipps doubtfully, while Chaloner acknowledged that the gaoler was telling the truth about the kitchen, because he had seen food stacked in its basement himself. 'The warden is usually the first to be shot when things turn sour, as I am sure he knows.'

Akers shrugged. 'Well, something dark and nasty is unfolding here, and I am worried. As I told you before, there have been odd comings and goings.'

'Prostitutes,' said Chaloner, recalling what Tooker had claimed. 'Sneaked in for those inmates who can afford them.'

Akers snorted his disgust. 'You mean for Spring and his fellows – the rest would never be granted such favours. But I do not refer to the whores, I mean *other* goings-on.

Moreover, the spectre roamed again last night, and I know *she* is up to no good.'

'She?' pounced Chaloner. 'How do you know?'

'Because I heard her talking – she was muttering something about dawn on Wednesday. She has a light voice and is very nimble. Although I suppose the same can be said of some men . . .'

Chaloner's interest quickened. 'Muttering to whom?'

'I tried to eavesdrop, but she and her companion heard me coming, and I was hard-pressed to escape. For God's sake do not tell anyone it was me they chased. If you do, I am a dead man. After all, I voiced my concerns to Underhill, Cocke *and* Parker, and look what happened to them.'

'Why pick those three for your confidences?' asked Kipps suspiciously.

'Because Cocke was our accompter, Parker our physician, and Underhill was always asking questions and so was interested. Something nasty *is* bubbling here, and it will boil over in less than two days. You do not have much time if you aim to stop it.'

'This spectre,' said Chaloner. 'If she is a woman, then who is she? One of the guests at Buckingham House? A local?'

'Someone who is more ruthless than any man. She must be, if she has throttled four people. Strong, too. Unless it is her companion who does the strangling while she looks on . . .'

'What do you know about him?' asked Chaloner. 'I assume it *was* a man, not another lady?'

'He was larger and heavier, so yes, although it was difficult to be sure in the dark. And I did not hear him speak, only her.'

'Do you have any theories or suspects?' pressed Kipps.

'One: Rector Wilkinson held grudges against all the victims – he considered Nancy a whore, Underhill a spy, Kole a voyeur, Cocke a thief, while Parker was the man who brought lunatics to his village. You should speak to him as soon as you can.'

Having had his say, Akers turned abruptly, and began climbing the stairs again. Chaloner and Kipps followed in silence, mulling over what he had said. They reached Tooker's office to find the warden at his desk. He wore his trademark cloak and tall hat, despite the heat of the day, and Chaloner supposed he had been glad to get them back. Rather wickedly, Chaloner had hung them on the village maypole when he had finished with them – a public statement that it had been the warden's own clothes that had let the intruder escape from the prison with such ease.

'What, again?' Tooker sighed with exaggerated weariness. 'What do you want *this* time?'

'To see the Garden Court,' replied Chaloner promptly.

Tooker grimaced. 'How many more times must I repeat myself? It would be a reckless breach of security to venture in there without good cause.'

At that moment Samm arrived, pistols in his belt and a rapier at his side. The firearms made Chaloner uncomfortable, not only because it was unwise to sport them in a place where they might be grabbed by inmates, but also because his own blades were no match for bullets. He moved his coat slightly, so the butt of Mrs Bonney's dag was visible, aiming to let Samm know that he was not the only one with a gun. It was unloaded, but the chief gaoler was not to know that.

'We have reason to believe that the Garden Court

330

holds English rebels,' Chaloner said baldly, watching both for a reaction. 'Regicides, rabble-rousers and men with wild religious opinions.'

'What nonsense!' cried Tooker angrily. 'Whoever told you such a foolish thing?'

'It is common knowledge,' lied Chaloner. 'People gossip in the taverns.'

'That intruder,' muttered Samm venomously, treating Chaloner to a cold and angry glare. 'He failed to unearth anything untoward when he broke in, so he is resorting to invention instead. Does he not understand that spreading reckless falsehoods might do a lot of harm?'

Chaloner pressed on. 'You have the care of Will Say, Andrew Broughton, Ned Dendy—'

'No!' snapped Tooker. 'There are no prisoners here by those names. We only have Dutchmen.'

'Other than Spring and his crew,' put in Samm. 'But you have already met them.'

'Then prove it.' Chaloner nodded to Kipps, who slapped the warrant on Tooker's desk. 'This document gives us the right to go wherever we please. Refuse to comply, and you will spend the rest of your short lives as traitors in the Tower.'

Tooker eyed it warily, then spent several minutes inspecting the seal. Chaloner held his breath, readying himself to answer the accusation that the writ was a forgery, although Kipps remained nonchalant, clearly confident that their handiwork would pass muster. The warden opened it eventually, and spread it out on his table, even going as far as to use a magnifying glass to examine it in more detail. At that point, Chaloner noticed that Samm had disappeared.

'Enough,' he snapped, unwilling to stand by stupidly while Tooker gave his chief gaoler time to prepare. 'Take us there immediately.'

Tooker stood slowly. 'Very well. Follow me.'

Chaloner was aware of being watched as he and Kipps followed Tooker across the baking yellow expanse of the yard. He glanced around and saw faces at almost every window. Why? Because the prisoners were bored, and official visitations were a departure from their dull routine? Because they sensed that something was about to happen, as Akers had claimed, and intended to be part of it – a mass escape, perhaps? Or because other men had gone into the Garden Court, and had not come out again?

He was glad of the stalwart presence of Kipps at his side. The Seal Bearer marched with military precision, his bearing regal, and no one who saw him could fail to believe anything other than that he was there with the full support of the King, the government and the law. Chaloner supposed the ability to strike a pose was why Kipps had won two lucrative ceremonial posts.

Tooker bought Samm yet more time by stopping to talk every so often, and adopting a very measured pace. Two burly soldiers were on duty at the Garden Court gate, and conspired to take an age to find the right key. The moment they did, Chaloner shoved past them to enter a short tunnel, which opened into the College's second yard.

It was a pretty square with buildings on all four sides and a garden in the middle. The buildings were crafted from honey-coloured stone with ivy climbing pictur-esquely up them. The windows were glazed, and

Chaloner saw faces at several on the upper floors, although all pulled back when they saw him looking at them. The delicious aroma of cooking issued from the far corner – of baked fish, and of cakes containing nutmeg and cinnamon.

'Your dangerous Dutchmen must love this,' remarked Kipps, as he looked around with his hands on his hips. 'Indeed, I could live here myself.'

Tooker scowled at him. 'Before you go any further, I have rules. Touch nothing and talk to no one. And keep a firm hand on your weapons. Everyone is locked in cells, of course, but one cannot be too careful.'

When Chaloner and Kipps nodded acquiescence, he walked to the nearest door. It led to a hallway, which had stairs leading to the upper floor, and a corridor running in both directions with more doors leading off it. The building smelled pleasantly of wax and wood, and Chaloner knew immediately that it was no prison.

'Stand well back,' instructed Tooker, as Samm produced a key. 'These rogues are not in here for nothing. They are villains to a man, who would slit your throat without a second thought.'

Samm unlocked the door to reveal six men. There was no furniture of any description, not even a bucket for sanitation, and it was improbably clean. The prisoners were bewildered, and Chaloner could tell that they had just been herded in to play a role in a game they did not understand. Samm unfastened a second door 'at random' to reveal more bemused inmates.

'When were you brought here?' asked Chaloner in Dutch.

One prisoner started to reply, but Samm slammed the door closed before the man could speak more than two or three words, although they were enough for Chaloner to hear the beginning of a demand to know what was going on.

'I told you,' said Tooker sharply. 'No talking to the inmates. Especially in their own tongue.'

'Open that door,' ordered Chaloner, pointing to one at the far end. The corner of a rug protruded from underneath it, and he was sure it was crammed with all the items that had been hastily removed from the two 'show' cells. Samm had done wonders in the short time he had been allotted, but mistakes had been made even so.

'No,' snapped Tooker. 'I have cooperated, but now you try my patience.'

'And you mine.' Chaloner started to walk towards it, but found his way barred by Samm and a henchman. The hands of both rested on the butts of their guns, ready to draw if there was trouble.

'What was delivered here recently?' demanded Kipps, frustration loud in his voice. 'In carts that you would not allow your other gaolers to inspect?'

Chaloner winced, and hoped the blunt question would not endanger Akers. Samm's eyes narrowed, and the gun started to come out of his belt.

'Food,' replied Tooker promptly. 'Lest the plague comes, and we find ourselves short. You clearly have an informant here, so tell him that the wagons contained victuals. And if you do not believe me, ask Commissioners Doyley and Reymes. It was their idea – as was keeping it secret. I said it would be better to do it openly, but they disagreed.'

'We shall show you the latrine now,' said Samm tightly. 'Then you cannot accuse us of being obstructive.'

'But you *are* being obstructive,' argued Kipps. 'And our report will—'

'What else is in the Garden Wing?' interrupted Chaloner, unwilling to challenge men with guns, even if Kipps thought he could face them down. 'Other than cells, kitchens and a latrine?'

'A hall,' replied Tooker, and led them to the building directly opposite the gate, where he opened the door to a large, airy chamber that was being cleaned by more Dutch prisoners. Again, the inmates were baffled and frightened, and Chaloner could tell it was nothing they had been told to do before.

'We use it for theological instruction,' said Tooker. Chaloner glanced at him sharply: the warden thought he had won the encounter, and so was amusing himself at his visitors' expense. 'After all, we cannot deprive our charges of religion, enemies or no.'

'You mean you hold services?' queried Kipps. 'Holy Communion and the like?'

'Not exactly. Wilkinson declines to bring the sacraments here, because he does not want to minister to men who mean his country harm, so we reached a compromise: he provides pamphlets, and our prisoners are encouraged to read them.'

He gestured to a pile of leaflets – all in English – but when Chaloner saw their titles, he was sure no inmate should be allowed anywhere near them. All were inflammatory, and would do nothing to promote peace. Had Wilkinson done it on purpose, aiming to incite a riot, so that the prison would be forced to close and revert to its original purpose, with himself at its head?

He nodded that he had seen enough of the hall, so Tooker led them back to the garden, where Chaloner noticed that the faces at the windows were back again. He pointed up at them.

'I want to inspect *their* quarters.'

Tooker grimaced. 'Well, you cannot. You have seen two, and that should be plenty.'

'We will tell Clarendon that you flouted his warrant,' threatened Kipps.

'And *I* shall tell him that you put the security of a nation at risk with gratuitous demands,' flared Tooker. 'Why must you pry, anyway? No one has escaped, and no one has complained about the conditions. Considering the pittance we receive from the Treasury, we have worked miracles.'

'That is for us to decide,' argued Kipps. 'Which we cannot do as long as you refuse to cooperate.'

'I *am* cooperating,' Tooker snapped back. 'Besides, I know why you are really here – because your master wants to use the prison to strike a blow at Reymes. Well, he should be ashamed of himself. All our commissioners are dedicated and generous, and they deserve better than to be used as pawns in his political machinations.'

'Yet you lie to these "dedicated and generous" men,' said Chaloner. 'They are under the impression that the Garden Court holds food and nothing else, but it contains prisoners who—'

'It holds both,' interrupted Tooker sharply. 'We have stored victuals all over the College – anywhere with cellars to keep them cool and safe. And of course the commissioners know about the dangerous inmates. If they claim otherwise, then I am afraid they are fibbing.'

'A likely story!' exclaimed Kipps. 'Do you take us for fools?'

While Kipps and Tooker sparred, Chaloner inched

away. Then before anyone could stop him, he tore up the stairs to the top floor. He bent to pick the lock on one of the rooms that had had faces at the window, and was startled when the door swung open before he could insert his probes. Two men were inside, watching the altercation in the yard below. Both whipped around in alarm when they heard him behind them.

The chamber was beautifully furnished, and the remains of a substantial meal lay on the table, but before Chaloner could register more, Samm hurtled into the room after him, pistol in his hand. Chaloner braced himself for the shot, but the gaoler's eyes flicked to the inmates, and the weapon was lowered. Chaloner turned quickly to look at them, but there was no indication that either had cautioned Samm not to fire.

'The door was open,' Chaloner said, when Tooker and Kipps arrived seconds later. The warden was breathing hard, and his face was white with anger. 'How remiss for a place where security is said to be so tight.'

'It *is* remiss,' said Samm through gritted teeth. 'I shall have words with the guards, and it will not happen again. We are fortunate that this pair of butter-eaters did not notice, or they might have escaped to terrorise the people of Chelsea – and perhaps even London.'

The 'prisoners' were well-fed and middle-aged, more like merchants than sailors. Neither wore the kind of clothes currently favoured by Hollanders, and there was a hardness in their faces that suggested both were individuals who believed in the power of their own convictions.

'From where in the United Provinces do you hail?' asked Chaloner in Dutch.

They regarded him blankly, revealing that they did not know the language.

337

'I told you – no talking to the inmates,' snapped Tooker, jabbing him sharply in the back. 'And it is no use babbling in Hollandish anyway, because these two are French. Not everyone in the Dutch navy hails from the United Provinces, and these are Breton mercenaries.'

Chaloner promptly switched to French. 'How long have you been in the Dutch navy?'

He was gratified when he saw the irritation on Tooker's face, but again, he sensed the prisoners sending their minders a silent signal, warning them against doing anything rash. The older of the two gave a brief smile, and answered in the same tongue.

'A few months – since war broke out, and we saw an opportunity to make some money.'

There was something odd about his accent, which Chaloner supposed might result from his first language being Breton, but that also might mean he was English. He stared at the fellow, taking in his fine clothes and haughty bearing, then addressed the second, still in French.

'On which ship did *you* serve?'

The first replied on his crony's behalf. '*Stad Utrecht*, under Captain Oudart. We were taken together.'

'Does he not speak for himself?' asked Chaloner, suspecting the 'Breton' did not understand a word that was being said.

'He has been mute since the battle,' came the glib explanation. 'Shock can do odd things to a man. You have the look of the warrior about you, so you must be aware of this phenomenon.'

'Does religion help?' Chaloner wondered if these two men were on the lists of names he had found. He had met some of his uncle's fellow regicides, but not all, so

338

the only way to tell whether they held revolutionary opinions was by needling one into an incautious response. 'Particularly that of a controversial nature?'

The first prisoner smiled again. 'Religion always helps, and I do not know where we would be without it. Now, is there anything else, or may we return to our chess?'

The pieces sat on the table, and although the two men had been nowhere near them when Chaloner had entered their cell, they made a show of settling to them now. He watched them for a moment, but could tell they would be persuaded to say no more. He allowed Samm to usher him out.

'Well?' asked Kipps in an undertone, once they were out on the road again. 'Did you learn anything useful? I did not, although I can tell you that prisoner was not Breton. My old nurse was Breton, and they have a distinctive accent. I would recognise it anywhere – and he did not have it.'

'You are doubtless right,' said Chaloner, 'and their clothes were English-made.'

'Regicides, then,' said Kipps in distaste. 'No offence to your uncle, Tom, but king-killers are a vile breed, and should be locked in the Tower, not playing chess in Chelsea.'

'I will write to Spymaster Williamson today, and ask for reinforcements. If there really are a dozen dangerous dissidents in there, we cannot tackle them alone.'

'Are you sure that is wise?' asked Kipps uneasily. 'Tooker did say that these men are guests of the government, and Williamson is a dangerous man himself.'

'He is,' acknowledged Chaloner. 'But he cannot know what is happening here. If he did, he would have warned me to stay away, not urged me to investigate.'

339

'If you say so,' said Kipps, unconvinced. 'But I shall write for help, too – from our Earl, who I trust far more than Williamson.'

Chaloner inclined his head. 'And while we wait for their replies, we will visit Wilkinson.'

'Fair enough,' said Kipps genially, then frowned. 'Why, exactly?'

'Because I saw him trailing Cocke in London; he was spotted arguing with Cocke last night; and now we hear that he gives polemical pamphlets to prisoners. He has been a suspicious character from the start, and it is time we interviewed him properly.'

Chapter 12

Chaloner and Kipps hurried to the Swan, where the spy composed a letter to Williamson, and the Seal Bearer wrote to the Earl. Then Chaloner gave two of Landlord Smith's fat sons a shilling each, and ordered them to deliver both messages as quickly as they could.

'My money is on Clarendon responding first,' said Kipps, watching the boys waddle off in opposite directions. 'If Williamson was going to help, he would have done it by now.'

It was an interesting point, but Chaloner was sure the Spymaster would be as eager to thwart a plot involving rebels as he was, and it was just a case of the earlier missive going astray before it was read. Hopefully, the second one would have better luck.

'We should tackle Rector Wilkinson now,' he said. 'We may not have time later, if we are embroiled in armed confrontations with rebels, and the Earl will be vexed if we lose the man who committed murder in his house.'

The market was still busy as he and Kipps trudged towards the rectory, but the atmosphere was testier than ever. The animals and birds were uncomfortable in the heat, and their objections were unsettling their owners, who felt pressure to sell. Foodstuffs wilted, and arguments broke out about their quality, while even those selling non-perishables were irritable and short with their customers. The Strangeways were the only ones to have done well: all their fish had been sold, and their apprentices were sluicing out the stall, ready for next time.

Chaloner chose a route that would take him past Eleanore's table, although his casual change of direction did not fool Kipps, who smirked knowingly. Eleanore was selling Mrs Bonney some parsley, but she abandoned the sale to an assistant – a gawky lass of fifteen or sixteen – when she saw Chaloner. The spy felt his stomach give a peculiar flip as she came towards him, something it had not done since he had fancied himself in love with his first wife. It had certainly never happened with Hannah. Eleanore, however, was angry, and Kipps backed away, unsettled by the flashing eyes and tight-lipped mouth.

'I shall leave you to it,' he gulped. 'Collect me from the White Hart when you are ready.'

'You upset my brother-in-law,' said Eleanore accusingly. 'After you agreed to let him be.'

'I did not agree,' corrected Chaloner. 'You issued an order. And I delayed the interview for as long as I could, but we needed answers.'

She regarded him frostily. 'And did he provide them?'

'He certainly made me wonder whether Nancy baulked under his suffocating care,' Chaloner shot back. He might find Eleanore attractive, but that did not mean he was prepared to let her ride roughshod over him or his investigation.

She sighed crossly. 'I knew you would think that, which

is why I tried to prevent you from speaking to him. However, he would never have hurt Nancy, while she liked having a protective husband. It would have stifled me, but she always said it made her feel safe.'

'Are you sure? And please think very carefully before you reply, because we will never catch her killer if you lie.'

'Yes, I am sure,' she said, meeting his eyes with a level gaze. 'They were devoted to each other, and neither would have looked elsewhere for affection. Some people *are* happy with their spouses, so you should not judge everyone by your own unsatisfactory experiences. And I can prove it, although I had hoped it would not be necessary. Come.'

She began to walk away, so Chaloner followed her to a small, unassuming house overlooking the market. The door was open and she walked inside without knocking, calling for 'Father O'Shea'.

O'Shea was a diminutive, gentle-faced man who scrambled up from his knees in alarm when Eleanore burst into his kitchen with Chaloner in tow. It took the spy no more than a glance to surmise that here was a Catholic priest, not illegal in Restoration England, but nothing to advertise either.

'Tell him, Father,' said Eleanore, nodding towards Chaloner. 'Tell him that Nancy loved her husband, and would never have contemplated violating her marriage vows.'

'It is true,' replied the priest softly. 'I break no sacred trust by assuring you that there was nothing of that nature in their confessions. She loved him, and he loved her. He would never have done her harm. Or anyone else harm, for that matter.'

343

'I beg to differ,' said Chaloner coolly. 'He tried to strangle me today.'

O'Shea smiled. 'But I wager anything you like that there is not a mark on you. It is always the same with him – he surges forward in fighting fury, but there is never a serious desire to hurt.'

Chaloner wanted to argue, but the old man was right: Janaway's attack had been fierce and sudden, but the big hands had done no damage. Moreover, he sensed an inner goodness in O'Shea that was sadly lacking in most of the people he met, so he was inclined to believe that the priest was telling the truth about the affection that Nancy and Janaway had shared. He grimaced. It gave him no pleasure to eliminate Janaway as a suspect, because he had not taken to the bell-founder at all.

'Are you happy now?' asked Eleanore, once they were outside again. 'Poor Father O'Shea! I had hoped to spare him that ordeal. He is old, and has enough to worry about without being grilled by agents of the government.'

'I was happy before,' lied Chaloner, aiming to regain her good graces, and feeling anyway that the brief time he had spent in the priest's kitchen hardly constituted an 'ordeal'.

She stared at him. 'There is a rumour in the village that Mr Cocke killed Nancy. Is it true?'

'It is a possibility, but there is no evidence to prove it, and I am inclined to keep looking for the culprit.'

Eleanore continued to gaze at him. 'Yet it would be a tidy solution – Mr Cocke is dead, and so not in a position to object. You could declare your investigation a success, and ride off to Hampton Court to accept your Earl's thanks for a job well done.'

'I could,' acknowledged Chaloner. 'But unlike Kipps, I do not think Cocke was the killer. I cannot explain why. Call it a hunch.'

Eleanore smiled. 'Good, because I do not think it was him either – he was more interested in seducing women than killing them. And now, as we are being honest with each other, I shall tell you what I learned from spying on the rectory last night.'

'Go on, then,' said Chaloner warily.

'There is definitely something odd going on in that place, but it is nothing to do with stockpiling food, which is what you were told. Those chests were too small and heavy to have been victuals, which you would have known if you had watched them for as long as I did.'

Chaloner frowned. 'You heard us talking to Doyley?'

'Yes – I was in the bushes by the gate.'

'So Doyley lied to us?'

'Probably not – I suspect that he just repeated in all innocence the tale he had been spun. However, Rector Wilkinson knows the truth, so you should go straight to him and demand it.'

'Kipps and I are on our way to do exactly that now.'

'Good. But not on an empty stomach. Will you eat bread and cheese with me first?'

She looked very pretty in her cornflower-blue dress, and Chaloner thought it would be churlish to refuse; besides which, he was hungry. She retrieved a basket from under the table, ordered her assistant to mind her stall, and led the way to a secluded spot on the riverbank. It was a lovely place, and peaceful after the cantankerous hubbub of the market. He watched her set out the food, admiring the curves of her body as she moved. There was something about her strong chin that reminded him of Hannah, although the two could not have been more different.

While they ate, she talked about life in the village, and how her neighbours had helped her after the death of her husband. Her voice was lilting and melodious, and he felt himself relax for the first time in days.

'Tell me about yourself,' she said eventually. 'Or better yet, your investigation.'

Feeling a need to talk anyway, to clarify his findings in his own mind, Chaloner recounted all he had learned since arriving in Chelsea, revealing far more than he would have done to anyone else. Like a moonstruck schoolboy, he thought wryly, although he was pleased when she hung on his every word. Hannah had always been more interested in talking.

The sun was low in the sky when Chaloner eventually bade farewell to Eleanore. He had enjoyed the respite, and found himself thinking that Chelsea was a charming place, and not too far from Clarendon House. He could see himself living there, travelling to London only when necessary for his duties to the Earl.

Kipps was in the White Hart's garden, throwing scraps of bread to a flock of ducks. 'I hope Hampton Court will be cooler than this,' the Seal Bearer grumbled, as he heaved himself to his feet. 'Because if not, I might be tempted to go to Russia. You said it was full of nice cool snow.'

'Yes, but only in the winter.'

Chaloner began to walk back to the road, and smiled grimly when he saw Wilkinson coming towards them, an incongruously feminine basket over his arm. They would interrogate the rector there, where he might be less comfortable than on the familiar territory of home.

'What do you want?' Wilkinson demanded, trying to push past them.

'Cocke is dead,' began Chaloner. 'And you followed him very slyly in London—'

'I have already explained that,' snapped Wilkinson. 'I was afraid he would visit plague-infested areas, and bring the disease to Chelsea. However, I did not kill him.'

'Yet you quarrelled with him shortly before he died,' pressed Chaloner, although a glance at the rector's hands told him that they had not killed the accompter, as they were too big. 'Why?'

'Because he was a loathsome worm – lecherous and sly – and I disliked having him in my house last night. When I ran across him later, I told him so, and he took exception to my honesty.' Wilkinson's expression grew vengeful. 'He will be burning in Hell as we speak. Assuming there *is* an afterlife, of course, and it is not something cooked up by the bishops, to keep us in line.'

'Speaking of radical beliefs, why do you give incendiary pamphlets to Tooker's prisoners?'

Wilkinson glared at him. 'Because it is a *theological* college. Ergo, its residents should read *theology*. And if the government disagrees, they can damn well find somewhere else to house their dangerous foreigners. How dare they snatch it away from me!'

So Wilkinson was a spiteful, petty man who did not care what the consequences of his actions might be, thought Chaloner, eyeing him in distaste. He returned to the murders.

'I am told that you disliked everyone who has been

347

strangled: Nancy, Underhill, Kole, Cocke *and* Parker. They are—'

'Yes, I disliked them!' snarled Wilkinson. 'However, if I dispatched everyone who does not deserve to live, then I would be the only man left on Earth. Besides, I have better things to do than soil my hands with blood, so you can take your nasty insinuations somewhere else.'

And with that, he shoved past them, and stamped away. Chaloner watched him for a moment, then turned to Kipps.

'Do you have a gun?'

'I am afraid not, Tom,' replied the Seal Bearer. 'I cannot abide firearms. Their bangs and pops always frighten the life out of me, regardless of who is pulling the trigger. Why? Do you want to shoot Wilkinson? I do not blame you – he is an irritating little man.'

Chaloner loaded the one he had confiscated from Mrs Bonney, glad he had thought to avail himself of her powder and shot, as well as the weapon itself. 'Take this. I need you to create a diversion while I break into the rectory. I know Doyley showed us around last night, but I want to explore it on my own.'

Kipps refused to touch the dag. 'Why can I not use my sword?'

'Because the idea is for you to shoot towards the marshes, and yell that you have spotted a robber. A loud report is essential, or you will not attract sufficient attention.'

Kipps accepted the piece and the wherewithal to reload it, and went to stand at the crossroads. Chaloner had only just reached a good hiding place, when the shot rang out, rather sooner than he had expected. People immediately hurried towards the sound, and he heard Kipps babbling excitedly. Several brown-coats emerged from the rectory and joined those who flowed towards the commotion.

'Robbers,' growled one angrily. 'We do not want *them* around here.'

Chaloner had already noted that Wilkinson's home was unusually secure, which was why it had been chosen to stockpile the food, of course. However, it was not until he had scaled the garden wall and was examining the outside of the house that he appreciated quite how resistant it was to invasion. The locks on its doors were exceptionally sturdy, and the window shutters were new and fastened from the inside.

In the end, he discovered a rusty grating, which he prised from its moorings. He slithered through it, and found himself in an enormous cellar, one that comprised a veritable maze of rooms and corridors. He turned left, and saw one of the brown-coats standing outside a door at the far end, vigilant and armed with a musket. A murmur of voices and the click of dice told him that others were in a guardroom nearby.

He retraced his steps, and found a flight of stairs that led to the kitchen above. The kitchen was empty, so he padded through it to the hall. Doyley had already shown him some of the rooms on the ground floor, but now he explored the rest, hurrying, as he was sure that Kipps' commotion must be subsiding by now. He discovered nothing of value, so he aimed for the main stairs.

The first floor boasted a number of gracious bedrooms with fine, if somewhat shabby, furnishings. One was obviously Wilkinson's, as it contained clerical vestments, although a quick rummage through them revealed nothing of import. Finally, Chaloner ascended to the attics, where

349

he discovered that each room there contained three or four mattresses with blankets – barracks for the brown-coats. He rubbed his chin. Was it really necessary for Reymes to bring an army from his country estate to stock-pile the food, or was something else going on?

He glanced out of the window. The sun had set and the villagers were beginning to trickle back, although Kipps continued to shriek and jabber like a madman. Then a second shot rang out: the Seal Bearer had reloaded, and had fired again at his imaginary felon. The excitement regained momentum, especially when Strangeways howled that *he* could see the villain, too. From his elevated vantage point, Chaloner saw the 'culprit' was actually Wadham, who had wandered away for some peace and quiet, and who had been sufficiently alarmed by the shots to take to his heels.

By this time, Wilkinson had returned to his domain, although he did not enter the house and loitered instead by his compost heaps, a place that seemed to hold some fascination for him. He was not the only one: Chaloner recalled Hart and Bannister confiding that Kole had lurked there, too.

He ducked into a cupboard when footsteps sounded on the stairs. Two brown-coats marched past, one with a handgun tucked into his belt, the other with a cudgel. They seemed so comfortable with their weapons that Chaloner could only assume that they had fought with Reymes during the wars, when farmers had been forced to turn themselves into warriors.

'I am glad Doyley has moved to Buckingham House,' the one with the gun was muttering. 'He was a nuisance around here, to be frank – always poking his nose into everything.'

'Reymes gave him Cocke's room,' said the other. 'Well, why not? Cocke does not need it.'

They disappeared into one of the attics. The moment they were out of sight, Chaloner hurried back down to the cellar, and it was not long before he found what he had predicted would be there: a trapdoor in one wall. He slipped the bolts and pulled it open, but the tunnel beyond was pitch-black and narrow, and there was no time that day to see where it went. He replaced the panel, although he left the bolts undone, to give himself the option of coming in from the other end, should he have the opportunity to explore it later.

He groped his way through the darkness to where the brown-coat still stood outside his designated chamber, illuminated by the lantern that hung above his head. The door to the chamber he was guarding was unusually sturdy, and Chaloner was under the distinct impression that it was a strongroom. More light spilled from the door opposite, along with the low voices of additional guards.

He knew he had to look inside the strongroom, but how? He ducked deeper into the shadows when he heard footsteps approaching, then peered out to see a familiar figure: Reymes.

'Come quickly,' the commissioner called urgently to his men. 'There is a robber in the marshes, and it is imperative that you lay hold of him. Hurry!'

Half a dozen brown-coats obeyed at once, although Reymes did not join them and the sentry stayed at his post. The commissioner entered the guardroom, where he began a low-voiced conversation with someone inside. Chaloner rubbed his chin. The odds were unlikely to get any better – just the sentry, Reymes and what sounded to be one other man – and if he wanted to know what was being so carefully guarded, he had to act now.

He emerged from the shadows, and walked confidently towards the sentry. The man regarded him uncertainly, but by the time it occurred to him that there was a problem, Chaloner had felled him with a sharp blow to the head. Chaloner let him down quietly, then tiptoed towards the guardroom. Reymes was sitting at a table with a pile of papers, while another brown-coat peered over his shoulder.

'You see, Vincent?' Reymes tapped a document with his finger. 'Spring and his friends were *not* captured at the Battle of Lowestoft, but were taken a week later.'

'Because they had been drifting.' Vincent was a shaven-headed person with peculiarly feminine features. 'Huddled in a boat for days before our navy picked them up and brought them here.'

'So they claim, but look at the report on their condition. They were fit, well-fed and unburned by the sun. I think they allowed themselves to be caught deliberately, just to get inside the prison.'

'But how could they know they would be brought to Chelsea?' Vincent sounded dubious. 'There are other gaols for captured Hollanders besides this one.'

'Not for sailors from the Battle of Lowestoft,' argued Reymes. 'They *all* came here, as anyone who frequents a London coffee house will tell you. Ergo, Spring could have gone to the coast, rowed a boat into the area patrolled by our ships, and waited for "rescue".'

'And all because of . . .' mused Vincent wonderingly.

'Yes,' said Reymes with finality. 'Which I should have guessed a lot sooner.'

They began discussing a consignment of barley at

that point, causing Chaloner to clench his fists in exasperation. All because of *what?* But it was no time to ponder. He returned to the strongroom, swearing under his breath when he discovered not one lock on the door, but two. They were good ones, and took him longer than usual to pick. Each time there was a squeak or a click, he paused in an agony of tension, sure that Reymes or Vincent would hear.

But he succeeded in the end, and the door swung open. He stepped inside, acutely aware that the sentry was beginning to stir. The lantern outside shed just light enough to show him that the chamber was full of wooden boxes – ones that were the same size and shape as those that had been unloaded from the carts the previous night. The lid on one had been flipped back, and he looked inside it to see a neat line of small cloth bags. He grabbed one, and heard the distinctive clink of coins within. Not food then: Doyley had been lying. Or had he? Eleanore had pointed out that the commissioner might just have repeated what he had been told.

Chaloner shoved the bag in his pocket to examine more carefully later, and turned to leave, stepping over the sentry as he did so. Unfortunately, the man was not as groggy as he thought, because a hand fastened around his ankle. He tried to pull loose, but the grip was powerful.

'Help!' the sentry croaked. 'Intruders!'

Chaloner wrenched free and ran as the heads of Reymes and Vincent snapped towards him. Had they seen his face, or was the corridor too dark? Regardless, he heard their footsteps hammering after him as he tore up the stairs and made for the front door. Unfortunately, he reached it at exactly the same time as Wilkinson, who was just arriving home. Chaloner pulled his hat low over his eyes as the rector hauled out a pair of handguns, glad the house was dimly lit, although recognition would hardly matter if he was dead.

Wilkinson took aim, but Chaloner had already turned, and was sprinting up the stairs towards the bedrooms. There was a deafening report, and splinters flew from the banister next to his hand. The rector spat a curse, and his next ball pounded into the wall above Chaloner's head. Chaloner did not stop, although clattering footsteps told him that at least half a dozen brown-coats had joined the race to catch him.

The only way to escape from the upper floor was to climb through a window and jump down into the garden, so Chaloner dived into Wilkinson's bedchamber and tore open the shutter. But the mullions were too narrow for him to squeeze through, and there was no time to try another room. He ducked behind a bureau when Vincent appeared in the doorway, although he knew the game was up. He was trapped, and there would be no escape now. Then Reymes released a triumphant cry from the chamber next door.

'I have him! He is here! Jem? What are *you*—ouch! Vincent! To me!'

Obligingly, Vincent hurtled to Reymes' rescue, and there came the sounds of a scuffle – grunts from the commissioner, an angry bellow from Jem, and Lil's distinctive whine. Chaloner sagged in relief, waited a moment to catch his breath, then tiptoed out into the corridor. He glanced into the next room as he crept past it, and saw an unexpected tableau.

The Colliers had clearly been in the act of rifling through a chest, because it lay open in front of them.

Both were being firmly held by the brown-coats, while Reymes regarded them with icy anger. Wilkinson was there, too, waving his guns in a way that suggested he itched to use them.

'The front door was wide open, so what do you expect?' demanded Lil, apparently of the opinion that her transgression was someone else's fault for providing the temptation in the first place. 'It was an invite, so we took it.'

'You are common criminals?' asked Wilkinson dangerously. 'You, who have accepted the charity of Mrs Bonney and her staff?'

'We ain't common,' declared Lil, aggrieved.

'And we ain't criminals neither,' added Jem. 'This is the first time we done any burgling, and only then because the door was open. But we weren't going to take nothing, honest.'

'Look,' said Lil, holding out the sack she still held. 'There's hardly nothing in it. Just a few candlesticks and a bowl. You can spare them, being a Christian man.'

'I did leave the front door open,' acknowledged Wilkinson, and glared at Reymes. 'I assumed it would be safe with all your guards around. How could these rogues have come all the way up the stairs without being seen? Were your people asleep?'

'Their eyes are on the basement,' replied Reymes shortly. 'For obvious reasons.'

Footsteps on the stairs prompted Chaloner to dash back to Wilkinson's bedchamber to hide. It was the sentry, white-faced and reeling from the blow he had suffered.

'They were in the strongroom,' he gasped, clutching the doorframe for support. 'They knocked me over the head, and made off with a bag of coins. Search them.'

'Here!' said Lil indignantly, as Vincent began to oblige.

355

'Watch where you put your hands! And we never went down no basement. We just came up here.'

Chaloner slipped away as the commotion intensified, padding into the dusk-shadowed garden and scaling the wall at the back. When he reached the top, he glimpsed someone hiding in the nearby trees, but by the time he reached the spot, the figure had gone. Was it the spectre? He knew one thing, though: it had moved with an uncanny lightness of foot, so he was sure it was someone who knew the area well. He began to poke around, and there in the last light of the dying day, he saw a strand of wool caught on a bramble. It was cornflower blue.

Since Chaloner had been inside the rectory, the courtiers had swung into action, and there was a terrific rumpus emanating from Buckingham House. He walked to the gate, where the usual cluster of interested villagers stood, all staring agog at what was happening – which was some sort of hide-and-seek that involved the losers dispensing with items of clothing. Chaloner pushed through the gawpers and hurried up the drive, knowing instinctively that Kipps would have gone to join his friends there when he had finished staging his diversion.

'Well, Tom,' the Seal Bearer asked with a happy grin, his eyes fixed on a scantily clad Lady Castlemaine. 'Were my efforts any good? I was able to keep the ruse going much longer than I anticipated, because some hapless fisherman happened to be out in the marshes.'

'Yes – Wadham,' replied Chaloner, and told him what had happened.

'Then thank God for the Colliers,' breathed Kipps when Chaloner had finished. 'Or I might have been left to solve this nasty business alone. Lord! The very thought of it is enough to make a man yearn for a drink.'

He hurried away to get one, ignoring the closer jug in favour of the one that was next to the object of his lust. Yet wine was a good idea, and Chaloner felt better when he had availed himself of a cup. He looked around and saw Brodrick, Greeting and Hungerford sitting despondently nearby. All looked haggard, and Greeting was complaining about a sour smell. He had good cause: there was a vinegar-dipped sponge under the chair in which he sat. Clearly, someone was still afraid of catching the plague, even in elegant company like that at Buckingham House.

'I have never known such wild frolics,' said Brodrick hoarsely. 'I would not have imagined that Reymes had it in him. He does not seem like that kind of fellow.'

'He is not,' chuckled Hungerford tipsily. 'That is why he paid Greeting and me to—'

'Hungerford!' barked Greeting urgently. 'It is a secret, remember?'

'Paid you to what?' demanded Chaloner, although he had already guessed the answer. 'To make the activities in Buckingham House as noisy and boisterous as possible?'

'No,' said Hungerford in a way that made it plain the answer was yes. Greeting rolled his eyes, while Brodrick gaped his astonishment. Chaloner was only disgusted that he had not put two and two together sooner, because it was obvious what was happening: Reymes was using his debauched guests to attract attention away from the rectory. Tales of odd happenings there had still leaked out, but they were mostly eclipsed by talk about the antics at Buckingham House.

'It was too good an offer to refuse,' said Greeting defensively. 'Although it was conditional on us keeping the matter to ourselves.' He scowled at Hungerford. 'He might refuse to pay us now that we have broken the terms of the agreement, and I need that money.'

'I need some, too,' put in Brodrick, while Chaloner thought Reymes was a fool to have recruited Hungerford for the task, a drunkard who barely remembered his own name most days. 'Perhaps he will hire me instead – *I* can keep a secret. And yet it is a curious business. Why would he want his entertainments to be raucous?'

'He declined to say,' replied Hungerford. 'That was another condition of the arrangement – no questions asked.'

Chaloner regarded the courtier thoughtfully. 'Your family estate is near Bath, is it not? Did the Collier family ever work for you?'

'No,' replied Hungerford shortly, 'and they are lying when they tell people that they did. I meant to mention it to Parker, but I kept forgetting. And it is too late now, given that he is dead.'

In a pensive frame of mind, Chaloner returned to the Swan.

Chapter 13

Chaloner woke early the following day, his thoughts churning in agitation long before he was fully awake. There had been no reply from either the Earl or Williamson, and he sensed that he and Kipps stood alone against whatever was unfolding in Chelsea. However, he had answers to some of his questions, including understanding at last the connection between the strangler's victims.

Nancy's window had a good view of the rectory, and she had spent a lot of time looking out of it with Martha's Dutch telescope. Meanwhile, Underhill had been one of Williamson's spies; Kole had been a peeping Tom; and Parker's coffee-induced madness had caused him to wander about at odd times. All had been in a position to witness the peculiar happenings at the rectory – happenings almost certainly related to the money in the cellar.

Cocke, however, had been killed by a different hand, and Chaloner was fairly sure that he had been dispatched for reasons wholly unconnected to the business at Wilkinson's home.

He had been too tired to give the bag he had stolen more than a cursory glance the previous night, so he pulled it out of his pocket now, and emptied it into his hand. It contained about a hundred shillings. All were grubby, which meant they were probably real – shiny new ones were more likely to be counterfeit. If each of the wooden boxes in the strongroom contained fifty purses, then a veritable fortune was in there. No wonder it was so well guarded, and that the carts bringing more of it had arrived in the dead of night!

So where had it come from? The Treasury? Reymes was prefect, so had he ferried it to Chelsea for safe-keeping? But then Chaloner remembered what he had learned about the Treasury at White Hall – that it was stored mainly as gold, and that its boxes were smaller and made of metal. Then was it the money that the goldsmiths had donated for the war? But that had come in sacks, and there had not been nearly enough of them to fill the boxes in the rectory. Chaloner racked his brain for other large caches of money, but no answers came.

As Kipps and Wiseman were still asleep, he worked on the cipher he had found under Cocke's mattress. It took him an hour to decode, but he succeeded in the end. It read:

Tayke 40s for sheetes, 10s for fyrewood, and 3d for each playte.

He opened Cocke's ledger, and saw the accompter had done just that – and that all three amounts were in excess of what Mrs Bonney's receipts showed had been paid. He frowned. Did it mean Cocke had been following orders to steal from Gorges? But why would he do such a thing when suspicion would inevitably fall on him? And who would be in a position to issue such instructions? Chaloner stared at the note, but the writing was unfamiliar.

He prodded Kipps awake, feeling the need to discuss what he had reasoned, and was pleased when Wiseman stirred, too. The surgeon's sharper wits would be far more useful. Unfortunately, neither man had any great insights to offer.

'Well, I can tell you for certain that the chests we saw being unloaded in Wilkinson's garden did not come from the Treasury,' averred Kipps. 'I would have recognised them at once. I *am* Messenger of the Receipt, you know.'

Chaloner supposed that was true. 'Then where else could they have come from?'

'The Dutch?' suggested Wiseman. 'We captured nine ships during the Battle of Lowestoft, and I know for a fact that there were coins aboard some of them.'

'Or perhaps Reymes filched them from another courtier,' said Kipps, eyes gleaming hopefully at the notion that his Earl's enemy could be exposed as a felon. 'Doyley and Wilkinson will not know they are helping to conceal stolen goods, of course. Those brown-coats are Reymes' men, not theirs.'

Their opinions served to confuse Chaloner even further.

Having had their say, the pair of them settled down to the game of chess that they had started the previous night, after Wiseman had declared himself the best player in London, and Kipps had decided to prove him wrong. The truth was that neither was very good: the surgeon was all reckless aggression, while Kipps favoured 'cunning' tactics that did not work. Both were determined to win, however, and the atmosphere around the board was poisonous. Kipps concentrated in icy silence, but Wiseman cursed in Latin, and some of his insults were

361

so ripe that Chaloner was surprised that the Seal Bearer did not surge to his feet and call him out.

While they played, Chaloner's mind seethed with questions. What should he do? The Earl would be delighted to hear that Reymes was involved in something untoward, but Chaloner felt he needed to learn exactly what it was before sending a report that would see the prefect in trouble.

And what about the College? *Were* the men in the Garden Court the ones on the lists he had taken from Tooker and Cocke, and if so, what did they intend to do? Something on Wednesday – tomorrow – as Akers believed? Did it involve the money in the rectory? And what was meant by 'elephants'? Were they guns, and a lot of very dangerous rebels intended to make an assault on London while the King and his government were away?

Was the spectre involved, and if so, who was he? Chaloner had been told it was Wilkinson, Sutcliffe, Reymes or a woman, with Lil going so far as to accuse Eleanore. Dorothy had drawn what she had seen, a visage that was uncannily like the description Parker had supplied – 'lithe, hook-nosed and brooding with evil'. Or was the 'apparition' just one of the brown-coats, prowling around the village as part of the security arrangements put in place to protect the rectory?

The first item on the agenda that day was to visit Gorges. There was ample proof – in the ledger and the note that Chaloner had just decoded – that Cocke had made off with the missing thirty pounds, but what about the thefts from the residents? The Colliers being caught stealing had muddied the waters, and Chaloner was loath to declare the case solved until he was sure exactly who had taken what. And hopefully, by the time he had sorted that out, Williamson would have sent reinforcements to deal with the other problems that were bubbling in Chelsea.

Night was only just fading into day, and it was still too early to call at a respectable place and expect to be allowed in, so Chaloner ate the stale bread and cheese that Landlord Smith provided, although he chafed impatiently at the delay. Kipps joined him, gloating because he had won the chess, while a sulking Wiseman remained in the bedchamber to heft his stones.

At that moment, Reymes and Doyley arrived, claiming that the revels at Buckingham House were still in progress, and they wanted to breakfast in peace. Chaloner felt his pulse quicken. It was an excellent opportunity for an interrogation, although his questions would have to be put with care, given that Reymes had a private army at his command.

'You were right yesterday, Kipps,' said Doyley amiably, approaching their table. 'There *were* thieves at large. Unfortunately, you sent everyone off in the wrong direction – the villains were the Colliers, and while we all hunted in the marshes, they sneaked into the rectory. They are now lodged in Gorges, which is the only house in the area with a cellar secure enough to hold them.'

'I would have thought that the rectory had plenty,' said Chaloner innocently.

'Much of our stockpiled food is in those,' replied Reymes, holding his gaze in the way liars do when trying not to appear shifty. 'But it would not remain secret for long if the likes of Lil and Jem got wind of it.'

'I agree,' nodded Doyley. 'That pair is better off in Gorges.'

'Why did they target the rectory?' asked Kipps, feigning nonchalance.

'Apparently, they saw the door had been left open and that was enough.' Doyley grimaced in disgust. 'The home of a cleric! Is nothing sacred?'

'I have been told that Wilkinson is very wealthy,' said Kipps. 'And that he keeps boxes of coins in his basement.'

Alarmed, Chaloner kicked him under the table. They would never thwart whatever was brewing if Reymes guessed that they suspected him and took measures to have them silenced.

'*Wilkinson* is wealthy?' asked Doyley in disbelief. 'Whoever told you that?'

'I cannot recall,' mumbled Kipps. 'One of the villagers, probably.'

'Well, he is mistaken,' stated Reymes firmly. 'The rectory is a grim and shabby place, as you must have noticed on your visit. The only thing of value is the food.'

The brazen lie was more than Kipps could stomach, and he lurched to another contentious subject, stubbornly ignoring Chaloner's second warning kick.

'Hungerford said that you *pay* him to make as much noise as he can during your parties at Buckingham House,' he announced accusingly. 'Why? It is an odd thing to do.'

'I know he told you – he confessed to betraying my confidence last night,' said Reymes coolly. 'However, there is a perfectly innocent explanation: I am not a man for frivolity, but I should hate my guests to be bored, so I asked him and Greeting to guarantee a lively atmosphere. Does that satisfy your prurient curiosity in my domestic arrangements?'

'Not really,' replied Kipps stiffly, while Doyley regarded his fellow commissioner askance, and Chaloner aimed a third kick at the Seal Bearer's ankles. 'I repeat: it is an odd thing to do.'

Reymes gave a harsh, braying laugh. 'And this from a man who has lived in White Hall! You know perfectly well that far stranger things happen at Court.'

'Perhaps they do.' Kipps shifted positions, so Chaloner's boot could not reach him. 'But—'

'When are you leaving Chelsea?' Reymes cut across him. 'You have identified Cocke as the Gorges thief, so your work here is done. Clarendon will be delighted with your efforts. Not only have you exposed the culprit, but he is spared the expense of a trial.'

Chaloner looked at Reymes' hands, noting that they were considerably smaller than his own. Had *he* strangled Cocke, so that the Gorges investigation would end and the Earl's men would leave? It was an extreme solution, yet it would certainly suit Reymes for them to be gone.

Doyley shook his head sadly. 'Cocke the culprit! I still cannot believe it. I am ploughing through the prison accounts, to see if he stole from us as well.' He gave Reymes a sympathetic smile. 'You must be concerned about the Treasury for the same reason.'

'Not at all,' replied Reymes coolly. 'We do not allow accompters access to the gold itself, so the King's hoard is perfectly safe.'

'What kind of food was in the boxes we saw last night?' asked Kipps, returning to the original subject like a dog with a bone, safe in the knowledge that his ankles could no longer suffer the consequences. 'Because they were too small for beans, peas and the like. Indeed,

365

it occurred to me that they might hold coins – perhaps ones that you will use to buy more victuals.'

'If only they did,' sighed Doyley, while Reymes' face was suddenly impossible to read. 'Then we should have funds to spare. Unfortunately, we are obliged to rely on my personal reserves at the moment, because the other commissioners are temporarily strapped for cash. They will reimburse me as soon they can, of course.'

Reymes gave an uneasy smile that made Chaloner suspect that Doyley might be waiting for some time. 'The chests contained eggs,' he told Kipps shortly, 'which we transport in boxes to prevent them from cracking. But this interrogation has quite spoiled my appetite, and I no longer wish to eat here. Good day to you.'

'We heard that something terrible will happen here tomorrow,' said Kipps quickly, as the commissioner turned to leave. He sounded desperate, unwilling for the conversation to end before he had shaken something loose. 'It involves the rectory.'

'The plague food,' gulped Doyley, and glanced worriedly at Reymes. 'I *told* you we should have stored it in the College with the supplies for our prisoners. The rectory might be secure, but I do not trust Wilkinson. He must have gossiped, and now some villain aims to steal it.'

'No one will touch it,' vowed Reymes, and glared at Chaloner and Kipps. 'And if I learn that *you* have been blabbing our secret, I will string you up.'

'I hope you are wrong, Kipps,' said Doyley unhappily, watching his friend stalk out. 'I cannot afford to buy more food if this lot is stolen. At least, not until the other commissioners pay their share. Unfortunately, they have

366

grown alarmingly slow at obliging of late, probably because there have been more bills than any of us anticipated.'

'When did you last visit the Garden Court?' asked Chaloner.

Doyley rubbed his chin. 'It must be several weeks ago now, because Tooker is loath to open it up any more than absolutely necessary, lest the prisoners see the delights stacked inside and try to storm it. Why? Are you still concerned by that silly tale about it being full of radicals?'

'Can you be sure it is not?' demanded Kipps.

Doyley smiled complacently. 'I think I would notice if the institution under my care was home to a lot of rebels! But I had better go, or Reymes will assume I am plotting with you. He has grown fearful and uneasy these last few days – his lively guests must be tiring him out.'

'Why did you not tell him, Tom?' whispered Kipps, as Doyley hurried away. 'He deserves to know about the men we saw in the Garden Court – no Dutch sailors, but regicides and the like.'

'Because if I had, he might run straight to Reymes and start demanding explanations, which is something I am keen to avoid until we have a clearer understanding of what is happening.'

'We know enough,' argued Kipps. 'It is *obvious* that Reymes is at the centre of something sinister. Him and Wilkinson.'

'Yes,' acknowledged Chaloner. 'But there is no need to warn them just yet. Surprise may be the only weapon we have – unless Williamson and the Earl send help.'

He went to the window, and saw Reymes regaling Doyley with a barrage of hissed opinions. Doyley was nodding without enthusiasm, his attention on treating himself to a large pinch of snuff. Chaloner pushed the window open a little further, and was able to catch some of the words.

'Clarendon will be blamed,' Reymes was whispering triumphantly. 'And it serves him right. My plan will bring us all we hope for – old grievances settled and ancient enemies repaid.'

'But I do not have any enemies,' protested Doyley, alarmed. 'Ancient or otherwise.'

'You will soon,' chuckled Reymes viciously.

Although there were several routes to Gorges from the Swan, Chaloner chose the one that took him past Eleanore's house, and was rewarded by the sight of her in her garden. She was sitting on the doorstep shelling peas. He stopped to talk to her, while Kipps loitered at a tactful distance.

'I shall be working at the College alone today,' she said. 'Lil and Jem have been arrested, and Una has run away. They were caught burgling Wilkinson's house.'

Chaloner held up the strand of blue thread he had found in the trees outside that particular abode the previous night. 'This matches your dress.'

'So it does.' Eleanore smiled thinly. 'I am always catching it on things.'

'I found it outside the rectory, near where I saw a shadow lurking. I thought I had warned you to keep your distance from the place.'

Eleanore grimaced. 'You did, but I am not Mr Kipps, bound by your orders, and I wanted to find out what is planned for tomorrow.'

'And did you?' asked Chaloner, aware that if she had, it was more than *he* had managed.

Her expression turned earnest. 'Well, I heard Wilkinson talking about it to a man he addressed as Vincent, and I would waylay them and put a knife to their throats, if I thought it would make them talk. Unfortunately, I doubt they would break.'

Chaloner doubted it, too, especially if the weapon was in the hands of someone like Eleanore, who would not know the first thing about intimidation. He advised her again to stay away from matters she did not understand, but although she nodded acquiescence, he could tell from the gleam in her eye that she was unlikely to comply. He left her and returned to Kipps.

'You should continue to court her, Tom,' advised the Seal Bearer brightly. 'She likes you.'

'How do you know?' Chaloner had always considered himself fairly adept at reading people, but he had detected nothing to make him think his growing affection was reciprocated. He had enjoyed the previous afternoon, but the coldly rational part of his mind knew that her real aim had been to quiz him about his enquiry into her sister's murder. He wished it had been otherwise, but self-delusion had never been one of his failings.

Kipps gave a long, slow wink. 'Experience, lad. Just trust me.'

The party in Buckingham House was still audible as Chaloner and Kipps neared Gorges, although it was quieter than it had been. There were still plenty of whoops and cries, though, along with a lot of laughter, and Chaloner was impressed by the courtiers' staying power.

By contrast, the atmosphere at Gorges was sombre, and there were tear-stained faces among residents and staff alike. There was also a good deal of unease. Franklin was doing his best to quell fears by summoning everyone to the ballroom for comforting speeches, but the names Nancy, Underhill, Kole, Parker and Cocke were on everyone's lips anyway. The dancing masters stood at the back, tense and watchful.

'Dorothy had a bad night,' Mrs Bonney told Chaloner and Kipps unhappily. 'Perhaps she saw the Colliers brought here under arrest. She never did like them.'

'She was right to be wary,' averred Kipps. 'They are nasty folk, and I am glad for Chelsea's sake that they are safely behind bars.'

'She has been asking for her husband,' the housekeeper went on. 'We have sent for Mr Wiseman, but will one of you call on her in the interim? A visitor may comfort her.'

'I will come with you,' offered Martha, who had been listening. 'She is always calmer with me to hand.'

'You go, Tom,' said Kipps hastily. 'I shall wait down here.'

Chaloner did not have time to play nursemaid to lunatics, but Mrs Bonney looked tired, drawn and anxious, while Franklin was clearly buckling under the strain of performing Parker's duties as well as his own – Wiseman had offered to help, but there was little a surgeon could do in a place where all the residents suffered from ailments of the mind and his brusque personality meant he was unsuited for the task anyway. Reluctantly, Chaloner handed all his visible weapons to Kipps, and followed Martha and Mrs Bonney upstairs.

The housekeeper tapped on Dorothy's door, which was opened by the nurse. The room was the same – bed, chairs, table and heavy chest – but Wiseman's garish mural had been covered with sketches of the garden. Chaloner suspected the kind-hearted Martha had obliged. Dorothy herself was in the process of climbing into bed, apparently convinced that it was night time.

'The batman,' she whispered drowsily. 'He stalks this sorry arbour, and he has eyes in the near garden. He prowls in the night.'

'You will go mad yourself if you try to understand her,' warned Mrs Bonney, seeing Chaloner's puzzled frown. 'She is incurably insane, and her words rarely make sense.'

But the glimmer of a solution was beginning to glow in Chaloner's mind. 'Do you think she could write these things down?'

Mrs Bonney blinked. 'She has not put pen to paper in years. And we would not be so foolish as to give her one – she could do a lot of damage with a nib. Oh, Lord! Mrs Young is sobbing again. I must go to her. The nurse will be outside, should there be trouble.'

She had gone in a flash, but Chaloner barely noticed. He tapped one of the drawings, which had a legend beneath that was printed in bold, confident letters, and addressed Martha.

'This is the same writing as on Dorothy's letter to Wiseman, begging him to come. *You* penned it. You added symbols and wild scrawls in the margins, to make it look as though a madwoman had produced it, and you used Dorothy's own words. But it was actually from you.'

Martha held his gaze steadily. 'I had never met Surgeon Wiseman before last week, so why would I send a message to him?'

'You wrote to a number of people,' Chaloner pressed

371

on. 'For instance, I know you contacted Mrs Thompson, urging her to bring her husband.'

'I *did* contact Gertrude,' acknowledged Martha. She indicated the picture. 'But I did not write on that. Dorothy must have done it in a lucid moment, when it was deemed safe to give her a pen.'

'Then why is it signed with your name?'

Martha flushed, caught out, and glanced towards the bed, where Dorothy was fast asleep. 'But she *can* write! Mrs Bonney is mistaken. *Everyone* can write.'

'Not everyone,' Chaloner said gently. 'Although probably everyone *you* know.'

'What do you mean by that?'

'You hail from a noble household, which is why you struggle with menial tasks, like making and serving chocolate. Martha Thrush is not your real name.'

The blush deepened. 'Yes, it is. My father is a tanner in Southwark.'

'You told Wiseman that you are unrelated to that particular clan.' Chaloner lowered his voice. 'We have never met, but I know who you are. Your eyes give you away – they are identical to Lady Clarendon's. Wiseman saw it, too, because he said you looked familiar.'

Martha regarded him in alarm. 'I know no ladies! I am a simple girl—'

'There is a walnut cabinet in your room. At first, I assumed it was similar to the one in Clarendon House, but it is actually the same piece. The Earl or Frances lent it to you, to make you feel at home here. You are their daughter. I guessed he was holding something important back when he ordered me to investigate the thefts, and I was right.'

'No! I have never met Clarendon.'

'Thrushes are his favourite bird,' Chaloner went on, recalling the Earl say so as they had strolled in his garden. 'And his kinship to you explains his curious insistence on referring to Gorges' inmates as songbirds. When he ordered me to protect them from harm, he was thinking of you.'

'Oh,' gulped Martha. 'But I—'

'You are here to recover from the recent death of a brother – Edward. The Earl lost a son named Ned in January, to smallpox.'

Tears began to fall. 'Poor Edward . . .'

'You did not write to your family for help when Nancy was killed, because you did not want to worry them. So you appealed to virtually everyone else you knew instead.'

Martha sniffed miserably. 'But no one came.'

'Eventually, you were reduced to telling your father about the thefts, hoping that those might prompt him into sending an investigator.'

'You, Mr Chaloner,' said Martha softly. 'I hoped he would send *you*. He thinks you are clever, and capable of solving anything.'

Chaloner doubted his employer thought any such thing. 'But then Kole was murdered, and you were frightened into begging for his help directly. He refused to tell us who had sent the letter he received that Friday – to protect you.'

He recalled the Earl's reaction when it had been delivered: relief that his daughter was well, followed by anger and fear that she might be in danger.

'It is shameful to have a child in an asylum, you see,' mumbled Martha, staring at her feet. 'And his enemies would use it to harm him. Moreover, I will never find a suitable husband if word gets out . . .'

'You must be Frances,' said Chaloner, running through a list of the Earl's children in his mind. He smiled kindly. 'You look like your mother.'

Which was not entirely true, as Lady Clarendon was delicately built, whereas poor Frances had taken after her father, and was inclined to portliness.

Frances rubbed the back of her hand across her nose, a gesture which reminded him that she was still very young. 'Yes, people say we are similar.' Then she looked at him, her face full of misery. 'I miss her, and I want to go home.'

'Kipps will take you to Hampton Court today. But before you go, do you know anything that might help me catch the killer?'

'No, but I think Dorothy does. She can see the orchard *and* Buckingham House from here, and she spends a lot of time standing at the window, looking at them. That is why I kept urging you to talk to her. The culprit is almost certainly the spectre, which she calls the batman, because she thinks it can fly.'

Chaloner took down the drawing that covered the crudely depicted face – paintbrushes were evidently deemed less deadly than pens – and studied it thoughtfully.

'You wrote the letter to Wiseman, but you used Dorothy's own words,' he began. 'Words she repeated verbatim just now – that the batman *stalks the sorrie arbor*. I think she was referring to the orchard where Nancy died.'

Frances nodded eagerly. 'Yes. And *hee has Eyes in the Neare Gardenn* probably means the grounds of Buckingham House, where the courtiers play. She must have seen him lurking there, spying on them.' Fear turned her voice unsteady. 'I hope he is not someone from Gorges.'

374

'No,' said Chaloner. 'There *is* something nasty going on here, but it does not involve murder.'

'It is nothing to do with Hart and Bannister, is it? They often come up here to give Dorothy her dancing lessons, but they always do it without music, which is rather odd.'

And with that, answers snapped clear in Chaloner's mind, and he knew exactly what Dorothy had meant by *theeves in Gorgess with Goldenn Eares and Fingers, and a Tyme that Singeth, and they put great storre in my coffin*. She had not said *coffin*, but *coffer* – Frances had misheard.

He picked the lock on the iron chest and flung open the lid. Beneath a blanket lay a pile of treasure – a silver plate, several watches, a selection of jewellery, and any number of purses. Frances gave a cry of delight as she pounced on a ring.

'Edward gave me this before he . . . I thought it had gone for ever!'

'Go and pack,' instructed Chaloner, eager to have her away from Chelsea as soon as possible, for his sake as much as hers. The Earl would likely execute him if any harm befell one of his beloved children. 'You leave as soon as we can commandeer a coach.'

'Sir Alan Brodrick,' said Frances. 'My father's cousin. He will find us one.'

Chapter 14

Before he returned to Kipps, Chaloner stood in Nancy's chamber with the Dutch telescope, and made a careful note of exactly what she had been able to see. Like Dorothy and Frances, her room overlooked the rectory and Buckingham House, but being on the corner, it also had an uninterrupted view to the north, where a break in the trees showed the track that wound through the marshes towards Knightsbridge. He walked down the stairs, tying together strands of information that had seemed unrelated at first, but that now made sense. He met Mrs Bonney at the bottom.

'I have been talking to Martha,' he said in a low voice. 'Or should I say Frances?'

The housekeeper's ugly face hardened. 'You should say *Martha*,' she whispered fiercely. 'You might know her real name, being a member of her father's household, but no one else here does. I was ordered not to tell a soul – not even Dr Parker and Dr Franklin. And nor have I.'

And she had done an admirable job, Chaloner thought, proving herself worthy of the trust the Earl had invested in her. He changed the subject as Kipps approached with his weapons.

'We need to speak to the Colliers.' He gave a seraphic smile when he saw Hart and Bannister standing nearby. 'Your dancing masters will escort us to them.'

'Us?' gulped Bannister in alarm. 'No, thank you! They are criminals.'

'They are,' agreed Mrs Bonney angrily, beginning to unclip the keys from her belt. 'And I shall never forgive them for abusing my charity.' She fixed the dancing masters with a gimlet eye. 'Be sure to lock up afterwards. I intend to see them tried in a court of law for what they did to us.'

'It is not a good idea to have further dealings with them,' said Hart uncomfortably. 'They are dangerous and—'

'They are deceitful,' interrupted Mrs Bonney curtly, 'but hardly dangerous. Now take Mr Chaloner and Mr Kipps to see them before you make me cross.'

With poor grace, Hart accepted the keys, and Bannister led the way to a flight of steps that looked like the entrance to a dungeon. Chaloner felt his stomach turn to acid as he began to descend, but he pushed his terrors aside – he did not have time for them that day. Eventually, they reached a room with a stout door. Hart stopped a short distance from it.

'This is stupid,' he said with a nervous grin. 'They will try to escape if we open it, and Gorges has enough trouble already.'

'They should have been hanged last night,' added Bannister, 'when they were caught red-handed in the rectory. It is a travesty of justice that they are still alive.'

'Of course you want them dead,' said Chaloner coldly. 'Because then no one would be alive to reveal *your* dishonesty.'

'Ours?' asked Hart, although Bannister swallowed hard. 'What are you talking about?'

'When we first met, you told me that you had worked in Bath,' began Chaloner. 'No one needs to ask where the Colliers come from – it is obvious from the way they speak.'

'So what?' shrugged Hart. 'Or are you suggesting that everyone who lives in the West Country knows each other?'

'You knew the Colliers,' said Chaloner. 'And their testimonials prove it. They are from Monsieur le Raille and Mr Dere, which are recklessly brazen puns on Bannister and Hart.'

'What nonsense!' cried Hart. 'It is just a coincidence.'

'It was a good arrangement for you all,' Chaloner went on. 'The Colliers enjoyed a life of indolence in the almshouse, and in return, they stole for you.'

'If that were true, then Jeffrey and I would be rich,' countered Hart. 'But we are not. Look at us! Our clothes are old, and our shoes will not see another winter.'

'You contrive to be modest in your dress, but you cannot resist a few luxuries, confident in the belief that no one will notice.' Chaloner pointed to Bannister's earring, then at the diamond on Hart's finger. 'But Dorothy did. She talked about *theeves with Goldenn Eares and Fingers, and a Tyme that Singeth*.'

'You cite Dorothy as a witness?' asked Hart with a mocking bark of laughter. 'Then you are as mad as she is! Singing tyme indeed! It is meaningless babble.'

'On the contrary, she was referring to the chiming

French clock in your room, an expensive item that your salaries are unlikely to cover.'

'The clock and jewellery were gifts,' said Bannister, licking his lips nervously. 'From grateful patrons in Paris.'

'You stayed at the Greyhound when you were in London, too.' Chaloner was relentless. 'A costly inn that should have been beyond your means.'

'Search our rooms,' challenged Hart. 'You will find nothing to incriminate us there.'

'No, you are too clever for that. But the chest in Dorothy's room tells its own story.'

'I imagine it contains her belongings,' said Bannister. His tone was casual, but a flash of dismay lit his eyes.

'She has none – at least, none that need locking away. You store your ill-gotten gains there, entering her quarters on the pretext of giving dancing lessons. But the truth is that you go to pore over what you have stolen. Or to add more.'

'But we have alibis for the thefts,' protested Bannister. 'Ask anyone. We were in full view of all the residents *and* the staff when those items went missing.'

'Which is where the Colliers come in. They are your accomplices. You provide music or some other entertainment to keep residents and staff in the ballroom, which enables Lil and Jem to move around the house undetected. Martha was suspicious of them, but you were there to protect them with lies – claiming that you could see them in the garden or the hall. But it was all untrue.'

'How sly!' spat Kipps in disgust. 'Preying on the feeble-witted. How perfectly vile!'

'But you should have chosen more sophisticated

helpmeets,' Chaloner went on. 'Lil and Jem stole rings, plates and thimbles, but overlooked items of greater worth, because they have no notion of what is valuable. As Martha said – the thieves are stupid.'

'You are mad,' said Hart contemptuously. 'As if we would demean ourselves by throwing in our lot with them. We, who have been fêted in the finest houses in Paris and Bath!'

'You tried so hard to lead us astray,' said Chaloner. 'For example, by claiming that Kole was in the orchard when Nancy was killed, and then by saying that he was your first suspect for—'

'But that was true,' cried Bannister. 'Kole *was* in the orchard that day, and he *did* dig around in the rectory garden. We thought it *was* him who killed Nancy and Underhill.'

Chaloner could only suppose that Kole had been spying on Nancy with a view to producing more of his obscene drawings. He indicated that Hart should unlock the door. 'Shall we see what the Colliers have to say about the arrangement they have with you?'

'Go on, James,' said Bannister defiantly. 'Open it. Lil and Jem will not betray . . . will not tell lies about us.'

But Hart refused, so Chaloner snatched the key and did it himself.

Jem and Lil sat on a bench, calmly playing dice. They were smugly complacent, clearly expecting their masters to rescue them from their predicament. Chaloner decided it was time they learned the truth.

'You will hang,' he said harshly. 'Not only were you caught burgling the rectory, but there is evidence that you stole from Gorges as well.'

'There is not,' countered Bannister quickly. 'Do not listen to him.'

'This pair will leave you to take the blame,' Chaloner pressed on. 'And you will face the gallows, while they go free. Is that what you want?'

Lil and Jem regarded him in alarm.

'You will not hang,' said Bannister, moving forward to smile reassuringly. 'We will help you, just as we helped you before. Although we did warn you to confine your sticky fingers to—'

He yelped when Hart jabbed him angrily.

'You have two choices.' Chaloner continued to address the Colliers. 'The gibbet or the truth.'

Lil did not hesitate. 'They *made* us do it. We were happy in Bath, but they dragged us here with the promise of great riches. But all we got was a poxy house and a lot of hard work.'

'Hard work!' sneered Hart. 'You do not know the meaning of the words.'

Lil ignored him. 'Set us free, and we will tell you everything. It was all their idea. They *ordered* us to steal. They wouldn't sully their own fine hands, of course.'

'They kept everyone busy with songs and dancing, then sent us to thieve,' elaborated Jem. 'But we never kept nothing for ourselves. They took it all, to put in a safe place.'

The contents of Dorothy's chest, along with Chaloner's search of their home, suggested they were telling the truth about that at least. However, there was something far more important that he wanted to discuss.

'I found a letter in your tobacco pouch,' he said, pulling it out to show Jem.

'I told you to get rid of that,' cried Lil, regarding her

husband in angry dismay. 'We couldn't read it, and I said it would bring us trouble.'

'It brings *them* trouble.' Jem stabbed an accusing finger at Hart and Bannister. 'We don't know no French, but *they* do, because they were in Paris. It proves us innocent and them guilty.'

'Guilty of what?' asked Chaloner.

'Of knowing foreigners,' replied Jem, and when Chaloner failed to look impressed, added, 'Or something equally serious.'

'This is a nonsense,' said Hart impatiently. 'How could that letter be ours, when we know no French either?'

'Then how did you work in Paris?' pounced Chaloner, using that language. All four looked blank, so he repeated the question in Latin, only to be greeted by more uncomprehending stares. He reverted to English, and homed in on Jem. 'How did you come by it?'

'*They* dropped it.' Jem glowered at the dancing masters. 'In the orchard, after they went to plot there with that lecher Cocke. I picked it up and hid it, ready to use against them if they got awkward with us. But someone came along and stole it. You, by the looks of it.'

'We dropped nothing,' said Bannister, bemused and alarmed in equal measure. 'It is not ours.'

Given his ignorance of Latin, Chaloner was inclined to believe him, and it reinforced what he had already surmised – that the note had belonged to Cocke. And as the accompter was not in a position to explain what it meant, this particular line of enquiry was now dead.

'You had better say your prayers,' he said, frustration making him testy. 'All of you. There is nothing more reprehensible than stealing from the sick, and any judge will agree. You will hang.'

'No!' cried Jem, frightened and panicky. 'Stop him, Mr Hart. Please!'

'Do not fret,' said Hart briskly, whipping out a pistol. 'He will not be talking to any judges.'

Chaloner eyed the dag in disdain. Such weapons were prohibitively expensive, and Hart should not have been able to afford one – yet more proof that the dancing master supplemented his income by dishonest means. The gun was unusually compact, which had allowed him to conceal it in his pocket, and it fitted perfectly into his delicately proportioned fingers. And with that observation, another piece of the puzzle fell into place in Chaloner's mind.

'Small hands,' he breathed in understanding. '*You* killed Cocke!'

'What?' Bannister gazed at his friend in horror. 'You did *what?*'

'Never mind that now.' Lil struggled to her feet and waddled towards the door. 'Shoot this pair, and let us out. Me and Jem will go back to Bath, and you won't never have to see us again. We'll take half the treasure, of course. Like you promised.'

'You are not going anywhere,' declared Hart. 'You will betray us the moment you are free.'

'You got no choice,' said Lil cunningly. 'Or will you kill us all with one bullet?'

'I can reload.' Hart pointed the gun at her, and pulled the trigger.

Nothing happened.

'You should have tested it,' said Chaloner, calmly removing it from his hand. 'Then you would have realised that it will never work without a frizzen spring.'

'In other words,' put in Kipps with a smug smile, 'it

383

seems you bought a weapon with an important piece missing. Fools!'

'Why did you kill Cocke?' asked Chaloner, keen to learn what he could from them and be away. 'Did he catch you stealing?'

Hart swallowed hard. 'We do not have to answer these questions. You cannot make us.'

Chaloner drew his sword. 'Oh, I think I can.'

'He caught *them* stealing,' bleated Hart, capitulating abruptly at the sight of naked steel and pointing at Jem and Lil. 'So we met him to discuss the terms of his silence. Twice – once when Jem tried to eavesdrop, and again yesterday at dawn.'

'But he was alive when *I* left him,' put in Bannister hastily, stepping away from Hart, as if to distance himself from what his friend had done.

'It was an accident,' shouted Hart, pale and frightened. 'I chased him to the orchard, aiming to give him a scare, but he struggled, and I must have squeezed harder than I intended . . . But I *had* to do it! He said that Parker was the Chelsea Strangler, and that he planned to get Gorges closed down, leaving us without work. He was a terrible man . . . a monster!'

'He *was* an extortionist, as I know to my personal cost,' said Kipps, opening the door to an adjoining cell, and indicating that the dancing masters were to step inside. 'But that does not give you the right to kill him.'

'There are four of us and only two of you,' shouted Hart desperately, taking up a fighting stance that made Chaloner want to laugh. 'We will not surrender without putting up a—'

Kipps pulled out his sword and feinted at him. Hart gave a shrill screech of alarm, and darted through the

384

door. Bannister was quick to follow, and Chaloner shut them in.

It was an unsavoury affair, and Chaloner felt no satisfaction at having winkled out the truth. Moreover, he could not escape the unsettling knowledge that the business at Gorges was nothing compared to what else was brewing. He sent Kipps to ascertain whether 'Martha' was ready to leave, then went back to the cellars to make sure that the four prisoners could not escape.

'Wait,' cried Hart through the locked door. 'I have valuable information to share with you. Such as that the real crimes – the *other* murders – are the work of the spectre.'

'And you wait until now to tell me?' asked Chaloner archly. 'Why should I believe you? Especially after you have both claimed that you have never seen it.'

'Because I was too frightened then,' shouted Hart. 'He would have strangled me, too. I could tell by the look in his eyes. But now I have nothing to lose—'

'*His* eyes?' pounced Chaloner. 'It was definitely a man?'

There was an uncertain pause. 'I could not tell. But the eyes were like shiny beads.'

'Could it have been Sutcliffe? Or Wilkinson?'

'I met Sutcliffe once,' hedged Hart. 'He sat in the Swan all night, holding forth about Shakespeare. He was an assassin during the wars, but you would not think it to look at him.'

'Why not?'

'Because he is delicately built, like a lady. But to return to the spectre, I decided to follow it once. I am not sure why, as I am not usually brave. I trailed it to the prison, where it knocked on the door and was admitted.'

385

'Really?' said Chaloner flatly. 'And why would it go there?'

'Well, if the spectre *is* Sutcliffe, it would be to visit the place he considers his by right.' Hart's voice went high with panic as he heard Chaloner start to walk away. 'Please! I am telling the truth! This is information that might help you, and you should remember it when I am charged.'

'Elephants!' cried Bannister frantically, when Chaloner kept going. 'We will tell you about the elephants.'

Chaloner stopped, thinking about the note. 'Go on, then.'

'They live in the Tower of London,' gabbled Bannister, 'but there are plans afoot to move them to Chelsea because of the pestilence. They are coming tomorrow. I heard Reymes tell Cocke.'

As the last elephant in the Royal Menagerie had died some years ago, as a result of being fed a diet of meat and wine, Chaloner knew the hapless beast was well beyond worrying about the plague. He left the cellar in disgust, and rejoined Kipps, who was helping himself to wine in Gorges' kitchen.

'Well done, Tom. I shall tell the Earl of your cleverness when I deliver Frances to him today – she has just told me that she is cured, and that I shall be escorting her to Hampton Court.'

Chaloner looked sharply at him. 'You know her real identity?'

'Of course I do. I am his Seal Bearer, a trusted member of his household.'

'And I am *not* trusted,' said Chaloner bitterly. 'But even so, you should have told me.'

'I begged him to take you into his confidence, but he

would not listen.' Kipps shrugged apologetically, then his expression grew smug. 'He did not tell Wiseman either, and *he* is the family surgeon.'

Chaloner was irked. 'There is no aunt who became a Parliamentarian during the civil wars, is there? It was just a ruse to explain his interest in Gorges.' When Kipps nodded, he added sourly, 'Will you ask Warwick when I can start work at the Treasury? I have had enough of Clarendon and his damned secrets.'

'Do not take him to heart, Tom – it is just his way. Ah, here come Frances and Mrs Bonney. I am afraid you have been nursing a nest of vipers in your bosom, madam.'

He began to summarise what had transpired in the cellar, giving himself rather more credit for cornering the thieves than was accurate, but Chaloner did not care. He was more interested in pondering why the spectre had been allowed inside the prison – the tale had the ring of truth about it, and he was inclined to believe that Hart had been honest about what he claimed to have seen.

'I do not believe it,' whispered Mrs Bonney, when the Seal Bearer had finished. She was ashen with shock. 'Mr Hart, Mr Bannister, the Colliers, Mr Cocke . . . All rogues!'

'I told you to be wary,' said Frances, and Chaloner was astonished at the change in her. Now she was no longer frightened, she was her mother's daughter, with intelligence sparking in her eyes and the confident bearing of one used to authority. 'You should have listened.'

'I should, and my obstinacy has led me to make terrible mistakes,' whispered Mrs Bonney wretchedly. 'I shall tender my resignation at once.'

'No, you will not,' countered Frances firmly. 'You will stay and make amends. Gorges is a *good* place, especially now that Dr Parker is not here to force coffee on everyone.'

Chaloner left them debating the matter, and went outside, his mind a whirl of unanswered questions. Kipps followed, frowning worriedly.

'While I am delighted to be going to Hampton Court and seeing my friends, I do not like leaving you here alone in this den of thieves and killers. Perhaps we should send Brodrick with Frances instead. Or Wiseman.'

'The Earl would never forgive us if anything happened to her,' said Chaloner. 'And you are the only man I trust with her safety. Just hurry back as soon as you can.'

Kipps nodded a promise, and set off to solicit Brodrick's help in commandeering a carriage. Chaloner trailed after him, trying to decide what to do next. They met Wiseman en route, downcast because he had found a full report about Dorothy among the notes that Chaloner had taken from Parker's secret drawer, and it was clear that she would never recover. Kipps told him about Frances.

'I once remarked to the Earl that I would send Dorothy to Gorges, should the plague ever come to London,' said Wiseman. 'I was impressed by Parker's theories at the time, and must have waxed so lyrical about them that he decided it was the best place for his daughter, too. I thought she looked familiar.'

'*I* knew who she was,' gloated Kipps. 'He trusts me, you see.'

Wiseman was more interested in railing against Parker than acknowledging the Seal Bearer's taunts. As he spoke, he fiddled restlessly with the coin that Reymes had given him – the payment for bleeding his guests.

'I suspect all his assumptions were in error – there is no verifiable evidence that coffee can cure madness, and his conclusions are based on insufficient data. He was a— Damn!'

The coin spun out of his hand and flashed towards a drain, although Chaloner managed to stamp on it before it rolled in and would have to be retrieved from the filth that had accumulated there. Chaloner picked it up and examined it idly. He rarely saw gold, because Clarendon always paid in shillings, and milled guineas were a relatively new invention that had only made an appearance in the last eighteen months. The King's head was on the obverse, and underneath it was a symbol.

'Christ!' he blurted. 'There is an elephant on this.'

'Of course,' said Kipps. 'To show that the gold came from Guinea, which is how the coin earned its name, of course. Why do you think we at the Treasury refer to them as "elephants"? It is not just some random custom, you know.'

'Then why did you not say so?' demanded Chaloner, exasperated. 'Because if you had, I would have understood all these references to elephants arriving.'

'What elephants arriving?' asked Kipps in confusion. 'What are you talking about?'

'The letter Cocke dropped,' snapped Chaloner, pulling it from his pocket to wave under the Seal Bearer's nose. 'I showed it to you, and you should have told me at once that elephants might refer to . . .' He faltered as understanding dawned. 'You have no Latin! If you had, you would have reacted when Wiseman insulted you at chess this morning. Nor did you understand the epitaph on Thomas More's tomb.'

'Yes, I did,' objected Kipps, blushing scarlet with

mortification. 'I am just a little rusty. And what is this about insults at—'

'Then what does this say?' Chaloner shoved the note at him.

'I do not have my eye-glasses with me,' said Kipps, refusing to take it.

'You do not wear them,' countered Wiseman, smirking his delight at the Seal Bearer's discomfort, while Chaloner was disgusted with himself for not guessing sooner. He wondered how the Seal Bearer had managed to conceal his ignorance, given that he would need some Latin to fulfil his ceremonial functions at Court.

'I improvise,' said Kipps curtly, although the question was unspoken. 'And I know French, which is a lot more useful.'

'I should have translated it for you,' said Chaloner tiredly. 'Then we would have known.'

'Known what?' asked Wiseman.

Chaloner tapped the note. 'That a quantity of gold coins will arrive tomorrow at dawn.'

'*That* is the essence of this deadly plot?' Kipps sounded relieved. 'Then it is not so terrible! I do not need to abandon Hampton Court and race to your assistance after all.'

'Oh, yes, you do,' said Chaloner. 'I imagine they represent an enormous sum of money, and the fact that people know it is coming almost certainly means there is a plan afoot to steal it.'

'Could it be the King's gold?' asked Wiseman. 'I did hear that was to be moved out of White Hall at some point.'

'But not until August,' said Kipps. 'And I am Messenger of the Receipt, so I would know if Reymes planned to

390

do it sooner. Besides, it will go to Hampton Court, not Chelsea.'

Chaloner sincerely hoped that Kipps knew what he was talking about, as the loss of the Treasury in its entirety would likely plunge the country into another civil war.

Chapter 15

Chaloner was relieved when the carriage carrying Frances was finally ready to depart. White Hall's indolence had evidently permeated Buckingham House, because the business took an inordinately long time to arrange, and it was evening before all was set. Brodrick was to ride in the coach with her, while Kipps accompanied them on horseback. The Seal Bearer was armed with a pistol borrowed from Greeting – Chaloner had insisted on keeping Mrs Bonney's – and his sword was loose in its scabbard. Brodrick was delighted with the opportunity to inveigle his way into the royal presence again.

'I hate to admit it, Chaloner,' he whispered, 'but Buckingham House is too much for me. I like a little fun, as you know, but it is relentless here. Moreover, I dislike being ordered to enjoy myself at specific times, and would sooner let the revels develop naturally.'

Chaloner was thoughtful. 'So Reymes tells Hungerford and Greeting *when* to make merry, as well as ensuring that the company is noisy and rambunctious?'

Brodrick nodded. 'I felt from the start that it was contrived, and I was right.'

'You know Reymes quite well. Does he ever mention elephants?'

Brodrick regarded him askance. 'What a peculiar question! Is there a reason why he should?'

'Has he mentioned a consignment of them being delivered here?'

'No, and I seriously doubt that even he will go to that sort of expense – it is common knowledge that they consume vast quantities of meat and wine. They will be better off staying in London, where those commodities are more readily available.'

'They are readily available here,' said Chaloner drily. 'Especially wine, if your antics have been anything to judge by.'

Brodrick lowered his voice. 'Drink yes, but not food. The portions are meagre, and I had to snag a few cherries from Gorges' orchard yesterday, just to stop my stomach from growling. Incidentally, I saw that ghost when I was there – the spectre. It was talking to Franklin.'

'Then why did you not tell me at once?' demanded Chaloner, irked. No wonder the pace of his enquiries had been so frustratingly slow – no one bothered to talk to him! 'You know I have been trying to hunt it down.'

Brodrick looked furtive. 'Because Gorges does not encourage casual visitors, so I had no legitimate reason to be there now that you are investigat—'

'You went to see Frances,' surmised Chaloner. 'And you did not want me to find out, lest I put two and two together. Damn it, Brodrick! Will your family never trust me?'

Brodrick spread his hands in a shrug. 'It was not my decision to keep you in the dark. Indeed, when the Earl told me that she was here – which he did only because

393

he needed someone to watch her until you arrived – I urged him to be honest with you. As did Kipps.'

'This spectre,' said Chaloner, not much mollified. 'What were it and Franklin doing?'

'Talking,' replied Brodrick, and shuddered. 'I probably should have rescued him, as I cannot imagine the poor man enjoyed the experience.'

'Did he look frightened, then?'

'No, but it is never wise to advertise one's terror to the enemy – it damages the dignity. Oh, Lord! Now what?'

Wiseman had arrived with Dorothy in tow, announcing that there would be two extra passengers in the coach. His hapless wife had been dosed with so much soporific that she could barely stand.

'I shall install her at an asylum in Richmond instead,' the surgeon said, as he packed her into the vehicle. He lowered his voice. 'Be careful, Chaloner. I cannot decide who is on the side of the angels and who is a devil in this village. Trust no one. And that includes Eleanore Unckles.'

'I hardly think—' began Chaloner.

'It is just a hunch, but my instincts are usually right, so watch yourself. I never thought I would say it, but I wish Kipps was staying with you.'

Kipps heard his name spoken, and came to join them. 'Perhaps I *should* stay. I am sure Frances will be safe with Wiseman. He is always telling me how good he is in a brawl.'

'Protecting the Earl's daughter is more important than anything happening here,' said Chaloner, although he disliked losing the only men he could trust. 'We have no choice.'

394

'I shall return as soon as I can,' promised Kipps. 'With reinforcements, as I am sure the Earl will expedite matters when I tell him that gold is at stake. And with luck, we shall have troops from Spymaster Williamson by then, too. We will thwart these villains, Tom, never fear.'

It was a round journey of more than twenty miles – and they might be forced to stop if the road became too dark for the driver to see – so Chaloner doubted if Kipps would arrive back before mid-morning at the earliest. He felt oddly bereft as the coach rattled off with an important clatter, Kipps trotting behind on his nag, already urging the coachmen to hurry.

With a sigh, he pulled himself together and considered his next move. He had three leads to follow, two of which involved the spectre. First, he needed to ask Franklin about the discussion that Brodrick had witnessed. Second, he wanted to explore Hart's claim that the spectre had entered the prison. And third, he had to find Reymes, to see what more could be learned about the elephants – hopefully without warning the commissioner that his plot was about to be exposed.

'Dr Franklin has gone to the gaol,' said Mrs Bonney, when Chaloner returned to Gorges and demanded an audience with the physician. 'He works day and night now that Dr Parker is no longer here – he is *medicus* to the prisoners, as well as here, you see.'

Chaloner left Gorges, walking faster than was pleasant in the heat of a sultry summer evening. There was not so much as a breath of wind, and the air felt hot and heavy. The sky was clear, but there was a prickle of something in the offing – a thunderstorm, perhaps, massing out of sight over the horizon. Or was it just the unshakeable sense that something bad was about to happen, something he might be powerless to prevent?

He had not gone far, when he saw Eleanore sprinting towards him, skirts gathered in her hands to reveal strong and shapely legs.

'Come quickly,' she gasped, grabbing his arm. His skin tingled at her touch, although it was hardly the time for such fancies. 'Something is happening at the prison. Hurry!'

Eleanore was wrong: the prison was still and forbidding in the fading light, and not so much as a peep from a bird or a bark from a dog broke its oppressive silence. The Thames slithered greasily along its back, while clouds gathered in the distance, and Chaloner thought he saw a flash of lightning, although there was no accompanying thunder.

'There *was* something,' she insisted, when several minutes passed and nothing changed. 'People were coming and going far more than usual, and when I tried to go and chop vegetables in the kitchen, Samm told me that I was not needed.'

'Perhaps they are awaiting a delivery of more food supplies to cache,' suggested Chaloner. 'Or prostitutes have been booked to come and—'

'No, it was something more important than that, because Tooker and Samm are on tenterhooks. But we cannot stay here – someone will see us. Come.'

She led the way to a thicket of shrubs that grew by the College's south-east corner. It was an excellent vantage point, and allowed them to see not only the main entrance, but a little gate in the eastern wall that Chaloner had not noticed before. Then Eleanore hissed softly, and pointed with an urgent finger. Franklin was stealing along in a distinctly shifty manner.

'He has no need to creep about,' she whispered. 'As the prison's physician, he has every right to go there openly. So what is he doing?'

They watched Franklin reach the little gate and knock in what appeared to be a pre-arranged pattern of raps. It opened at once, and Tooker and Samm emerged. The three of them began a muttered conference.

'Can you get close enough to hear what they are saying?' asked Eleanore in an undertone. 'Yes? Then go. I shall wait here – you are used to this sort of thing, but I am not, and it is too important a matter for inadvertent bungling.'

Chaloner was pleasantly surprised by her sensible attitude to espionage. In his experience, amateurs tended to be annoyingly insistent on being included in anything risky.

With one hand on the hilt of his sword and the other clutching Mrs Bonney's dag, he eased through the undergrowth, struggling to move quietly over the dead leaves that littered the ground, all burned to crunchy crispness by the summer sun. Fortunately, the evening was now full of thick shadows, so at least he could keep himself invisible, even though he felt as if he was making more noise than a herd of cattle.

He went as close to the gate as he dared and stopped, but the trio were no longer talking and stood in silence. Had they heard him coming? Then the gate opened a second time and twenty or so men filed out – Spring and his cronies. Spring carried a lamp, which allowed Chaloner to see that all were heavily armed. Were *these* the weapons that Akers thought had been delivered to the Garden Court? Regardless, there was not much he could do against such a horde, other than watch, listen and learn.

'I told you – no!' Spring was snarling. 'We need time to prepare. Next week will—'

'It must be tonight,' interrupted Franklin sharply. 'Or not at all.'

'Are you sure this is wise, Franklin?' Tooker was clearly nervous, too. 'Our other operations have been carefully planned, but this smacks of undue haste. We will all hang if they are caught.'

'Yes, *all* of us,' spat Spring viciously. 'Because we will not protect you if your greed puts us in danger. We are in this together, for profit *and* for failure. Besides, if you want us to go now, we will not have time to take the back roads – we shall have to use the main one. And folk look hard at anyone going *towards* London these days.'

'Tonight's work will not be in London,' said Franklin. 'It will be here, in Chelsea.'

'No!' snapped Tooker. 'We agreed not to operate here. It is too dangerous.'

'But in this instance, the rewards far outweigh the risks.' Franklin addressed the prisoners. 'In fact, you will win enough to keep you in comfort for the rest of your lives, and these nocturnal forays will be a thing of the past. Unless you choose to continue them, of course.'

'You want us to visit Buckingham House,' predicted Spring heavily. 'Well, you can think again. It is packed with courtiers and their servants; we would get nowhere near it.'

'Oh, yes, you will,' said Franklin smugly. 'Because I have dosed their wine with a soporific, and everyone

398

will be sound asleep. Listen – the place is normally buzzing with activity by now, but what do you hear? Nothing. They are already drowsy, and will be asleep within the hour.'

With sudden, startling clarity, Chaloner recalled the vinegar-soaked sponge under the chair in the ballroom. It was Franklin's favoured remedy against the plague, and was a strong indication that the physician had indeed been inside Buckingham House.

'It is quiet,' conceded Tooker. Samm was a silent hulk behind him, but Chaloner could see that the gaoler was also tense and uneasy. 'But I thought it was because Brodrick has left.'

'I do not care,' said Spring firmly. 'It is too chancy, and we are not going.'

'Think of the riches that would be yours if you did,' coaxed Franklin. 'Reymes' guests may not have as much money as the others you have preyed upon, but they still own all manner of priceless trinkets.'

As Franklin continued to tempt, Chaloner recalled all the people who had mentioned burglaries that targeted the homes of the rich – homes that had been abandoned as the plague had spread. He, like everyone else, had assumed the culprits were local villains, but he had been wrong. They were Spring and his cronies, slipping out of the College under cover of darkness and slinking back with the dawn. Moreover, Stephens at the Treasury had noted that all the crimes had occurred on the western side of the city. Of course they had – it was the part nearest Chelsea.

But how did they know where to strike? Chaloner rolled his eyes. He knew the answer to that, too: Franklin had a courtier brother – the Admiralty Proctor, who had been left in the disease-infested capital and was bitter about it. What better way to avenge himself on his absent colleagues than by providing his sibling with a list of who was away? And Chaloner knew the proctor was dishonest, because Captain Lester had said as much when *Swiftsure* had docked in Harwich.

Chaloner looked back at the men by the gate. It was clever to use prisoners to burgle, as who would suspect men who were thought to be incarcerated? And it explained why Spring and his friends had better food, spacious accommodation and the freedom to lounge in the yard – being spokesmen for the inmates had nothing to do with it.

So was this the deadly plot that was brewing? Reymes' guests losing the gold guineas they had brought to Buckingham House? Chaloner sagged in relief. It was not so dreadful.

'We are not doing it,' Spring was insisting, growing angrier by the moment. 'Empty houses are fair game, but you want us to invade one that is bursting at the seams with people.'

'So this job is too challenging for you?' taunted Franklin. 'You, who brag that you are the best in the business?'

Chaloner found he was disappointed in the physician, who had seemed an amiable, decent sort of man, genuinely concerned with the welfare of his patients. However, as the argument progressed, he witnessed an unsettling change: Franklin's friendly affability gradually evaporated, and he became caustic and sullen, much like his odious sibling.

'We are the best because we are careful,' Spring snarled. 'And being careful does *not* entail working in Chelsea, where we might be recognised.'

400

'So what if you are?' Franklin flashed back. 'Being arrested the last time was not so terrible, was it? Good things happened – you met my brother.'

Another snippet of an overheard conversation returned to Chaloner – the one between Reymes and the brown-coat in the rectory, about Spring and his friends being picked up a week after the Battle of Lowestoft, but in better health than they should have been after days in an open boat. Criminals were often offered a choice of execution or naval service, so it was obvious what had happened: Spring's talents had snagged the attention of Richard Franklin at the Admiralty, who had suggested a third option.

'Yes, but I doubt even he could save us from the noose if we were caught stealing yet again,' said Spring sourly. 'I repeat: we are not doing it.'

Franklin's voice turned icy. 'Then my brother will hang you tomorrow. He made our terms perfectly clear – you either follow my orders, or our alliance may be considered at an end.' He stepped back smartly when Spring started forward with murder in his eyes. 'And you will definitely die if I fail to report back to him by morning.'

There was a moment when it looked as though Spring would take the risk anyway, but then the felon inclined his head stiffly. 'Very well. But bear in mind that if we are caught, we shall have nothing to lose – *we* will consider our alliance at an end, and you and your stinking brother will hang next to us.'

'No one will hang if you do your work properly,' said Franklin crossly. 'Now go to Buckingham House and wait for me in the grounds. I will slip into the house first, to make sure everyone is asleep.'

The discussion was over. Spring and his cronies

401

melted away into the night, while Franklin lingered a few more moments, whispering to Tooker and Samm, then he, too, disappeared. When he had gone, the warden and his henchman exchanged a glance that revealed the depth of their own concern about the scheme, then stood in silence, smoking their pipes in the warm glow from Spring's lantern.

Hiding in the shadows, Chaloner was not sure what to do. Should he go to Buckingham House and attempt to wake the drugged courtiers, with a view to catching Franklin and his burglars in the act? Or should he confront Tooker and Samm about their policy of allowing inmates out to steal?

'What is wrong?' came a soft whisper at his side, making him jump. 'I just saw a lot of prisoners sneaking through the trees. Why did you not stop them?'

Disconcerted that Eleanore had moved stealthily enough to startle him, Chaloner told her what he had overheard, finishing with the fact that he could not challenge twenty-plus heavily armed men on his own.

'So which of them strangled Nancy?' asked Eleanore, clearly unimpressed by his timidity. 'Not Tooker – he does not have the courage. Samm, a prisoner or Franklin?'

'Franklin, probably. He was in Clarendon House when Underhill died, and he was in Chelsea when Nancy, Kole and Parker were murdered.'

Eleanore was thoughtful. 'But he will not confess on the basis of what you heard here, so we had better start with Tooker. We shall tell him that he will hang unless he turns King's evidence and gives us what we need to charge Franklin with Nancy's murder.'

402

Chaloner did not think it was a good idea to tackle Tooker when Samm was with him, but Eleanore was insistent, and he was foolishly loath to disappoint her again. He extracted a promise that she would stay in the bushes until he told her it was safe to come out, then strode forward quickly when he saw the warden and his henchman finish their pipes and prepare to re-enter their domain.

'You have a lot of explaining to do,' he said, watching them leap in shock at the sound of his voice. 'I know exactly what you have been doing.'

The blood drained from Tooker's face. Samm reached for the gun in his belt, but Chaloner held Mrs Bonney's dag, and the chief gaoler froze into immobility when he saw it levelled at him.

'Throw it down,' ordered Chaloner.

'We are only taking the air,' blustered Tooker, watching Samm toss his weapon on the ground. 'As we always do of an evening.'

'That is perfectly reasonable,' said Chaloner. 'What is not, however, is allowing your charges out to do the same. How much money have you made from sending Spring to steal?'

'Christ!' gulped Tooker, white with horror. Then his voice went from indignant to wheedling. 'It was Franklin's idea. Him and his brother.'

'It is true,' nodded Samm. 'We did not want to do it, but they made us.'

'They threatened to kill our wives if we did not follow their orders,' elaborated Tooker.

'You are not married,' said Chaloner, recalling Akers' contention that neither cared if plague-infected prisoners put gaolers' families in danger, because they had no

403

spouses of their own. 'So do not lie. You will only make matters worse.'

'Did I say wives?' asked Tooker desperately. 'I meant sisters. They—'

'Enough!' snapped Chaloner. 'I heard your conversation with Franklin and Spring. You—'

Tooker staggered suddenly, hand to his heart, and Chaloner's split second of inattention allowed Samm to make his move. The gaoler hurtled forward, and crashed into Chaloner with such force that both went flying. Chaloner landed hard enough to make his head spin, and by the time his vision cleared, Samm was looming over him with a heavy stone. Chaloner jerked to one side, and felt the ground vibrate as the rock plummeted down next to his ear. Enraged and determined, Samm fastened his hands around Chaloner's throat.

Chaloner had been in many desperate situations in his time, but never one that was quite so pathetically mundane as lying flat on his back while a brute of a man choked the life out of him. One of his arms was trapped beneath him, and it was, of course, the one he needed to reach his knives – the gun was lost in the grass. He flailed with the other, scoring several vigorous punches and even a jab to the eyes, all of which Samm stoically ignored.

He knew the most useless thing that anyone could do in his situation was to grab his assailant's hands in the hope of prising them off, but he did it anyway. While he struggled with Samm's diabolical strength, a distant part of his mind asked whether this was what had happened to Nancy, Underhill, Kole and Parker. It made sense that Samm was the strangler – Franklin would have more exotic means at his disposal.

He was weakening, and knew he had to do something fast. He kicked upwards as hard as he could, aiming for the chief gaoler's groin, but although it must have hurt, Samm did not release his deadly hold. Where was Eleanore? Watching in horror from the bushes, bound by her promise to stay there until he called her? Or had she tried to come to his rescue, but had been overpowered by Tooker?

With a massive effort of will, he let go of Samm's hands and scrabbled on the ground, hunting for something, anything, that he could use as a weapon. There was nothing, not even a twig. He managed to snag a handful of dust, though, and flung it straight into the gaoler's eyes. But Samm did not flinch, and the pressure only intensified.

And then Chaloner knew he was defeated.

Chapter 16

Chaloner heard a distant roaring. Was it thunder or the sound of approaching death? The sky was dark above him, and he could no longer see Samm's silhouette. But the pressure was gone from his throat and Samm's weight was no longer crushing his chest. He drew one deep, rasping breath, then another, and gradually his normal senses began to return.

'Stand against the wall, Tooker,' a man's voice was saying. Chaloner turned his head to see Samm lying face down next to him. 'Now, if you please.'

'This outrage will cost you dear, Akers,' hissed Tooker. 'Interfering with matters that do not concern you. You will pay with your life when Samm wakes up.'

'Samm is dead,' said Akers flatly. 'And I will not tell you again – stand against the wall, or he will not be the only one to meet his Maker tonight.'

Chaloner blinked in an effort to dispel the lingering blurriness. Akers held the lamp, which illuminated Tooker's furious face. It also revealed that Samm had been killed by a blow to the head. Confused and wary, Chaloner groped on the ground for Mrs Bonney's gun.

'Some of the prisoners are missing,' Akers was saying to the warden. 'And I am told that *you* gave orders for their release.'

'If you want to live, walk away,' urged Tooker. 'Why antagonise powerful and dangerous men by meddling in their affairs? They will crush you like a fly, so drop that cudgel and leave. In return, I shall not tell anyone what happened here.'

'And find myself throttled one night?' Akers glanced at Samm. 'Or will you find another way to dispatch your victims now that your pet strangler is dead? I saw what he tried to do to Chaloner.'

'We had nothing to do with the murders,' said Tooker. 'Listen to me, Akers. I can give you money – lots of it. Take your wife and go somewhere far away. Altrincham, perhaps.'

Chaloner struggled to his feet with the dag in his hand. He had still not fully recovered, and would likely lose a fight if Akers accepted Tooker's offer. He only hoped the sight of the gun would provide enough of a deterrent.

'Tooker lets Spring and his friends out to burgle,' he rasped. 'It has been going on for weeks. You do not want to be associated with—'

'Lies,' snapped Tooker. He appealed to Akers again. 'You can become a wealthy man tonight, and nothing will ever be said about the fact that you brained my chief gaoler.'

'Your chief gaoler was the Chelsea Strangler,' said Akers coldly. 'And I caught *you* watching him attempting to claim his next victim. Now tell me what is going on. Not with Spring and his minions – they are nothing. I want to know what is happening in the Garden Court.

407

Who are those prisoners? Or should I say those *guests*, given that they were no more captive than I am?'

'I do not know,' replied Tooker impatiently. 'They did not tell me, and I did not ask. All I can say is that I was under orders to keep them hidden, and to do whatever they wanted.' He glanced at Chaloner. 'Which did not include being interrogated by him – they were vexed about that. But forget them, Akers. The *real* money comes from my arrangement with Franklin.'

'You are a fool,' said Akers disgustedly. 'The business in the Garden Court is far more important than Franklin's antics.'

'Not so,' insisted Tooker. 'I am paid a pittance for housing those men, a mere fraction of what Franklin's operation brings me.' He blanched when Akers raised his cudgel. 'It is true!'

'Answer my questions, or I will knock your brains out, like I did Samm's. Now, who are those guests, and where have they gone?'

Chaloner regarded Akers in alarm. 'They have gone?'

'An hour ago,' replied the gaoler, hefting the bludgeon higher as he glared at the cowering warden. 'And this villain had better explain what is happening or—'

'But I do not know,' bleated Tooker. 'Soldiers arrived with three carriages, and off they all went. The soldiers had the proper paperwork, and it is not for me to question the government's secret dealings.'

'Regicides and rabble-rousers,' croaked Chaloner. 'I have the list from your office – ten names, with two more that were illegible because the bottom was burnt off.'

'That was me,' confessed Akers sheepishly. 'I knocked over a candle when I was searching Tooker's desk – fear made me clumsy. But what is this about regicides?'

'They are not regicides,' objected Tooker. 'You met them, Chaloner – they are just harmless, middle-aged men in need of refuge. Besides, the *government* charged me to keep them here. They would not have done that for king-killers.'

'*Who* in the government?' demanded Akers. '*Who* signed these documents that you keep mentioning?'

'The Lord Chancellor.' Tooker's eyes were calculating as he felt himself on firmer ground, and he pointed at Chaloner. '*His* master, and if he tells you otherwise, he is lying. Now, shall we say fifty pounds, Akers, to dispatch Chaloner and say no more about this unsavoury matter? I hear that Altrincham is a *very* beautiful place . . .'

Chaloner held his breath. It was a lot of money, and Akers worked in the prison because his farm had failed and he had no other source of income. But Akers scowled indignantly.

'How dare you try to bribe me! That will go in my official report, too.'

'All right, I should not have done that,' conceded Tooker hastily. 'But the business with those guests is perfectly above board. Look – here are the deeds, all signed by Clarendon himself.'

Chaloner and Akers studied them in the flickering lamplight.

'Old customs certificates,' said Chaloner. 'Someone probably fished them out of the Admiralty's rubbish heap.' He regarded Tooker appraisingly. 'You cannot read, can you? *That* is why Samm's initials, rather than yours, were on the ledger in your office.'

'Of course I can read!' cried Tooker, affronted.

Chaloner held out one of the certificates. 'Then tell me what this says.'

Tooker folded his arms. 'No. And you cannot make me.'

The warden's illiteracy, not uncommon in an age where education had often been interrupted by civil war and political upheaval, made several things clear to Chaloner.

'If Tooker could not read the names on that list,' he said to Akers, 'then I imagine he really is ignorant of who was in his Garden Court.'

Akers grimaced wryly. '*I* read them, but I had no idea either. I memorised them, though.' He began to recite them like a mantra. 'Price, Broughton, Dove, Dendy—'

'Oh, Christ!' blurted Chaloner, as understanding shot into his mind like a bolt of lightning. 'Dove and Dendy! The Peacemaker and the Dandy!'

Akers blinked. 'What?'

Chaloner's thoughts whirled in confusion, and it took an effort to articulate them. 'Hannah's letter . . . *the ghost-man will leade the Peace-Maker and the Dandey to Stryke the Sicke and the Hurte.* She meant Dove and Dendy. '

'He is deranged,' said Tooker. 'Ignore him, Akers, and listen to me. I—'

'Shut up,' snapped Akers, and turned back to Chaloner. 'Who is Hannah?'

'My wife.' Chaloner's heart was pounding. 'She caught the plague in a theatre. The "ghost-man" is the spectre. She was not raving – she was sending me an important message!'

But the realisation raised more questions than solutions. How had Hannah known what he would be investigating weeks into the future? And why had she chosen to write her warning in such an abstruse way?

Akers nodded towards Samm's body. 'He is the stran-

410

gler, which means he must be the spectre, too. Your Hannah was referring to him.'

'I chased the spectre,' said Chaloner. 'It was too small and fast to have been Samm, while you have been under the impression that it is a woman. However, it was seen visiting the prison, so I imagine Tooker knows its identity.'

'I admit that a person who *may* be the spectre has been staying in the Garden Court with the other twelve,' hedged the warden. 'But it was government business, and none of mine.'

'But it is *not* government business, is it?' said Akers, brandishing the worthless certificates. 'However, it is not for us to decide whether you are a conspirator or just a fool – that will be determined at your trial. Now tell us this spectre's name. And lest you think to lie, remember that cooperating with us may save you from the gallows.'

'The spectre is Sutcliffe,' predicted Chaloner. 'Hannah probably saw the "ghost-man" at the theatre, a place that Sutcliffe liked to frequent. Cocke told us that Sutcliffe stopped going when an actor dropped dead during *The Indian Queen*, which was probably where Hannah caught it.'

'All right,' whispered Tooker, glancing around uneasily. 'The spectre is Sutcliffe. But *please* do not say I told you. He is an assassin, and his strangling hands will find me, even in the Tower.'

Chaloner thought about what Thurloe had said – that Sutcliffe was a vicious malcontent, dissatisfied with everyone and everything around him. Who better to bring like-minded fanatics together? And he had a motive, too: to repay the government for laying claim to a building

411

he thought should be his. Thinking about Thurloe made something else clear, too. He glanced at Akers.

'You were brave,' he murmured, 'to send Thurloe reports about the prison.'

Akers was honourable, and exactly the sort of man with whom the ex-Spymaster would correspond. Wearily, Chaloner recalled his friend's advice – to concentrate on the prison for answers. As usual, Thurloe had been right, and Chaloner should have listened to him.

'I cannot tell you how relieved I was when you arrived,' Akers whispered back, then smiled wryly. 'I imagine you were suspicious when I tried to tell you everything that I had learned.'

Chaloner nodded. 'But I would not have been, if you had also mentioned that you know Thurloe.'

'But I do *not* know Thurloe – we have never met. I chose him as the recipient of my reports because I could not decide who in the current government might be involved. However, I was a staunch Parliamentarian in the Commonwealth, and I sometimes sent him information about my more radical Royalist neighbours, so I felt I could trust him with this, too.'

'So he does not know your name?' asked Chaloner, supposing it explained why Thurloe had neglected to mention that there was someone at the prison who would be on his side.

'He does not, and nor is he aware that I work here. It was cowardly to remain anonymous, I suppose, but these are dangerous times, and a man must take what precautions he can to protect himself and his own. But we should not discuss this now. Not when you have rebels to hunt, and I have a prison to secure.'

'Never mind the prison,' said Chaloner. 'The dissidents are far more pressing.'

'Unfortunately, resentment has been festering among the inmates ever since Spring was appointed as their spokesman, and it has reached crisis point. A firm hand is needed tonight, or we shall have two thousand angry Dutchmen on the loose. My duties lie here.'

'Christ!' muttered Chaloner. A mass escape would make tracking Sutcliffe and his rebels all but impossible. 'Do you need help?'

'We can put our own house in order, thank you. Do not worry – there are more good men than bad here, and they will follow me once Tooker is behind bars. It is the least I can do, given that I inadvertently misled you about the spectre – I should have known that no woman would be involved in such dark business. Of course it was Sutcliffe.'

'You know him?'

'Enough to tell you that he might be small and possessed of a peculiarly feminine voice, but that you should not underestimate him.'

Despite his brush with death, Chaloner found himself oddly light-hearted. The knowledge that Hannah had tried to help him in her dying hours meant more to him than he would have imagined, and the more he thought about it, the more certain he was that the note had been her way of telling him that he was forgiven for being away when he should have been at her side.

He hurried back to the place where he had left Eleanore, only to find her gone. He looked around in alarm. Had Franklin or Spring caught her? Then he became aware of someone creeping towards him in the

413

darkness, and heaved a sigh of relief when he heard Eleanore call his name.

'Where have you been?' he asked. 'I was worried.'

'I went to the village to fetch help, lest things went awry for you. Unfortunately, everyone was asleep except the Strangeways men, although it seems you did not need help anyway. So what happened with Tooker? Will he turn King's evidence against Nancy's killer?'

Chaloner told her all that had transpired, including Akers' timely intervention, and watched her eyes grow wide with shock.

'So Spring and his men are robbing Buckingham House as we speak? We must stop them, Tom! We cannot stand by while they commit a crime that will make them rich. You say it was Samm who strangled my sister – *he* might be beyond the reach of justice, but his thieving cronies are not.'

Chaloner caught her hand before she could dash off. 'And do what? There are twenty of them, all armed. Besides, I need to find Sutcliffe and these so-called prisoners.'

'They will be long gone, and you cannot track them in the dark. But the crime at Buckingham House *can* be thwarted, and if you will not help me, I shall do it myself.'

'Wait! I will ask Akers to—'

'He cannot – you just told me that he has his hands full with the prison. We are the only ones who can challenge Spring now. Or are you afraid of him?'

'No, but—'

'Then come *on*.'

Chaloner trailed after her only because his near-strangulation had left him muddle-headed, although

414

a persistently nagging voice at the back of his mind told him it was entirely the wrong thing to do.

The village was silent, and the air hung heavy, oppressive and sultry in the dark streets. Chaloner saw lightning again in the distance. Perhaps a thunderstorm would break the heatwave, and bring some cooler weather. He only hoped that he and Eleanore would still be alive to appreciate it.

They passed the rectory, where one or two lights still shone, despite the late hour. He thought he saw someone in its garden, and would have stopped to investigate, but Eleanore pulled him on. Eventually, they reached Buckingham House.

'Wait,' he whispered, as she began to open the gate. He took a deep breath in an effort to clear his wits. 'We cannot just march in. We need a plan.'

'Then think of one.' Eleanore sounded fraught and impatient in equal measure.

'We shall rouse the sleeping courtiers, and let *them* tackle the men who aim to steal their elephants. Although we shall have to avoid Reymes, of course.'

'Why?' asked Eleanore, puzzled. 'He will not want his guests robbed.'

'Because he is involved.' Chaloner rubbed his head, wishing he could think more clearly. 'Perhaps not in the burglaries, but in something unsavoury, and we cannot trust him to be on our side. Ergo, he is not the person we should wake first.'

But Eleanore shook her head in exasperation. 'Your plan is flawed. You said that Franklin has dosed everyone with a soporific. We will not be able to wake Reymes or anyone else.'

415

'He cannot have fed them too much, for fear of killing them, while there will certainly be servants who are awake. So you warn the staff, while I look for Greeting and Hungerford – they will help us.'

'I do not like this scheme,' declared Eleanore uneasily. 'You do not know who to trust, so why rouse anyone? It is better to deal with Spring and his cronies ourselves – pick them off one by one in the dark. They will not know what is happening until it is too late.'

That stratagem was even shakier than his own. 'One mistake would see them all turning on us at once, and I doubt we will escape alive, which will leave Sutcliffe's dissidents free to do whatever they like.'

Eleanore was silent for a moment, then inclined her head. 'Very well, we shall do it your way, although I hope for your sake that it works.'

He was puzzled. 'Why for my sake?'

'Because there will be trouble if Spring does manage to make off with these courtiers' elephants, and it emerges that the Earl of Clarendon's spy failed to stop them.'

She had a point, although Chaloner could think of no way around it. She opened the gate, but the notion that all was not right persisted, and this time it was powerful enough to keep him rooted to the spot.

'Now what?' she hissed, turning back irritably.

'This is wrong.' Again, he wished his wits were sharper. 'Something is amiss . . .'

'Yes, something *is* amiss – a burglary in progress! Now, come *on*, or it will succeed.'

Chaloner still did not move. 'You were not reckless with your safety outside the prison just now. What has changed?'

416

Eleanore sighed softly. 'The knowledge that these rogues are in league with the man who killed my sister. I did not know it then, but I do now. *Please*, Tom. We waste time by chatting here.'

The urgency in her voice started him walking again, but his sense of impending disaster grew stronger with every step. He struggled to analyse what was bothering him, and wished he could stop for a moment to think.

'It is quieter than it has been in weeks,' whispered Eleanore, as they neared the great house. 'Franklin's potion has done its work well.'

Chaloner saw a shadow by the porch, and hauled Eleanore behind a tree, out of sight. He was only just in time, as several figures emerged from behind the fountain to converge on the front door where Franklin was waiting to wave Spring and his friends inside.

Chaloner and Eleanore crept into Buckingham House to be greeted by a very bizarre sight. Lamps were lit in the ballroom, where a dozen courtiers were slumped. Lady Savage still held her wine goblet, although her companions had managed to set theirs down before they had nodded off. Chaloner assumed that the remaining guests – Hungerford and Greeting among them – had retired to bed when they had felt lethargy descend.

'Wait!' whispered Eleanore, baulking suddenly. 'What if the guests or their staff accuse us of being in cahoots with the robbers?'

It was a little late to be thinking of that, thought Chaloner irritably. 'Hungerford and Greeting will not. I will look for them, while you speak to the servants.'

'But I do not know the servants – they have no reason to trust me. I know Hungerford, though, so I will rouse

417

him, while you fetch Greeting – who lodges on the second floor, third room on the left.'

She had disappeared before Chaloner could demur. Swearing under his breath, he tiptoed up the stairs, hoping he would not meet a burglar, because he was still unsteady on his feet and in no state to do battle. He pulled Mrs Bonney's gun from his belt and checked it was loaded. Perhaps the sight of a firearm would dissuade anyone from wanting a swordfight with him. He ducked behind a curtain when Spring passed. The felon was scowling, perhaps because all he carried was a mock-gold jewel box that appeared to be empty. Chaloner reached the next floor, and was just passing Cocke's old room when he saw a light.

The door was ajar, and he peered around it to see Doyley sitting there, writing by candlelight. Of course! The commissioner had recently abandoned the rectory for the greater comfort of Buckingham House. Chaloner heaved a sigh of relief. Doyley would help. He pushed open the door and quickly slipped inside. Doyley looked up in surprise when Chaloner put his finger to his lips, warning him against calling out.

'There are burglars in the house,' he whispered. 'We must—'

The tap of approaching footsteps in the hall outside caused him to peer back around the door to see who was coming. All his attention was on watching Spring pad past, so he knew nothing of Doyley's intentions until the gun was wrenched from his hand. He sighed: he did not have time for lengthy explanations.

'There are burglars in the house,' he repeated, trying to inject sufficient urgency into his voice. 'We need to stop them before your fellow guests lose all their elephants.'

'How do you know?' Doyley sounded angry.

Chaloner appreciated why the commissioner was wary of someone who invaded his room in the middle of the night with a firearm, but it was exasperating even so. 'Just trust me.'

'Shut up,' snapped Doyley, pushing him back with his free hand. 'You will ruin everything.'

Chaloner was about to explain further when he saw that Doyley's shove had left a brown mark on his shirt, one that looked like a muddy fingerprint. He looked at it more closely. It was snuff. And then many things suddenly became horribly clear.

He had seen similar smudges on the package of documents that Doyley had handed Evelyn in Deptford, and was disgusted that it should have slipped his mind. Then he would have made the connection between Doyley and the dirty smears on the list of rebels in Tooker's office *and* on the elephant note – a message that Doyley must have sent to Cocke. Which meant that Doyley was involved! Chaloner felt physically sick. His stupidity would see the plot succeed!

'Did you move from the rectory to oversee the crime in person?' he asked tiredly.

'No talking,' ordered Doyley. 'Or I will shoot you.'

Desperately, Chaloner wondered if Eleanore had managed to alert Hungerford, but she was taking a long time over it, and he could hear the thieves moving from room to room, increasingly confident when no one stirred. Then came Reymes' indignant voice, followed by an answering groan from a drowsy woman. Chaloner felt a surge of relief. The courtiers were waking up without outside help. The plot might yet be thwarted.

'Stop,' ordered Doyley sharply, as Chaloner took a step towards the corridor.

'Why? People are coming to now. The alarm will be raised, and Spring and his friends will run to save their skins. It is over.'

Doyley smiled coldly. 'It is not over at all. In fact, it is only just beginning.'

And then Chaloner understood at last. 'This is a diversion! The real crime is taking place elsewhere – and involves regicides and other dangerous dissidents!'

Chapter 17

Doyley made no reply to Chaloner's accusation, while out in the hall Reymes was yelling at the top of his voice. His howls were punctuated by indignant squawks from Lady Savage and the distant sound of a skirmish: the burglars were meeting at least some resistance from their intended victims.

'You sent us to sleep with cheap wine,' bawled Lady Savage accusingly, 'in the belief that we are sots who will not notice. Indeed, everything here reeks of miserliness and thrift.'

'How dare you!' bellowed Reymes indignantly. 'Do you have any idea how much it costs to house you and keep you in revels? And do not say I can afford it, because I cannot – not with a fortune to pay for the "privilege" of being a commissioner. Now drink your wine, woman, and shut up. I have work to do.'

His voice grew closer, then Doyley's door was flung open and he strode in, although he stopped abruptly when he saw Chaloner held at gunpoint.

'He came to steal,' explained Doyley. 'But he chose the wrong room.'

'Hah!' exclaimed Reymes, gratification lighting his eyes. 'So Clarendon's spy is a common felon. Excellent! I shall not let the old goat forget this.'

'I shall keep him here until you are free to take him into custody,' said Doyley.

Reymes nodded his thanks and was gone, leaving Chaloner blinking in confusion. If Reymes was part of the plot, he would know that the thieves hailed from the prison, so why did he believe that 'Clarendon's spy' was one of them? He turned back to see Doyley smirking at him.

'You have no idea what is happening, do you? But do not think you will find out, because you will make a grab for this gun soon, so I shall have to shoot you. No questions will ever be asked, and you will be dismissed as a grubby little felon who tried to rob his fellow courtiers.'

Bewildered, Chaloner rubbed his head, although he was not at all perplexed about Doyley, who obviously intended to dispatch him as soon as a suitable interval of time had passed. So where were Sutcliffe and his rebels while Buckingham House was in turmoil? Stealing the money from the rectory? But of course they were! There had only been shillings in the bag Chaloner had taken, but there could well be guineas in the others.

'Your note to Cocke was a fiction,' he said, aiming to see if he was right. 'The elephants are not arriving at dawn – they are already here.'

Doyley frowned. 'Cocke claimed he had lost that, but I had a feeling it had been stolen. I should have known it was you – a man sent to pry into matters that do not concern him.'

'He dropped it in the orchard, where it was picked up by Jem Collier.'

Chaloner could tell Doyley did not believe him, not that it mattered. He glanced at the door, wondering if he could dive through it before the commissioner pulled the trigger.

'You can die in here quickly, or out there slowly,' said Doyley sharply. 'I strongly advise the former. Do not underestimate me, Chaloner. I *will* carry out my threat.'

'I do not understand,' said Chaloner, fraught with tension. 'What is—'

Doyley raised the gun and squinted down the barrel. Fortunately, Chaloner's instincts were still sharp, even if his wits were sluggish. A distant part of his mind remembered the way Mrs Bonney's dag had pulled to the left when he had fired it in the orchard, so he jerked in the opposite direction. The bullet cracked harmlessly into the wall.

He leapt at Doyley before the commissioner could rearm. Doyley stumbled backwards, and Chaloner had just managed to push him against the wall when Reymes hurtled in.

'Thank God!' cried Doyley. 'Help me, Bullen!'

Reymes obliged his friend by slashing at Chaloner with the flat of his sword, blows that hurt enough to force him to release his prey. Chaloner scrabbled for his own weapon, but too late. Reymes' blade was at his throat, and the savage look in his eye warned against fighting back.

'He rushed me and the dag went off,' said Doyley in a voice that was unsteady with genuine shock. 'He would have murdered me had you not arrived. Kill him, before he tries it again.'

'I am not in the habit of skewering unarmed men,' retorted Reymes. 'Besides, I want to see Clarendon's face when I present him with evidence that a member of his household is a felon.'

'Then I will do it.' Doyley grabbed a knife from the table. 'He is too dangerous to leave alive, just so you can gloat.'

Doyley wanted him silenced before he could reveal what was afoot, Chaloner realised with quickening hope. Which meant that Reymes was *not* part of the conspiracy, or Doyley would not care what was divulged.

'This burglary is a diversion,' he said urgently, flinching when Doyley swiped at him. While Reymes pushed his friend back with an irritable scowl, Chaloner knocked the sword away from his throat. 'Listen to me, Reymes. There is a plot to—'

'Ignore him, Bullen,' ordered Doyley. 'And you cannot hand him to Clarendon alive – if you do, he will pose a serious threat to security. Let me kill him, and you will be well rewarded.'

Reymes regarded him in surprise, which allowed Doyley to stab at Chaloner a second time, a blow the spy only just managed to evade. Chaloner fumbled for a knife of his own, but his fingers encountered the Dutch telescope instead, which was far better for blocking slashes. In the distance, a woman squealed. Was it Eleanore? Regardless, it meant the thieves had moved to another part of the house, and so posed a less immediate danger to him.

'Doyley arranged for you to be burgled tonight,' he said to Reymes. 'By prisoners from—'

'Doyley did not – *I* did,' interrupted Reymes shortly. 'Although they are not prisoners. They are locals, eager to earn a shilling for a bit of easy work. Never let it be said that life here is dull.'

'They are prisoners!' insisted Chaloner urgently, dodging yet another swipe from Doyley's blade. 'And while you waste time here, different thieves are stealing the elephants.'

'What elephants?' demanded Reymes, eyes narrowing.

'Enough, Chaloner,' snarled Doyley furiously. 'You will be silent or—'

'The ones in the rectory.' Chaloner still had no idea who was in league with whom, but he knew he had to convince Reymes, or Sutcliffe and his radicals were going to succeed. 'Doyley fabricated a tale about stockpiling food in readiness for the plague, but the cellar contains coins, not victuals. I saw them the evening you caught the Colliers.'

Reymes' expression hardened. 'I had a feeling that they were telling the truth when they claimed they had never been downstairs. Was it you we chased then?'

'It must have been,' yelled Doyley, almost beside himself. 'So dispatch him before he tells everyone what he knows, and we have every criminal in the country at our doors.'

'That money is for the relief of injured sailors, Chaloner,' said Reymes sternly.' The Sick and Hurt Fund. You would not be so unscrupulous as to put that at risk.'

'The sick and hurt!' Chaloner's understanding coincided with a flicker of lightning. 'Hannah wrote that the Peacemaker and the Dandy would strike at the sick and the hurt. She must have overheard Sutcliffe say that the rebels were going to—'

'He is deranged,' cried Doyley. 'He cannot be trusted. For God's sake, Bullen, *end it*!'

'You rented Buckingham House, and invited the most debauched courtiers you could find to stay with you,' Chaloner forged on when Reymes wavered uncertainly. 'It was to attract attention away from the rectory. You hold noisy parties at specific times, with Greeting and Hungerford under orders to make as much racket as possible.'

'Bullen!' howled Doyley, lunging again. 'Enough!'

'It worked,' Chaloner went on. 'The villagers are fascinated by what happens here, and watch intently. Yet despite your best efforts, the rectory is still the subject of gossip. Wilkinson has a suspicious number of visitors for an unpopular man, and shadows move around it at night to—'

'Doyley explained that,' interrupted Reymes sharply. 'We are laying in food for the village, lest the plague—'

'There is not enough of it to supply a whole parish,' argued Chaloner. 'What he showed us was victuals for your brown-coats.'

'Brown-coats?' echoed Reymes, his eyes wary.

'That is enough,' snapped Doyley. 'Either dispatch him yourself, or get out of my way and let me do it.'

'The Sick and Hurt Fund was being delivered at the time.' Chaloner still addressed Reymes. 'You were probably here, overseeing the rumpus that would allow it to arrive unnoticed. Doyley *pretended* to take us into his confidence with the yarn about food, expecting that we would ask no more questions, but—'

'Go and manage your burglary, Bullen,' ordered Doyley, struggling to control his anger and frustration, 'or it will peter out into nothing, and you will have wasted your money. Leave Chaloner to me.'

'You told the Treasury men that the King's gold cannot

426

be moved before August,' said Chaloner, ignoring Doyley as he continued to appeal to Reymes. 'But that is not true, is it? It is a fiction, put about so that thieves will not ambush it when—'

'Stop!' breathed Reymes in alarm. 'Please, no more!'

'It is the *Treasury* that is arriving at dawn,' finished Chaloner. 'The Sick and Hurt Fund was a dry run, the final test of your careful arrangements. Everything is in place now – a team of guards, their victuals, a way of diverting attention from the place where the King's gold will be stored—'

'You are wrong,' said Reymes, although his horrified eyes suggested otherwise. 'Why would we bring it to Chelsea?'

'Because it cannot stay in White Hall while the plague rages, and nor can it be toted around the country every time the King decides to move. It needs somewhere secure and permanent, and conveniently close to where you can fulfil your obligations as commissioner. But it is not safe here, Reymes – it is being stolen as we speak.'

'Ignore him,' barked Doyley. 'He is trying to unsettle you for sinister reasons of his own. Now kill him, for God's sake. We have wasted enough time on his nonsense.'

But Reymes' attention remained fixed on Chaloner. 'Stolen by whom?'

'By the rebels who have been hiding in *your* prison – not as inmates, but as pampered guests. After all, who would think of looking inside a gaol for them? It was a stroke of genius to use the Garden Court to house them until the gold arrives.'

'What rubbish is this?' spat Doyley in disdain. 'No

one lives in the Garden Court. How could they? There is no room – it is full of food.'

'It is not,' countered Chaloner, 'although you let Kipps and me believe it was when we asked, with your coy winks and enigmatic remarks. And all to protect dissidents – enemies of the state.'

'You are the one with the regicide uncle, not me,' hissed Doyley. 'So do not—'

'Shut up!' Reymes turned back to Chaloner. 'What dissidents?'

'Ones who are in league with a man who thinks the College should be his, and who has been moving about Chelsea secretly, watching all that happens. People call him the spectre.'

'You mean Sutcliffe?' asked Reymes, frowning. 'I thought I saw him lurking near the College one night, and I always said that the government was rash to annoy an assassin by turning "his" property into a prison.'

'Sutcliffe!' sneered Doyley. 'A worn-out nobody, who spends all his time at the theatre. How can a man like him pose a danger to us? Chaloner is lying, Bullen.'

'He aims to steal the King's gold, and he has recruited a dozen men to help him,' Chaloner told Reymes, acutely aware that Sutcliffe's chances of success rose with every passing minute. 'Agitators and radicals, who will use it for rebellion. And if they do, *you* will bear the blame.'

Reymes blinked. 'Me? Why?'

'Because you arranged for your guests to be drugged and your house to be burgled. You did it to ensure that no one will be watching the rectory when the elephants arrive, but that is not what the King will believe when his hoard disappears. Was it Doyley's idea?'

428

'The burglary was.' Reymes cast a sidelong glance at his fellow commissioner, who was vehemently shaking his head. 'But we have not drugged anyone. Why would we? We need the guests awake to make a fuss over the robbers.'

'Listen!' urged Chaloner, trying to control his rising agitation. 'We have been howling loudly enough to wake the dead, but are your guests awake? No, they are not – other than Lady Savage, and even she has gone quiet. Doyley arranged for Franklin to dose everyone with a soporific that—'

Doyley lunged at Chaloner so hard that sparks flew from the telescope. 'Kill him *now*,' he screamed. 'I will hear no more lies.'

'But he is right,' said Reymes worriedly. 'My guests should be swarming all over the house by now and—'

With a roar of frustrated fury, Doyley leapt at Reymes instead. Reacting instinctively, Reymes raised his sword to protect himself, and Doyley's face contorted with agony as he ran on to the point. He collapsed on the floor, clutching his chest.

'My God!' breathed Reymes, staring at him with a mixture of horror and confusion. 'Everything Chaloner said is true! Why else would you attack me?'

Doyley was struggling to breathe. 'You . . . killed me . . . Your friend . . .'

'No friend of mine,' countered Reymes unsteadily. 'Not if you have conspired to steal the Treasury. Why would you do such a terrible thing?'

Doyley no longer tried to deny it, and the fight went out of him as his life ebbed away. 'I also resent . . . burdened with . . . costly commission . . .'

'So you threw in your lot with rebels?' asked Reymes

in a strangled voice. 'You, who were knighted for your loyalty to the King?'

Doyley closed his eyes. 'I deserved better . . . Then you said his gold . . . coming here . . . you asked my advice . . . to keep it safe . . .'

'What have you done?' Reymes was whiter than the dying Doyley. 'Tell me!'

Doyley's voice was barely audible. 'The plan . . . in motion . . . cannot stop it now.'

It was not long before Doyley's laboured breathing stopped, and despite frantic attempts by Reymes to make him reveal more, he died with sealed lips. When it was over, Chaloner opened the door and peered into the corridor. It was still and silent, and he wondered if the burglars had finished their raid, and were already traipsing back to the College with their loot. If so, they would be in for a shock when they arrived.

'Now we must try to thwart the greatest theft the country has ever known,' said Reymes, standing slowly, and rubbing a shaking hand over his eyes. 'Although God knows how.'

'Summon your men,' ordered Chaloner briskly. 'The brown-coats from your country estate.'

'I do not have a country estate – it was sold years ago, to pay for the civil wars. And *Doyley* hired the brown-coats, so obviously they cannot be trusted. On the contrary, they will likely fight against us.'

Chaloner regarded him askance. 'Why would you let Doyley, a man who has nothing to do with the Treasury, recruit the men who will guard it?'

'Because he offered, and I was low on funds.' Reymes' expression grew more wretched than ever. 'I assumed it was a gesture of friendship, but I should have known that no one does anything for nothing in this world. Damn him to Hell!'

'Then who do you trust in Chelsea?'

'No one. Doyley, Franklin, Cocke . . . they have all betrayed me. No, wait! I trust Kipps. He is a Treasury colleague, even if he is another Clarendon man. Where is he?'

'Gone to Hampton Court.'

Reymes closed his eyes in despair. 'Christ God!'

'Lend me a fast horse,' instructed Chaloner, aware that vital moments were passing. 'I will ride to White Hall, and tell Warwick to keep the King's gold there.'

'It is too late – it has already left,' gulped Reymes. 'And Doyley recommended that Warwick take an indirect route of his own choosing, for added security, so you are unlikely to intercept it.'

'Warwick!' pounced Chaloner. 'He can be trusted. What does he know about your plans?'

Reymes looked ill. 'Nothing – he is an empty-headed fool, which is why I turned to Doyley for help. I went secretly to White Hall on Monday night, and told him to load the carts ready for a quick getaway, but I declined to reveal anything else.'

So that was why Reymes had been striding into Chelsea from the east the previous morning, thought Chaloner; the tale about taking a walk to cure a headache was a lie. 'Was it your idea or Doyley's to keep Warwick in the dark?'

'His – he said it would be safer. Indeed, nearly all "my" ideas came from him: the noisy revels, bringing the gold here, pretending to stockpile food . . . Christ! I have spent every penny I own on this scheme, because

431

he said the King would reward me with a lucrative post when it succeeded. He played me for a fool, and even if I am not executed, I shall be ruined financially.'

'So will the King,' Chaloner pointed out.

Reymes screwed up his face in anguish and took a deep, shuddering breath. Then he released it slowly, and resolve took the place of despair.

'No! I shall not allow these bastards to destroy me. We are going to stop them.'

'How, when there is just you and me?' asked Chaloner. 'And Eleanore Unckles.'

While Reymes opened the door and peered out to check the coast was clear, Chaloner reloaded Mrs Bonney's gun and shoved it in his belt. Then the commissioner led the way towards the stairs. He was as nimble as a rhinoceros, and Chaloner was sure they would be heard as he blundered along. There was no sign of the burglars, but far too much was at stake to risk running into them.

'Did you really not know that the thieves were to come from the prison?' Chaloner asked softly, indicating that Reymes was to hold back while he looked around a corner.

'The agreement was for Franklin – whom Doyley insisted on taking into our confidence – to recruit a few trustworthy villagers. Dosing my guests with soporifics was never part of the plan. I would have refused.'

'But why bother with such elaborate subterfuge? Why not just bring the gold here in the dead of night, when the village sleeps?'

'Because some nosy soul would be awake, and then the elephants would be vulnerable for as long as they are stored here. Believe me, there *had* to be a distraction.'

Chaloner was finding it hard to credit Reymes' gullibility. The commissioner had agreed to let Franklin hire villagers for a task that was manifestly peculiar, so how could he possibly think that they would do it without asking questions? Moreover, the rectory was near Buckingham House, so what if the false burglary attracted a crowd, all hoping to witness more lewd revels? The Treasury carts could never arrive unnoticed then. And Reymes accused Warwick of being dim-witted!

'Tonight's theft was never intended to pull attention away from the rectory,' Chaloner explained, struggling not to sound contemptuous, 'but to distract *you*. I imagine Doyley expected you to be killed or incapacitated, leaving him free to heap all the blame for the theft on you.'

'But all the blame will *not* be heaped on me,' countered Reymes. 'Some will go to Clarendon, because it was *his* idea to move the Treasury from White Hall. So if you want to save his neck, you had better devise a plan. Fast.'

Unfortunately, Chaloner's mind was blank, and he had started to worry about Eleanore, too. Where was she? Still trying to rouse Hungerford? Or had she encountered a thief and suffered the same fate as the two servants? Then they reached the main stairs, and his heart sank when he peered over the balustrade to see Spring and his men gathering in the hall below. Two bodies lay nearby – footmen who had bravely attempted to repel the invasion.

'Him!' breathed Reymes, eyes fixed furiously on Spring. 'As soon as I clapped eyes on that fellow, I knew he was no Dutch sailor. His transfer here was almost certainly contrived.'

Chaloner recalled him saying as much in the rectory,

and was unimpressed that he had failed to follow up on his suspicions, given that he intended to install the Treasury nearby. It was unforgivably lax, and told Chaloner that he should never have been appointed prefect.

'Are we all here?' Spring was so confident that no one could hear him that he did not bother to whisper.

'Moor is still searching Reymes' quarters,' replied one of the thieves. 'The man must be rich, because he rents this fine house, but I found nothing of value, so I told Moor to keep looking.'

Chaloner felt Reymes stiffen with rage, and shot him a warning scowl. It would serve no purpose to mount an assault when the two of them were so heavily outnumbered.

'Moor is wasting his time,' said another sullenly, 'because the pickings here are paltry. Franklin risked our lives for a few jewels and some fancy clothes that will be difficult to sell on. He lied to us. We cannot live in luxury on what we found here tonight. We are—'

He stopped grumbling abruptly when another crony arrived at a run.

'I just saw Franklin,' the crony reported breathlessly. 'He says Tooker is caught, and is telling Akers everything. We cannot go back to the College now, but he wrote down a place where we can hide until he finds us somewhere better.'

He handed over a piece of paper, and as Spring was directly under the balustrade, Chaloner had a good view of it. He could not read the words, but he certainly recognised the writing. It was the same untidy scrawl as the cipher message in Cocke's room. In other words, *Franklin* had told the accompter how to cheat Gorges.

434

'Hah!' came a voice from the door, and everyone turned to see Hungerford, who held a sword and wore an eclectic array of improvised armour. He was followed by five similarly attired courtiers, including Greeting, the redoubtable Lady Savage and – to Chaloner's relief – Eleanore.

Spring gaped at them. 'You are meant to be asleep.'

'Eleanore woke us,' said Greeting. 'I fled for my life when I saw the dead footmen, but then I met Dr Franklin in the garden, who assures us that we can defeat you with ease.'

'So you had better put up your weapons,' added Hungerford, brandishing his blade.

'Franklin is creating yet another diversion,' murmured Chaloner to Reymes, noting that the physician had slyly stationed himself outside, so he would not be caught up in it. 'The Treasury must be close, so a battle here will—'

'Attack the bastards, Hungerford,' screamed Reymes, making Chaloner, courtiers and burglars alike jump in shock. 'For King and country!'

The skirmish that followed was one of the most ridiculous Chaloner could ever recall. He and Reymes had six courtiers and two women to fight twenty felons who were desperate not to be taken. Hungerford and Lady Savage comported themselves adequately, but the rest – on both sides – were more of a danger to their friends than the enemy. Those with guns fired without taking proper aim, while the others flailed recklessly and clumsily with whatever happened to be to hand – swords and knives in some instances, but also pokers, walking canes and part of a fire-screen.

Chaloner did his best, but was acutely aware that he

435

should be trying to save the Treasury, not doing battle with petty thieves, which did nothing for his concentration. Reymes had played right into Franklin's hands with his foolish yell, making Chaloner wonder afresh whose side the commissioner was really on.

But luck was with him. The shots, howls, thumps and clashing blades roused more guests, who stumbled in to see what was happening. Some brought weapons, but others, assuming it was a game, lobbed books, plates and even furniture at anyone they did not recognise. Chaloner staggered when a vase struck him on the shoulder. It jolted him forward, which allowed the scything blow that would have decapitated him to pass harmlessly over his head. He glanced up at the balustrade, and saw that Eleanore had thrown it.

And then it was over. With a howl of pain and bitter frustration, Spring tossed down his cudgel. Seeing him defeated, his cronies did likewise. Only half of his men had survived the encounter unscathed; the rest had been injured, two seriously. Three courtiers lay unmoving on the floor, although whether dead, drunk or drugged was impossible to say.

'I will turn approver,' cried Spring, one hand to a bleeding elbow. 'I will tell you about Tooker and Franklin in exchange for my life. I also learned things about Dutch shipping from the other inmates, which could help England to win the war.'

'It might,' cautioned Chaloner, stepping forward quickly to prevent an enraged Reymes from running the felon through. 'At least give Spymaster Williamson the opportunity to decide for himself.'

Reymes scowled, then turned to his victorious guests. 'You are in charge here, Newport – lock these rogues in the cellar and see to the wounded. The rest of you, come with me.'

'Come with you where?' asked Greeting warily.

'To save your country from ruin, if we are not too late,' replied Reymes shortly.

Chaloner watched Newport begin to herd the sullen burglars towards the basement, although it was Lady Savage's jabbing sword – stained with someone else's blood – that convinced them to go without a fuss. Then Eleanore appeared.

'I just saw Franklin racing towards the rectory,' she reported. 'We must stop him.'

'How did you see him?' demanded Reymes, eyes narrowing in suspicion. 'You were in here with us, fighting thieves.'

'Does it matter?' Eleanore sighed irritably when she saw it did. 'I spotted him through the window. Now, let us catch him before he causes even more trouble.'

There was thunder in the air as Chaloner trotted after Reymes, Eleanore and their rag-tag band of helpmeets, who comprised Greeting, Hungerford and two courtiers whose names he had forgotten. Then lightning lit the land as bright as day, before plunging it back into darkness again. It illuminated figures on the road ahead. The dissidents! Chaloner hauled out his sword and broke into a run, aiming to prevent the novices at the front from falling quite so early in the game. But it was not regicides and rabble-rousers who blocked the way.

'Strangeways!' spat Reymes. 'I might have known! He and his vile kin are part of this damned plot, and I shall kill them where they stand.'

He surged forward, and Chaloner was hard-pressed to keep up with him. Strangeways wore an old metal breastplate from the wars, and carried a fish-gutting knife, while young Wadham had what appeared to be a basin on his head, and brandished a stick that was far too thin to be of any use. Giles was unsteady on his feet, and the way he held his musket would have been dangerous if it had been loaded. They looked ludicrous, like characters from a comedy at the theatre. Reymes clearly thought so, too, because he faltered when he reached them, wrong-footed.

'What plot?' asked Strangeways, when the commissioner repeated his accusation.

'Stealing the King's gold,' replied Reymes tautly. 'As you know perfectly well. You joined it to harm me, you malicious bastard. You know I am prefect, and thus in charge of its security.'

'Actually, *I* asked them to come,' said Eleanore. 'I ran to the village for help while Tom eavesdropped on Franklin and Tooker earlier. Unfortunately, Franklin dosed *them* with soporific as well, because everyone was fast asleep except these three. I told them to arm themselves, and prepare to defend Chelsea's honour.'

'Franklin must have doctored the wine he gave away in the Swan tonight,' said Strangeways. He nodded towards Giles. 'He only had one cup, but look at the state of him – reeling about like an old sot. I warned folk against drinking it, but no one listened.'

'Franklin poisoned an entire village?' asked Greeting, aghast.

Strangeways nodded. 'Once word spread that free claret was available, everyone flocked to the Swan to have some.'

Reymes surveyed his troops disparagingly. 'So here is the army that will save the King's gold from dangerous radicals: an ancient fishmonger, a drunk, a pimply youth with a twig, a woman, Clarendon's spy, four debauchees and me.'

'You are lucky to have us,' objected Strangeways indignantly. 'Not everyone would abandon his principles to fight by the side of an ass like you.'

'So what is the plan?' asked Giles genially, propping his musket against Reymes in order to relight his enormous pipe. 'March up to the rectory and let rip?'

'Why not?' asked Hungerford, eyes gleaming wildly. 'I cannot think of a better idea. We shall probably die, but that will not matter if we save the Treasury.'

The other courtiers exchanged uneasy glances. The sycophants at White Hall were not noted for their valour, and Chaloner could tell by the way they held their swords that most had never been drawn in anger. He swallowed hard. It was going to be a disaster!

'We need a diversion,' he said, thinking fast. 'Two, in fact.'

'Yes,' growled Reymes. 'A dose of their own medicine. I like that!'

Chaloner turned to Giles, whom he adjudged to be the least useful person present – he was too intoxicated to move quietly, and would be a liability in a skirmish. Moreover, the reek from his pipe would warn anyone of his presence from miles away.

'Go to Buckingham House and tell Lady Savage to make as much noise as she can. The objective is to make Franklin think that Reymes is frantically fighting burglars, and that the racket has woken his guests. Franklin will then assume that everyone at Buckingham House is occupied, which will give us the advantage of surprise.' He turned to the others. 'Who has guns?'

There were five in total, including Mrs Bonney's unreliable pistol and Giles' musket. Chaloner loaded them himself, not trusting anyone else to do it properly. Then he took the remaining powder and fashioned a crude bomb, using the scant equipment to hand – a metal flask from Giles, a strip of cloth from Eleanore's skirt, and the pin from Hungerford's brooch.

When he had finished, he glanced up to see nine faces looking at him with eager anticipation, and realised they were expecting a miracle. It was unsettling, as he could provide no such thing. He gave the weapons to Strangeways and Eleanore, and explained what he wanted them to do.

'Will it work?' asked Strangeways doubtfully.

Chaloner nodded confidently, although the truth was that he had no idea. 'The ground is tinder-dry.' A sudden rumble of thunder mocked his words. 'But it *must* be done before it rains.'

'Then we had better hurry,' said Wadham, 'because it will pour soon. I can smell it in the air.'

So could Chaloner, and he winced when several flashes of lightning illuminated them as they stood in the road, sincerely hoping that no one from the rectory happened to be looking their way, or the encounter would be over before it had begun. He turned to the others, and outlined the rest of his plan, before ensuring that everyone was armed with at least one weapon with a decent point. He glanced at Reymes, who was unexpectedly acquiescent. Was this suspicious, or was the commissioner merely glad that someone had an idea that might save his skin?

'Lord,' gulped Greeting. 'I do not think I am equal to this. I am a musician, not a warrior.'

'Nonsense,' said Hungerford, as the beginnings of a rumpus began to emanate from Buckingham House. 'Comfort yourself with the knowledge that you die for King and country.'

'Follow me,' ordered Chaloner, before Hungerford could make any more unsettling remarks.

He set off fast, aiming for the rectory's back gate, where he picked the lock. Then he led his helpmeets into the dark garden.

Chapter 18

The racket emanating from Buckingham House was impressive – Lady Savage was doing herself proud – and masked admirably the sound of snapping twigs and muffled curses as Chaloner led his troops through the rectory's overgrown garden. His stomach churned with tension, and he was sure they would have been caught instantly had he not arranged the din. He indicated that everyone was to wait near a derelict shed, while he went to reconnoitre.

'How do we know we can trust you?' hissed Reymes, belligerent again. 'You might decide to throw in your lot with the villains for a cut of the proceeds. I am coming with you.'

'Very well,' said Chaloner, manfully ignoring the insult to his integrity and thinking it would be better to have Reymes where he could see him anyway: the commissioner was not the only one who distrusted his allies. 'Wadham can come, too, lest we need a message carried to the others.'

Before Reymes could argue, he began to creep through the tangled undergrowth towards the back of the house.

His heart sank at what he saw: twenty men – a dozen middle-aged fellows in nondescript clothes, and another eight whose hard-edged demeanour suggested mercenaries.

'Christ God!' breathed Reymes. Chaloner could feel him shaking with outrage, and hoped he would not launch another anger-driven assault, or all would be lost. 'Regicides from the list that you found in Cocke's room. You were right after all. I cannot believe it!'

'And the "soldiers" who collected them from the College,' surmised Chaloner. 'They gave Tooker old customs forms, and told him they were official documents of transfer.'

'I recognise some of the bastards.' Reymes pointed to the one who had spoken French in the Garden Court. 'That is John Dove. The man by the door is Will Say, while Andrew Broughton, John Lisle and Ned Dendy are next to him. King-killers, the lot of them, just like your uncle.'

'And all guests in *your* prison,' Chaloner shot back, feeling that Reymes was hardly in a position to cast aspersions.

Reymes opened his mouth to argue, but Chaloner waved him to silence, and led the way to the front of the house, where three wagons had just arrived, all covered with tarpaulins. The carts were accompanied by Warwick and six liveried guards, who Chaloner suspected had been chosen for their smart uniforms rather than their martial abilities. Reymes was right, he thought in despair: Warwick *was* a fool who could not be trusted with such matters. The mercenaries would cut him and his pretty men to pieces in moments.

'Look,' growled Reymes, pointing. 'That scheming villain Franklin.'

The physician, sleek and smug, was talking to Warwick, whose teeth could be heard clicking together in agitation, even from a distance.

'But I am uncomfortable leaving it out here,' the secretary was saying. 'I want to see it locked safely in the cellar. And where is Reymes?'

'Busy masking your arrival with a rumpus,' replied Franklin smoothly. 'As you can hear. And you cannot come in, because it would compromise our new security arrangements. I am not doubting your integrity, you understand, but what you do not know, you cannot later be forced to reveal. Here is the receipt to say that you have done your duty.'

'All sealed and official,' said Warwick. He sounded unhappy as he peered at it in the gloom. 'But I am Secretary of the Treasury! You cannot expect me to leave the—'

'Orders,' interrupted Franklin crisply. 'From high-ranking members of government, so not for the likes of you and me to question. Now, if there is nothing else, we must get on.'

Lightning flashed again, revealing Doyley's browncoats in the upper windows, all with weapons trained on the yard below. Chaloner swore under his breath. Racing out and warning Warwick that he was about to hand the gold to thieves would see him shot long before he could explain – and Warwick and his men would quickly follow him to the grave.

'We have never met before, Rector Wilkinson,' said Warwick, still reluctant to abandon the precious cargo. 'But Reymes told me that you were . . . slimmer.'

'Strain,' explained Franklin shortly. 'I eat when I worry. But all will be well now that the elephants are here. Goodnight.'

There was not much Warwick could say after being so summarily dismissed, so he mounted up, flung a last, anxious glance towards the carts, and led his guards out of the gate.

The moment Warwick had gone, the rebels and mercenaries who had been waiting at the back of the house poured out of the front, and the brown-coats were not long in joining them. At their head was a slender figure in a long coat. Chaloner recognised him as the person he had chased two nights before – the so-called spectre.

'You see, Sutcliffe?' said Franklin smugly, as the thud of hoofs faded into the night. 'I told you I could do it. That asinine Warwick was putty in my hands.'

Sutcliffe flung back the cowl that shadowed his face, revealing darkly forbidding features that were unmistakably the same as the 'batman' on Dorothy's wall. His eyes gleamed oddly, visible even in the gloom.

'Change the horses on the carts,' he instructed the mercenaries. His voice was high for a man, although there was nothing gentle about it. 'A barge is waiting, and I want these crates on it before dawn. Hurry! The longer they are on land, the greater the chances that someone will see us.'

His men raced to do his bidding. Chaloner turned to whisper to Wadham.

'Go after Warwick. Tell him what is happening and bring him back. Quickly!'

The lad nodded, then proceeded to lumber through the garden so clumsily that Sutcliffe and Franklin cocked their heads in his direction. Fortunately, both relaxed when there was a sudden renewed cacophony from Buckingham House.

445

'Spring and his fellows are putting up a better fight than I expected,' remarked Franklin. 'But the racket should not last much longer. Even Reymes' drunken libertines should be able to trounce that lowly bunch.'

Sutcliffe was visibly angry. 'You said there would be a minor ruckus – just enough to occupy anyone who refused your wine – but this uproar will bring the whole village here to gawp.'

'Hardly – I gave *them* enough soporific to drop a horse. And the battle in Buckingham House is all part of my plan anyway. Spring and his crew have outlived their usefulness, and this is an easy way to be rid of them. No loose ends, as we agreed. Stupid Reymes! He thinks he is working for the King, but instead he is dispatching burglars for me. What a joke!'

'No joke,' said Sutcliffe coldly, while Chaloner sensed that Reymes was having difficulty in controlling himself. 'And you have miscalculated. There is too much noise, and someone is bound to come and see what is happening. We cannot afford to be spotted.'

'No one will come,' said Franklin dismissively. 'And if they do, we shall just repeat the tale that has worked before: that we are stockpiling food.'

'And loading it on a barge?' asked Sutcliffe archly. 'Besides, Reymes will know it is a lie.'

'Then I shall poison him. He will not hinder us, never fear.'

Both turned as one of the rebels approached – the man Reymes had identified as John Lisle.

'You have served us well, Franklin,' he said amiably. 'Both you and Cocke.'

'Cocke was a liability!' spat Franklin. 'He was all for

446

stealing Gorges' money openly – and would have done it, if I had not taught him how to do it discreetly.'

'I thought the dancing masters did that,' said Sutcliffe, frowning. 'At least, that is the rumour in the village.'

'They stole from the inmates,' corrected Franklin. 'But I refer to funds filched from the coffers – another mystery, designed by me, to draw attention away from this place, although, as I say, Cocke would have fouled it up if I had not intervened. He also told Clarendon's men that you and I were friends, Sutcliffe.'

'He would never have done that,' said Sutcliffe shortly. 'Do not lie.'

'I am not,' objected Franklin. 'It is true. He also urged them to speak to Parker, who knew enough about my activities to be a danger to us. Fortunately, the Chelsea Strangler got to Parker before they could act on the advice. But Cocke was a drunken fool, wholly incapable of holding his nerve, and I am glad he is no longer in a position to harm us.'

'He was a loyal ally,' countered Sutcliffe. 'And the only man in London who could converse intelligently about Shakespeare's comedies – unlike you, who knows less than a gnat.'

'We enjoyed our stay in the College,' said Lisle quickly, after a short and obviously uncomfortable silence. 'Tooker could not have been more accommodating, and it was a fine place to hide and wait.'

'I arranged it all,' boasted Franklin, pointedly turning his back on the surly assassin. 'Good food, lovely rooms, deliveries of weapons. Some of the gaolers were suspicious, but I told Tooker how to assuage their concerns.'

'You should not have let him send burglars to London,'

447

said Sutcliffe accusingly. 'It might have been a lucrative caper for you and your brother, but it posed an unnecessary risk to us.'

'Rubbish! Besides, they will all be dead soon, and we will be on our way to France.'

'You are coming with us?' asked Lisle, surprised. 'You will not continue your work at the asylum?'

'There is no point. Parker was mistaken when he said coffee can cure insanity, and I am not wasting any more of my time on his mad theories.'

'And you, Sutcliffe?' Lisle turned to the assassin. 'Will you accompany us overseas, or will you stay to press your claim on the College? Living in it these past few weeks must have made you want to try – to retrieve your rightful inheritance from this corrupt government.'

'I shall return to Greenwich and bide my time,' replied Sutcliffe darkly. 'It will—'

'When will I be paid?' demanded Franklin, demonstrating his dislike of Sutcliffe by cutting rudely across him. 'Today or at the—'

Sutcliffe moved fast, and the physician gave a gasp that was part pain and part astonishment, before crumpling to the ground. Chaloner saw a flash of metal as the assassin sheathed his blade.

'He was right about one thing,' said Sutcliffe flatly. 'No loose ends. Do not gape at me, Lisle – such worms can never be trusted, as you know perfectly well.'

'I cannot imagine how you persuaded him to join us,' said Lisle, staring down at the body. 'He had a good job, the respect of his colleagues, the satisfaction of curing the sick . . .'

'Greed,' replied Sutcliffe, loudly enough for his fellow

conspirators to hear. 'It corrupts the most steadfast of hearts.'

He eyed them one by one. They shuffled uneasily under his basilisk gaze, although Chaloner thought he need not worry about betrayal from them. Exiled regicides were the most dedicated radicals alive, with nothing left to live for but the prospect of another revolution.

Chaloner and Reymes crept back through the undergrowth to their remaining troops. Hungerford was raring to go, but the others were hesitant and apprehensive, and Chaloner knew he had to set his plan in motion before they lost their nerve completely. Quickly, he repeated what he wanted each of them to do.

'But how do we get in?' gulped Greeting, openly petrified. 'I can see from here that the back door is guarded, while you have just told us that a dozen deadly dissidents are outside the front one, along with the spectre, so that is obviously unavailable.'

'Through the tunnel that leads from the garden to the cellar,' replied Chaloner.

A flash of lightning showed Reymes gawping his astonishment. 'What tunnel? Wilkinson never mentioned any tunnel. Of course, I was never happy including *him* in our plans – he will be part of this plot, you can be sure of that, the damned fanatic!'

'Yes, what tunnel, Chaloner?' asked Greeting uneasily. 'And how do you know about it?'

'Because I saw it when I explored the rectory the other day,' explained Chaloner. 'It exits by the compost heaps, which is why Wilkinson spends so much time there – either keeping the door free of weeds, or making sure that no one else tries to use it.'

'That is interesting,' mused Hungerford. 'Because Kole liked to poke around there as well. I saw him several times, and so did the Gorges dancing masters. We often discussed it in the Swan.'

'Kole was a spy,' confided Greeting. 'I caught him searching Underhill's room once, and do you know what he said? That it was *Underhill* who was the spy! I did not believe him, of course.'

'Perhaps Kole was afraid that Underhill might unearth something to harm his claim on the College,' said Reymes. 'I knew I should not have invited a person like him to stay in my house – he was obviously a dishonest rogue.'

'So why did you?' asked Hungerford curiously.

'Because he offered to pay rent and I needed the money. Not that he honoured the agreement.'

'Follow me,' instructed Chaloner quickly, before Reymes could work himself into a lather about that too. 'Quietly, if possible.'

Although the noise from Buckingham House was beginning to flag, it was still enough to mask the racket that Chaloner's chosen helpmeets – Reymes, Greeting, Hungerford and the two courtiers whose names he could not recall – made as they edged towards the place where Wilkinson had so often knelt. Even so, Chaloner winced at every curse, scrape, crack and snap.

When they arrived, he removed a strategically placed log to reveal an iron handle set into a rectangular stone. He grasped it and pulled. It opened easily, suggesting that Wilkinson had gone to some trouble to keep it in good working order. Beyond was a dry, airless space filled with floating dust. He climbed in, wincing when Hungerford, who was behind him, began to cough.

450

'Cover your mouths and noses,' he ordered, and there was another agonising delay while they obliged, taking longer than they should have done because their hands were unsteady, either through excitement or terror.

It was an awful journey. The tunnel was low and narrow, obliging them to crawl, which was not easy over a floor strewn with sharp stones. There was a constant medley of expletives, which intensified when the passage tapered further still, and their progress brushed loose earth from the ceiling, creating more dust and less breathable air.

Just when Chaloner was beginning to think he might be wrong about where the tunnel went, they reached another trapdoor. He listened intently for a moment, then gave it a shove, relieved beyond measure when it swung open to reveal the cellar beyond. He had harboured an unspoken fear that Wilkinson or one of the brown-coats might have re-bolted it.

The basement was in darkness. He scrambled out, lit a candle and explored quickly while his companions caught their breath and brushed themselves off. But the cellars were empty, and the boxes of coins gone. Predictably, Reymes was hot-eyed with anger.

'The Sick and Hurt Fund!' he spluttered. 'How *could* they? Is the King's gold not enough?' He turned furiously to the others. 'They have stolen the money intended for the relief of those maimed in defence of the realm. Will you allow them to get away with such an outrage?'

'We shall not,' declared Greeting stoutly. 'And if I survive, I shall write a song condemning them, one that will be sung in taverns and ale-houses for years to come.'

The others hissed vehement agreement, which was encouraging, so Chaloner led them to the stairs before their righteous anger could wane. And if luck was on his side, Wadham would return with Warwick and his men. He grimaced. Of course *they* would be of scant use, and what he really needed was Spymaster Williamson and a contingent of loyal, well-trained soldiers.

The rectory appeared to be deserted, and Chaloner could only suppose that everyone was outside with the carts. He sent the four courtiers to reconnoitre the bedrooms and attics, while he and Reymes took the ground floor. Three brown-coats were in the kitchen, packing the kind of rations that were taken on long journeys, but that was all. He and Reymes returned to the cellar, where the others were waiting to report that the barracks upstairs were devoid of bedding, clothes or personal belongings. The thieves were ready to depart.

'We should strike now,' said Greeting, pale with anxiety. 'Or it will rain and our plan will—'

'Strike?' came a soft voice. 'You will not be striking anything. And what are you doing in my house anyway? You have no right to be here.'

Wilkinson stood there with a brace of pistols, and Chaloner cursed himself for sending amateurs to search the building. He should have done it himself, because although the rector could not shoot them all, the sound of a firearm discharging would bring Sutcliffe running, and that would be the end of their effort to save the country from poverty-induced anarchy.

He tensed, assessing whether he could surge forward and disarm the priest without the guns going off. But Wilkinson's hands shook with the thrill of cornering officials from the government he so hated, and Chaloner knew that overpowering him quietly would be impossible.

A knife, then? Chaloner drew one, but then felt the weighty bulk of the telescope in his pocket. He shifted the dagger to his other hand, and eased the instrument out.

'What you are doing is disgusting,' snarled Reymes, regarding the rector with contempt. 'You aim not only to steal from your King, but from the men who fought the Dutch on your behalf.'

'Not *my* behalf,' countered Wilkinson, while Chaloner winced at the rising voices. 'It is a wicked war, and I argued against starting it. Not that anyone listened. And as for the King, I hate him. He took my lovely college and turned it into a prison. How dare he! It could have been the envy of Oxford and Cambridge had it been allowed to flourish.'

'All *you* want is to court controversy,' sneered Reymes. 'But we have had enough of religious strife, and His Majesty is right to turn the place into something useful.'

'It will not be a prison for much longer,' vowed Wilkinson shrilly. Chaloner glanced uneasily towards the door, half expecting to see Sutcliffe there. 'I am going to buy it with the King's own gold, and become provost of the greatest theological foundation the world has ever seen. I shall create such schism and debate—'

Reymes cut across him with a bark of scornful laughter. 'You think no one will notice you purchasing a large estate when the Treasury has just gone missing from your house? Besides, I imagine Sutcliffe will have something to say about your plans. He thinks the College belongs to him.'

'He agreed to relinquish his claim in exchange for my help.' Wilkinson's eyes blazed madly. 'Which I gave willingly – to thwart men like *you*.'

'Not now, Reymes,' murmured Chaloner, but the commissioner ignored him.

'I might have known *you* had no honour,' he spat at Wilkinson. 'And I was right to accuse you of lying when you claimed to have followed Cocke all over London on our behalf last week.'

'Oh, I followed him all right! I never did trust him. But it was not for your benefit, it was for mine. I *want* the gold here, and I needed to make sure he did not do something to put the scheme in jeopardy.' Wilkinson jerked his thumb at Chaloner. 'I lied to *him*, though – I could not care less whether Cocke brought the plague to Chelsea.'

'So you are just another filthy money-grubber,' said Reymes contemptuously. 'You pretended to be accommodating, lending us your home and helping with our plans, but all for selfishness. You are a snake, who does not deserve to call himself an Englishman. A rebel, in fact.'

'I am no rebel,' shouted Wilkinson, and Chaloner cringed, sure the dissidents would hear. 'I shall serve my country by making Chelsea famous for theology. Which is a lot more worthy than storing Dutch prisoners and hiding the King's gold.'

'Reymes, please,' whispered Chaloner sharply, as the commissioner drew breath to respond in kind. 'This is not the time.'

But Reymes had been obliged to suppress his temper for too long already, and it began to erupt like a volcano. 'You will never be provost of anything,' he screeched. 'Sutcliffe will dispatch you, just as he dispatched Franklin. And it will serve you right for joining ranks with an assassin.'

'He has already tried.' Wilkinson's face was alight with

454

the power of his convictions. 'But his blade missed, although I let him think he had succeeded.'

Chaloner did not blame the Garden Court dissidents for asking Franklin to play the role of rector when Warwick had arrived – the secretary was likely to have taken one look at Wilkinson and hauled the gold straight back to London. He tried again to silence Reymes, but the commissioner was beyond reason.

'*I* will kill you!' Reymes howled, fists clenching in fury. 'You are scum, and God will help me strike you dead.'

Incensed, Wilkinson pointed a gun at him, hatred suffusing his face. Chaloner hurled the telescope as hard as he could, heart hammering as the rector's finger tightened on the trigger. Just when it seemed the dag would go off, the telescope landed, hitting the rector right in the middle of the forehead. The gun clattered harmlessly to the floor, landing just before Wilkinson himself.

'Lock him in the strongroom,' ordered Chaloner, as the courtiers clustered around to congratulate him on his aim. 'No, do not leave him his guns, Greeting! Take one yourself, and give the other to Hungerford.'

When the rector was safely secured, Chaloner led the way upstairs, where a flash of lightning and an almost simultaneous clap of thunder told him that the storm was virtually overhead. It would start to rain soon, and unless he acted fast, his plan would fail. He turned to Greeting.

'Go upstairs and use a lamp to signal Eleanore. The rest of you, come with me.'

It was so long before Eleanore and Strangeways fired their first shot that Chaloner began to fear that they had either been caught or had run away. Out in the yard, the crack caused immediate consternation among the rebels, which intensified when the second shot rang out. Then the bomb ignited with a boom that sent several scurrying for cover, and others falling to the ground with their hands over their heads. A dead tree caught fire, sending flames leaping high into the sky. Suddenly, there was a yell.

'The road north!'

What did that mean? And had it been Eleanore's voice?

The third shot killed the regicide Dendy outright, which had not been part of the plan, although a victorious whoop from Strangeways told Chaloner that the fishmonger had used the delay to secure himself a better vantage point. At the same time, smoke billowed across the yard. It frightened the horses, which began to dance and fret. All three carts swayed precariously.

Sutcliffe, who had been standing in open-mouthed shock, suddenly swept into action. He whipped around, and screamed at his mercenaries to counter-attack. When they hesitated, uncertain where their assailants were hiding, he led the charge himself, but a fourth shot dropped him to the ground, clutching his leg. Most of the dissidents, more used to causing trouble than stopping it, promptly fled to the safety of the house. Only Lisle and Dove stood their ground, howling frantically as they tried to rally their bewildered troops.

Chaloner surged forward with a battle cry that he had not used since the wars. Overhead, thunder clapped so loudly that he did not hear the shrieking clash of metal as his sword met its first opponent. Then all was a chaotic mêlée as weapons flailed in the darkness, not helped by the lightning that flickered or the smoke from the fire, which made it difficult for the combatants to see. More than one fell to the blade of a friend, aimed in error.

'The road north,' howled someone a second time.

Chaloner was not in a position to ask what it meant. He was heavily outnumbered, forced to give ground again and again, and he could see at least one courtier dead on the ground. He battled on, although with the sinking sense that he had overestimated his ability to stop what had been set in motion. His only hope was that Eleanore or Strangeways would escape to tell everyone what had happened. He coughed as smoke rolled across him, distantly aware that Wilkinson's tinder-dry garden was now well and truly alight.

The clamour of fighting, along with the stench of burning and the almost continual lightning, unnerved the horses further still, and one pair bucked so violently that their wagon lurched to one side. Several of the metal chests fell off and burst open, spilling their contents across the ground.

They were full of dirt.

Chapter 19

Most of the brown-coats abandoned the skirmish to race towards the carts, howling their shock and dismay, but Chaloner was being pressed hard by three resolute mercenaries, and dared not turn to see what was happening. He heard Lisle's bellow of frustrated disbelief, though.

'We have been betrayed! There is no gold.'

Sutcliffe hobbled forward, careless of the swords that flailed around him, and kicked open another crate. Gravel trickled out, clearly visible in the glow from the approaching fire.

'Did you know, Reymes?' he demanded.

'Yes, of course,' declared the commissioner defiantly, although it was patently obvious that he was as stunned as everyone else.

Sutcliffe was silent for a moment, then started to laugh – a harsh sound that drew glances of consternation from his men. The dissidents abandoned the sanctuary of the house and ran to join him, while Chaloner's mind was a chaos of questions, even as he fought for his life. Had Warwick guessed that the Treasury was at risk, so had delivered decoy chests instead? Then why had he not returned to catch the would-be thieves red-handed?

Then a gunshot rang out, louder than the thunder that pealed overhead, and one of Chaloner's attackers fell dead. Another bang saw a second follow suit. It was Eleanore, striding towards them and tossing away the guns as they were spent. Chaloner summoned every last ounce of his remaining strength and drove the last mercenary back in a frenzied assault, not stopping until the man was staggering in the burning grass. The fellow shrieked as his breeches ignited, and Chaloner left him frantically trying to bat out the flames with his hands.

'Behind you!' screamed Eleanore.

Chaloner turned to see Dove, sword poised for the kill, and only just managed to block the blow. The force of it knocked him off his feet, though, and he fell awkwardly. Dove came to stand over him and the blade began to descend again, but Eleanore swept forward and Chaloner heard her gasp as the weapon entered her body.

Dove was in the process of hauling it out of her when Hungerford appeared. The courtier was a terrifying sight, blood-splattered and savage-faced, and Dove fell under a brutal flurry of blows. Without a backward glance, Hungerford lurched away to kill someone else. There was a ripping crack as thunder rolled overhead, and the air was scarcely breathable from the fire that danced across the garden. The surviving dissidents were clustered around the carts, voices shrill with disbelief, but Chaloner only had eyes for Eleanore.

'What a pity,' she murmured. 'I hoped you might stay here with me when all this was over. Chelsea is a pretty place, and you would be safe from the plague.'

'I still could,' said Chaloner, stomach churning as he watched her life slip away. 'You are right: it is a pretty place.'

'The Treasury carts,' she whispered. 'There are five of them, not three. I saw them while we were waiting for your signal. The other two took the road north. I tried to tell you, but you did not hear . . . *They* carry the King's gold. These are a ruse.'

'How do you—'

'I followed them, which is why our bomb was late. Warwick had caught up with them . . . he was laughing with his friends . . . saying the ploy had worked.'

'He is Secretary of the Treasury.' Chaloner tried to stem the flow of blood from her wound, although he knew it was hopeless. 'He will be taking it to Hampton Court.'

'Hampton Court is west,' she whispered, barely audible. 'He went *north* . . . He is stealing it.'

Chaloner did not care. 'Never mind that. Concentrate on breathing.'

She nodded, but her eyes had a glazed, unfocused look. She smiled briefly, then her face went slack and her head lolled. He shook her gently, but there was no response.

Chaloner was not sure how long he knelt in the rectory garden, cradling Eleanore's body, but he gradually realised that the sounds of battle had faded away. Dazed, he glanced around him.

The fire still raged, but it had rolled past the house, and the smoke had blown away, so it was possible to see. Most of the brown-coats and all Sutcliffe's mercenaries had gone, unwilling to linger in a place of danger now it was clear that the promised riches would not be forthcoming. But the rebels remained, and they outnumbered Chaloner's surviving helpmeets two to one. Grimly, each side waited for the other to make the first move, while Lisle stayed by the carts, doggedly smashing open box after box in the hope that one might contain something other than soil.

With another flicker of lightning and the loudest roll of thunder yet, the first drops of rain began to fall, hissing as they hit the fire-scorched ground. Then Wadham staggered through the gate. He gazed around wildly before stumbling towards Chaloner.

'Warwick was not on the King's Road,' he gasped. 'You can see along it for miles at the Bloody Bridge, even in the dark, but it was empty, so I ran west, to see if he was aiming for Hampton Court instead. He was not on that track either, which means he must have gone north . . .'

'He has outmanoeuvred us,' Sutcliffe told his companions in grudging disbelief. 'Who would have thought it of such a stupid fellow?'

Chaloner glanced at Reymes. The prefect was blinking his shock, astonished to learn that Warwick had done something clever.

'Then we shall ride after him,' determined Lisle. 'We risked a great deal by gathering here, and I am not leaving empty-handed. The time is perfect for rebellion, with the King driven out of London by the plague.'

A couple of his cronies clamoured their agreement, but most shook their heads. The one Reymes had identified as Will Say was the first to make his objections heard.

'This was an ill-conceived venture from the start, and

461

I was a fool to think it might work. What use will a disease-ravaged city be to us? How will we raise an army when people are too frightened to look at strangers, let alone fight next to them? I say we take the boxes of shillings, and quit this benighted country while we can.'

'He is right,' said the man named Broughton. 'And we should not forget the storm . . .'

'What about it?' asked Lisle belligerently.

Broughton pointed upwards as lightning flashed. 'It is a sign from God, warning us against throwing away our lives when the odds are stacked so heavily against us. There will be other opportunities, and I would rather wait until the auspices are more favourable.'

His remarks prompted the radicals to go into a huddle, discussing their options in tense, agitated whispers. Sutcliffe did not join them. He limped to a nearby trough, where he sat and inspected his wounded leg. Reymes took a firmer grip on his sword and stepped towards him, murder in his eyes, but Sutcliffe showed him the dagger he held – and would throw if the prefect went any closer. Reymes faltered.

'Cocke told me not to underestimate Warwick.' Sutcliffe sounded amused, which Chaloner found far more disconcerting than anger or frustration. 'I should have listened to him. No wonder Warwick wanted to carry these chests to the cellar himself – he was afraid we would notice something amiss if he let us do it.'

'You must be disappointed.' Chaloner laid Eleanore gently on the ground and climbed slowly to his feet. 'Given that you have been planning this night since June. All those arrangements and expenses – and for nothing.'

'Hardly for nothing,' objected Sutcliffe, mock-indignant. 'We still have the Sick and Hurt Fund, which was our original objective, after all. We never imagined that the King's gold would fall into our laps – not until a few days ago – so I am not unduly distraught about losing it. But how do you know we started planning our operation in June?'

'My wife overheard you discussing it, probably during a performance of *The Indian Queen*. You must have gone to watch it with Dove and Dendy.'

Sutcliffe frowned. 'A small, pert lady in a green dress, who eavesdropped on us, even after one of the cast fell down dead? I tried to catch her, but she escaped. Was she a spy, too?'

Chaloner did not answer. Hannah had been brave, risking her life to monitor dangerous men, and he felt a sudden surge of affection for her. She had even told him what Sutcliffe and his cronies had intended to steal – not the Treasury, as Reymes had only decided to move that when he had seen how safe the Sick and Hurt money was in the rectory.

Then Strangeways stepped forward. 'Which of you bastards is the Chelsea Strangler?' he demanded. 'Nancy was a good lass, and I will not let her murder go unpunished. I owe that at least to her sister.'

'I am afraid you must look elsewhere for him,' replied Sutcliffe evenly. 'We aimed to avoid suspicious deaths in Chelsea, lest they brought unwanted attention.'

Before the fishmonger could ask more, the rebels finished their conference and came to cluster at the assassin's back. The rain began to fall harder.

'We have made our decision,' announced Say. 'We will take the shillings from the cellar and quit the country. The Treasury . . . well, we are disinclined to chase it. The risk is just too great.'

463

'You are not having the Sick and Hurt Fund,' declared Reymes angrily.

'You will lose if you fight us for it,' warned Say. 'But you might be able to save the Treasury. It is your choice, of course, but think very carefully before you decide.'

'Do not take me for a fool,' snarled Reymes. 'Even if we did manage to defeat Warwick, you would just come along and take the gold from us. Well, we are not fighting your battles.'

'We will not take it,' said Sutcliffe. 'You have my word.'

'The word of a traitor,' spat Reymes in rank contempt.

'You *can* believe us,' Say assured him. 'Sutcliffe is wounded, and is in no condition for another skirmish, while the rest of us have had enough. All we want now is to leave unmolested.'

'Although England has not seen the last of us yet,' growled Lisle, suggesting that *he* had been willing to pursue the men who had outwitted them, but had been overruled by his more cautious companions. 'Not by a long shot.'

'Warwick cannot have gone far,' said Sutcliffe to Reymes. 'His carts will be slow, weighed down with heavy guineas. However, allow me to give you one piece of advice: do not roar your accusations at him like lions, or you will have half the thieves in the country after you. Whisper, if you can.'

'What nonsense is this?' demanded Reymes suspiciously. 'If we whisper in this storm we—'

The rest of his sentence was lost in an ear-splitting crack of thunder that proved his point.

'Go,' said Sutcliffe briskly. 'And when you return, we will be gone.'

Reymes started to refuse, but Strangeways approached him, rain bouncing off his breastplate with metallic pings.

'Go after Warwick,' he urged softly, 'or all our efforts and sacrifices tonight will have been for nothing. You *must* save the gold.'

Chaloner watched an inner battle rage within Reymes: the Sick and Hurt Fund or the Treasury? Unfortunately, there was only one real option – the one the King would want him to take – so Chaloner spoke before the commissioner could make the wrong decision.

'We shall need horses,' he said, although he resented the immediate flash of satisfaction in Sutcliffe's eyes. 'Fast ones. If you cannot provide them, we will stay here, and so will you.'

He touched the sword at his side, to ensure they took his meaning, and Say hurried quickly towards the stables before they could change their minds.

'Ride quickly,' instructed Sutcliffe. 'And make sure you kill the man who was a colleague and a friend, but who betrayed you without a qualm.'

'Yes, Warwick *will* die tonight,' spat Reymes. 'Although I assure you, he was never a friend.'

'Warwick is not the driving force behind this mischief,' said Sutcliffe with a sly smirk. 'Cocke was wrong to suspect him. Think rather of someone who can wrap Warwick around his little finger with his bluff good nature and charm. Someone who has two Court posts, but who is still fearful for his future.'

Chaloner gaped at him. 'You mean Kipps? No! He would never . . .'

But then Hannah's letter flashed into his mind yet again: *Beware of smokey half-fisshe and Candels in Battell.*

465

The *smokey half-fisshe* – Kipps, the first part of the word kipper! And the *Candels in Battell* meant War-wick. Chaloner's stomach lurched painfully. Surely she was mistaken! Yet she had been right about Sutcliffe, Dove and Dendy. With a sick, sinking feeling he supposed she must have overheard Kipps and Warwick plotting at Court, and sincerely hoped it had not been marriage to a spy that had prompted her to listen to conversations not intended for her ears.

'Yes, Kipps,' said Sutcliffe softly. 'There is a sharp mind behind that bumbling exterior. How else could he have survived so long in the snake pit that is White Hall?'

'No,' said Reymes hoarsely. 'He has gone to Hampton Court. If he had hatched such a terrible plot, he would be here to see it through.'

'Believe what you like.' Sutcliffe began to limp away. 'But you will see.'

Rain lashed down as Chaloner, Reymes and Greeting – the only three still capable of riding – galloped along the north road. The storm had turned it treacherously slippery, and lightning flashed almost continuously.

Chaloner's horse stumbled, almost unseating him, and he wondered what they would do if they did catch the carts. Try to reason with the culprits? But why would they listen? They would have professional soldiers to do their bidding – he was sure the *real* gold would not be guarded by peacocks who thought more of their uniforms than their martial abilities – and three tired men would pose no threat to them.

Reymes forged ahead, fuelled by rage, and Chaloner knew he would be more liability than help in the skirmish

466

that was to come. Then the commissioner reined in so abruptly that Chaloner almost crashed into the back of him. On the track ahead were two wagons, the front one tilted at an angle. At first, Chaloner assumed it had skidded into a ditch, but the lightning told a different story: a wheel had sheered off, and its guards were milling around it in dismay. They rallied at the sound of approaching hoofs, though, and all drew weapons.

'Damn it, Tom!' cried Kipps. 'What are you doing here?'

'I might ask the same of you,' said Chaloner, and although he had resigned himself to his friend's treachery, he still experienced a sharp pang of regret at the sight of him there.

'Was it you who sawed through the axle to prevent our escape?' asked Kipps, eyeing him reproachfully. 'How very unkind!'

'Someone sawed through—' began Chaloner, bemused, but Reymes cut across him.

'So it is true? You do not deny it? You *are* stealing the King's gold? I might have known! You are in Clarendon's employ, after all, and he only ever hires rogues.'

'And you are a better judge of character, are you?' retorted Kipps archly. 'You who trusted Doyley, Cocke, Tooker, Samm, Wilkinson, Franklin and all those brown-coats, when even a child could have seen that they were rogues.'

Reymes opened his mouth to respond, but then could think of nothing with which to refute the charge. All Chaloner's attention was on Kipps.

'You must have been delighted when the Earl ordered you to help me with my investigations,' he said bitterly.

'It allowed you to stay one step ahead of me the whole way.'

When the lightning flashed again, he saw that the Seal Bearer held a handgun. So did Warwick, who was gesturing for Reymes and Greeting to dismount. The secretary was grim-faced but determined, and Chaloner saw a resolve that had been absent in White Hall, when he had been nothing but a badly treated servant of the Crown.

'Not really, Tom,' Kipps was saying generously. 'Most of your enquiries were irrelevant, because I had already guessed that Reymes would try to move the Treasury secretly, taking Warwick and me into his confidence only at the very last moment. It was obvious: keeping it in London while the plague edged ever closer was just *too* reckless, even for him.'

'He said it would stay until August,' added Warwick. 'But we are not stupid – we knew it was a lie. And when Kipps saw the arrangements that had been put in place at the rectory, he understood exactly what was going to happen.'

'You treacherous worms,' snarled Reymes, clenching and unclenching his fists in impotent rage. 'I was right to distrust you.'

Kipps ignored him and continued to address Chaloner. 'So do not feel too badly about failing to predict what we intended to do. We are clever, not like those fools at the rectory, and you did your best.' Then he smirked, unable to resist a gloat. 'Of course, you never came close to learning anything that mattered.'

'Anything that mattered,' repeated Chaloner, climbing slowly off his horse when Warwick wagged the pistol at him. 'Like murder.'

'Murder?' echoed Kipps, although the unease in his

468

voice gave Chaloner all he needed to slot the last pieces of the puzzle into place.

'Yes – it was *you* who strangled Nancy, Underhill, Kole and Parker. To protect yourself.'

'Kipps is the Chelsea Strangler?' Reymes eyed the Seal Bearer with renewed contempt. 'Is no filthy deed beneath him?'

'Nancy spent a lot of time looking out of her window with Frances' telescope,' Chaloner continued when Kipps made no attempt to deny the charge. 'Not at the rectory, as I first assumed, but at the north road, which you would have surveyed thoroughly before using it to escape.'

'I am a careful man.' Kipps glanced ruefully at the damaged cart. 'Although not careful enough, it seems. I was sorry about Nancy, but I could not have her telling Frances about me.'

'Underhill was Spymaster Williamson's man, and you certainly did not want *him* poking about in Chelsea,' Chaloner went on. 'It was a godsend when he visited Clarendon House, allowing you to dispatch him in a place you know better than your own home. Meanwhile, Kole liked looking through keyholes, hoping to see naked women—'

'A nasty habit,' said Kipps. A flash of lightning illuminated his hands, which were strong and capable – a strangler's hands. 'And one I was unable to ignore, given what we planned to do.'

'The spectre never visited Kole in his room the night he died. You made that up to confuse me. What about Parker? Did he deduce the truth in his coffee-aggravated delirium? Is that why you stole whatever he was writing?'

Kipps inclined his head. 'He was putting his suspicions

about me in a letter to the Earl when I arrived. Thank you for not rushing to speak to him at once, by the way. That would have been awkward. And thank you for disappearing on business of your own early that morning, giving me the opportunity to dispatch him at my leisure.'

'Cocke knew you were a man with secrets, and I should have listened to him. Did he really blackmail you about Martin, or was that a lie, too?'

An expression of pain crossed Kipps' face. 'No, that was true. He was a vile man – a thief, who stole Gorges' money and plotted with rebels.'

'Yes,' agreed Chaloner. 'But no worse than one who could not look his victims in the face when he squeezed the life out of them, and so attacked them from behind.'

Kipps shuddered. 'It was not something I enjoyed, so I hope I shall not be obliged to do it again.' Then he brightened. 'So why not come with us? I have no wish to harm a friend, and you are as weary of White Hall as I am. Nothing holds you there now that Hannah is gone.'

'That is a tempting offer,' said Greeting quickly, although Chaloner doubted he had been included in the invitation. 'I would not mind—'

'No,' barked Warwick, teeth clacking angrily. 'None of them can come. It is too risky.'

'We would not demean ourselves anyway,' said Reymes, all haughty contempt. 'We would sooner die than throw in our lot with scum like you.'

'That can be arranged,' muttered Warwick.

Chaloner was struggling to understand why Kipps was willing to abandon all he professed to hold dear. 'You have two good Court posts, a nice family, you are popular . . . you have so much to lose.'

470

'We were left behind to die.' It was Warwick who answered, and the words emerged as a snarl. 'We have given the best years of our lives to the King, but he left us in plague-infested London without a qualm. Well, we are *not* expendable. This money will allow us to live comfortably for the rest of our lives, and to Hell with him.'

'Besides, better we have it than those lunatics in the Garden Court,' added Kipps. 'They aimed to use it to start another civil war.'

'You are fools if you think you will get away with this,' said Reymes tightly. 'Do you really imagine that no one will notice your sudden riches? You will be caught in an instant!'

'No, we will not,' stated Warwick. 'And if you had not sawed through the axle, we would not even be having this stupid conversation. We would be long gone.'

'We did not touch the carts,' said Chaloner. 'That was Sutcliffe. I wondered why he was so sure we would catch up with you. He knew something would happen to slow you . . .'

He trailed off, recalling what else the assassin had said: that they should speak in low voices so that no one would hear them. But who would be listening in the marshes in the middle of the night? The answer was that no one would, and that Sutcliffe had wanted them close to the vehicles for some other reason. He began to back away, and as he did so, he saw the Treasury's Sergeant at Arms darting away through the trees.

'Stephens!' bawled Warwick. 'What do you think you are doing? Come back here at once!'

'What is he—' began Kipps, then his eyes narrowed. 'Stop him, Warwick! Shoot!'

As one, he and Warwick took aim and pulled their

471

triggers. His shot went wide, while Warwick's weapon failed to discharge – rain had leaked into his powder.

The remaining Treasury men began to babble in confusion, so Chaloner used the opportunity to turn and run, pulling Reymes and Greeting with him. Two musket shots followed, but neither came close to hitting their targets. Then there was an explosion so violent and massive that the ground bucked beneath their feet, sending them all sprawling. They cowered, hands over their heads, as a lethal hail of coins and debris hammered down around them.

It felt like an age before it was safe to get up. Chaloner stood cautiously, aware of Reymes and Greeting doing the same. Several trees were alight, which shed enough light for them to see that one of the carts was no longer there. It had been replaced by an enormous crater in the ground.

'Christ God!' breathed Reymes. 'How did you know that was going to happen?'

'Sutcliffe's parting words,' explained Chaloner. 'He should have resisted the temptation to gloat, because I guessed what he had done, even before I saw his spy haring away after lighting the fuses. He wanted everyone dead – the thieves *and* us.'

'But how did he guess what Warwick and Kipps intended to do?' asked Greeting shakily. 'I thought he was as astonished as the rest of us when the crates at the rectory contained dirt.'

'Not quite,' said Chaloner, 'because Cocke had already warned him that Warwick was untrustworthy. Indeed, I suspect that Cocke's concern prompted Sutcliffe to recruit a spy from among the Treasury men.'

472

'Stephens!' Reymes looked around quickly. 'Who seems to have escaped.'

'And who probably informed Sutcliffe that the convoy was to be divided in two,' said Chaloner. 'Which means that Sutcliffe would have guessed that something was afoot, so he planned his revenge in the event of a trick. He ordered Stephens to saw through the axle and put gunpowder in the "non-rectory" carts—'

'And blow the whole lot to kingdom come,' finished Reymes. 'No wonder he was unwilling to give chase!'

'Well, look on the bright side,' said Greeting, stooping to retrieve a guinea from the ground. 'None of the thieves have the elephants – they are here, with us.'

'For now,' said Chaloner soberly. 'However, I have a bad feeling that Sutcliffe is not far away, and when he hears the blast, he will know it is safe to come and see what might be salvaged.'

They crept back to a scene of carnage. Some men groaned, others were dead, while the remainder hunted frantically for the scattered gold, desperate to redeem something from the disaster. Kipps lay on his back, his clothes in shreds and his eyes closed. Then there came the sound of drumming hoofs.

Greeting sagged in defeat. 'Here comes Sutcliffe now. He will kill us *and* have the gold.'

Reymes whipped out his rapier. 'I shall not sell my life cheaply. Come, stand with me, and we will give them something to remember. Christ God! I never imagined that I would die with a toady of Clarendon at my right hand, and a Court debauchee on my left.'

'One more remark like that, and you can die alone,' muttered Greeting acidly.

Numbly, Chaloner drew his sword, and stood shoulder-to-shoulder with them. The horsemen drew closer, then wheeled to a stop. Chaloner blinked his astonishment when he saw the lead rider.

'I told you Kipps was a rogue,' said Wiseman smugly. He snapped his fingers, telling the soldiers he had brought with him to round up the survivors. 'I am never wrong about people, and I sensed the villain in him from the first. You should have listened to me.'

'He was my friend,' said Chaloner tiredly.

'*I* am your friend,' corrected the surgeon. '*He* is a thief. I suspected he was up to no good last night, when he installed Frances, Dorothy and me at an inn in Chiswick, and took off alone. So I rode hard to White Hall, collected these fellows, and came back here as fast as I could.'

Chaloner went to kneel next to Kipps, whose eyes had fluttered open.

'Tell Martin . . .' the Seal Bearer whispered. 'Tell him . . . think of something, Tom. I know you will do that for me . . . as I saved Hannah's last letter for you.'

'She guessed you would find it,' said Chaloner softly. 'It is why her message was so abstruse. She used a code, which she expected me, as an intelligencer, to understand. She named you as a traitor.'

'Did she?' Kipps shook his head slightly, a smile playing about his lips. 'Women! They make fools of us all. Of course, they are not the only ones . . . It makes sense now . . . It has been so easy . . . I should have been suspicious. His Majesty is not stupid . . . no one will ever steal *his* coffers.'

Chaloner glanced around him. 'Is that so?'

'But he and his favourites are devious . . .' Kipps' voice was growing weaker. 'Why was it left to the Earl

474

to suggest moving the Treasury? Why were you and I sent to investigate . . . shedding his writs and warrants with gay abandon? He has become a nuisance in the eyes of many . . . they long for him to fall . . . How much will they pay to see it happen?'

Chaloner's blood ran cold. 'Are you saying this business has royal favour?'

Kipps shrugged. 'You will never know . . . not now it has failed. But I imagine there will be some angry men in Hampton Court tomorrow . . .'

Epilogue

London, a week later

It took days to collect the guineas that had been scattered by the blast, although Chaloner, Reymes and the palace guards retrieved most of them in the end. Chaloner had been more than happy for Reymes to take the credit for their rescue, given what Kipps had claimed, but the unrestrained joy with which the gold had been received at Hampton Court left him uncertain of the truth.

'It is a pity Reymes transpired to be innocent,' the Earl had said, disgruntled. 'You should have worked harder to uncover evidence of malfeasance. And I wish you had managed to conceal Kipps' role in the affair. There are those who think I put him up to it.'

Then he had sent Chaloner to Piccadilly, with orders to mind Clarendon House. It was meant as a punishment, to deprive him of the pleasures of the King's company, although Chaloner had been glad to go. The only bright spark during his brief stay in Hampton Court had been smiles from Frances and her mother.

476

He had arrived in London that morning. Unfortunately, the violent thunderstorms that had lashed the region had not broken the heatwave, and the city was hotter and more sultry than ever. Virtually everyone who could leave had gone, and the streets were disconcertingly empty.

He went to make his report to Williamson, but the Spymaster's offices were closed. A lone guard informed him that the whole operation had moved to Kent.

'After one of his clerks died of the plague,' the man explained, then added in an angry mutter, 'He should have taken *all* of us with him. What did I do to deserve being left here to rot?'

Supposing it explained why no troops had been provided when they had been so desperately needed, Chaloner trudged on. He reached Fleet Street, sorry when he saw the Rainbow was closed, and that the building next to it was marked with a red cross. He thought he glimpsed Farr's face at an upstairs window, but the coffee-house owner did not return his wave.

He turned up Chancery Lane and entered Lincoln's Inn, because its garden was the only place he knew where the plague was not in evidence. The closed-up homes, tolling bells and constant graveyard processions were painful reminders of Hannah, and he wanted to escape them for a while. Then he saw a familiar figure sitting on a bench in the shade.

'I thought you had gone to Oxfordshire!' he exclaimed, delighted to see Thurloe, but also worried that something terrible had happened to keep his friend in the city.

'One of the other passengers in the public coach kept sneezing, so I leapt out at Highgate and raced back here as fast as my legs would take me. I am now waiting for my wife to send our personal carriage, which is the only safe way to travel these days.'

'But you are well?'

'Quite well, thank you, although I am not sure the same can be said of you. Was Chelsea not the quiet retreat you envisaged?'

Chaloner slumped next to him and told him all that had happened, although the ex-Spymaster's lack of surprise suggested that much of it was not news. He could only suppose that Akers had obliged with one of his anonymous reports.

'I liked and trusted Kipps,' he concluded unhappily. 'He always took my side at Clarendon House, even when it made him unpopular with the other staff, and he introduced me to his son. He was the last man I would have suspected of . . . whatever happened in the marshes.'

'I can see why you are confused,' said Thurloe sympathetically. 'It is not at all clear whether he acted for himself or was a puppet of the King. However, the incident will certainly damage your master, which should be enough to earn your disapprobation.'

'I know,' sighed Chaloner. 'For a start, his antics resulted in Sutcliffe running off with all the money intended for wounded sailors.'

Thurloe smiled. 'Not so, Tom. Several boxes of shillings were left anonymously at Sayes Court in Deptford five days ago. Perhaps the rebels are not such scoundrels after all.'

'Everything was returned?' asked Chaloner, astounded.

'Not quite everything – a small percentage was retained to cover expenses.'

'But they had been planning that theft for months! What made them change their minds?'

'The deaths of Dove and Dendy, apparently, who were the driving force behind the scheme. The rest maintain that their war is not against maimed seamen but the Crown, and they did the decent thing. They have now quit the country, although Sutcliffe did not go with them. His wound was more serious than anyone realised, and he died.'

'Are you sure?'

Thurloe nodded. 'I saw the body myself.'

'That is justice of a sort, I suppose.' Chaloner sighed. 'So now the government is free of all the claimants to the College – Sutcliffe and Kole are dead, while Wilkinson is locked in Bedlam.'

'The best place for him,' declared Thurloe. 'But at least he is alive, unlike Nancy, Underhill, Kole, Cocke, Parker, Doyley, Sutcliffe, Warwick, Kipps . . .'

'And Stephens,' said Chaloner. 'He doubled back to get some of the gold, at which point the palace guards shot him. He made a full confession before he died – Sutcliffe *did* order him to rig the carts with explosives, which were to be ignited after the axle broke.'

'But only if they contained none of the King's money, presumably. Sutcliffe had no reason to wreak revenge on the Treasury otherwise.'

'He wanted them blown up regardless, although I suspect he knew by then that Kipps and Warwick *were* planning to make off with it.'

'Well, I did warn you that he was dangerous, and while I am not a man to delight in the death of another, I feel the world is a safer place without him. Of course, Stephens would not have retained his post even if he had been innocent. Reymes has made a clean sweep of the Treasury, and appointed a whole new set of officials.

Unfortunately, you will not be one of its Sergeants at Arms.'

'I imagine not, given my association with the Earl.'

'On the contrary, Reymes is impressed with your integrity. However, he feels it is wiser to make a fresh start with men he can train from scratch.'

'Then let us hope he recruits better ones than Kipps and Warwick.'

Thurloe sighed. 'Yet I understand why they acted as they did. They were left to take their chances in a plague-ridden city, while others – perhaps less deserving – were whisked to safety. No one likes to think of himself as expendable.'

'*I* am expendable,' said Chaloner gloomily. 'My orders are to mind Dunkirk House while the Earl and his family enjoy Hampton Court.'

'He will send for you soon enough,' predicted Thurloe. 'You are more useful to him than you know. But Chelsea was a sorry business, Tom. Reymes' ploy to turn Buckingham House into a minor White Hall, to distract attention from the rectory, almost worked in the rebels' favour.'

'He was not the only one who created diversions: Sutcliffe set about frightening folk as the "spectre", while Franklin ordered Cocke to steal money from Gorges' funds . . .'

'Although sending prisoners to burgle London houses was not a smokescreen for the business at the rectory. That was just Tooker and the Franklin brothers seizing an opportunity for profit.'

Chaloner nodded. 'Tooker should never have been appointed warden. You knew he was corrupt, and the government should have done, too.'

480

'The Earl was right to send you to investigate Gorges,' mused Thurloe. 'Of its governors, Franklin and Cocke plotted to steal the King's gold, Underhill was a spy, Kole was a voyeur, and Parker was experimenting on his charges.'

'And himself, which is why he took to wandering around Chelsea in full plague costume, even though it must have been fearfully hot.'

'Then there were the Colliers and the dancing masters,' Thurloe went on. 'All thieves, living under Gorges' roof.'

'I suspect Franklin guessed what they were doing, but turned a blind eye, because it was something else that stopped people from looking too closely at the rectory.'

'And in the end there were *two* schemes to steal His Majesty's gold,' said Thurloe. 'The ridiculously elaborate one orchestrated by Doyley, Sutcliffe, Franklin and the dissidents, and the equally ridiculously simple one devised by Kipps and Warwick.'

'But both failed – fortunately.'

'Thanks to you and your helpmeets,' said Thurloe. 'Especially Eleanore, who saved you from Dove's sword. I am sorry I did not have the chance to meet her.'

Chaloner said nothing. He had not known Eleanore well, yet her death was a sharp pain in his heart that surprised him with its intensity. It made him feel guilty, as he had not experienced anything nearly as strong for Hannah. Did that make him a poor husband, who quickly allowed other women to rise high in his estimation? Or were the two inextricably tangled in his mind, and distress for one was really grief for the other?

'Come to Oxfordshire,' said Thurloe kindly. 'There is room in my carriage, and your company would be

481

welcome. Then you can defend me from any rogue who tries to breathe on me.'

'I wish I could, but my orders are to stay here. I doubt the Earl will appreciate me abandoning Dunkirk House.'

'Why? London is much safer now that Spring and his surviving cronies are installed in Newgate. Besides, the Earl will not refuse a request from me, and I am disinclined to leave you here while your spirits are low. It has not been long since Hannah died, after all.'

'Hannah,' sighed Chaloner despondently. 'I failed her in so many ways. I did not even understand her letter until it was almost too late to matter. I cannot imagine what it must have cost her to write as she lay dying.'

'She loved you,' said Thurloe gently. 'Or she would not have bothered. Just be grateful for it.'

'She died while I was at sea,' said Chaloner unhappily. 'So how could she have known that I would be involved in the matter?'

'I doubt she did. She was just letting you know that Kipps was not all he seemed, and that if the Sick and Hurt Fund ever disappeared, you should look to Sutcliffe and his regicide friends Dove and Dendy for the culprits.'

'Well, she was brave, and I am proud of her, so I have decided to erect a monument to her in our parish church at Westminster. A gaudily expensive one, just as she would have liked. I will not leave London until it is done.'

'Any mason worth his salt has fled the city. But why not commission one in the place where she was born, where it is more likely to stand out?'

'I suppose the Westminster church is already stuffed with them,' acknowledged Chaloner. 'And she always did speak fondly of her childhood home . . .'

'It is decided then,' said Thurloe. 'We shall do it together on our journey to Oxfordshire.'

Chaloner left Lincoln's Inn in a much happier frame of mind. He returned to Covent Garden, and began to pack for the journey. He would enjoy relaxing in the easy company of Thurloe's family, and if the Earl did not like him leaving Clarendon House, then that was just too bad.

When he had finished, he glanced at his new viol. He grabbed it, sat down and launched straight into one of his favourite pieces – a lively air by Lawes. He played better than he had done in weeks, the instrument finally yielding to his touch, and for the first time, he began to feel at one with it. It sang in his hands, and he bowed for a long time before setting it down with a feeling of enormous satisfaction.

Then he took a pen and began to draw, and soon had a whole series of sketches that caught Hannah perfectly, from the jaunty angle of her head to the merry twinkle in her eyes. Afterwards, he drew Eleanore, a darker, more shadowy portrait of a woman he had known barely at all. He gathered them up carefully, and put them ready to take to Oxfordshire.

His garret was hot, so he sat on the windowsill to read Hannah's letter for the umpteenth time. Thurloe was right: she had loved him enough to spend her last moments trying to pass him important information, and he should not doubt the strength of her feelings for him. As he gazed at the words through eyes that were suddenly misty, a gust of wind plucked the worn paper from his fingers, and he almost toppled out of the window trying to catch it. It sailed across Fleet Street, where an upwind snagged it, and it fluttered out of sight.

483

Historical Note

The Great Plague of London is so well known that it needs no explanation here, other than to say that by July 1665, it had people well and truly frightened. Those who could leave the city went in droves, to places like Woolwich and Deptford, which were regarded as safe. Some doubtless fled to Chelsea, then in the country and surrounded by fields and market gardens. It was known as the village of mansions for its large number of stately homes – at least eight, some of which had hosted monarchs. One was known at that time as Buckingham House, although it had several different names in its history.

Another mansion was Gorges House, which started life as the family home of Arthur Gorges, son-in-law to the Earl of Lincoln, in the early 1600s. It later became a boarding school for girls, and was demolished in the early eighteenth century. Chelsea was famous for its lunatic asylums at this stage, and one was run by Mrs Bonney. Dancing was thought to be beneficial for those in delicate mental health, and two dancing masters in seventeenth-century Chelsea were James Hart and Jeffrey Bannister.

The rectory, rebuilt and restored several times through the ages, was sold into private hands in the 1980s. Its incumbent in 1665 was Samuel Wilkinson, who was also the last provost of Chelsea's infamous Theological College.

The foundation stone for this particular institution was laid by King James I in 1609. It was intended to promote the study of radical divinity – a contemporary archbishop dubbed it 'Controversial College' – but it was expensive to run, and the see-sawing religious opinions in the seventeenth century ensured it was doomed to failure. It was all but ruinous by the mid 1660s, at which point the Royal Society decided it might make a rather nice headquarters. Permission was granted for them to use it, but then war was declared on the Dutch, and the building was hurriedly put to use as a prison for captured sailors.

Some of these seamen had been taken after the Battle of Lowestoft on 3 June 1665 (Old Style). We will probably never know the real number of the dead and wounded, and modern estimates vary widely. However, the official reports of the time record English losses as fewer than seven hundred, while the Dutch are alleged to have suffered between six and ten thousand killed or taken prisoner. Jacob Oudart was master of *Stad Utrecht*, which was set alight by a British fireship sent by Admiral Berkeley from his flagship HMS *Swiftsure*.

The diarist John Evelyn was one Commissioner for the Care and Treatment of Prisoners of War, while the others were Sir William Doyley, Sir Thomas Clifford and Colonel Bullen Reymes, a gentleman of the Privy Chamber and MP for Weymouth and Melcombe Regis (although he was never associated with the Treasury).

The treasurer for the Commission was Captain George Cocke, who had a reputation for drunkenness and dishonest accounting.

Conditions in the gaol were said to have been grim, with a number of prisoners dying from malnutrition, poor medical care and eventually the plague. The warden was Mr Tooker, who allowed some of the prisoners out to work, to earn money for their keep. John Spring was one such inmate. He does not sound Dutch, but perhaps he was a merchant sailor caught on the wrong side. Regardless, he seems to have been trusted not to escape and start fighting again.

Not everyone was pleased to see the College used for non-religious purposes, and several men stepped forward to stake claims on it. One was the rector, Wilkinson, who was a bit of a character. He is said to have stolen books from College patrons, and was reviled by contemporaries as 'a man of very scandalous report'. Another claimant was John Sutcliffe, nephew of Dean Matthew Sutcliffe, the College's instigator and major financer. Yet another was Andrew Cole (or Kole), a speculator who had been renting the place.

The College was intended to be a splendid affair, built around two courtyards akin to the grander Oxbridge colleges. In reality, probably little more than the first quad was ever completed. The Royal Society never did move in, and later plans to turn the place into a market garden, an observatory and a glass factory came to nothing. The grounds were eventually sold back to the Crown, and became the Royal Hospital Chelsea, home of the Chelsea Pensioners.

Records show that Commissioner Reymes had a serious dispute with the Strangeways family that lasted several years. The Strangeways included John; his son Giles, a noted smoker, drinker and enemy of dissidents, according to Parliamentary records; and his grandson Wadham.

Other people in *The Chelsea Strangler* were also real. The landlord of the Swan was Francis Smith, and Chelsea residents in the 1660s included Thomas Janaway the bell-founder, Curtis Akers, Richard Samm, Thomas Franklin, John and Eleanore Unckles, and James and Elizabeth (Lil) Collier. Richard Franklin was an Admiralty Proctor, known to the diarist Samuel Pepys (who never went to a party in Clarendon House in July 1665). Dr Parker died of the plague in London in 1665, after which his lodger, Mr Underhill, claimed that their house had been burgled.

The Earl of Clarendon did have a daughter named Frances, although she was younger than portrayed here. His other children included Henry, Lawrence, Anne, James and Edward, the last of whom died of smallpox in January 1665. He also had a cousin named Alan Brodrick, who was one of the Court's most lively debauchees. Other colourful courtiers of the day include Sir Edward Hungerford, Henry Savile, Richard Newport, Thomas Greeting the musician, Lady Elizabeth Savage, and the King's mistress, Lady Castlemaine, who was pregnant with her fifth child in the summer of 1665. Betty Becke was the Earl of Sandwich's mistress.

The dissidents and regicides also existed. William Cawley and William Say signed Charles I's death warrant; Sir John Lisle and John Dove did not sign, but still sat on the tribunal; Edward Dendy was the Court's Sergeant at Arms; and Andrew Broughton and James Phelps helped to prepare the paperwork. All except Dove – who

487

made a grovelling apology and was pardoned – fled to Switzerland at the Restoration, and all except Broughton (who died in 1687) were dead by the mid 1660s. Evan Price was a fiery Fifth Monarchist who was active shortly after the Restoration.

The King and his Court did decamp from White Hall when the plague grew serious. They went first to Syon House, and then to Hampton Court, where they arrived in July. As the disease showed no sign of abating, arrangements were made for a move to Salisbury in August. When Salisbury proved unsatisfactory, they descended on Oxford, where they commandeered university colleges for their living quarters.

The King liked to have his money to hand, so the Treasury was moved as well. It had been in White Hall, but followed him on his travels, which must have been a cause of concern for those whose task it was to mind it. Sir Philip Warwick was Senior (Parliamentary) Secretary to the Treasury from 1660 until 1667, and Francis Stephens was its Sergeant at Arms. Thomas Kipps, who was also the Earl of Clarendon's Seal Bearer, held the post of Messenger of the Receipt.